Auslander

Auslander

a novel by

Mary Powell

TCU Press
Fort Worth, Texas

Powell, Mary Curtner
Auslander : a novel / by Mary Powell.
p.cm.
ISBN 0-87565-215-8 (alk. paper)
1.German Americans-Texas-history-20th century Fiction.
I. Title
PS3566.O83266A95   2000
813'.54-DC21
99-32491
CIP

Illustration and design by
Barbara M. Whitehead

For John,
my constant friend

PART I

I depart voluntarily from my teaching position.
I leave Germany, exchanging comfort for toil,
the familiar pen for the unfamiliar spade,
but I will be a free man
in a free earth.

Professor Ernst Kapp
Emigrant to the Texas Hill Country, 1840s

Vera

It was spitting rain when I stepped from the plane in San Antonio and made my way across the steamy tarmac. I covered my head with the magazine I'd been reading and looked up through the large glass of the terminal, where it wasn't difficult to spot Uncle Benno. He stood to one side of the others gathered to greet arriving passengers. Dressed in suspenders and bow tie, silver hair all slicked down, he looked as out of place as a calf in the sheep pen. Every few seconds he fingered his mustache and adjusted his glasses. When our eyes finally met, he gave a quick, unsmiling nod. Welcome home, I thought.

It was a short, sticky walk to the truck. Once in, I rolled down the window and lifted the hair off my neck.

"It's hot enough to be summer."

"Not so," he corrected me. "Just humid. Been gone so long, Missy, you've forgotten what a Texas spring is like." He waved a hand toward a sack on the floor at my feet. "Queenie sent lemonade and sandwiches."

I lifted out the thermos and filled two paper cups. "They fed me on the plane."

"I told her they would, but she sent some anyhow."

Benno's truck was the same old '47 Ford I remembered from forever. Twenty years old now, I figured, not air conditioned but clean inside and it ran surprisingly well. On the tray beside the driver's seat he still kept a pad and pencil. He claimed it was for figuring gas mileage, but then he always did the calculations in his head. When we were children, my cousin Fritz and I had used Benno's pad to play hangman, on occasions when he took us into town and we were told to wait while he tended to some business or other.

"So, how many miles on Old Bessie now?" I asked.

"Past two hundred thousand," he said without looking at the odometer.

A silly thing to be proud of, I thought.

The threat of rain had passed as Benno turned north and headed out Highway 281. I rested my arm on the back of the seat and followed the familiar route past the outskirts of town. It was a gentle climb from the shallow bowl of the city up onto the outer rim of the escarpment. Before long, fields and hills stretched out as far as I could see in all directions, punctuated by rocky outcroppings, stands of juniper and live oak, an occasional fence, a farm house, a barn. Where the road cut through a hill, limestone cliffs on either side displayed layers of rock in patterns that appeared to have something to say, if only one knew the language.

The trees and earth were sprouting new growth, green like the grass of Easter baskets, a welcome contrast from the dull landscape I'd left. It was unexpectedly sweet to the eye—a huge sky dotted with the puffy clouds of a child's drawing, some with dark underbellies. And wildflowers, pink, blue, yellow, and lavender, lay sifted across the countryside in thin blankets of color.

"In Philadelphia, we have frost through the end of May," I said, almost to myself, as if there was some need to justify the pleasure I found in the scene.

Benno only nodded.

"So, how have you been, Onkel?" I wanted to break the silence between us.

"Well, and you?"

"Very well. Sorry I haven't kept in better touch."

"What's it been? Five years now since you were home? People that live as far away as you do only come home for weddings and funerals.

Guess you're lucky this time, Missy. Guess that makes us all lucky, come to think of it," he chuckled at his small insight.

"I was in Europe for a while," I tried to change the subject.

"Ja. And didn't go to see your mother. Now she comes here."

The old faultfinding. Here it came again, the list of my obligations, the tally of my omissions. Certainly I had wanted to see her as long as I could remember, but it wasn't as simple as he wanted to make it. On my nightstand I kept her picture, a black and white snapshot of a thin, serious woman standing in a grove of trees, a woman with short, dark hair, frowning into the camera as if the sun were in her eyes. A hundred times I had searched that face looking for signs of myself.

"I felt uncomfortable, looking her up, when she's never come to see me."

"Uncomfortable," Benno repeated, as if that were a lame excuse.

When I took the cigarettes and lighter from my purse, Benno looked across with a frown. I lifted up the pack to offer him one but he shook his head.

"So, all grown up now."

I lit the cigarette and took my time exhaling the smoke.

"Are you happy about Fritz's wedding?" I asked.

"She seems like a good enough girl."

I tried not to let his choice of adjectives irritate me. "From around here?" I asked.

"From Houston."

"They'll settle in Houston?"

"Not so. He's coming back to work with me."

"What about the engineering degree?"

"What about it?"

"I'd think he'd want to use it."

"Lots of engineers looking for work these days. He's going to stick around here 'til something good turns up."

"Is . . ." I groped for the name, "Carol Anne happy about that?"

"Should be."

"Schoenberg may be hard for a city girl."

"She's a lucky girl. Fritz will see she gets along," Benno announced bluntly, as if that made it true.

3

I shrugged and kept my thoughts to myself. We made small talk about people in town, his insurance business, the wedding plans, everything but what concerned me most at that moment—my mother, how she looked, how long she would stay, whether she was anxious to see me. He didn't offer and I didn't ask.

Still, I hated sitting in this hot truck together and having so little to say.

Shifting into German I said to Benno, "I've been thinking about the pony you gave me for my birthday."

He looked sideways at me.

"I loved that pony, but I was too mad to thank you properly."

"You were mad at me," he repeated. "I built you a room of your own and it made you mad."

"I didn't like it."

"So you didn't." He chuckled. "*Esel*, you called me."

"I heard the word first from you."

"It wasn't proper."

"And you whipped me."

"You deserved it."

I shook my head. "You're a stubborn man, Onkel."

"Look who's talking now. How many years you stayed mad?"

"Well, I think we should make peace."

"Good enough."

"Want to smoke on it?" Again I offered him a cigarette from my pack. I knew he liked store-boughts even though he insisted on rolling his own. He unclipped his bow tie, put it in his pocket and looked over at me again, still without a smile.

"Just once," he said.

The house where I grew up sat near the center of town. It was white frame and freshly painted, with a long porch across the front and a wooden swing at the far end. The Jahn name stenciled on the mailbox was unnecessary. Everyone in Schoenberg knew who lived there. The grass was trimmed and edged and Queenie's roses bloomed along the walk. The front door stood open. While Benno lifted the bags from the back of the truck I checked my hair, wiped my palms against my skirt, and willed myself to look calm.

"Come, Missy, she won't bite you." Benno opened the truck door, suddenly jolly, and I felt another flash of irritation. You are an esel, I thought. He seemed to be enjoying watching me struggle with this meeting, as if I were some creature he had come across in the field, trying to shed its outgrown skin. He steered me through the front door, down the hall, and into the living room where she was sitting, heavier now, with short hair the color of steel, looking older, and more stern than I had imagined.

"Well, Greta, here is Vera, all grown up," he said with a chuckle.

She didn't get up, but held out her hand and beckoned me toward her. When I got close enough she raised her eyebrows to look out over her glasses.

"You don't look much like your pictures."

"I hope that's a compliment," I said. We spoke in German.

"Well, you're a nice looking girl," she said, inspecting me like a piece of furniture, "but too thin."

She turned to Benno.

"I thought she'd have curly hair."

"I did when I was little," I said.

"Too bad I couldn't see you then." She sat back and put her feet up on the ottoman. "The trip over made my ankles swell and I've spent the last three days on that sofa over there. Only managed to dress this morning since you were coming but I can't walk too well. I hope I can make it to the wedding."

Queenie came from the kitchen then, wiping her hands on her apron and rushing forward to gather me up in a hug.

"Vera, Vera, let me see you. It's been so long." She took my face in her soft hands and held me out at arms length, her eyes shiny with tears.

"Even you look like a professor now! I am so proud."

I started to stop her, to explain once again that I wasn't a professor, just a graduate student with teaching duties, but she had already turned to Greta. "What do you think of our girl?" she asked.

5

"She looks tired. Why don't you put your things away, Vera, and then we will talk."

Benno glanced out the window toward the street. "Better make it quick," he said. "Fritz and his girl will be here for supper."

In the back room I hurriedly changed into cooler clothing and low-heeled shoes, but my hands continued to shake. On the dresser a familiar family picture confronted me—Uncle Benno, Queenie, Fritz, in his letter sweater, looking like the All-American boy, and me, with my chin down, looking meek and hopeful. I stood before the mirror, buttoned the sleeveless white blouse, and concentrated on formulating my thoughts in German. I had waited so long to meet this woman. The language would be our bridge.

When I returned to the living room, my mother motioned me to sit down beside her on the sofa and began to speak in English. She was more fluent than I had expected.

"I worked for the Americans after the war," she told me, "I managed very well but could never afford to leave my job. A woman alone must think about herself."

"That's true," I said. But she had found a way to come this time. Why not before? She had kept in touch with Queenie and Benno. Why had she never written a letter to me or sent a gift? Was my father still alive? I knew she didn't live with him, but did she see him? Did she have a picture? I had come hungry for explanations. She wanted to talk about her music club and her job in city government, the important people she knew, the Volkssportverein she belonged to when she was younger, before her knees went bad and she could no longer keep up with all that walking. Her speech was sprinkled with opinions, little hard seeds she appeared to have been saving to pass on to me. The best of them were ordinary and the worst were bitter. But I listened. I smiled and nodded in the right places. Then I began to let it go, the idea I had held to for so long, the foolish hope that we would someday be happily, even joyously, reunited.

"What would you like me to call you?" I asked.

"Greta is fine."

"Well, Greta," I decided to change the subject, "I've brought something I thought you might be interested in."

"Oh?" she said and sat up.

I fished a scholarly magazine from my purse. "An article I recently published on German settlement in Pennsylvania."

"Oh," she said. "Very nice. I'll read it tonight. I like to read before I go to bed."

"Keep it," I said. "I have other copies."

We were waiting in the front room when Fritz and Carol Anne arrived. She was young. Twenty to his twenty-seven. Blonde and blue-eyed. Motion-picture pretty but a bit flashy, I thought, for a bride-to-be, in short shorts, halter top, and clear plastic sandals that showed off bright red toenails. She wasn't at all the type I thought Fritz would choose. But what did I know? It had been years since we'd talked, and the letters we wrote at first had dwindled to Christmas cards.

He was a man now, with his hair short and military but still bleached by the sun. He had grown taller, or maybe it only seemed that way because he looked so serious. I liked the straight way he carried himself. Well, like they said, within two weeks he would become a husband and provider. There were expectations.

First he shook hands with Benno, and then hugged Queenie. He was introduced to Greta next and finally turned to me, smiling as if truly glad to see me. I hoped my face didn't reflect the ambivalence I felt. I offered to help unload the car. Back and forth we marched from the driveway to the house, carrying their things, Carol Anne watching Fritz, Fritz watching me, me watching Carol Anne.

"How are you, Vera?" He held out a box tied with string and our hands brushed.

"Better," I said.

"Better than what?" he grinned.

"Better than ever, I suppose."

He studied my eyes as if to make certain I wasn't pretending. "It shows."

"Thanks, cousin," I smiled back, thinking the cleft in his chin was even more distinctive than before. "It looks as if things are going well for you, too," I nodded my head in Carol Anne's direction.

He squinted into the distance beyond me, as if checking the weather. There was a hint of concern on his face. "I hope so," he said.

Carol Anne was staying in Fritz's old bedroom. Fritz was staying at the cabin on the river, and Greta, claiming disability, had taken over my bedroom. After supper Queenie slipped me some money and Fritz gave me a ride to the hotel but first through the park and up around the square. Carol Anne sat between us like a little sister, with her bright eyes taking in his every move. We made small talk.

"That's where we learned to swim," he told her and pointed to a bend in the river bordered by giant cypress trees.

My pulse accelerated, but I sat quietly. Was he baiting me? She had her head resting on his shoulder, her fingers drumming on his leg.

"Speak for yourself, cousin," I told him. "You were the swimmer. I mostly watched."

I turned to Carol Anne. "He was about ten and all legs, like a spider. He'd scramble up that big tree on the other side, the one that leans out over the water, and then come crashing down with a huge splash."

Fritz looked at me over her head.

"And she'd sit right there, at the base of the tree, reading her book, and dare me to get her wet."

"I didn't dare you. I warned you," I corrected with a smile.

"You liked it. You just wouldn't admit it."

We had been talking about childhood, but suddenly, something else. The ring of his words hung in the silent car. I turned to Carol Anne. "He always thought he knew what I was thinking."

She looked over at him and smiled suggestively. "He's never sure what I'm thinking."

Fritz ignored us both and drove on, stopping again at the low-water crossing. "It's high," he said.

I nodded. "I hope they don't get any more rain for a while."

"What is it with you all, talking about the weather and how high the river is?" Carol Anne reached forward and switched on the radio.

Fritz rubbed his hand along her bare back. "That's what you do in the country. Before long, you'll be doing it too."

"That'll be the day." She sat in the dim light with her eyes closed, head bent to one side, slowly twisting her creamy shoulders back and forth to the music.

Back at the hotel, I unpacked and tried to sort out the day's happenings. I thought about my mother, this woman who wanted to be called Greta. Years ago I found her letter in Queenie's dresser drawer, a single sheet of blue paper, thin as tissue, postmarked Berlin, November 1939, and it was about me.

"Hitler's Germany is not a place for a newborn and so I am asking you to take this child until the fighting is settled. If the U.S. gets in the war, who knows what may happen to Americans living here? Her father is no help. Sometimes he goes to meetings and ties my legs to the bed, like a crazy man. I am afraid for her safety on many counts. As my younger brother, you are the one I trust the most. You must help. I have no place else to turn."

"What's this?" I asked Queenie. I was maybe fifteen.

"The letter your mother sent Benno after you were born."

"Ties her legs to the bed. What does that mean?"

"It means he is sick in the head."

"Why would he do that?"

"To keep her from leaving."

"What about me?"

"He did nothing to you, *leibchen*. When we got you, you were perfect—a little colicky, only, from the trip and all those strange hands."

"She wrote just Onkel and not you?"

"Ja. Me she didn't know so well. Only a few times had we met before she went to Germany to marry a stranger."

"Why would she marry a stranger?"

"It was arranged."

"Arranged?"

"Agreed between the man and her father."

"Ugh." I stuck out my tongue and wrinkled my nose at the idea.

"So, did Onkel ask you?"

"Ask me what?"

"If you wanted another child. Wasn't that just before Fritz was born?"

"It was a good time for it. Two babies can't be much more trouble than one was what he thought."

"And what did you think?"

"I thought it was a privilege."

"And when the war was over, did you expect her to come and get me?

"Expect? Ja, but I hoped not."

I carried the clothes from my suitcase to the bathroom, hung them on hangers, and suspended them from the overhead shower-curtain ring. Then I filled the old, claw-footed tub with hot water, eased in, and let myself remember.

Queenie and Benno raised me, right along with Fritz. She taught me to call her Queenie and him Onkel and she treated us the same, except that Fritz was a boy and everyone expected more from boys. Early on, we lived at the cabin outside of town. I remember happy days, Fritz and me playing in the sandpile, chasing butterflies, filling our toy wagon with acorns, floating cottonwood leaves down the river. "A mother has eyes in the back of her head," Queenie told us, and we believed it. Wherever she was, house or garden, she knew what we were up to. Before lunch, she stopped her chores to teach us our letters. At the kitchen table, we watched as she created for us samples of old-world script. Then, using turkey quills and ink we struggled to reproduce them. When I became discouraged, she put her hand over mine and guided gently. In the evenings she read to us from German story books saved from her own childhood.

I can't remember ever seeing Queenie or Benno lying in bed. They were up, no matter how early we awoke, with the fire going and the water drawn. Cold mornings, Fritz and I snuggled under the same blanket and waited to be called to the table. Sometimes we pretended we were puppies, imitating growls and yips and licking each other's necks and faces. While Benno fed the animals, Queenie fixed breakfast and, with the heavy flatiron that was heated on the stove and that we were forbidden to touch, she ironed his white shirt. After breakfast Benno washed up, changed into town clothes and went to sell insurance for the Sons of Hermann. In the afternoon, he returned, changed into overalls and worked in the fields until dark. Queenie rinsed out the white shirt and hung it on the line to be ready for the next day.

Benno's business began to grow after the war. We moved into town in 1947, and Fritz and I started public school in the same grade. Life for Queenie was easier then, with running water, electric lights and a gas stove, but she seemed to work just as hard. Mornings and evenings Benno drove back and forth to the ranch to tend the cattle and crops. Neighbor children came knocking on the door once we were in town, but still I preferred Fritz's company.

On rainy days, we turned chairs upside down and spread covers over the top to make a playhouse. He arranged mazes and doors and skylights, and I drew pictures and pinned them to the inside walls. We played house, Fritz and I, and no one thought anything of it. We shared the same bedroom and bathed in the same tub until we were in second grade. Then one night Benno came in and saw us together. I remember him standing in the bathroom doorway, his face in a terrible scowl, like the giant in one of our books.

"Queenie," he called, and when she came to the doorway he began to speak to her in a gruff voice, and they spoke in German. Queenie lifted me from the tub, wrapped me quickly in a towel and took me to the bedroom to put on my nightclothes. After that, Fritz and I bathed separately. Benno put a lock on the bathroom door and we were taught to use it.

What did Benno see that bothered him? I recall no feeling of shame. Nevertheless, he built a new room, a little square off the kitchen that became my bedroom. I didn't like the little cupboard room and told him so one day when Queenie was at the market.

"Missy," he told me back, "you're lucky to have a home and people who will take care of you, so pay attention to your chores and don't be a complainer. There's much to be done and we must all put up with things we don't like."

I stuck out my tongue at him and stamped my foot. I screamed the worst words I knew. *"Du esel!"* I said. Literally, I was calling him a donkey, but in a seven-year-old way I was aware it was a serious insult.

He went outside and cut a green branch from a mesquite tree, stripped the leaves, held me between his legs and switched my behind until it raised red welts that stung beneath my hand. Alone in my room, full of fury and self-pity, I stood on the dresser to look in the mirror at those stripes on my backside. It wasn't long after that, on my birthday, that Benno took me to the ranch to see the pony he had bought. It was his way of saying our quarrel was over, but I pretended I wasn't interested.

In the dark hotel room I raised the window and sat on its broad sill. The night air was filled with a sweet fragrance—honeysuckle, or maybe it was jasmine. I always confused the two. From a car radio in the parking lot I could make out a familiar melody, and as I strained to hear it, the courthouse clock began to announce the hour. Eleven deep chimes resounded across the square. They could be heard at least as far away as Queenie's house and, though I knew what time it was, I counted each, as I had often done in the past. In the silence that followed came the growl of a truck pulling out from the mill over on River Street. The night was fertile and familiar for me, evoking a kind of body memory that comes with the places of one's childhood.

I felt no overpowering sadness about the meeting with my mother. In fact, I felt less burdened. Whatever imaginary bond I had tried to create between us was a cobweb, spun of childish dreams. To clear it away would be a relief.

Early the next morning I walked from the hotel down along the river bank, until I came to the place. If Fritz remembered our days here, then he remembered our last time here. He had made me uncomfortable when he pointed it out last night in front of Carol Anne. Would he tell her? I hoped not.

A giant cypress tree at the river's edge stood mounted in its own satiny roots. I stooped and ran my hand across the gnarled surface. The year I was sixteen I spent every spare moment from April to October in this place, sitting in first one indentation, then another, dangling my legs in the water, escaping in daydreams of triumphant trips to Germany where, according to my mood, I would be claimed by my own heartbroken mother, or an older man, someone at least twenty-five, handsome and imperious in his uniform, which, as I recall, resembled something out of *The Nutcracker*.

That idea of going to Germany turned me into a serious student. In high school I was with the eggheads, all boys, studying German, Latin, and chemistry. Fritz and I had many of the same classes and spent time together at the library or around the kitchen table, worrying over trig problems or English assignments. When he wasn't looking, I studied the stubs of hair sprouting from the side of his jaw. I wanted to fit my finger in the cleft of his chin, hold it there, and feel it move when he talked.

The night of our graduation was a culmination of so many things, and the fact that we happened to end up together in this favorite spot was unplanned but hardly a coincidence. The yearbook had come out that day, page after page of girls in white blouses with barrettes in their hair and crew-cut boys in dark jackets. Fritz, in addition to being quarterback on the football team, had been named Senior Favorite and Most Likely to Succeed. I, who had the better grades, had been chosen to deliver the invocation at the cap and gown ceremony.

"God, Our Father," I heard my shaky voice amplified across the open field. "Let this moment be not our finest hour, but the beginning of a long and worthy journey. May we each become a voice for good and truth." It had taken hours to come up with those two sentences. I had little experience with public or private prayers, and, unlike most of the kids in town, no church life to draw from. I had finally gone to Queenie for help and she told me she didn't see much use in out-loud praying, but, if there was a God, and if he happened to be listening, he would require honest and simple words.

The party that followed was almost as uncomfortable for me as the praying. Fritz stood in a circle of friends, laughing at pointless stories and filling up on Pearl beer. The girls teased and tossed their hair and looked over their shoulders at him, like always. I slipped away early and walked home. Queenie and Benno were already asleep. I pulled on my bathing suit and headed for the park, knowing better than to swim alone, but on graduation night we were supposed to break rules.

The park was deserted. In the distance I could hear occasional singing and shouting and tires squealing, kids whose idea of celebrating was to drive around the town square until someone got brave enough to jump out and dump soapsuds in the fountain. Sometimes dye. I hung my feet in the water, craned my neck to locate the moon over the tree-tops, and tried to ignore the uneasiness of being alone in the dark. I couldn't help looking back at every crackling twig and rustling leaf. Then, suddenly, a strange voice moaned "Ve. . . ra. Ve. . . ra."

I slid into the water and started swimming with all my strength. Something came crashing behind me. Almost to the other bank I looked back, just in time to see Fritz grab my legs and pull me under. I came up furious. *"Esel!"* I sputtered the insult. "You scared the skin off me!"

He stood in the shallow, still fully dressed and bent over with laughter.

"I called out," he told me, spreading his arms in innocence. "I called your name."

With the flat of my hand I bombarded him with sheets of water until he finally managed to grab my arms.

"What do you mean following me, anyway?"

"Looking out for your interests," he said. "You shouldn't swim alone."

"I don't need you watching out for me."

"It's my job."

"Who says?"

"Benno."

"Benno?"

Fritz leaned forward and stuck his finger in my face. He spoke in Benno's soft accent. "Two kinds of women there are, son. The kind you look at and the kind you look after. Vera, now, is your sister. She is the kind you look after."

"He said that to you?"

"Would I make it up?"

"When?"

"When we were in seventh grade and he caught me watching you."

"Watching me what?"

"Hanging out the wash, I think it was."

I pictured myself and laughed.

"It's true," he said.

"I'll take care of myself," I told him, no longer amused. "Leave me alone, Fritz. Don't butt in on my life."

"You butt in on mine."

"Like when?"

"Like in my dreams."

It was not something Fritz would say to me. Not something he should say. A blush spread up my face. Good that it was too dark for him to see. He let go my hands and changed the subject.

"It's a big night, Vee. Let's do something."

"Like?"

He climbed up on the bank and looked down at me. "Wait and watch," he said. They were words from our childhood, the invitation to a game.

Before long I heard a familiar whistle upstream and started toward the sound. At the overhanging tree, I saw Fritz balanced high above the water, luminous in the moonlight, stripped to his underwear, long legs, broad chest, toes curled over the edge of the thick trunk. My heart pounded, part fear, part excitement as I watched him push from the tree, arms extended, like a bird flies over the water. As he fell, he straightened and broke through the still surface with a splash, then came up beside me.

"Not bad," I told him, trying to act unimpressed, "for someone who's been drinking beer all night."

"Just enough," he grinned proudly. "Your turn now."

"You know I don't dive."

"You don't have to. I dare you to stand up there."

I crawled from the water and made him swim downstream while I struggled up the tree. Even with boards nailed for climbing, it was hard going, and I had watched enough novices attempt it to know how awkward one could look. I held to a branch and inched my way out on the large limb. At least twenty five feet down. When I saw his head below me, very small, I gathered myself as tall and tight as possible, plastered my hands to my sides, took a deep breath and stepped off. He was there when I surfaced, pulling me up, holding me until I caught my breath.

"I didn't think you'd do it," he said.

"I'll do anything you do."

"It's not a competition."

"Not for you. No competition with a girl."

"Not true. You beat me in grades."

He slicked his hair back with both hands, relaxed against the water, looked up through the trees and ignored my bad temper.

"God, I love this place," he said. "And I hate for it to end. You know, Vera, after today, things will never be the same."

"I heard kids saying that tonight at the party," I said. "I think they were trying to act sentimental. You know what I thought? I thought that for some of us, things will get better." I started toward the bank.

He followed me from the water and caught me by the shoulders, then pulled me gently to him and held me close.

"Vee," he said, and now it was his turn to be serious. "Seems like you're always mad. What the hell is the matter?"

I shook my head.

He continued to hold me. I felt his heartbeat and the chill bumps on his skin. And the swelling below. And he smelled of the river, and shaving lotion, and beer from the party. I buried my head in the curve of his neck and felt the slick drops from his hair fall on my shoulders and run down my back. I had dreamed of this. I wanted to freeze the moment, make it last forever. I put my arms around his waist and turned my face to his, but he turned away. The thought of Benno was there between us, a presence, impossible to ignore. I pressed against him and stood on tiptoe to match his height.

"I don't care," I whispered.

"Then neither do I."

What followed was awkward and disappointing. Standing on the spot, almost ten years later, I couldn't remember his kiss, or his hands on my body, or mine on his, only a rush of activity, the sloping river bank, dirt, and gravel, and cypress needles, me struggling from my wet suit, the heaviness of him, the difficulty of entry. I remembered wanting it to be over. When he laid back finally, quiet, I slipped into the water to rinse off, thinking now I understood why female animals tried to get away from the males and when they did give in, they didn't seem too happy about it. He came to the water's edge.

"I can do better," he said.

"You've done it before?"

"Well, you know."

"No, I don't." But I had heard about initiation trips the boys took across the border into Mexico. "All I know is that isn't what I expected."

"It'll be better next time. I promise."

There won't be a next time, I thought. I was disgusted and ashamed and wished we could forget it. We'll never be friends again, I thought, not like before. As for the haunting mystery of sex, it seemed like a bad trick.

I hurried along to Queenie's house, where everyone had gathered for wedding preparations. Benno was bragging to Greta about the Octoberfest he had helped plan ten years before, while Fritz was giving his version of the event to Carol Anne.

"It was one long party," he told her. "Music every night. Food. Beer. Dancing. They let us out of school a couple of days, even though we were lowly freshmen. Remember, Vera?"

I nodded. Laughter, that's what I remembered, and singing, accordians, costumes, women in embroidered, tight-waisted dresses, men in *lederhosen*. And a stranger, a visitor named Hans, two years older than I, with slick, dark hair, and eyes like coals. They burned my skin when he looked at me, and every time I looked up, he was looking. On his last night we walked down along the river. The moonlight spread across the water like pools of silvery paint and we stood watching the fish jump for lightning bugs. I told him about my plan to go to Germany and look for my mother.

"If you come, I will be your friend," he said, very serious. "And you will be my American cousin." Then he leaned down and gave me my first real kiss, a kiss I relived a thousand times, except I imagined it coming from Fritz.

"You should have been here then," Benno was saying to Greta as we all sat down to lunch. "A celebration to rival the best, I tell you." He stood up to fork a slice of ham off the platter, then helped himself to butterbeans and passed the bowl to her. "My club raised $5,000 in contributions. Sent it to our sister city in the old country, with a promise that whoever would come could stay in our homes for free. Fifty people came, some with families. They stayed for three weeks. Our German cousins, we called them." He took a forkful of food and washed it down with water. "Ha! They were quiet in the beginning, but after some singing and some beers they began to loosen up."

Fritz passed me a bowl of new potatoes and green beans.

"Remember that fellow who had a crush on you? What was his name?"

"Hans Mueller," Queenie volunteered. "His mother writes still. He and Vera were companions in Germany last year," she added proudly.

"Companions," Fritz nodded and repeated Queenie's word, managing to turn it into a subtle question.

I avoided his eyes and stirred my iced tea. "He was very helpful."

"So, is there anyone in your life right now?" Carol Anne asked. "Anyone special?"

"No one special. I'm concentrating on my thesis."

She raised her eyebrows as if that were a new idea. "What's it about?"

"The mythology of the Master Race." I looked at Greta, wondering if she would have something to say, but she studied her plate.

"Like what?" Carol Anne asked.

"It's complicated," I said, sorry I'd broached the subject. People like to ask what you're working on and when you tell them, they get a bored expression like they didn't really expect you to talk about it.

"Try me," she insisted.

"I'm collecting stories, songs, cultural clues that would help explain how good, thinking people could be caught up in Nazi atrocities."

"That's easy," Benno said. "A hungry man follows a donkey if he thinks it leads to food. There was a depression there, just like here. A crazy paperhanger talked himself into power and everyone paid. That's what happened. Don't waste your time with something that's over and done with."

"Should never get so busy you can't come home," Queenie said, as if to change the subject.

Fritz turned to Carol Anne. "She was always too smart for the boys here."

"Too sophisticated, I bet," Carol Anne said. "Tell me what it's like in Philadelphia?"

"Quite different from here. The weather. The scenery. The people."

"Maybe we'll come see you," she said and smiled at Fritz. "I always wanted some family to visit."

Carol Anne

I was sitting on a stool at Dirty Martin's Cafe watching this cute character behind the counter cooking on a big, greasy griddle. He wore his hair in duck tails, had a package of cigarettes rolled up in the sleeve of his tee shirt, and was flipping the patties real graceful, like it was some special trick. He knew I was watching, but I kept looking at my book and pretending to study. Then this other guy with a crew cut came in, sat down at the stool next to mine and ordered.

"You come here often?" he asked me.

"Yeah. I like the music they have on the jukebox." I nodded in the direction of the cook. "Everything here's kind of old-fashioned."

"Good, old-fashioned food," he told me. "And reasonable."

He looked too old to be a student but too young to be a teacher. And I liked how natural he was when he told me he liked to eat there because the prices were good. So many guys trying to be cool act like money is no problem.

"What are you studying?" he asked me.

I looked at the cover of the book. "Economics," I said, and made a face.

We talked a little and he managed to finish eating about the same time I did and then he asked if he could walk me to my dorm.

"Getting dark. And it's not as safe on the drag as it used to be," he said, looking serious.

I nodded. None of us could forget about that kook that had climbed up in the tower a few years before and shot all those people. I just tried not to think about it.

"Will I be safe with you?"

"You bet you will," he told me and grinned. He was definitely cuter than the guy behind the counter. "My name's Fritz," he said, and he held the door for me, real smooth, not like it was something he was supposed to do, but like it was something he'd been doing all his life.

Well, I've never had a problem attracting boys but when I let Fritz pick me up that Thursday night, and two months later he was asking me home for the weekend to meet his parents, and stay in their hundred-year-old river cabin, I realized that the University of Texas, like they told us at orientation, could open up new worlds. I packed two bathing suits and a church dress, just in case, and prayed my period wouldn't come.

Schoenberg, the sign said. Established 1850. Population 15,000.

"It means beautiful town," Fritz warned me while we drove through in his Mustang, with the top down. "But it's pretty tame. Old-fashioned. You'll see, when you meet my parents."

At a stop sign someone called his name and he waved. We drove down the main street, which was extra wide and lined with trees, past a couple of churches, a movie theatre, a grocery store, and a bunch of little shops with strange names, like the one that said Doeppler's.

"Doppler's," I read.

"Deppler's," he corrected me. "When you see two vowels together in a German word, if you pretend the first one is silent, you'll get it right most of the time. So, what's that one?" he pointed to a street sign that said Baenz.

"Bens," I said.

"You're quick," he told me. I'd never been told that by a guy before.

He touched my arm and motioned at a little man in a white shirt and tie, bent over, sweeping the sidewalk. "The shopkeepers do that when business is slow," he said. It was cute how he wanted to show me things, like the bandstand in the center of town, and the fountain, and the statue in front of the old stone courthouse. "Pop says there's too much traffic in town. He and my mom usually spend weekends out at the cabin."

"But they have a house in town?"

"Right over behind that big stone church," he pointed down the block.

"Is that your church?"

"We're not exactly church people," he said real matter-of-fact.

I've never heard anybody say it exactly that way, no apologies or anything, just 'we're not church people.' Which was fine with me. I went with a Baptist boy for a while whose parents expected us to go to the early service with them, and then they liked to take a drive and go someplace nice for lunch, which takes up exactly one-fourth of the weekend when you think about it, counting getting up early and getting dressed and all that. We broke up because he didn't like me to smoke. And then I went with a Catholic who told me some of the things he had to confess, which had to be embarrassing, and he also said a priest had paddled him once with a piece of linoleum with pennies glued to it, so it would whip around and hurt like hell, but still he went to mass regular as clockwork. So I figured this was something Fritz and I had in common, not being churchy, even though I would have expected different, what with him saying his parents were old-fashioned, and them being German, and all.

I pulled my legs up in the seat beside me, tightened the scarf around my head and tried not to ask dumb questions. This place was different from Austin, and really different from Houston, where I'd grown up. They called this traffic? When cars honked, Fritz waved, real friendly, even when he couldn't see who it was. I felt like Grace Kelly touring Italy with a local driver. "It's charming," I told him. "How much farther?"

"About half an hour. Only twelve miles, but the road follows the river the whole way and you can't make very good time on it."

The cabin wasn't wooden, like I'd imagined, but stone, with a screened porch on three sides and cots on one end. His mother put on fresh sheets while I watched, and she spread a quilt across the end of the bed in case it got cold. Fritz said they got electricity out there about ten years ago, and before that his mom had cooked on a wood stove that they still kept out at the hunting camp for heat and because it made good biscuits.

"Bathroom?" I asked. Surely plumbing had come in with the electricity. He pointed to a small closet by the kitchen.

"The old outhouse is still standing, if you're daring," he grinned.

About midnight Fritz was beside my bed.

"You awake?"

"Shhh."

"They never hear a thing after they've gone to sleep. Come on out and look at the river. The moon's almost full."

We tiptoed out through the screen door, me in a short cotton nightie I had bought especially for the occasion.

At the bottom of the steps Fritz grabbed my hand and we ran down to the river. He twirled me around and hugged me.

"Bad boy," I laughed and shook my finger in his face, then turned around and leaned against him. His arms were around my waist and I kept my arms folded and resting over his, like a nice girl.

"Want to skinny dip?" he asked.

I hesitated because I wanted to play it cool. Fritz looked like the kind of guy who wouldn't stick around long if he thought you were easy. But, it wasn't like I'd never tried it before. I had done a lot of stuff because Sheila said young people should experiment with life and not get stuck in ruts. Sheila, my mother. A musician.

"Jazz never goes out of style," she told me once, and I guess she's right. It kept us in a nice apartment in Montrose, with good clothes and something put away for college. Her tip jar was a brandy glass labelled, "College for my baby." It embarrassed me but she said to get over it.

Sometimes she took me on gigs with her group. Three black men and a blonde woman. Sheila and the Nights, they called themselves. In sixth grade I went with her to a little bar in west Houston where a sign in the restroom said, "Don't put your butts in the can." I sat at a table by myself up front and drank Shirley Temples while she smiled down at me.

"Six extra children just from getting french-kissed," the bass sang. The crowd hooted and wheels in my head started turning. I knew about being french-kissed. At a Christmas party a junior high boy had taken me out on a dark porch. It started like a regular kiss, then the tongue that I thought I would hate, but it was better than it sounded when the girls talked about it on the playground. Sheila roared when I asked if you could get pregnant doing that.

"Where'd you get that?"

"From that song Bo sings," I repeated the words.

Sheila fell over laughing. "He's saying frisky, not french-kissed. He got six extra children just from getting frisky. Like a puppy. Playing around, having fun, making love without being careful. Get it?"

She went into the other room and came back with a little square package. "This is a rubber," she said, biting off the corner of the package and taking out a round thing the color of old chewing gum. She poked in the center and began to unroll the edges. "Men buy them at the drugstore. Sometimes they're in machines in their restrooms at filling stations."

I was beginning to get it. She had told me about intercourse a while back. Now she began to act out the putting on of a rubber. I put my hands over my ears and ran out of the room, but I could still hear her laughing. Later, she came to my bedroom.

"Honey," she told me. "You can't stay a child forever. A girl needs to know these things. There's a diaphragm, too."

I shook my head.

"Later," she said.

I nodded.

Fritz had a country way about him. He didn't pretend to be somebody else, like most of the boys I'd met at school. But, also, he was older, and smart and good-looking. The perfect catch, I thought.

"Too cold to swim," I told him.

"I could throw you in."

"You couldn't." He looked at me like I was daring him.

"You wouldn't," I tried again.

"Bet I could. What do you weigh?"

"With my clothes on?"

"Like that," he stared down at me like he was glad to have an excuse to look.

"A hundred and thirteen."

"I could do it with one hand tied behind me. Come here," he said and pulled me over to the picnic table. "Sit." He put me between him and the moonlight and I could tell he was trying to look through my nightshirt.

"You do this with all the girls you bring home?" I asked.

"I try," he said. He was honest, too. He wasn't wearing a shirt, only blue jeans that hung low on his hips, and I couldn't stop looking at how the muscles across his stomach wove in and out like a loose, fat braid. I reached out and ran my hand along the tight skin.

"How do you get that?"

"Sit ups," he told me, and I could tell he liked the attention. "Baling hay, mowing, setting fence posts. I help with the ranch work every weekend I'm home. Want to come with us tomorrow?"

I rolled my eyes. "You just want to get me over to that camp where the stove is so I can bake some biscuits." Then I let him kiss me because I didn't want him to be mad. Sometimes I make guys mad, being sassy.

Fritz joined the army after high school, he told me. Said three years of his life in exchange for college expenses had been a fair trade and he was lucky to have gotten out before Vietnam got as bad as it was, or he might be there now.

"So, do you expect to move someplace exciting when you graduate?" I sure didn't want to talk about the war.

He was tracing letters with his finger on my leg.

"No," he said. "Maybe San Antonio. I want to stay close enough to help keep the ranch going. It'll be mine someday. Part of it, at least."

"So why'd you choose something as hard as engineering? I mean, if you maybe aren't going to use it."

"Pop thought it was a good idea."

"But he wasn't even paying for it."

"Doesn't mean I don't ask him."

He seemed really sure of himself, about what he planned to do and all, and also couldn't keep his hands off me, but I was used to that. After I scooted away from him the second time, he picked up an old pocket knife stuck in the end of the table.

"Five letters," he said.

"Huh?"

"In your name. C-A-R-O-L. I'm going to carve it here for posterity."

It's there on the picnic table all right. My name with a heart around it.

Sheila wanted me to go on the pill when I left for college, but I was determined to manage my own business. So when Fritz and I started seeing each other, I went to the campus doctor who wouldn't give me a prescription unless my mother came in with me. Fat chance of that! Not that she'd mind; she just wouldn't schedule a trip for it. The next thing I knew, I was pregnant. I guess I was careless, but so was he, and always in a hurry. We used rubbers most of the time, but neither of us liked them much.

The first thing Fritz did when I told him I was pregnant was go talk to Benno. I said why don't we go to the courthouse, get married, and then tell them. But no, he insisted on doing it his way. The next thing I knew we were sitting down with his mother to make wedding plans.

When I walked in the door Queenie jumped up and hugged me to her big feather pillow bosom. "So there's to be a wedding," she said and I swear she was rubbing her hands together. "And soon?"

"Fritz thinks Easter would be good, but it's only six weeks away. Is that too soon?"

"Soon is good," she said, like that was something I should know, and then she turned to say something to Mr. Jahn in German.

"My aunt's coming from Germany for a visit," Fritz interpreted the conversation. "The first one in something like thirty years."

"So, does that make it a bad time for a wedding?"

He laughed. "We couldn't have planned it better."

I guess I looked confused because he leaned down and whispered in my ear, "The more, the merrier."

"Ja," Queenie turned back to me. "And your mother?"

"I haven't talked to her yet."

"Well, you must. You want to call now?"

"No. No, thank you. I'll call her after we've made our plans."

"Well, if you say so." Queenie looked surprised, but it didn't last long. "Now Fritz says not many people. That's hard here, where we know everyone, but perhaps we have the words for just the family here in the house and then the party in the park and decorate with the flowers from the yard, and we will make sandwiches and have someone to take the pictures for the newspaper, and . . ."

"Mother," Fritz had to interrupt her to make her stop.

She turned to him and put her hands on either side of his face like he was a little boy. "Excuse me, Fritz, I'm so happy. A daughter, and soon. . . ." she hesitated and looked over at me like we were in this together. Then she really caught me by surprise. "You will sing at the wedding?"

"Me?" I swallowed and remembered my manners. "I don't think so." I looked over at Fritz for help.

"Some girls do. Sing to their husbands after the words are said. Fritz tells me you sing."

An image popped into my head, something á la the version of "Oklahoma" we'd done in high school, me in a sunbonnet, him in cowboy boots, but I held back on the joke and kept on smiling at his mother while I shot darts at Fritz with my eyes.

He grinned and shrugged his shoulders and tried to explain his way out. "I told her you had a nice voice. Music's important around here."

I shook my head. "Fritz was just teasing," I told her. "I sing a lot with the radio, but not much in public."

"I think he likes it," she reached over and patted my hand. "Else he would not have told me."

His father never said a word, but Fritz said later if Benno was willing to pay for the food and the beer, that meant he approved.

Fritz stood beside me while I dialed the phone.

"Hey, Sheila," I said bravely

"Baby. What's going on?"

"I called to tell you the news."

"You made the dean's list?" I could hear music and talk in the background.

"You wish," I told her, and we both laughed. "No. Fritz and I are getting married."

"Fritz?"

"Fritz Jahn. I told you about him. His parents have that ranch in the Hill Country where we stayed last Fall."

"You didn't tell me it was serious." She lowered her voice. "Are you pregnant, Baby?"

"Sure 'nuf," I told her, hoping Fritz wouldn't understand our shorthand.

"You want an abortion?"

"No."

"Are you sure? What's tomorrow, Wednesday? I can be there tomorrow. Just a minute." I heard her put her hand over the phone and call out, "Do we have a gig tomorrow?" Then, "Shit!" Then, back to me. "Baby, if you can you wait 'til next Monday, I'll come. We'll take care of it if we have to go to Puerto Rico."

"No. Thanks, Mom."

"Hmm," she said, and then nothing for a while. "Grandmother Sheila. I'll have to write a song about this."

Fritz was pressing my waist, wanting me to get to the point. "Fritz has asked his pop to stand up with him and I was wondering if you'd stand up with me."

She laughed, hard enough that Fritz could hear her over the phone. I smiled at him and shrugged. Sheila wasn't much for tradition, but I couldn't expect him to understand.

"This going to be a big church thing?"

"No, just a little ceremony in the back yard."

"With a priest?"

"No. Why would you care?"

"Catholic would be a pretty hard jump for you to make."

"You don't need to worry about it."

"So they're Protestants, huh?"

"Why is this so important?"

"Not important to me. But, they're all something. It might be important to you, in the long run."

"No problem, Sheila."

"No problem it is."

"She said she'd like to. She'll check her calendar and get back to me," I told Fritz when I hung up the phone.

"Check her calendar?"

"Yeah. Like the group might be committed for that Saturday."

"For our wedding?"

"Well, Sheila's not too big on weddings. But, then, she don't do funerals, neither."

He didn't smile. "Will she be here, or not?"

"She'll let us know."

"When?"

"Who knows?" I threw my hands in the air. "Who cares?"

Seemed like I was always trying to explain her, our relationship. "I raised myself," I once told a strange guy I wanted to impress. I had my own key from the time I was ten, which was what she called the age of reason. Fixed my own sandwiches. Cleaned my own bathroom. On Sundays, around noon, I fixed her a Bloody María, tomato juice and tequila, and served it with cheese toast on a bed tray.

"If my bedroom door is closed, knock first and wait for an answer," she told me, "in case I've brought a friend home. I'm here for you," she told me, "but I've got my own life, too."

On Monday nights she never took a gig, so we could go out to dinner, a different place every time. She talked to me about school and homework and clothes and boys, and men in her life and music and on Tuesday mornings she got up and fixed cinnamon toast for breakfast. I still think of Monday as the last day of the weekend.

She never made it to the cheerleaders' mothers' meetings. Other mothers, the kind that wore denim skirts and carried basket purses, decided things like the color of our tights and whether we should be allowed to wear lipstick.

By eighth grade, it was a routine we had worked out. I told people that my mother had to work nights, so she couldn't do carpools or chaperone on field trips, even though she'd really like to, but she'd be glad to send a check to help with expenses.

"Money talks," she always told me. "It forgives a lot of trespasses, real and imagined." I never liked the tough look she got on her face whenever she gave that little speech.

"It's not the end of the world if she can't make it to the wedding," I said to Fritz, setting the telephone in its cradle. Then I had to tease the worried look off his face. "What's important is how happy I'm going to make you." I put my arms around his neck and rubbed my blue-jeaned pelvis against his in a slow, wide circle. "When we have a big house and a boat and two beautiful kids and you're the mayor and I'm the mayor's wife, we'll see if she wants to sing at the inauguration ceremony." I took a few steps away from him, then looked back over my shoulder, like Marilyn Monroe. "Money talks, you know."

He folded his arms, leaned back against the door frame and grinned. He was easy.

"Don't worry about it," I said, mostly to myself. "She'll be here if she can."

Meanwhile, I called Angie and worked out an escape plan.

"Banzaii," I said over the phone, our code word for big trouble.

"What's up?" she said.

Angie and I had been friends since seventh grade, since her father ran away with his secretary, and her mother stayed in bed and cried all day and drank everything in sight. Other girls' mothers frowned when they found out mine left me alone in the apartment at night, but Angie's mother suggested I come to their house. It made her feel valuable again, she told my mother, "taking the girls shopping, cooking for them, hearing those innocent giggles. I'd like to shelter them a little longer before the goddamned world eats them up." My mother smiled sympathetically and handed her a card.

"Call me Sheila," she told Angie's mother. "If I get an out-of-town gig, would it be all right for Carol Anne to stay here?"

Angie's mom nodded.

"It wouldn't be more than once a month," my mother said.

"Any time," Angie's mom said. Behind their backs, Angie and I gave each other the high sign.

I knew Angie would walk barefoot over hot tar to my wedding. She'd do whatever I asked.

"If Sheila doesn't make it, I want you to be maid of honor," I told her. "If she does come, I want you to do the guest book."

"Can you feel the baby?" she asked.

"Too early." I didn't mention that I forgot about it for days at a time. Pregnant was just a word, and a baby was more than I could think about, like trying to get interested in Christmas shopping in August.

I hung up the phone. "That's it," I announced. I was tired of wedding talk.

"My cousin, Vera," Fritz said. "She's coming. Queenie thought maybe there was something you could ask her to do."

"Someone I don't even know? What'll she think?"

"She'll think it's good to be included." The words sounded like they came from his mother.

"Where's she coming from?" I asked.

"Back east. She's in German Studies at the University of Pennsylvania. Went there on scholarship."

"And never came home?"

"Not often. Queenie calls her a professor, but I figure she's a TA, like the grad students at UT."

"Hmm." A female teaching assistant. In German? I got a vision of thick ankles and stringy hair. "Not married?" I asked

"No."

"Is she pretty?"

"I wouldn't call her pretty."

"What would you call her?"

He thought for a minute. "An excellent cake-server."

"Are we back to the cake?" I was getting irritated.

"I thought it was important to you," he told me. "Women want those things."

Three days before the wedding Sheila called.

"Baby," she said. "I've got good news and bad news."

"Tell me the good."

"A gig on a cruise ship! Someone cancelled at the last minute and guess who they called? Us. Two weeks in the Bahamas, and if they like us, maybe more. It's my dream come true."

"And the bad part is?" I saw it heading for me like one of those torpedos out of a World War II movie.

"They need us this weekend." She stopped for a minute and I heard her light a cigarette. "How much would you mind?"

"I'll get over it," I told her. I couldn't act with her.

"And I might not," she laughed. "I promise I'll make it up to you."

"I know. I have to run, Mom," I told her. "We were supposed to get on the road an hour ago." If I stayed on the phone one more minute she was going to hear me crying. Tears are one of the few things Sheila doesn't approve of.

At Fritz's house, Vera and her mother from Germany were waiting to meet us. The mother was having trouble with her ankles and wanted to tell us everything that had gone wrong with her in the past ten years, but Vera was cool. She helped unpack the car and then I caught her in the kitchen.

"I need to ask a favor."

"Yes?" she said, and looked at me with her eyes open wide and her brows raised, kind of half-smiling, like I was somebody's kid she wanted to be nice to.

Fritz walked into the kitchen. He put his arm around my waist and rested the other arm around Vera's shoulder.

"Carol Anne wants you to be in charge of the book," he said, and he pulled the three of us together in a tight little circle.

Vera beat around the bush. "I really should look after Greta."

Fritz made a sour face in the direction of the living room. "Come on, Vee. You know everyone who's coming. It would help us out." He grinned at her and I felt envious. She shot him a funny look, and then turned to me with a smile, "Sure. If that's what you need."

Two hundred people were invited to our reception. Queenie and Benno's friends, distant cousins, people Vera and Fritz had grown up with, and our friends that drove over from school. The morning of the wedding Queenie and Benno's sister, Greta, were up at dawn, bustling around the kitchen, turning out tuna fish and pimento cheese sandwiches, and potato salad and cole slaw, and fruit punch and iced tea.

Vera, Angie and I went to the park in the rain to decorate the pavilion with fresh flowers and crepe paper. We arranged chairs and benches and set up a table for the cakes and one for the gifts. In the far corner by the bandstand we put a table for the beer. I thought it was funny, beer at a wedding, instead of champagne, but Vera said it was more important than the preacher.

"I'm worn out," I said, and plopped myself on a stone bench. The sky was clearing and Angie had wandered off in search of cokes. Vera finished bunching white net around the edge of the cake table and came to sit beside me.

"I get tired quick these days," I said.

She turned and looked at me with the question on her face.

"Sorry," I said, and patted my still flat stomach. "I figured you knew."

"How would I know?"

"Your aunt."

"Queenie doesn't tell other people's business. Actually, Benno and those men down at Otto's cafe are more interested in town gossip. But if I were you, I'd keep it to myself. If you don't say anything, no one else is likely to."

"No one's going to act shocked when I start pooching out?"

She kind of laughed. "It won't be the first time they've seen it. With something like that, people here are pretty forgiving."

I looked over at the pavilion. "Looks like we're about through here. Wonder what I've forgotten that Fritz told me to be sure and do."

"Do you have a nice pen for the guest book?"

"Oh, hell no! Do we have to have one?"

"I'll borrow something from Queenie," she said. "Some of your guests are quite adept with a quill pen. I think you'll enjoy looking at their signatures later."

I nodded. Adept with a quill pen. The words rolled around in my head, and I couldn't help wondering what someone who talked like that thought of me. Probably that I was too young and not serious enough for Fritz. But she didn't know me. I could be whatever he wanted.

"Angie's mother is going to help us dress," I told her. "I want to do something special with my hair."

She came over, slipped her hands into the hair along my temples and pulled it up puffy on each side. "Maybe a couple of combs here," she said, "then fresh bridal wreath tucked across the top." She studied my face. "It would be striking."

I liked the way she took charge. She must have changed a lot since high school. Too big a nose, too square a jaw to be pretty, but I wouldn't call her plain. Olive skin. Straight brown hair. A good blunt cut, longer on the sides. Tall and thin. She had what the magazines called the natural look. All she needed was a little makeup and to shave her legs.

She offered me a cigarette.

"No thanks. I quit."

"Good for you," she said and lit one for herself.

"Glad to be back home?" I asked.

She looked away and pulled on her cigarette again. "Back in the provinces?" She hesitated, "Oh, I don't know."

"What about me?" I laughed. "Fritz tried to teach me some word they say here for people that aren't German?"

"Auslander?"

"That's it. That's me," I said.

"Try not to let it bother you," she told me. "It means outlander, someone who comes from a different region and either doesn't understand or won't bend to the local ways. Sometimes I feel like one myself."

Actually, it hadn't bothered me at all. I liked the idea that people recognized I was different. They even had a word for it.

QUEENIE

wo Germans together, my grandfather used to say, make for three opinions. That's to show, I suppose, how important are opinions. So many ways to see something. At Fritz's wedding, we all had our ideas. Greta thought the girl was a *schmeichelkachen*, a sweet talker who would say what anyone wanted to hear. But Greta was a sour person and glad as I was that she finally came to see the family, I didn't have to agree with everything she said. Benno liked the girl's pretty face. She was Fritz's choice, he said, and time would tell. Me, I couldn't stop thinking she carried in her belly my grandson. So maybe it wasn't what they say a marriage made in heaven, but we would make it work.

Benno and I married because of the land. I had it and he wanted it. And I wanted children and chose him to be a father. That's not so bad a reason, and makes more sense to me than the fairy-tale ideas the young girls have these days. When I think on our courtship and wedding, I see how changed things are since the day I stood before the preacher, my head torn between worrying whether my cooking would be good enough to please him and wondering what was to happen in the bedroom.

36

I met Benno when I went to Houston in 1933 to sell the lace Mama and I had been making during the drought and bad times that came after my second papa died. Frightened I was to ride the train by myself, far from home, not knowing what I should find.

I stayed at the boarding house of Mrs. Voigt who kept rooms for travelers. At supper the first night seven of us sat around a fine table with a white tablecloth and ate off hand-painted dishes. I was glad to be wearing my nice dress, though I had thought to save it to be fresh for market. Everyone spoke in German.

"Queenie has come to sell her lace," Mrs. Voigt announced. "She could use some help."

"That is your work?" one of the ladies at the table asked. She was pointing to the bodice of my dress, where I had sewed an inset of fine lace.

I looked down and nodded. So much attention.

When I looked up everyone it seemed was looking at my bodice except for Benno who was sitting across from me, busy eating he was, with big square hands that looked stronger than the rest of him and weren't too good with the knife and fork. He was a middle-sized man, past thirty years I guessed, with a serious face, and eyes that I couldn't find very well because of the glasses. Not a friendly face, just ordinary, like a picture in a newspaper, with dark hair parted almost in the middle and a little straight mustache that stopped here above his mouth.

"Benno knows the market," Mrs. Voight said. "He used to stay with me when he drove the freight. Now he sells insurance with Mr. Nowotny, but still he knows the market." She looked over at him and he stopped his eating and looked back at her. "You'll take Queenie there in the morning?" He nodded and looked down at his plate, and when he swallowed I saw the pieces going down.

At the marketplace the next day he carried my lace box to where a man who bought such things looked at it and offered me fifty dollars. I looked to see what Benno thought but he was across the way talking to someone else.

"This is good work," I told the man. "No mistakes." My mother learned from her mother, who came from the old country. "Should be worth seventy- five." I had hoped to get one hundred. A year's work of nights it was.

"Fifty dollars," the man said.

Benno was at my shoulder. "Take it, it's a fair price," he told me.

I didn't know what to do.

"She'll take it," he told the man and held out his hand.

I said nothing on the way home but was angry and sore inside, feeling I had been cheated. When I complained to Mrs. Voigt she told me, "If Benno said it was a good price, it was a good price. He may be lacking some polish, but he is as smart and honorable as any man I know. You are lucky."

Now I was feeling more foolish than ever. I waited until after supper when Benno went out on the porch to smoke, and followed him outside.

"It's hot out yet," I said.

"Ja," he said.

"Cooler where I live."

"Ja," he said.

"I'll be going back tomorrow."

"So?"

"*Danke schön* for your helping."

"You weren't liking it much this morning."

"Mrs. Voigt, she said it was a good price."

"Ja."

"I was hoping for more."

"Everyone hopes for more," he said.

"But I need it."

'Everyone needs it. What makes you so different?"

"Taxes."

"Taxes?"

"Ja."

"Land?" says he, and for the first time I see his eyes bright, like river stones.

"Ja," I said and held my tongue.

"You have land?"

"In the hills, four hours by train, beyond San Antonio, to the north and west. It's cooler there. Not so green all the time, but cooler."

"Your land?"

"My mother's."

"You have brothers and sisters?"

"Four, but they are from my second papa. My mother's land all comes to me and we are paying the taxes."

He put out his cigarette. "Are they much these taxes?"

"Eighty-two dollars."

"A lot of land."

"More than three hundred acres. Good for cattle and feed and pretty in places down by the river where the big trees grow."

"River land?"

"Some," I said. I stood up then and he stood too. "I must be getting to bed. I catch the early train."

"I can take you to the train," he said.

"*Danke*," I said. "I must be leaving at 8:00."

"Pecans?" he said.

"What?"

"Pecans. Do you have pecans on your land?"

"Ja. Many pecans." I held my skirt out wide. "We gather them in the fall like this, apron after apron full, and eat them all year round."

When I went down the next morning Benno was in the dining room drinking coffee and reading the newspaper. He put my suitcase in the back of the truck and I saw there was another one already there. I looked at him.

"I thought to ride with you. Looking for a place to start my own business and . . . well, they say it's cooler in the Hill Country."

I laughed then, partly because I felt happy for his company and partly because I could see how even smart men have a hard time saying what they think. Especially to women. And I was surprised to see him laughing too. He had strong, white teeth. A good sign in a man.

On the train he told me his story. What a courtship that was. More talking than we ever did after. Once said, he told me, things didn't need to be repeated. It went this way. His family's farm was in the Texas lowlands near to the coast. Four older brothers and three sisters he had and not enough land to go around, so at eighteen he traded his part for a truck and started carrying goods from town to town, supplies to soldiers, lumber and materials for building.

He was thirty-one now. His father had died, he had money in the bank and wanted to do something else. He thought to be a Texas Ranger but his eyes were weak, so he found work selling life insurance for the Sons of Hermann Lodge. Every German knew the name. A lodge brought over from the old country. Their motto—friendship, love and loyalty—many times my *opa* told me it.

"The lodge sells insurance?" It was strange to me.

"Since 1890," Benno told me proudly. "We help the man who wants to help himself." Now that he had done his training, he wanted a place to settle.

I saw it in his eyes, the wanting, looking out the train window as he talked, then back to me, then again out the window. Six rivers we crossed, and in between, fields of rice, cotton, and corn.

"Good land," he told me and nodded his head, like so. "My papa was a farmer. Always, the land," he said. "All us kids worked in the fields. In spring, he'd reach down and get a handful of fresh-plowed field, crumble it, and hold it in our noses. Said a rich field made him think of chocolate cake, almost good enough to eat."

What would Benno be saying, I wondered, when soon the fields would start to spread out tall with grass and the black earth came dotted with rock, seeing how things must work harder to grow. Out of San Antonio and moving to the north, the hills were beginning when I saw again his looking.

"Different land," he said.

"Ja."

"Good, though, on the eyes."

"Queenie," he said, later. "Where did such a name come from?"

I told how my *opa* had made it.

"Mama, she looked for a boy, which she would name after Prince Otto von Bismarck, the great German hero. Then I came instead, and Mama and Papa thought to call me Ottilie, like Otto, but for a girl. *Opa*, he said I deserved better, something more American, with a better sound, but important still. He called me Queenie from the earliest I can remember. One day, when I was older, to the town records he went, marked through Ottilie and wrote in Queenie."

"Easier back then," Benno told me. "Now, in the big cities, one is supposed to have a piece of paper to prove he was born."

"No."

"Ja. Can't account for people otherwise, so much moving around. And when *Opa* changed the name to Queenie, what did your mother say to that?"

"She said he might as well because I would never answer to Ottilie."

"My mother's name was Ottilie," Benno told me.

"Ja?" It was good, I thought, to share his mother's name.

I told Benno more of my *opa*, how tall and straight he was, even as an old man, with a full, curly beard that smelled like the smoke of wet leaves. I told of his white teeth that he kept clean with splinters of cedar, chipped fresh every day and kept in the pocket of his shirt. When he talked, I said, his bushy eyebrows danced up like everything was a question, and across his forehead came rows of curving lines, like the pictures of birds at the seashore.

I told how my *opa* had been a schoolteacher in the town called Comfort where I grew up. People from all around came to him with their questions and visitors stopped their wagons at our house for talk and music that went on until the candles burned away. How *Opa* kept bees so that we always had honey. How he organized a singing club and started a library, with some of his own books. How he wanted that I should learn to speak perfect English, but at home we used the mother tongue, and still I did not like to let it go.

I told Benno of my father, Frederick von Roeder, who was one day in San Antonio when a man in a bar jumped onto the table and asked who would follow him to Cuba to fight a war. My father signed to leave that day, only eighteen he was, and two years later back a hero and took a job with the railroad and married my mother. The man he followed turned out to be the first President Roosevelt, before he was president, which made my *opa* proud.

"This is how you got the land?"

"The land comes later." Benno is impatient, but he must hear the whole story, in order, if I am to tell it only once.

Papa von Roeder died in a train crash when I was too little to

41

remember. There was a little money from the railroad and a little from the government, and Mama and I moved in with her people to make ends meet. My *oma* was sickly and *Opa* had much to do. He was head of the school for many years."

"You told that already," Benno said.

"Back when school was taught in German and English," I paid no mind to his interruption. "He had read all the fine books and knew parts of them by heart. Sometimes he stopped in the classroom and asked us questions, just to see how it was going with our studies. That was when he was the mayor."

"Mayor, too?" I saw Benno liked this better than the teaching part.

"At funerals it was *Opa* who stood up and listed the person's good deeds, for he knew everyone, then 'rest in peace,' he said, and it was time to eat and drink."

"A preacher too?"

At this I shook my head and wanted to laugh. "Not my *opa*. Early on his people came, and such strong feelings they had about too much governing and too much religion, even they built a town without churches. Freethinkers, they called themselves."

"No churches?"

"Not for forty years, and after some were built, even, we never attended."

"Freethinkers," Benno said, like talking to himself. "Never heard of such."

"So now you have."

"Couldn't have been so many of them."

"Enough to settle Comfort, and others, yet, in Bettina and Sisterdale."

"Hmmm," he said, like thinking. "And these freethinkers didn't follow the church? So, what then would they think of the afterlife?"

A strange question, I thought, but I told him my mind.

"Not so much. We say we live on through our children and our deeds. You are a church man?" I asked, worried to hear the answer.

"Brought up Catholic, but that was a long way back."

"I'm not one who goes to church," I said again, to make it clear, "though there are many such in Schoenberg. Catholic, mostly."

"Nor me. Only weddings and funerals. Christmas and Easter, sometimes, for the music."

"The music is good," I agreed.

We were coming into the Schoenberg station before I got to the part of the story I knew he wanted most to hear.

"One day a man comes to our door, looking for someone to help with his children. His wife has died, he tells my *opa*. He has four small children and has come to ask for the hand of the widow who lives in this place.

"That is up to her," says *Opa*, and calls for my mother, who comes from the kitchen with me, ten years old, watching from the other room.

"This is Peter Zipp," he says, "who is looking for a wife."

"What have you to offer?" my mother asks.

"I have land, sheep, cattle, a ranch house, a Sunday house in Schoenberg, four children to be taught and cared for, and I am a hard worker."

From my place behind the door I see a heavy man with a red face who wipes his face with a handkerchief as he talks.

"Queenie comes with me," my mother says and motions me to come out. Peter looks down and gives a wink.

"You good with babies?" he asks.

"Could be," I tell him, "if they're good babies." This makes him laugh.

Benno has been listening close to my story. "You liked this Peter Zipp?" he asked me.

"Ja."

"And your mother liked him?"

I nodded. "She said he was a simple man, but with a good spirit."

"And you got the land from Peter Zipp?"

I nodded.

"And this Peter Zipp, with the Sunday house in Schoenburg, he was a church man?"

"Not so much after he married my mother. She was backwards, he told her in a joking way, because so many weekdays we spent in town for the children to get their lessons, but always she wanted to be at the ranch house on Sundays for cooking in the big kitchen."

"And why did he leave the land to the second wife, and not his sons?" Benno wanted to know.

"There was some for them, too."

"A lot of land."

"You need a lot in the Hill Country."

He looked out the window then. "Not so rich as in the lowlands."

43

"Ja."

"Easy on the eyes, though."

"You said that before," I told him.

By the time we got off the train Benno and I had agreed to marry. These were the things I liked about him. I listed them in my mind for I knew Mama would ask. He was smart enough, he would be a good provider, he had his fill of wandering, he did things and not just sit and dream. He wasn't a heavy drinker, he told me, and he was respected as a man of his word, Mrs. Voigt told me that. He was willing to take care of Mama, too, as long as she lived.

Mama didn't complain. I guess she was thinking, like I, that it was time. Twenty-six years I was, and good that I chose someone who wasn't against her staying on. After she met Benno all she said to me was that he seemed a serious man.

"I know," I said.

"Have you seen him laugh?"

"Once," I said.

"Has he kissed you?"

"Once, on the cheek," I said.

"Well, there's more, you know."

"I know. But I don't know what to expect."

"It's a private thing," she said.

"Is there anything I need to know?"

"How can I say? Every man is different."

So that is how I was thinking with this wedding. My own son a man now, an educated man, and the times are better and what we think isn't so important. The children are the future. Who doesn't know that?

"Rain on the wedding day means the bride will shed many tears," Greta told me.

"Oh, shush, Greta," I said. "You and I both know a bride will shed many tears, no matter what the weather."

44

Carol Anne

Sheila's wedding present was a honeymoon trip to Acapulco. Fritz said it almost made up for her not coming to the wedding, which is of course what she wanted him to think. Me? I figured she'd do something flashy. Still, I wasn't about to turn it down. It was exciting, flying off with my new husband to the land of sun and sand.

In Mexico, I learned right off that Fritz likes things to be predictable. The first morning he went down to breakfast at 7:00 a.m., which is when they were supposed to start serving. All he really wanted was a cup of coffee because he had drunk a lot of beer the day before, like people had told us—don't drink the water, just beer. So he had. I only had a couple and then switched to Cokes because of the you-know-what we were trying not to talk about but kept being there between us anyway. We were both worried about getting sick. Fritz's Aunt Greta had warned that someone she knew had to be flown home from Mexico in diapers.

Anyway, Fritz woke up early that first morning and went down for coffee and nothing was open. Then he stormed back to the room and hunted up the card.

"Right here, it says, they serve from 7:00 until 10:00."

"I guess they're running late."

"It's no way to run a business. These people never do anything on time, except start the music and take siestas."

"Hey! That's not such a bad idea." I invited him back to bed but he shook his head and headed for the bathroom.

"The toilet won't flush," he called out a few minutes later. "Call someone to come and fix it."

I put on my swim suit and laid his on the bed.

"Let's go to the beach," I told him. "We'll tell them at the desk and it'll be fixed when we get back."

"I'll believe it when I see it. Mañana, maybe."

He was still grumbling when we got down to the water so I didn't want to ask him to put lotion on my back. "I've already got sand in my teeth," he complained.

"That's the beach for you. Hey, let's get one of those drinks in a coconut shell." I waved at one of the little serving boys, but Fritz waved him away.

"How about a beer?" I asked.

"Not before I've even had a cup of coffee." He stood up and shook out his towel. "I'm going to look for a newspaper I can read," he said, like he was mad because they didn't print their newspapers in English.

"I'll catch some sun," I took off my dark glasses and rolled onto my stomach.

Married two days and he had turned into a grouch. Well, I knew something that always put him in a good mood. I dozed, thinking about dinner in our room, a shower, the candles I'd packed, and the black lace nightie Sheila had given me.

"Carol Anne," he woke me up shouting my name. "You're blistered," he said, and pressed his finger on the back of my leg to prove it.

I told him I wouldn't mention my sunburn if he'd stop complaining about the way they did things in Mexico. Still, he never acted like he was having fun until the day we went deep sea fishing and he caught that marlin. He looked so proud when they took his picture with a fish taller than he was. They cut off the end of the beak so he could take it back for a trophy but then he complained because they charged him almost twelve American dollars for it. He said it was his fish and I said then maybe he should have gone and bought a good knife for whatever that would cost him and cut the beak off himself.

"It would have been gone by the time I got back. They charge me for the beak at the same time they get the meat to pass around to all their family and friends."

"Yeah, they look like they're really getting rich off this fishing thing," I grabbed his arm and pulled him along down the dock, while I stuck the trophy on the end of my nose and hoped I could get him to forget his irritation.

We were on the plane home when Fritz picked up a New York Times someone had left on the plane. He was all worked up reading about President Johnson deciding not to run again, when I saw this headline on the back of the section he was reading.

"Look at this, Fritz."

"Just a second."

"No, look. It says, 'FLASH FLOOD HITS TEXAS HILL COUNTRY.'"

He flipped the paper around to see. "My God."

I read over his shoulder. It was the Guadalupe, all right. Kerrville, Comfort, Sisterdale, Schoenberg, Sattler, New Braunfels, and McQueeney. They listed the towns where people had drowned.

"It'll be okay." I patted his arm. His face was as gray as the airplane seat and he wouldn't look at me.

"You don't know," he said. Click, like that, he shut a door in my face and locked it. Didn't say anything until the plane landed and he could call home to find out for himself.

The news wasn't good. Fritz's parents had put Vera on the plane home and decided to spend the night at the cabin with Aunt Greta. In the night the water came up, so high they climbed to the attic and finally up on the roof and had to wait until neighbors came by the next morning in a motorboat.

For the first time, I saw traffic in Schoenberg. There were National Guard trucks and Red Cross and volunteers from all around who had come in to help. We had to show I.D. to prove we had a reason to be on

River Road but finally made it to the cabin, and that's where we found Benno and Queenie, looking really old and tired, like in those stories where people's hair turns gray overnight. The mud in the cabin was like three inches thick, and there was a dirty water line on the wall almost to the ceiling. While Fritz and Benno shoveled mud, Queenie and I carried out beds, mattresses, chairs, a dresser, everything we could lift. We hosed it all down and left it in the sunshine, the stuff we thought could be salvaged. There was one big pile of trash to be burned, once it dried out, and the dishes and clothes and things that needed to be washed went on the truck to be taken into town since their well water had gone bad.

Fritz and I went in search of the picnic table, the one with my name carved on it. We found it caught on a fence down from the house, along with rubber wading boots, plastic tablecloths, fishing tackle, an ice chest, and a pair of ladies' panties, really huge ones, caught way up in a tree, like a bad joke. When I laughed, Fritz frowned.

"It's not like they're your mother's," I told him and headed to the car for my camera. Benno followed me back and was chuckling while I took the picture. At least he got the idea.

Queenie said it was three times now the water had come into that house. She would never sleep there again, like an old log asking to be washed away.

"You're getting too old to work all that land," I heard her tell Benno. "Fritz has his college now. He's not interested in ranching. We should sell the land, most of it. Keep a little for picnics, over where the big pecan trees stand."

"Sell the land?"

"Well, why not? The tourists come and want the water near. They don't worry that their houses wash away, and their crops rot and the animals drown. They come to have fun. We will help them."

"Who would want to sell the land?"

"I would, Benno, and it was my mama's land, and she got it from my second papa . . ."

"I know, I know," he said and waved his hand at her to stop the talking.

Before long, it was Benno's idea.

"Getting too old to work all that land," he told Fritz. "Nowotny's son in Houston, he sells real estate. Says there's always a market in Houston for Hill Country property."

"Wouldn't hurt to see what they're looking for," Fritz told him.

That night when we were alone he said, "I can't believe they're talking about selling the land."

"You don't want them to?"

"It's not up to me. But, it's always been there, like something I counted on."

"Like you told your dad, it doesn't hurt to look into it."

"I guess."

I didn't know much, but I knew there were people in Houston with enough money to buy anything they wanted. Lots of them. And I thought Queenie made sense. What was the point of keeping all that land?

For the next few months the flood was all that people in town could talk about. They told the same stories over and over.

"The water was up, up, all the way in the house," Queenie was telling me.

"Two thousand dollars an acre," Benno was telling Fritz.

I was trying to hear both conversations at once.

"Benno's sister, Greta, she's sleeping in Fritz's room and her arm hangs off the bed like so, and all of a sudden she feels the water and she calls out, 'Benno, Benno, *mach schnell*.'"

"They want to build a golf club."

"A golf course?"

"Golf club. Golf course. You know what I mean."

"Don't sign anything until a lawyer looks at it."

"I know. I know."

"So Benno gets up and starts looking for his pants, and he can't find them because they've floated into the corner, so he pulls on my robe and takes the flashlight and goes out to see about his sister, and she's so upset he brings her back to our bedroom and the three of us we sit crosslegged on the bed and watch the water rise until we can't see the legs of the bed any more."

"Six hundred thousand dollars," Benno said. "What do I need with all that money?"

"What do you need with all that land?" Sounded to me like Fritz had changed his tune and turned businessman. "Improve the value and the thirty acres you keep may end up worth the three hundred you sell."

"I don't know. The money goes but the land is always there."

"They say the army engineers are going to build dams all up the river for flood control."

"Ja. I'm thinking maybe these golf people are thinking to get the land cheap when the flood is fresh in everyone's head."

"Then Benno he waded out to the kitchen and brought back two chairs and on one chair he stacks some books and helps us climb up into the attic. It wasn't easy, especially with Greta who has lived in the city all her life. Not even strong enough to lift herself up. Benno pulled and I pushed from behind, and all the while I'm wondering how high that water is going to come and do I want to be in that hot attic all night with the field mice and the scorpions and maybe a rattlesnake. Benno brings a little axe —how do you say? A hatchet, he brings, just in case, and good that he does, for we need it in the morning to cut through the roof when the boats come looking—"

"Didn't have much choice," Benno interrupted. "Lucky the house didn't wash away."

"Many hours, four or five maybe, we sat up there. Lie back, try to make yourself comfortable, I told Greta, save your strength, but she insisted on looking down into the bedroom, watching for the water to rise, listening in the dark. We just have to wait it out, Benno told her, but she was frightened and crying off and on. Finally Benno began to whistle and I began to hum and she was so angry that we would be singing while she was about to die, but after awhile she started to calm down."

"You call that calm?" Benno said.

"Do you think your mother likes me?" I asked Fritz.

"Mother likes everybody."

It was Sunday morning and we were on the bed in the apartment over Benno and Queenie's garage. We did it just about every night those first few months and sometimes in the mornings or when he came home for lunch. Daylight was the best because I got to look at him. I liked to take my finger and trace the line of his jaw. I'd stop and rest in that nice little dent in his chin, then back up to his temples where the hairline was moving back. I closed my eyes when we made love and when I opened them, sometimes I'd catch him looking out the window.

"What are you thinking," I'd ask.

"About the future," he'd tell me, "the good life we're going to have."

That would satisfy me.

The day I came home from the hospital with Georgie, Queenie was there, with the apartment shiny clean and smelling like cinnamon rolls just out of the oven. She had a vase of roses beside my bed. The covers were turned back and the pillows all plumped up and I crawled in and let her wait on me.

For two weeks she came two or three times a day, bringing fresh flowers and hot meals. She bathed the baby and rocked him when he cried and when I didn't have enough milk to satisfy him, she insisted I sit down, put my feet up, and drink a pitcher of beer. It worked, but it made me feel like a cow.

"Omie," I said, "I don't want to eat and drink beer. I want to get my figure back. It'll be summer before I know it and I have to get into my bathing suit."

"You're a mother now," she reminded me. "Time to think about more important things."

"But Fritz won't like me fat."

"He'll learn," she told me.

I was finally planted in a family and did my best to be nice and keep everyone happy—Fritz and Benno, their customers who rang the phone about business when I was bathing the baby or trying to take a nap, the doctor who told me it was time to be feeling better. How would he know? Keeping them happy wasn't easy, especially since it meant keeping my mouth shut. The men frowned on interruptions and anything that wasn't their idea. Like when I wanted to go shopping on Saturday afternoons or when I had the cramps and didn't feel like fixing dinner. I didn't remember Fritz being so bossy when we were together in Austin. In Schoenberg, he was just like the rest of them.

"It's hard," I told my mother when she showed up one Saturday for a visit.

She lit her cigarette. "I was afraid of that."

"Queenie says Georgie is a perfect baby, but if he is, I'd hate to have a bad one. I didn't know there'd be so much to do and I thought Fritz would help more."

"Thank goodness you have Queenie," she said. "It's a new world for you, Baby." She looked around the apartment. "Not that bad."

I made a face at her.

"Oh, cheer up, Sweetie. Honeymoons never last very long."

"Arbeit maks das leben suiss," is what Queenie told me. "Work makes life sweet." She had the words carved on a wooden plaque that hung in her kitchen. In Fritz's family the important things got boiled down to a few words.

Fritz got busy, working with his father, selling insurance and, of course, keeping up the land. Day and night, selling insurance, talking with Benno, maturity tables and retirement plans, mowing, baling, telephone calls, planting, paper work, calving. We moved into a little house on Franklin Street that we rented from his parents and he turned the empty bedroom into an office with a desk and chair and a daybed. Sometimes he slept there. Said the baby's crying kept him awake.

"You're nursing the baby?" Angie sounded surprised. "So, are you voluptuous?"

"Seriously volup," I told her.

"No kidding," she said. "Does Fritz think that's sexy?"

"He thinks he's died and gone to heaven," I told her, not about to admit my nursing embarrassed him. At least, I think it did. Still, I was glad I had decided to try. It was an easy way to keep the baby happy, and it was fun, having cleavage. One night I was getting ready to feed.

"Want to see what it tastes like?" I asked and offered Fritz a breast.

He looked at me like I was the world's worst slut-puppy and walked out of the room. I fed Georgie and put him down, then plopped on the bed and stared at the beam of light under his door, hoping any minute it would turn off and he'd come back and want me, like he used to. Things had changed too fast. I felt old and I wasn't even twenty-one yet.

Queenie stewed over me like I was something special. Every time she saw me she said how pretty I looked and what a good mother I was and what a good cook I was going to be. She taught me to fix rouladen and blaukraut and stollen.

"Fritz likes raisins and no fruits and Benno likes fruits and no raisins, so I put the raisins in this end and the fruits in the other, like this."

I liked to watch her big white hands work the dough. She tucked in the puffy ends and sealed the edge with one long stroke.

"You make it look so easy, Oma. How many times do you think you've done that?"

She looked at me surprised. "Oh, a hundred times a hundred. When I was a girl, I worked for the baker. My mother sent me off in the dark, before school. For my pay, a loaf of bread a day, which helped the family. I was very good help, such that he wanted to marry me, the baker man, but my papa said no, I was too young and he needed me at home."

"How old were you?'

She thought. "Fourteen, fifteen maybe."

"And how old was he?"

"The baker?" She cocked her head and thought back. Mrs. Santa, Angie called her, because of the way her eyes crinkled when she smiled.

"Oh, thirty, thirty-five maybe, very old I thought."

"And would you have married him?

"Well, if papa had said so, I guess I would have to."

I liked listening to her talk about the old days and about Fritz and Vera growing up. Stories about her mother and her opa and how she and Benno met. They still slept in the same bed. Did they do it, I wondered? I didn't really want to know, but it was hard to imagine, him with those big, blunt hands and serious face and the way he blew his nose like a foghorn. Still, he wasn't bad looking when he slicked up, and he had a good sense of humor, when he wasn't working. He liked it when I laughed at his jokes, so I tried to stay on his good side that way and not interrupt when the men talked business.

"Kissin' don't last, cookin' does." That's another old saying they have on the wall of the big restaurant in town and Queenie believed it. She cooked a hot meal at lunchtime every day. We served the men's plates and listened to them talk about what the lawyer said and whether the investors would get their financing and how everything rested on when the dam was completed, and in the meantime they needed to clear the prickly pear from the front pasture and repair the fences and build a new hay shed.

"If the ranch sale goes through, Benno wants to buy more land," Fritz told me. "He's looking at property around the edge of town for a housing development."

"A housing development?"

"The resort's going to put us on the map. We figure the town population will double by 1980."

Queenie said he and Benno were getting big ideas.

"Do you think the ranch sale is really going to happen?" I asked Queenie one afternoon in late summer. We were in the park at that spot not far from their house, where the cypress trees grow right at the water's edge and lean over to touch each other at the top.

She held Georgie in her lap, letting him wiggle his feet in the water.

"Who knows?" she shrugged.

"But you think so, don't you?"

"Benno says so. Me, I don't like counting chickens before they hatch."

"What would you do with the money, Queenie? Don't you think about that?"

She shrugged her shoulders and handed Georgie a little piece of bark to float in the water.

"Air conditioning, maybe," she said.

"I think you should have put a window unit in the kitchen a long time ago."

"Seems a waste," she smiled, "first to make cool the hot air, then to heat it up again with the stove."

"It's not a waste. It's a help. What about a maid?"

"Ha," she said. "What would I do with a maid?"

"Have her do the ironing?"

She smiled again. "Sheets and pillowcases, maybe, but I do Benno's shirts myself."

"You really like to do that?" I asked her. "It's such a pain."

"It's how I was taught."

"But don't you think it's kind of unfair? I mean, who says the women have to do the ironing and the cleaning and keep the kids quiet, and the men always get their plates served first and get to hand out the money and go off to meetings whenever they want. And when you go on trips, they always drive."

"No one says," she rearranged Georgie in her lap. "I never thought to mind such things."

"Vera says being a woman makes you a kind of auslander."

"And what would she be meaning by that?"

"It's not important." I took off my sandals and stuck my feet in the water. "I just wondered what you thought."

She was quiet for a while and I was feeling bad about bringing up the subject, like I was complaining or wanted to make Vera look bad.

"The girl is a good thinker," she said finally, "but the feelings don't come so easy for her. If one can't accept some things with the heart, an auslander he will always be."

"Or she."

"She?"

"Or an auslander she will always be."

"Ja. That, too."

Sometimes when Queenie and I talked, I wasn't sure whether we had understood each other, or just slid right by.

"Well, if this deal makes," I told her, "I want to build a house up on the hill and I've promised Fritz I'll treasure it and never, ever, ask for anything else."

"Here is your treasure." She reached down and kissed the back of Georgie's neck where the curls were sticking together in a damp little clump. "Last night, when the president said on the television, there'd be no more drafting of young men, I said to Benno, good that our Georgie won't be called to fight a war."

I fished in my purse and handed him a cookie. "He's only two, Omie."

"But grown before you know it."

When the deal went through, I had to read it in the local paper. "JAHN RANCH SOLD FOR GOLF RESORT," the headlines said. There was a picture of Benno and Fritz shaking hands with the new owners and a sketch of the proposed club house and home sites, and a five-year development timetable.

I waved the newspaper at Fritz. "Why didn't you tell me?"

He grabbed it from my hand. "They weren't supposed to announce it until tomorrow."

"How much?"

"How much what?"

"Fritz, don't tease me. How much money?"

"Mostly paper money. Two hundred thousand cash and a note to Queenie for the balance. Doesn't mean anything yet, except now we start buying land in town."

"So when did you plan to tell me?"

"Carol Anne, it's a touchy deal. When I'm told not to say anything until Friday, I don't say anything."

"Not even to me?"

"I was trying to do it right."

"And did you?"

He ran his hands through his hair and grinned at me. "You're darned right I did."

Oh, that grin. I hadn't seen it for months. I hadn't felt so much in love since the day we got married.

We stopped counting pennies then and started counting dollars, which doesn't mean we wasted any. Benno put the down payment into a company where he and Fritz were equal partners. By my figuring Fritz and I came out with $100,000 on the deal, a lot of money, but it wasn't time to ask for anything. I just listened while those two talked about land to buy and land to sell. They still acted like ranchers and insurance men, still wore cowboy boots and bluejeans most of the time, but they both bought new suits, for days they went to talk to their bankers.

People in town had frowned on the idea of the resort, selling the land, bringing in auslanders and all that, but then they got projections on the growth it'd bring the area, and the idea started looking better. Nothing succeeds like success, Sheila used to tell me, and now that my husband and father-in-law were local heroes, I saw what she meant. People came to them to talk about building subdivisions and a shopping center, and, maybe this sounds bad, but it made me feel important.

Fritz was happy and I was happy and, thanks to Queenie, I wasn't tied down by the baby. I saw what happened to the women here, turning into frumps with the first baby, but it wasn't going to happen to me, not when we were beginning to have some fun.

We started clearing brush from a plot Fritz picked out for a building site. Saturday and Sunday afternoons we left the baby with Queenie and headed for the property. Almost an acre on one of the hills that bordered the city. The low side was almost a thicket.

"Think there's berries in here?" I asked him.

"Not in a cedar brake," Fritz laughed at me and pointed to a can of turpentine. "Roll down your sleeves and put some of that around the bottom of your jeans. It'll keep the ticks off."

He got a chain saw and some long-handled shears from the back of the truck. "Cut whatever you can get these around," he said, handing me the shears. "And take it off as close to the ground as you can."

I put on the heavy gloves he handed me and wiped the perspiration from my forehead with my shirt sleeve. "Hot," I said.

"There should be a good breeze once we get some of this cleared away. Watch out for snakes."

Great, I thought. "Can't we pay somebody to do this?"

"We could hire some Mexicans," he said. "But I'd rather do it myself."

"I know," I said. *"Arbeit* makes life sweet."

"Now you're getting the idea."

I stuck out my tongue at him and started cutting.

Sheila

*L*ife's a crap game, my daddy used to say. You never know what the next roll of the dice will bring.

I never expected that my baby would end up in a place named Schoenberg, but I'll tell you this, people in Houston think the Hill Country's the next best place to Heaven. I tell them my daughter lives there and they get this far-away look in their eyes. "We like to go there every summer," they tell me. "Swimming, fishing, tubing the river. And that German sausage!"

I figure the area must have changed since I was there back in the Depression, riding along with my Daddy who was tryin' to get Lyndon Johnson elected to the U.S. House. I remember how hot it was trying to sleep curled up in the back seat of that old Pontiac with all the windows open and the wind blowing my hair in tangles. We stopped at church picnics and town squares and people cooled themselves, or tried, with paper fans from the funeral home and Johnson talked about how he was going to bring electricity to the area. I remember thinking they sure could use some help. All the women had what my daddy called "a passel of kids" and were stooped over from hauling water every day, Daddy said, and the men had big ol' rough hands and red patches on their lips and noses from too much sun. There were churches everywhere, but it didn't seem to me they were doing too much good.

That country wasn't a place I had much use for, until Carol Anne perched herself right in the middle of it. So, when Labor Day marked the end of my cruise ship gig, I made the overdue trip to see my daughter and my grandson.

"What a little doll," I heard myself cooing over the baby, sounding like a grandmother, for God's sake.

"I never thought you liked babies." Carol Anne watched me jiggle Georgie on my knee with a funny look on her face.

"Who doesn't like babies?" I urged another smile out of him before I handed him back to his mother. "They're just. . . ."

"A lot of trouble."

"You said it, Kiddo." I followed her into the kitchen. "Why don't we put him in the new stroller and you can give me a walking tour of town?"

"You interested?"

"I've done my homework."

"What's that?"

"Stopped and read a marker on the way in. Established in 1950 by the Adlerverien, whatever that is."

"1850," she corrected me, "and it's Adelsverein. Adler is an eagle."

"Sounds like you've been doing your homework, too." Carol Anne was a bright girl, but had never seemed interested in learning anything in particular. Maybe she wants to prove something to me, or somebody, I thought.

"It's a long story."

"Can you boil it down to fifty words or less?"

"Let's see." I could see her rising to the challenge while she settled Georgie in the stroller and pulled a cap over his head. "Okay. Here goes. These noblemen in Germany decided to set up a model colony here. They sold boat passage over and they promised free land, and building materials, and food to get through the first growing season, but when the people got here, nothing was like it was supposed to be."

"Isn't that always the way?"

"You can ask me questions," she said.

"Do I have to?"

"Yes, because I had to leave out a lot"

"So why'd these people want to leave Germany? Every German I ever knew thought wherever he happened to find himself was the best place to be."

"There were too many people and not enough land, Queenie says, and then some people got over here and sent letters back saying how great it was, that the Indians were friendly and the snakes didn't bite and lots of stuff grew wild, without having to be planted, and they made it sound like paradise."

"So it was one huge hoax?"

"Not exactly. Just a lot of goof-ups." Carol Anne closed the door behind her, and together we lifted the stroller down the steps.

"They landed in the winter, in Indianola, down by Galveston."

"I've been to Indianola. Not much there."

"There were supposed to be wagons to carry the people into New Braunfels. That was the original settlement. But the wagons never came, so they had to live in tents for the winter and the ones that weren't sick from the trip over got sick living outside in the rain."

"How do you know all this?"

"Queenie tells me," Carol Anne said. When she talked about Queenie, I kept imagining a large woman, with a crown on her head, who sat in a big chair and told stories all day long. "Her grandfather came with his parents on the boat when he was five. He told her how they all stood on the deck when they were leaving and sang the German national anthem while they watched the sun set on the home-land. These people are really patriotic."

"And really sentimental."

"Be sarcastic if you want, but I think it's sweet that they love being American. You should see what they do here for the 4th of July."

"So Queenie's people settled here?" I was fishing for information about this woman who was giving my daughter the mother treat-ment.

"Her people left the first settlement because it was too crowded and went to the edge of Indian country, first to Fredericksburg and later they started a town called Comfort."

"I went to Comfort once with my daddy, long time ago. Those were some optimistic farmers. Built a town on a rocky cliff in Indian country and called it Comfort."

"They weren't all farmers."

"They were by the time I was there," I told her, getting a little tired of the history lesson. "I thought everyone here was a farmer, like those two there," I nodded toward two heavy-set men standing in overalls beside an old pickup. One raised his cap as we walked by. "Mrs. Jahn," he said and nodded at Carol Anne.

"You know that man?"

"He's a customer of Benno's. Comes by the house sometimes."

"Mrs. Jahn?" I repeated, trying to get the sound of it placed with my Carol Anne.

She turned and gave me a smug grin. "What do you think?"

"I don't know what to think."

"Well that's a first."

"Give me time," I said.

We turned down a side street and were suddenly at the river. Carol Anne lifted the baby from the stroller and started down toward the bank.

"You going to leave the stroller here?"

"Sure," she said. "No one's going to bother it."

I pulled it behind a tree, just in case, and followed her.

"This is my favorite spot," she said.

So much for the white pants. I brushed off a flat rock and sat to face the clear, green water that rolled along like it had someplace it needed to be. "This is what they talk about in Houston," I said. "They're right. You don't find anything like this in our air-conditioned metropolis."

"I thought you'd like it. If you listen, the water has a kind of music to it."

We were quiet for a minute, long enough for me to hear what she was talking about.

"Queenie told me that," she said and I felt a little stab again.

I had to meet this Queenie. What the hell kind of name is that anyway? And Benno? I've lived almost fifty years and never heard of anyone named Queenie or Benno, not even in magazines or movies.

"When do I get to meet your new family?"

"Well, you kind of caught us off guard. This weekend is the Handel Festival in San Antonio and they went down for the day. It's a big thing they've been talking about for months."

"And Fritz?"

"Had to cover the office, but he'll be home at five."

I checked my watch. "I have to leave for Austin by eight, but I'd like to take you guys out for an early dinner."

"I hoped you'd say that. I'm not much of a cook, yet."

"You want to be?"

"I'm trying."

Carol Anne was trying, that was for sure. I thought about her all the way back to Austin. Trying to be a mother, and a wife, and even a friggin' cook. She's picking up the history, and all that damned determination that goes with it. Before long, she'll be speaking the language. Seemed to me these people were way behind the time.

I took one hand off the wheel and rubbed a tight place in my shoulder. Schoenberg's one of those nice places to visit, but I'd hate to try and live there. I didn't see one thing in the store windows that I'd be caught dead wearing and that sign over the counter at the soda fountain about not serving draft dodgers was pretty tight-assed, if you ask me. I wonder what they'd say if I walked in there with my black trio.

Fritz was a surprise. Somehow I'd pictured a cowboy type, but he's much smoother than that. Tall, dark, handsome, and serious, which is funny, because I always figured Carol Anne would end up with some unreliable jerk she'd run off with just because he made her laugh. Guess I made the mistake of thinking that because she was my daughter, I knew what she wanted. Fritz, now, is the kind that wants everything just so. I could tell that when he had her change the baby's clothes before we went out. And they weren't even dirty. He had a hard time letting me pay for dinner, too, even though I know they're strapped. He'll be a good provider, I imagine. I can tell more about him when I meet Queenie and Benno. Just hope I can keep a straight face calling them by name.

I told Carol Anne I'd be back before long, but I'm thinking she's got about all the family she can handle right now and I'll give those two some time to iron out the wrinkles before I show up again. She hinted things weren't going like she'd imagined. Well, I'm not one to give advice. Always comes back and bites me on the ass. But I wanted to warn her not to give too much of herself away. She may wake up one day and wonder who the hell she is.

Vera

Four linguists sat in a garden discussing the merits of their language when a butterfly flew by.

'For example,' the Italian gestured, 'we call that lovely creature a *farfarella*. Imagine a language that captures the sound of gentle flight.'

'We say *mariposa*,' the Spaniard said. 'Mine is a language of color and design.'

'*Papillon*,' the Frenchman whispered. 'A word as delicate as those tissue-thin wings.'

They turned finally to the German to give his name for butterfly. 'We call it *schmetterling*,' he told them, and when they had finished laughing, he shrugged his shoulders. 'It works for me,' he said."

The class erupted in polite laughter. The speaker leaned over and scanned the audience, pinning us with intense eyes. "People, we're going to talk in this class about political and cultural differences that shape the modern world. But we can't begin to talk about World War II, or The Holocaust, or the Nuremberg Trials without an attempt to understand the German mind. Extremely practical, not inclined to romanticize a butterfly—or a word. But an idea? That's something else."

He stopped for a moment and no one moved. "That's why we're here—to study ideas—and the men," he looked around again, "and women, who've managed to influence the course of history through those ideas. Keep in mind that I'm not interested in cramming facts down your throat, but I'm going to try my damnedest to stretch your perspective."

I was twenty, a sophomore at the University of Texas in 1960. The speaker was Dr. Donaldson, Associate Professor of History, and it was the opening day of class. I was excited by this man who dressed in shirt sleeves, instead of a jacket and tie. He wore his hair almost to his shoulders and spoke with a passion I hadn't seen in other professors. At the end of class he asked if anyone was looking for part-time work and I stayed behind.

"You're . . .," he looked down the roster.

"Vera Jahn," I said.

"A good German name," he looked up and smiled. "You from around here, Vera?"

"Schoenberg," I told him.

"I know the town," he said. "Beautiful town."

I nodded.

"So you have some time to work?"

"I'm working now, in food service at The Commons, but I'd rather do something more. . ."

"Interesting?"

I nodded again.

"Look, I can only pay you $2.50 a hour, and, if you're a student, they won't let me use you more than fifteen hours a week. It'll be mostly grading papers, filing, copying, stuff like that."

"I can do that."

"Sprecken ze Deutsch?"

"*Jawohl.*"

"Good. You can help me with some translations I've been fumbling over." He smiled again. "You a good student, Vera?"

"Yes, sir."

"Live on campus?"

"Yes, sir."

"Follow me back to my office and we'll get you signed on."

"Yes, sir."

"Look, Vera," he stopped and turned to face me. "You can call me Dr. D. That 'sir' stuff makes me feel old. I may seem like a fossil to you, but I haven't hit forty yet."

For the next two years, his office was like a second home. Student workers had permission to study there, when there was nothing that needed to be done. He loaned me books by new writers—Gunter Grass, Joseph Heller, James Baldwin ñ and wanted my opinion on what I'd read. He followed my studies and made suggestions on classes and professors, and a few times he tried to arrange dates for me, which I didn't appreciate.

I remember the afternoon he closed down the office and took us out for beers to celebrate the first American in space.

"You'll tell your grandchildren about this one day," he lifted his glass and looked around the table. "This one's for Alan Sheppard and the good ol' U.S. of A." We drank up. There were two other professors, four grad students, and me, the only girl, as usual. I mostly listened, but I knew I could hold my own in their conversations, as well as their beer-drinking.

Dr. D. picked up the pitcher and filled everyone's glasses again. Then he announced that he'd been offered a position at the University of Pennsylvania, his undergraduate alma mater, and he'd be leaving in about six months. I felt like someone had pulled a rug out from beneath me.

"Where I'm going, Vera," he told me the next day, "they have one of the finest programs in German Studies in the country."

"Um hmm," I was grading papers and only half-listening.

He walked over and waved some forms in my face. "There are scholarships available and I think you should try for one. If I know the

Quakers, they'd welcome a female candidate. You might lose some credits in the transfer, but it couldn't set you back more than a year and would put you in a good position for graduate school."

"I can't afford graduate school," I said.

"Nonsense. You can always afford what you want. The only question is, is this what you want?"

Was that what I wanted? A Ph.D. in German Studies, from an eastern university? My heart was bursting.

On the plane home from Fritz's wedding I had time to think and much to think about. There was my mother, and Fritz, and how my life had changed since leaving Schoenberg. I was glad to see Fritz married if it meant we could finally be friends again. And the fact that none of these people who were my family understood the least thing about me didn't seem to matter as much as it had in the past.

When the opportunity came for me to study in Pennsylvania, I had gone for help the only place I knew to go.

"What is wrong with The University of Texas?" Queenie wanted to know.

"Nothing. But this is a good opportunity. One of the best schools in the country for what I want to study."

She stroked her cheek, thinking.

"You will be very alone, way up there."

"I have a mentor."

"A what?"

"A professor who's going to teach there, who thinks I should go."

"A professor?"

I nodded.

"Is there something more, with this professor?"

"Something more?"

"I see a light in the eyes."

"Nothing romantic, Queenie, if that's what you mean."

"Romance grows."

I couldn't tell her what I suspected. "I need to borrow some money to get started," I said, "but I'll find a way to pay it back."

She said she'd talk to Benno, but when she came back to me, it was with cash that I suspected was her own. Benno had never appoved of my going to college. "Where are the boyfriends?" was all he ever asked. "Isn't that what a girl goes to school for?"

"We will say nothing of this, *leibchen*," Queenie told me when she handed me a fat, sealed envelope. It contained almost $800 in small bills. Household money, I thought. "I never spend it all," she had told me once, "just in case."

My introduction to Philadelphia began with a solicitation at the airport by a bald-headed man dressed in robes. If I had known he'd be there I could have avoided him, but in the crush of people exiting the plane I was pushed directly in his path. There he was, standing on one foot, chanting and hopping, and when I passed by, he thrust a book in my hand and continued to chant. I looked around for Dr. D. who had said he'd meet me.

"No thanks," I handed the man back the book, realizing he was no older than I.

"Any donation will be accepted," he said.

"I'm really not interested," I told him.

"Take it for nothing. It will change your life."

"Vera!"

Suddenly Dr. D. and another man were beside me. He took the book and handed it back to the boy who turned to one side and started hopping and chanting again. No one else was paying the least attention to him.

"Hare Krishna," he told me. "They're harmless." Then he motioned to his friend. "Say hello to Sam."

Sam smiled and took my hand luggage. We waited for the other bags and he sat patiently while I caught Dr. D. up on the department at U. T. since he had left. After a while I felt like we were excluding him.

"Do you teach at the university too?"

"Sam's in linguistics. He and I are roommates," Dr. D. said.

"I suppose you've heard the schmetterling story," I said.

"Many times," Sam told me. He looked over at Dr. D. with open fondness.

It didn't take long for me to understand that the two were a couple. "Queers," Benno would have said, but it didn't strike me like that. They didn't do anything flagrant, like others I saw on the streets, but over time it became clear. I accepted the fact without a considerable amount of discomfort. People on the East Coast, and especially on campus, were in rebellion against the old standards. The community accommodated a variety of lifestyles and it was difficult, perhaps dangerous, to appear to pass judgment. I found this "live and let live" philosophy very freeing, and also slightly unnerving.

Dr. D., or Donald, as I came to call him, continued to be a mentor, and Sam became a friend. In the year or so that followed the three of us spent a lot of time together. They took me to concerts and plays and out to dinner. One night at their house, we fixed spaghetti and drank a lot of wine. Sam was determined that night to teach us to dance the Watusi.

"Vera, you really should cut your hair," he told me.

"What's wrong with my hair?"

"Nothing. It's shiny and thick. Just boring."

"How about letting me cut it?"

I looked over at Donald.

"He's good," he assured me.

"What's the point?"

"Sam thinks you need a boyfriend."

"I don't need anything of the sort."

"Have you ever had sex, Vera?" Sam asked.

"Excuse him. He's had too much to drink," Donald said.

"Once. And I didn't like it."

They laughed at me.

"Things take time," Donald said.

"Let me cut your hair. Please," Sam begged.

It was ridiculous. A grown man, acting like a child. I told them good night and left. The next morning Donald called to apologize and a few days later I found a funny card from Sam in my mailbox and a note signed with a smiley face that said to lighten up. I shook my head at his inability to understand. It was my nature to be serious.

Perhaps his words were ringing in my ears a few months later when I went to New York to my first professional meeting. I was twenty-four, into the second semester of graduate school, and, I suppose, tired of watching a revolution go on around me without taking part. I ended up in bed with a stranger and found out I didn't have to love someone to do that. I also found out Sam was right. A little attention to how I looked could attract men. Back at work, I was suddenly being noticed. I went out with some of those who asked me, and some of those, I slept with. Finally I didn't have to bristle when someone asked the question that had become a common greeting on campus, "How's your sex life?"

The pill was freedom, and for a while I used sex like a lot of those around me, as a welcome diversion. Why not, the reasoning went, if you don't have to think about getting married or getting pregnant? Donald and Sam celebrated my liberation at first and then it placed a wedge between us. I lived alone, struggled with meager finances and was intensely occupied with my studies. The time I used to spend with them came to be spent with whomever I was sleeping with at the time. Few of my boyfriends were comfortable with Donald and Sam, so it naturally came about that we saw each other less and less.

Queenie sent letters, with money tucked inside, and news of home. Fritz was stationed at Fort Hood in Killeen, she wrote, and looked very handsome in his uniform. He would begin at the University of Texas as soon as he completed his national service. I smiled at her choice of words. In the midst of the complaints and mistrust I saw directed at our government daily, such respect seemed naive. And wasn't it terrible about President Kennedy getting shot? she wrote. Him and his young wife and all that blood on her pink suit. And did I see on t.v. when the dear little boy saluted his father's casket? Benno never wanted to see a Democrat in the White House, she wrote, but at least President Johnson was a Texan. From the Hill Country.

From my point of view, having LBJ in the White House during the years I had been in school had kept me on the defensive with my East Coast friends, trying to explain a kind of crudity and male power politics I found personally distasteful.

I shifted my seat to an upright position and looked down on the Philadelphia Airport, glad to be home, and glad to be back in the present. The wedding trip had been a excursion into the past. But it was good to have a fresh starting place. Fritz had become a man, an interesting man, and we were friends again.

When news of the flood hit the papers I called immediately and it was Fritz who answered. His voice was reassuring but ambivalent.

"Everyone's okay," he said, "but they're talking about selling the land."

"They'll never do that, cousin," I laughed at the thought.

He called again six months later to tell me an offer was under consideration.

"A golf course on the ranch?"

"And home sites. But we're setting aside ten acres for you."

I was caught off guard. "I can't afford to buy right now."

At that he laughed. "They want to give it to you."

"Benno wants to give land to me?" I was stunned.

"Actually, it's Queenie's land. But, yes, they want us each to have some."

I was speechless.

"He's a fair man, Vera, and he considers you a daughter."

"What do you think of this idea?"

"I like it. A family compound. Benno and Queenie are keeping twenty acres for themselves. He said if you don't plan on coming back, you could take yours in cash when the deal goes through."

"I want the land."

"Eight hundred feet of water frontage, Vee, from where the cabin stands to where the river turns. I'll work you up a plat and put it in the mail. If we can't all agree, we may draw for lots."

"This is for certain?"

"It's for sure, whether the sale goes through or not. You know how Benno is when he decides to do something."

For days a light in my head turned off and on. Land, it said in neon letters. Your land. It seemed a coincidence to be teaching Marx that week. Marx, and his theory that private property was responsible for the enslavement of women, replacing, as it did, a communal society with a competitive one. I considered confiding in my students. Look, I wanted to say. A century later, and the theory can be observed working in reverse. Private property placed in a woman's hands imparts power.

I picked up the phone and called Benno.

"Onkel, it's Vera."

"Ja."

"Fritz tells me you want to give me a piece of the ranch."

"It was Queenie's idea. Her stepfather set it aside for her mother. She sets it aside for you."

"Well, wherever the idea came from, I'm grateful."

"It's your inheritance. We give it to you in a will, you must pay taxes. This way we give it a little at a time. In five years, it's yours."

"Sounds like a good plan."

"It is a good plan. Fritz's plan."

"Okay. Well, what can I say? Thanks, Onkel."

"Ja."

Talking with him was like talking to a wall. Still, I was grateful and glad I had told him so.

Fritz and Carol Anne's baby was born the following January and I began saving for a trip home. Carol Anne sent pictures and Queenie sent reports on Georgie's development and Fritz called from time to time to keep me informed of progress on the land sale. It was more contact with family than I had had in years. Not only did I have a piece of land I wanted to see again, but a nephew, whose picture had replaced my mother's on the bedstand.

When school closed that next winter for Christmas vacation I found a ride with a student, a silly boy who insisted on showing me how fast his new Bel Air could travel for extended periods. He honked at every car with a girl in it, and talked incessantly about how drunk he planned to get on New Year's Eve. It was a relief when we reached his home in

Atlanta and I boarded a train for the remainder of the trip, anxious, for once, to get home.

On the afternoon of Christmas Eve, Fritz, Carol Anne and I drove to the ranch to cut a tree. We took our time, finally settling on a huge cedar with a fat, full center, and only one bare spot. Carol Anne and I laughed as we filled the spot with an empty nest from another tree and then left Fritz to top it out and skin the lower branches while we went to walk the river.

"Over there," I pointed to the opposite bank, "where the river begins to bend, that's where the old orphanage was."

"Queenie told me about it, a preacher and his wife that took in children whose parents died on the trip over."

The sun was low in the sky, spreading a wide, bright path across the water. We shielded our eyes to make out remants of a farmhouse and some collapsed outbuildings. "I grew up hearing about what a great man he was," I told her. "Well-educated. He left the church to take care of fourteen orphans and six children of his own."

"I bet his wife did most of that 'taking care.'"

"He also raised silkworms and experimented with new strains of tobacco and took a strong, unpopular stand against slavery before the Civil War. When I was a senior I did a long paper on him and in my research discovered there's a part of that story no one talks about."

"There usually is."

Carol Anne surprised me at times.

"After years of being a leading citizen, he got involved with one of his own orphan girls. Ended up taking her and two of his own sons off to Mexico."

"Does Queenie know that?"

"Of course. They all ignore it so they can have a mythical hero. I asked her about it and she said—"

"That no one's perfect."

"Something like that. She said that a man who gives so many years helping things grow shouldn't be remembered as bad."

"And he was probably horny. I'm sure his wife was all used up."

"Queenie said something like that too. 'A man has calls,' she told me. That's the kind of attitude that furthers the enslavement of women."

"Did you tell her that?"

"Of course not. I didn't even think in those terms ten years ago."

Carol Anne picked up a handful of stones and began tossing them in the river. "I don't feel enslaved, Vera. Do you?"

"Not enslaved. It's an outdated term. What I feel, what I've always felt, growing up here, is that being a woman makes you an auslander. You're always having to earn your citizenship in a place where men, white men to be specific, decide what's important and then make rules to ensure it doesn't change."

"You mad about that?"

"I try not to be," I told her and then the conversation shifted to the river lots. I said I had a preference for the end one, the one across from the orphanage. I liked the history of it.

"Fine with me," she said. "I probably ought to warn you about the peacocks."

"What peacocks?"

"Across the way. The guy that owns that place now raises them."

"I like that."

"You won't when you hear them."

"I know the sound. Sharp. Mournful."

She shivered and hugged her arms to her body. "And you like it? Makes me nervous," she said. "Like a baby crying."

I returned to Philadelphia following that holiday to find my apartment had been broken into and the old man who lived on the first floor had been beaten, a good man who sat by the window and waved to everyone who went by. At the hospital, he lay in the darkened room like a lump of wax.

"Mr. K, it's Vera, from upstairs."

"Vera," he opened his eyes and tried to smile.

"I brought you some kolaches."

He reached out a bruised hand and tapped the bedside table then motioned for me to come close. I set the bakery box down and leaned over all the tubes connected to his frail body.

"*Schwarze*," he whispered.

"The police arrested them," I told him. "Those kids that hang out on our corner when they ought to be working."

"I let them in," he said. "They admired my music box."

"And they took it."

"And my gold-headed cane" he said. "Hit me with my own cane. My papa's cane."

"Outlaws," I told him.

"*Schwarze,*" he said. "Black trash. An old man should know better."

"You wanted company," I told him.

"An old man should know better."

"The police said to put in window bars and deadbolt door locks."

"Such a pity," he said. "Such a pity."

I walked home with my purse held tight, looking over my shoulder every few steps. Three young blacks had already claimed the spot on the street corner where the others had stood. As I passed by their voices grew loud with words I couldn't understand. They reminded me of grackles, ugly, quarrelsome birds, bent on intimidating anything that happened by, and though I tried, I could summon no feelings of pity or forgiveness. The City of Brotherly Love had palpable anger on its streets. I felt angry too. Angry at the invasion of property, at the injustice of unprovoked attack, and angry with the shame of my own thoughts.

Schwartze. Black. Another word I had learned early. Queenie used it to denote color. In Benno's throat it was a term of disdain, delivered with a kind of slow growl, the sound that echoed now in my own head.

The officer who took the robbery report suggested I buy a gun.

"I can't believe the police would recommend such a thing," I told him.

"This is off the record." He looked at me with eyes like blue steel. "You live in a war zone, Miss. Shoot first and ask questions later. It's the law of the jungle."

"The law of the frontier," I corrected him, "on the way to becoming civilized."

"You call beating an old man for a $20 portable radio civilized?" he

76

asked. "I see it every day. A woman alone should look out for herself any way she can."

"The end doesn't justify the means," I said, quoting words which were lost on him.

He looked at me and shrugged his shoulders. "Suit yourself."

I bought a dog instead, a German Shepherd that I named Val for the Valkyries. Together we attended obedience training. Even before she was old enough to actually offer protection, her bark and her breed elicited respect in my neighborhood, and she was a quick learner. Val went everywhere with me. She stayed beneath my desk when I was at the university, waited for me on the library steps, and slept at the foot of the bed at night, attentive to my mood, alert at the slightest unusual sound.

On certain mornings when the air was clear, I could hear the lions over at the zoo calling for their breakfast. Val would lay her ears back and bare her teeth.

"It's okay," I had to continue reassuring her until the sounds stopped or were drowned out by the roar of freeway traffic.

It would be good, I thought, to exchange the confusion of this city for something more simple. My life was increasingly frustrating and I was forced to take extra jobs to supplement my teaching income. There were semesters when progress on my dissertation seemed to come to a standstill. I was in the fifth year of graduate school and a clock in my head had begun to tick.

When Donald was awarded his Fulbright Grant to lecture in England and Sam managed a sabbatical so he could go along, we went out to dinner to celebrate.

"It won't be the same here without you two."

"Only nine months," Donald reminded me. "We'll be back in time to see you graduate."

"If you ever finish the dissertation that has no end," Sam chided me.

"I plan to. Before the year is out."

"You've been saying that for how long now?"

"I mean it this time. I'm beginning to look at job postings."

"Which reminds me," Donald said. "Something came across my desk the other day I thought you might be interested in." He handed me a notice from a colleague, announcing the formation of an Institute of Texas Cultures in San Antonio.

"I always planned to teach," I told him

"I think you should send this fellow your resume."

"Because?"

"Because I suspect you want to go back to Texas and I don't want to see you end up teaching German in high school, or some second-rate college. You've almost educated yourself out of the marketplace, Vera, and this looks like a good opportunity."

"Listen to the voice of reason," Sam said.

"You think I should go back home?"

"I think you want to. I think you have unfinished business there. And people you care about."

"It might be a terrible mistake."

"Could be. There are no sure things."

"This place is getting to me. I remember when I thought I'd never want to leave the university, but it's more of a circus these days than a place to look for answers."

"Your aesthetics are changing," Donald smiled. "It happens to all of us."

"How old are you, Vera?" Sam asked.

I knew he knew. "Thirty," I told him, trying not to let something so neutral as a number bother me.

"Well, there you are," he said, as if it were settled. "Time to move on."

QUEENIE

After the flood my grandfather comes in a dream and says to sell the land. What is this, I ask myself? My grandfather died before it passed to me. He didn't even know about the land. But he was wise, my opa, and if there is some knowing after death, he would be the one.

"Things change," he used to tell me. "Things change. Four years of drought. Then it rains for that, or longer. Then it floods. Four, five more years of drought. The story is all there." I remember him showing me the rings on a freshly chopped cedar tree. I remember, and I begin to think of the circles of my own life.

Benno grows too old to try and run a ranch and a business too, and Fritz likes more to work with his head, I believe, than his hands. Our children are grown, with a child on the way, a child who may not choose a country life. So why do we keep the land and use our savings for the taxes that grow bigger while the crops grow smaller? It is time to change our thinking, but I know Benno will have a hard time with this, for it is not how he was taught. So I blame it on the river.

"The river is like a cat," I say one day at the lunch table. "Sometimes it licks your toes. Sometimes when you are sleeping it sneaks up and scratches you. Three of our townspeople drowned in the flood. Could have been us."

"Mother," Fritz tells me like I don't already know, "It's the twenty year flood plain. Maybe not so good a place to build a house, but ours is still standing. It can't be too bad."

"Easy enough to say," I tell him. "It feels different when you look from the roof and see the neighbor's cow wash by."

"With the new dams, it's not likely we'll ever see high water on our property again."

"Then it is a good time to sell," I say. "Keep a little for ourselves. Keep the cabin, even, for day visits, but no sleeping there. Not my grandchild."

Benno has not been listening. He looks up from the newspaper.

"Sell the land? Who would want to sell the land?"

"I would," I say. And it goes from there.

It was Benno's idea to give the ten acres to Vera. We talked with Fritz about the part we would all keep together.

"I thought to leave my part to Vera in my will," I tell him. "Like my mother left hers to me."

"I thought to give her some now," says Benno.

"Good idea," says Fritz. "You can avoid estate taxes that way."

"It was good of you, thinking of Vera so," I told him later.

"Only fair," he said.

"Still. She should know it was your idea."

"No need for her to know."

Those two. Will they ever get over their quarrel?

Vera wants the land across from the old orphanage, where The Reverend and his wife made a home for the children. So many there were, whose parents died on the crossing. Then others, that died of the cholera, after the boats had landed. Such a long walk to get here, poor children, and the good man and his wife took them in, nursed them, fed them, gave them first a tent, then a house.

It's the story of the barnyard. The girl is there, young and soft and fresh, like bread from the oven. Benno frowns to hear the man's name, so much he disapproves, but Benno has many rules for what goes on between men and women. He is glad Vera wants the land across from the orphanage. "I don't want to look at it," he says.

"So long ago," I tell him. "Who are we to judge?"

"You're willing to forgive? You forgive," he says. "Not me."

I say young girls have their ways. Perhaps she smiled sweet at him. Asked for special favors. The Reverend Mrs, she closed the house when she found out. Took the children, the younger ones, with her and left the others for him to find homes for. He told her he would follow. Promised, some say. I say who knows? But the direction he headed was toward Mexico, to be free. Of what, we do not know, but there is always something.

When Carol Anne has the baby, everything stops for a while. Benno is in a good humor. We had wished for Fritz to marry a girl from home, with a good family we would know, but this girl can't be blamed for our wishing. It is enough that she has so much to learn. But she has Benno on her side, which is a good thing. He liked the first he saw of her, like Fritz did, I suppose. Like they say, the apples don't fall far from the tree.

After little Georgie was born I spent much time with Carol Anne and the baby and could tell she was glad for me being there, but not nearly so glad as the day Benno rang the doorbell.

She answers the door and there he stands, looking up at the ceiling beams.

"Where do you want it?" says he.

"Want what, Pop?"

"Your new swing," says he. "Can't raise a baby without a swing." And he goes to the truck and carries back a new wooden porch swing he has made in his workshop. She is clapping her hands and jumping like a little girl. They get the baby and sit down on the swing. She hums a little tune to the baby and it stops fussing. Then he picks up the tune with a whistle and her eyes light up and she hums again, like a little test, and Benno gives harmony with his whistle. Too busy he was to know our little ones until they grew to follow him around and ask questions, but I can see he will take time to get to know this little one.

"Come to Opa," he says and holds out his arms.

The baby gives a little one-sided grin and makes a loud toot in his pants.

Benno cocks his ear and opens wide his eyes. "Thunder," he tells Carol Anne, and she laughs at his bad joke. I see them there together so and I am thinking the gift is a good one.

Everyone is busy with talk of land and money, buying and selling, building and moving around. I mop my floor and try to stay still, but I can't keep out of it. First, we are choosing lots, deciding who is to have what land on the river.

"It doesn't matter so much," I tell Benno. "I will not be building a house there. Not my children, either. No houses on the river."

"It's not for you to decide," he says, and I know it is true.

Here's something else. Snakes at the river. They come back in my dreams. My opa said if there is such a thing as the Garden of Eden, this is it, and the snake means we are responsible for what we know. What I know is, if you live by the river long enough, it may swallow you up and wash you away.

I was eleven when my mother married again. The year was 1918. My grandparents both passed that year. Oma went first, shriveled like a pickle and sour in her old age, and then Opa. They said he went because of her, but I believe it was the war. More than forty years he had lived here, but the homeland was in his heart and how do you go to war with your heart? During that time we had to be careful in many ways. It was not good to be speaking German on the streets. They say in other parts it was worse. Families were driven from their towns, we heard, because of their name. Some changed their names and stopped speaking German in the home. Good Americans we were, but there's no proving anything to those who choose to hate.

Mama and I came to live on the ranch of Peter Zipp, who became my second papa. His wife had died in childbirth and left him with four little ones. He owned a ranch outside the town of Schoenberg, many acres where he raised sheep and goats, and had, as well, a Sunday house in town, which we didn't visit so much at first because of the war.

Peter was a thick man with arms and legs like gate posts. After dinner he liked to lie on the floor and put us all upon his chest, me, the largest, first, then Emil on top of me, Walter next, then the twins, Tressie and Anna. He could give a big laugh that made us all bounce up and down on his huge belly.

My mama, who could have no more children of her own, was happy to be married to Peter, even though the seven of us stretched the corners of the little house, but there were plans to make it larger when the summer was over and the rains came. Then the well caved in and needed to be repaired and the tank went dry and Peter was busy cutting the prickly pear and burning the stickers off to feed the animals. The drought had come and we were not expecting it. Some said it was a message from God and those they went to church to pray for water.

Water. We had to be careful with every drop. Without rain to catch we hauled well water in buckets for washing. First we scrubbed the clothes, then the children, then carried the same water to the garden. Some people moved on, saying the land was no longer hospitable. We waited.

The town suffered and Peter along with it. Little by little he sold the rest of his herd and finally, when the war anger died down, we moved into town. He talked of selling the ranch but Mama said no, to sell in bad times would be worse than giving it away. That year I worked for the baker in the mornings for a loaf of bread a day, and I got to go to school some days. Mama kept us clean and fed and made lace, while Peter took what work he could find. I will say this. We never went hungry.

The drought lasted four seasons. By my seventeenth year the springs ran again and the wells gave water and Peter was back on the ranch with sheep and goats and people to buy them and the railroad to take them to market. He planted corn and cotton and when the crops were good he bought more land, down along the river and moved the old cabin there, hauling it in the wagon, stones and beams.

"When the water comes high," he told us, "and it will again, we go into town. For now, we stay here, with the cool breeze and all the water we need for the animals and ourselves." Even he arranged a bucket and pulley that ran from the top of the biggest tree beside the cabin, down to the river, for pulling up water.

On the wall of the cabin Peter nailed a piece of paper with a drawing of the ranch and where it touched the neighbors to the north and to the south. The river was a thick blue line to the west and the road to town was on the east. Down the middle he drew a line and on one side he wrote in big, black letters, Johanna, my mother's name, to show it was her land. She had earned it, was what he said.

I was nineteen when Peter died. Emil and Walter brought him from the field, where he had fallen over setting a fencepost. They were only boys themselves and white with fright, after having to pull him up and into the wagon and head the horses home. There he lay, with his big red face turned the color of young plums and the eyes open but not seeing. Us standing in the hot sun, not knowing what to do.

Mother got a mirror and held it to his mouth but there was no breath. From down on her knees she shouted in his ear but nothing happened. His fingernails were blue and his pants were soiled. It was an awful sight, like a drowned cow I found in the tank once. I took one hard look and then I turned away. Huge and helpless he was and smelling bad and in my mind I was thinking how a few hours before he had been at the table eating eggs and sweetcake and telling the boys what was to be done. One is never ready for such things, but what can you do?

After Peter died we worked the ranch, my mother, the other children and me. Mama and the boys worked the land and the girls and I kept the house and garden. It was not so bad, for there were many of us, all pulling together. After a few years the boys built themselves a cabin and moved up by the road. Too old, they said, to be living with the women, and time it was to be on their own. Still they would work the land and share the profits. Me and Mama, and the girls, were left in the cabin, but not for long. Two big brothers, the Henke boys, from across the river, came courting and they decided to marry at the same time and the same place. The brothers had a mind to start a brewery in Kerrville and when that failed they started a restaurant, keeping the girls busy in the kitchen, and from that to furniture-making and finally to shopkeepers. Well thought of, they became, in time, but without the girls so lonely was our home and we had come into another drought and there was little time for visiting. Only work. I was twenty-six then and thinking of marrying myself, but who would care for Mama?

One night my step brother Emil came knocking to the door. He had talked to the lawyer about dividing the land. This is how it went. Four parts, three hundred and twenty acres each. One part to Mama, one each for Emil and Walter, the other part to be shared by the girls. Mama and me, we were to stay in the house because that is where we belonged, he said. It wasn't half, like Peter had shown on the map, but the boys were older now and needed their own start. Mama thought it very fair.

"I will still work it for you," he said. "Grow feed and run cattle."

"*Danke,*" I said.

He took out his handkerchief and wiped the sides of his temples and then his neck. Then he gave his head a little jerk toward the door and motioned with his eyes for me to come outside where Mama was not listening.

"What is it, Emil?"

"I'm, I'm, I'm. . . "

Emil got stuck like that sometimes.

"Slow down," I told him, like always.

"I'm thinking," he said, "that you and I should get married, Queenie."

"Emil!"

"What's so bad with that?"

"I raised you from a little boy."

"Only three years difference between us."

"Four."

"Three and a half."

I looked up at him, now almost twice my size, blond and heavy, his eyes too close together, not blinking, looking, looking to me, a good boy but not so bright, like his father, Peter, my second papa, and I knew I wouldn't marry him, but what was I to say that would make it okay?

85

"No," I said.

He put his hands on my shoulders then. Sweet, fat hands of a child they looked, I thought, with the nails nibbled down to the pink.

"I'm a man now. Time to get married and you're the one."

"I'm not ready yet," I told him.

"I'll wait," he said.

When Benno and I married, Emil came to the wedding in a shirt I starched and ironed for him, but he wasn't looking in my eyes. He came so not to disappoint Mama and the girls, but he hung around the party's edges like an angry calf and drank too much beer. Even later, when he and Benno got to be friends, mending the fences and doing the branding together, Emil wouldn't come in the house when I was there, wouldn't touch my coffee or sweetcakes. What I think is he couldn't let go of his hurt, even when it didn't hurt any more.

Walter moved to California, but Emil stayed on the land and works it still. He never married and no one sees him much, though Benno sold him some insurance years back and checks on him from time to time. A hermit, he calls him, and says that's a man's choice. A nice boy, but not too bright. What can you say about someone who doesn't learn to read?

Before I know it I am an oma. Georgie is three years old, walking and talking and oh so smart, already showing me his letters, and Fritz and Carol Anne are busy all the time, planning a big, new house, and Vera is coming home to live. How quickly things change. I am thinking to give a big party for her but Carol Anne says no.

"Why not a picnic at the river?" she asks. "Fritz will invite a few couples she knows who have kids Georgie's age. You invite the Vogels and Tante Helen. We'll make it easy. Fritz can barbecue bratwurst. You do pinto beans, potato salad, maybe some sauerkraut. I'll do Jell-o salad for the kids and I've got a bunny mold for a cake. White icing, sprinkle it with coconut and stick in pink jelly beans for eyes."

She is so excited I cannot say no, and why should I? Still, a cake that comes in a package ? I am wondering how she knows what Vera would like better than I who raised her. Who is right? I only know I am glad for Vera's coming back, for I know it means the ties are strong.

Vera

What could I have been thinking? I sat crosslegged on the floor of the little house Fritz had located for me to rent. Perspiration rolled down my temples and the back of my neck. I pulled my hair into a pony tail, fished a glass from the box labeled "kitchen" and drew a drink of foreign-tasting water. My living room was crammed with boxes and furniture and as I sat waiting for the electricity to be turned on, I wondered how I had come to convince myself that this move was a good idea.

"Anybody home?" Carol Anne's voice came through the screen door.

"Body ome?" little Georgie echoed her call.

"Here," I said, pushing things aside to make a path.

She looked around and wrinkled her nose. "Should I ask how it's going?"

"Not unless you want to hear the truth."

In her pink tennis dress and hair tied back with a matching ribbon, she looked like an ad for Virginia Slims and I was suddenly conscious of looking wilted and grimy.

"I brought you a housewarming plant," she said. "Watch Georgie a minute while I get it." When she slid the child's hand into mine and started down the walk, he began to whimper.

"She'll be right back," I said. "Come sit with Tante Vera on the steps and we'll watch."

He did as I asked, holding to me with one hand and using the other fist to rub away a single tear that clung to his cheek.

Carol Anne struggled up the sidewalk carrying a round brass planter with a thick climbing ivy half as tall as she.

"Isn't that Queenie's plant?" I asked.

"Started as a cutting the day Fritz was born," she quoted the familiar recitation as Georgie and I held the door open for her.

She knelt, engrossed in clearing a spot by the window and pushing the container into position.

"You're looking very good," I told her. She glowed in the compliment, and reached down to smooth her dress across her flat stomach.

"Hard, keeping in shape with Queenie's cooking."

"You don't seem to have any trouble."

"Dexidrene," she confided. "It's great! Kills the appetite and still leaves plenty of energy for tennis. If you quote me, I'll swear I never said it."

She looked at her watch. "I've got a match in fifteen minutes. C'mon, Georgie," she reached out her hand for the child who had discovered my bean bag chair and was busy burrowing in.

"Leave him with me, why don't you."

"You sure?"

"We'll find something to do."

She blew him a kiss on her way out the door. "Okay, baby? "Mama will be back. You stay with Aunt Vera."

She was gone before the child could protest. He watched the car drive away, then turned back to me and pointed outside. "Go," he said, "le's go."

"Wait," I told him. "I have something to show you." We walked around to the back yard, where Val was busy exploring her new surroundings. The child wasn't the least afraid of her. We put her on the leash and started walking.

Walking with Georgie was an education for me. Like the dog, he stopped to inspect everything. Rocks, leaves, chewing gum wrappers, shiny bits of metal, dead bugs, he wanted to pick them up, and I allowed it. Most, he returned to the ground after a moment and brushed off his hands, as if to say "enough." Others, he handed to me with a look that said I was to keep these for him. It was surprising to discover intelligence and personality in so young a child. I caught myself feeling proud of him, and was reminded immediately of those tiresome people who can't stop talking about some child they're attached to. It was something I'd have to guard against.

"Hi," he called brightly to everyone who crossed our path.

"Well, *guten morgen. Wie gehts?*" a white-haired man stopped to shake hands. The child nodded his head and allowed his hand to be pumped up and down.

What's your name?" the old man asked.

"Georgie."

The man looked up at me sharply. "He looks like a Jahn," he said.

"He is. He's Fritz's boy."

"Benno's grandson?"

I nodded.

"I know your Opa," he said to the boy.

Georgie was staring at the man's cane.

"And you are?"

"Vera," I said.

"Little Vera?"

I nodded. "I've moved back."

"What took you so long?"

"I've been working out of state."

"No place like home," the man pronounced, fishing in his pocket. "Here, son, this is for you," and he handed the child a new copper penny. "What do you say?"

"Tank you," Georgie said.

"*Danke,*" the old man coached.

"*Danke,*" Georgie repeated.

"Ha! That's better," the old man said and walked on.

Georgie and I stopped for a Coke at the soda fountain on the square, then made our way to the park. We strolled along the river's edge, watching for the catfish that cruised regularly through the clear, green water. The dog and I rested beneath a tree while Georgie alternately chased and ran from the ducks, eventually returning to flop himself in my lap.

"Tired?" I asked.

He shook his head adamantly.

"Hungry?"

He looked up with eyes bright as buttons.

"Let's go see your Omie. She always has something good."

As promised, Queenie had lunch on the stove. Georgie stood on a chair to watch her, while I filled glasses with iced tea. Benno and Fritz arrived from their office on schedule and we all sat down together.

"So how's it going?"

I had to swallow my forkful of macaroni and cheese before I could answer Fritz's question.

"Georgie and I went to the library this morning."

"He told me."

"Mrs. Oberman asked to be remembered to you."

"Ottie Oberman?" Benno looked up from his plate, his mouth full. "Good woman."

"Takes her job seriously," I told him. "She frowned at my leaving the dog outside and bringing Georgie in. I assured her they were both well-behaved, but she watched us like a hawk. When I told her who I was, she relented a little."

I turned back toward Fritz to share my joke. "I asked if she had a copy of *Animal Farm* and she directed me to the children's books."

He grinned and shrugged. "Expect too much and you'll be disappointed."

"Who's disappointed?" Queenie came in on the end of the sentence, carrying a bowl of fresh sliced peaches.

"I'm disappointed that my air conditioning hasn't been turned on yet," I said. "It's nice and cool in here. Remember when we used to eat out under the trees because the kitchen was so hot?"

She smiled. "Ja. Better now, for sleeping, too. Still sometimes I turn it off and open up the doors."

"She wants it, then she doesn't want to use it," Benno grumbled.

"Kind of like your new car and your old truck, Pop," Fritz told him.

Benno looked over at Queenie and laughed. "That's what she told me."

"We stopped for a Coke at Otto's on the square," I said.

"Otto Kiesling?" Benno said. "Good man. Our new sheriff."

"So I heard. I wonder how he intends to enforce the sign on his wall?"

"What sign?" Queenie asked.

"We don't serve dogs, dopers, or draft-dodgers," I quoted.

Benno laughed a hearty laugh. "Otto, he don't waste words. Longhairs, floating our river, crawling out on anyone's property, taking what they want. He tells his people not to serve them and if they make trouble, he arrests them."

"He can't arrest someone for having long hair."

"He'll find a reason. Maybe scare them enough so's they go else-where. You think that's so bad? Think about your old neighborhood. Blacks camping out on the street corner until you had to get a dog to protect yourself. That won't happen here."

"They were criminals. They intimidated me."

"What do you think these fellows are? No honor for their country. Maybe you should hold your tongue, Missy, 'til you've been here awhile and seen some of them."

"The point is, everyone with long hair isn't a draft-dodger.

"You think every *schwarze* in your neighborhood was a criminal?"

"That's not what I'm talking about."

"Seems the same to me. Nothing wrong in wanting to be with your own kind."

"We're talking about Constitutional guarantees of liberty, Onkel."

"Otto takes the liberty to say who he serves in his place," Benno told me, pleased with his own cleverness.

"He's heading for trouble," I said.

"It won't be from me," Benno declared.

Carol Anne burst in the front door, flushed and radiant.

"Sorry I'm late," she announced. "The match kept going to love until I didn't think we'd ever finish."

"Hi, baby," she kissed Georgie in his high chair and Benno on the forehead, then slipped into the empty chair at the table beside Fritz and patted him on the leg.

"Help yourself, there's plenty," Queenie said.

"I'm not very hungry. "

The table was silent while we watched her drain a glass of water and spoon peaches into a bowl. She changed the energy in the room like a magnet. Benno obviously doted on her, although Fritz seemed distant. I wondered again, as I had the first time we met. Why her? Sometimes I think I'm the only one who looks for reasons. She certainly seemed deliriously unaware, still chattering about her new tennis teacher and her backhand lesson when Queenie lifted Georgie from his chair and carried him to the back room for a nap.

"Before you came in we were talking about the draft," I drew Carol Anne into the conversation, trying to elicit an opinion.

"If Georgie was old enough to be drafted, I'd help him get to Canada before I'd let him fight in some stupid war," she said.

Fritz turned to her, and I could tell he wanted to smooth things over quickly. It was, after all, Benno's dinner table. "Carol Anne," he said, "you always have to be so emotional."

"There is a case to be made against the draft," I said.

"Not here," said Benno.

Carol Anne shrugged her shoulders. "Vera asked me what I thought and I told her."

"I wish you'd think before you open your mouth," Fritz said.

She stood up all of a sudden and laid her napkin on the table. "And I wish you wouldn't put me down all the time." She turned and walked from the room and the next thing we heard was the squeak of the screen door. From the dining room window we could see her cross the lawn and get into her car.

"Better go make it right," Benno told Fritz. Fritz looked embarrassed, but didn't move. Queenie stayed silent and began to clear the table and I got up to help, wishing I hadn't pushed things. No one knew what to say, so we said nothing.

On Saturday Carol Anne called me to ride with her to San Antonio. "I want to get stuff for your party and thought it would be a good chance for us to visit," she said.

She picked me up in her red convertible with the top down and showed no sign of being upset over the previous day's scene at Queenie's house. I had dressed in jeans and was surprised to find her wearing a white sundress and pumps, no stockings. Her hair was pulled back and tied loosely with a red scarf the color of the car.

I took one look at her and frowned. "You didn't warn me."

She giggled. "Sorry. It's what everybody does here. You know, dress up and go to town. But look at me telling you."

"Give me a minute to change" I said and started back in the house.

"Buy a new outfit when you get there," she called after me. "It'll be fun."

"No thanks. I'm saving my money." When I came out, a policeman was leaning on the car, talking to Carol Anne.

She introduced us. "Donnie says this car invites tickets."

"Probably so," I agreed.

"Still, I've only gotten two in two years."

I put on my sunglasses and reminded myself she was still very young.

"And how many times have you been stopped?" Donnie asked.

"Five or six," she grinned.

"She's a fast talker," he said, looking at me with a knowing grin.

"I can talk almost as fast as I drive," she said and pulled away, waving at him in the rear view mirror.

"You seem to have made the adjustment to small town life," I said.

"I guess," she said. "It helps to be Mrs. Jahn."

"So it's been easy?"

"Not really," she said. "But you don't want to hear about that and I don't want to talk about it. Not right now, anyway." She pulled out onto the main highway, adjusted the sound on the radio, and accelerated the convertible so fast I was jarred back against the seat. "Hold on," she shouted with a smile. "I make it from here to Joske's in thirty-five minutes."

We had finished shopping and were eating lunch when she said, "I hope I didn't make too much of a scene yesterday. He makes me so mad sometimes. I was raised to think my opinion was as good as anyone else's."

"Fritz was wrong to talk to you like that," I said.

94

"Why does he act that way?"

"You'll have to ask him."

"I do, but he won't discuss anything. Was he always like that?"

"He was fairly quiet and serious."

"Popular?"

"Very."

"With the girls?"

I nodded, remembering how they used to befriend me in order to be around him.

"I know there must have been lots of girls, but he won't talk about them. And sometimes he's such a prude. I can't figure it out. He had to have me and now he acts like he's hardly interested."

I held up my hand to stop her. "I'd rather not talk about this."

"Why not?"

"It's between the two of you."

"Well, I need some attention. Why can't he see that?"

"Maybe because he's busy supporting a family."

She was quiet for a while. "I guess you're trying to tell me I have a lot to learn."

"You're doing fine," I told her, "except you should know better than to ask an old maid for advice on marriage."

"You're not an old maid, Vera."

"In this town I am."

"Well, I'm inviting some eligible bachelors to the picnic Sunday."

"I'd rather you didn't."

"C'mon, just someone to date? You're going to hook up with some-one eventually. Why don't you let me make it a little easier?"

"I start my job at the Institute on Monday. Meeting a man is the far-thest thing from my mind."

"Really?" She turned to look at me, as if confused. "So what are you going to do with yourself?"

"Work, save my money, and build a house," I told her.

"You really are different," she said. "I see why Fritz says he respects you."

Benno recommended someone to clear my lot. Harvey Weigel worked for the county highway department during the week and rented himself and his bulldozer out on weekends. He wouldn't expect to be paid until the job was done, he said, and I decided I could handle that. I met him at the river and tried to explain my idea.

"I want it to look like a park," I told him.

"It's not a park. It's a river lot."

"What I want is a series of berms," I rolled my hand in our mutual line of vision, "so it looks like the land ripples down to the lake, and the house will set back, about there, on a rise. Can you do that?'

"I can make you a rise. Push the side of that hill up?"

We agreed on a price and I told him I'd be out the next morning so I could watch how the work was going.

"Not much to watch," he told me. "I know what you want."

I showed up nevertheless. Harvey worked quickly and steadily, ravaging the land with no apparent sense of design. A desecration, but once begun, there was no going back. I came and went, bringing water and opinions. I sat under a tree and watched for a couple of hours at a time. He was a tireless worker. Whenever he looked my way, which was only when I was in the path of the dozer, I rolled my hand at him.

"Like a park," I shouted. His face remained expressionless.

"I have a man what works for me during the week," he told me Sunday afternoon "He will finish up. That okay with you?"

"As long as he does a good job." I told him, hoping for someone more amenable to my suggestions.

The next afternoon when I reached the site, the bulldozer was there and before I even met the driver, I was impressed. He handled the awkward machine like a sports car, shifting smoothly from forward to reverse. Here was someone with an eye, who sat forward in the chair, concerned with what was going down beneath his blade. When I got out of the car, he slipped from the yellow monster and came toward me, a young, brown-skinned Mexican with high cheekbones and dark, oval eyes.

"Miguel Villareal," he held out his hand. "Mr. Harvey said you would be coming." He motioned to the excavation area. "You like what I've done?"

I nodded. "I don't want to tear it up any more than necessary. I want it to look like. . ."

"A park?"

I smiled. "Harvey told you that."

"He said you'd be watching."

I was suddenly conscious of the sun in my eyes and shielded them, to see his face and the river behind him, flowing by like green ink.

He looked back at me. "It's a beautiful place, ma'am" he said, and waited for a response.

It felt strange to be addessed so. The deference seemed a little false.

"Can you make it roll down to the river?"

"I can do whatever you want, ma'am."

Just polite, I decided. He was striking. Skin the color of milk chocolate. Straight, white teeth and long, muscled arms with a prominent vein that ran up the inner forearm, through the bend of the elbow and across the bicep.

"I want berms," I told him. "A series of gentle rolls," I moved my hand like the motion of a wave, "to give some protection from rising water."

"You'll need a dock, too, and a rock retaining wall along the bank."

"We'll see," I told him, cautiously. "There's quite a lot to do here." All that week I watched Miguel sculpt the earth, and each day I liked him more.

I offered him a glass of water and a cigarette.

"Thank you, ma'am," he said. He made the word sound more like a title than a reminder that I was significantly older than he.

"Where did you learn to run a caterpillar?"

"Working for the highway department."

"You don't work for them any more?"

He smiled and straightened up. "I'm in college. This is my summer job."

"You like the river?"

"I've been fishing here in the mornings. I hope you don't mind."

"Have you been tubing yet?"

He shook his head. "Never. We don't go tubing in Kingsville."

One day I showed up at quitting time with Val, Georgie in his orange life vest and two inner tubes.

"Your son?" he asked me.

"My nephew. We're going for a float. Want to come along? It's the only way to see the river."

He glanced back at his pickup and looked hesitant.

"Georgie's mother will meet us at the bridge and bring us back for the cars."

The next thing I knew Miguel had slipped off his shoes and socks, rolled his khaki pants up above the knee and waded in. I floated him the smaller tube. "Put it around your waist, hook your arms over it and lay back," I told him, trying do the same for myself, but awkwardly, with the child in my arms. Georgie grabbed the tube as it passed over his head and held on.

"Look's like he's done this before," Miguel laughed. "Well, here goes," and he pushed off, his face serious with concentration at first and then, as the water carried him gently out into the current, he stretched his feet out in front of him and relaxed into a broad smile.

"This is great," he said.

"What'd I tell you? Now, hook on to my tube, so we can stay together," I instructed.

"Are there any snakes?"

"Not many," I said.

I saw his eyes scan first one bank and then the other. "I know that feeling," I laughed, "but it's quite safe. Val will let us know if there's one around. The dog ran in and out of the water, swimming along at times, following along the bank at others. Georgie bobbed against me like a cork in the center of the tube. "What are you studying, Miguel?"

"Communications."

"And you chose that because?"

"It sounded good," he said with an embarrassed laugh. "And I like to be in the spotlight. I come from a large family and always had to shout to get myself heard."

He liked college, he said, but wasn't sure he had chosen the right field. I told him most students felt that way at some point.

"You sound like a teacher, yourself," he said.

"I've done my share of teaching, but I've just taken a new job with an institute in San Antonio. I'll be organizing programs that highlight Texas culture."

He told me he was in school on an athletic scholarship.

"Football?"

"No," he laughed. "I'm not brawny enough. Golf is my game."

"I didn't know—"

"That Mexicans played golf?" he broke into my sentence.

"I didn't know U. T. had a golf team."

"Sorry, ma'am, I didn't mean to be rude."

"You weren't. Just defensive. And you don't have to call me ma'am. Call me Vera."

"How about *profesora?*"

"If it makes you more comfortable."

"My friends call me Mike," he smiled.

Georgie suddenly pointed to a log protruding from the water, decorated by a line of turtles with necks extended, sunning themselves like row of small tanks. When we had floated past them, Mike leaned back and rested his head on the water.

"My father thinks I'm a fool to try and break into a rich man's game, but I love it."

"I never could understand how one comes to love a game."

He laughed. "It gets in the blood. I've been caddying since I was old enough to carry a golf bag and started playing seriously in high school. I think I could make money on the tour, but there aren't many of us, Mexican golfers," he grinned. "Lee Trevino, they call him Tex Mex, he's my hero. Won the U. S. Open a few years ago."

"Times are changing," I said. "Are you good?"

"I'm very good," he said. "I hope that doesn't sound like bragging. You know that new course up the hill? I was thinking I'd see if I could work at the clubhouse."

"Georgie's father is involved in that project. I'll ask him to put in a word for you."

He looked me in the eyes, and I had the feeling he was checking to see how serious my offer was.

"What should I tell him, to recommend you?" I teased.

He reached out with one hand to capture a large, green leaf floating in the water, and placed it playfully on Georgie's head. The child shook it off and laughed. Mike put it on his own head and the child laughed again. I thought he had decided to ignore my question. "Tell him I have *sangre azul*," he said.

"Blue blood?"

"That's what my father told us. Whenever any of us complained about some job we thought we were too good to do, we got the lecture. 'Whatever your job, washing dishes, scrubbing floors, raking chicken yards, you do it with honor. Never forget the *sangre azul* that runs in your veins.'"

The river carried us in silence for awhile, and I looked up to watch two turkey buzzards circling high above. I was chewing on his words, wondering why he had chosen to tell me that.

"Your father sounds like a proud man."

"He is. Never had much schooling, but interested in lots of things, especially seeing his kids improve themselves."

"He could be a good German."

"He married one instead."

"Mexican father and German mother?"

"Yes," he laughed. "Constant clash of attitudes.

"I'd imagine so."

"My father tells a story about an old bridge down in San Antonio, near the Alamo. It was built back when the land belonged to Mexico, and when the city started growing, it was too rickety to handle all the traffic it was getting. So the city fathers put up a sign saying there couldn't be more than one cart at a time. Well, nobody paid any attention to the load limit sign, so they put up two more signs. One, in German, that said 'THE LAW FORBIDS MORE THAN ONE CART ON THIS BRIDGE AT ANY TIME,' and one in Spanish that said 'ANYONE WHO TAKES MORE THAN ONE CART ON THIS BRIDGE AT ANY TIME WILL BE PUNISHED BY GOD.'"

"Did it work?"

"What do you think?"

"Probably so."

"It reminds me of that rock, scissors, paper game. The Mexicans, convinced by religion. The Germans, convinced by the law. I bet some people ignored both signs and just trusted their luck."

When we reached the spot where Carol Anne was waiting on the bank, I lifted Georgie up to her and introduced Miguel while she was occupied drying off the child. I remembered how she had acted with the young policeman and was relieved that in this case she only looked up, smiled in acknowledgement, and turned her attention back to Georgie.

"There's an extra towel in the back seat of my car," she told Mike, "if you'd like to get it."

When he turned to walk away, she looked at me and raised her eyebrows in a question.

I ignored her.

"Would you help me put the top up, Miguel?" she called and started after him. "I don't want Georgie to get chilled. You all, either."

I heard him tell her it was a nice car.

"Gets good gas mileage, too," she said, as if that were something she was interested in.

"Wow!" she said, her word for all occasions, when she had dropped Miguel at his truck. "You're just full of surprises."

"A nice boy," I said. "Reminds me of one of my ex-students."

She cut her blue eyes sideways. "Looks like a man to me. Too bad he's a Mexican."

I stared at her.

"Well, you know, in this town. . . . "

"What are you trying to say?"

"The unwritten law. Like a caste system. White women and Mexican men, big no-no. I think it's silly, but, well, that's why I put the top up on the convertible. People see him with us and there'll be eyebrows raised. You know how they talk."

There was some truth to what she said, but I didn't like the brassy way she tossed it around. "I don't think you have the whole picture," I told her. "Anyway, it's irrelevant in this case."

"I think it's sexy," she said. "I bet Fritz would have a hissy fit."

It was beginning to irritate me, her way of reducing everything to the simplest common denominators of sex and money.

Carol Anne announced at Thanksgiving that she was pregnant. Queenie, flushed from the kitchen chores, poured everyone a glass of homemade wine and we toasted new life. Benno and Fritz finished the bottle and settled down to the football game while Carol Anne and I cleaned the kitchen.

"I hope it's a girl this time and I can be through with this childbearing thing," she confided to me. "I feel like shit."

"You look wonderful," I said, hoping to cheer her up.

"Yeah? Well, like they say, looks aren't everything."

I had never seen anyone try so hard to ignore a pregnancy. My concern turned to irritation when I learned she was leaving Georgie with Queenie almost every day. I approached Fritz about it.

"Maybe this isn't my business," I said, "but Queenie has been tied down all her life. I think she needs a rest."

"Georgie's no trouble," he said, a little defensively. "I can't watch him during the day and she loves it."

"She's not young any more."

He ran his hands through his hair. "Who is?" he said.

"I can't believe you said that."

"Damned if I know what's going on, Vera. Carol Anne's out of control. All she does is shop. I counted twenty-six pairs of shoes in her closet."

"Shame on you, cousin," I said. "It's no fun to be pregnant, they tell me."

He glared at me. "Sounds like another excuse to me. She's always begging off her responsibilities."

"You're beginning to sound like Benno."

"This baby is a mistake," he said.

"An accident," I corrected him.

"A mistake."

"Fritz, let up."

"I've got business," he said and turned away. Almost immediately he wheeled around. "Like Benno? What's wrong with that?"

As if he didn't know. I held hands beside my eyes, simulating blinders.

"Anyone but you tells me I'm narrow-minded, and I put them in their place."

"See what I mean?"

"Let's go get a beer," he said suddenly.

"There's some at the house."

And then we were sitting in my living room, talking about old times, close in a way we hadn't allowed ourselves before.

"You're a good sounding board, Vera. I'm glad you came back, even if you have to remind me I'm beginning to sound like my father."

"Only a little," I said, "and I like it better on you."

"He's a good man."

"I know. And officious Mrs. Oberman at the library is a good woman and the heavy-handed sheriff is an exceptionally good man."

He held up his hands. "Truce?"

I leaned over and put my palms against his. "Truce," I said, and touched my finger in the cleft of his chin.

When he stood to go, he hugged me. "Thanks, Vee," he said. "Thanks for trying to keep me straight."

"You need to have more fun, Cousin. Enjoy your family."

"But there's always more to be done," he insisted in a mock accent.

"Then, get on with it." I grabbed a broom and shooed him out the door like I used to when we were ten, an action which elicited concerned barks from Val who had certainly never seen me act that way before.

"It's okay, girl," I was calming her when Fritz stuck his head back in to have the last word.

"Next time you go to the store, get some dark beer!"

Carol Anne

*I*t happened the first Friday in September, the night of the first high-school conference football game. We had invited everyone we knew to come by after the game because our new house was finally finished and I was itching to show it off. The refrigerator was full of food and there were fresh flowers all around, even in the bathrooms. I talked Fritz into taking Georgie with him to the game to let me have the last couple of hours alone. I wandered through the house, checking details, like I was trying for an A in hostessing.

Outside on the patio I straightened the long table Fritz had set up with a white cloth to use as an outside bar. The night was clear enough to see stars overhead, but there was heat-lightning not far off. I crossed the fingers of both hands and held them to the sky, wishing first, it wouldn't rain, and second, that we'd win the football game. Bad luck on either count would have ruined the party.

The last thing I did was turn on every light in the house, upstairs and down, light the torches I'd put out along the the walk, and try to get a picture of the house like you see it from the street. God, it was beautiful in the viewfinder. A big old white-columned colonial that reminded me of the houses in River Oaks Sheila and I used to drive by at Christmas to look at the decorations. I liked the ones that kept their drapes open so you could see their huge, loaded tree, or sometimes, people walking around in red velvet dresses. One time, a dog with a bow around his neck had his paws up on the window, looking out. Happy family houses, Sheila called them, and I took her seriously until I got old enough to tell when she was being sarcastic.

The party started with a rush, a caravan of cars, straight from the game, singing, shouting, swarming over my house, maybe a hundred people, counting kids, all excited and full of compliments. I grabbed a beer and tried to let it happen, like it said in the magazines good hostesses are supposed to do.

Out on the patio Fritz and his buddies were replaying the game.

"They may have a better team than we had the year we went to state," someone said.

"Erlich is a damned good little quarterback. Pitched that bomb right before the half."

"The play of the game."

"Reminded me of that pass ol' Fritz got off the last two minutes of the quarterfinals."

"From desperation," Fritz shrugged.

"Down six points and he lets go with a long, high floater that hangs up there—"

"And Mondo takes off running and turns around just in time to see it coming square at him —"

"And he's so damned surprised to find the ball there, he lets it bounce off his hands—"

"And Udo comes up from behind, never breaks stride, catches that sucker, like it's rehearsed, and takes it in."

I had heard the story at least ten times before but I liked watching them tell it to each other, like it was yesterday, not twelve or thirteen years ago. Fritz's face was all smiles and he looked great in his white shirt with the collar unbuttoned.

"What's going on out at the ranch?" someone asked.

"Looking to open next year," he told them.

"They're saying the Arab oil embargo is going to hurt business everywhere."

"We're not going to have an energy crisis in Texas. Hell, man, we've got enough oil here to service the whole goddamned world."

I wandered into the kitchen to check on the food and there was Vera, talking to some guy about President Nixon.

"I think we'll find out, eventually, that he was involved in the Watergate break-in."

I put my arm around Vera's waist and leaned between them. "You two wouldn't want to spoil a good party with serious conversation, would you? Besides, I haven't met this man who's not talking about football or business." I held out my hand. "I'm Carol Anne."

"This is Bill," Vera jumped in. "We were in high school together and he's come back as the new history teacher."

"From?"

"San Francisco."

"Were you there for the Summer of Love?"

"History in the making," he said.

"Fritz really frowns on hippies," I laughed, "but I'm kind of fascinated."

"I was too."

"So why'd you come back?"

"Because most of the learning's going on in the streets, not the schools."

"And that's bad?"

"If you're a teacher."

"Look who's getting serious now," Vera pointed out. "Come on, Bill, you need a refill."

Later I walked through the living room and found Vera in another group. "There never was a good war," she was saying.

"Or a bad piece," I broke in with an old joke of Sheila's, and raised my eyebrows suggestively to show it was naughty, but no one seemed to get it.

"Great party, " Fritz told me when we were standing on the porch, waving the last car away.

"We'll have lots more," I said and rested my head against his shoulder. "Vera and Bill sure spent a lot of time talking to each other. You think we might have a romance in the making?"

"No way."

"Oh, come on, I can tell she likes him."

"They go way back to eighth grade, but take my word for it, there's no romance there. Vera just likes to be with people who carry on intelligent conversations."

"Does that let me out? I thought I was pretty sparkling tonight."

"You were sparkling, and pretty. And just to show you how impressed I was, I'll take Georgie to the park in the morning so he won't be under your feet when you're trying to clean up."

I nodded, happy and exhausted and we started up the steps.

"Wait!" I stepped back to admire the wide, circular staircase I had fought to keep in the house plans. "Isn't that beautiful? I walk in the front door, see that staircase and feel like Scarlet at Tara. Would you carry me up the stairs, Fritz? Just once."

He grinned. "For some *dummkopf* reason, I end up doing whatever you want."

"You like it, don't you?"

"I like you."

"Why?"

"Because you're my wife."

"Not a good enough reason. Tonight, pretend I'm not your wife, or that you're not my husband." He picked me up and looked down at me and I think he had drunk enough whiskey to get the idea.

So I was pregnant again. And devastated. Another huge belly, another little person to fit into my life, another something to demand my time and steal Fritz's attention. Selfish. I know. But it's dumb to feel guilty for feelings you can't help. Bad enough that I'd been careless about taking the birth control pills, which Fritz was quick to point out when I told him what I suspected.

"It's not a good time," I told him.

"If we're going to have another baby, this is as good a time as any," he said, looking kind of pleased with himself.

"You have it, then," I snapped. He had no idea how trapped I felt.

I played tennis with a vengeance, and hoped I'd pass out and wake up in the hospital with my doctor leaning over, saying, "Mrs. Jahn, I'm afraid you've miscarried."

I didn't tell the family until I was beginning to show. By then it was almost Christmas and after that we celebrated Georgie's birthday and then Fritz's birthday and in between I spent as much time as I could in Austin. Yeah, it was more than an hour away, but I liked to shop at those stores right across from campus. I liked watching couples acting romantic with each other, and guys on the green tossing the football around. Sometimes I'd go to the movie, especially when they had a sad one. Cry through a package of Kleenex. Weird how good that made me feel. One time I bought a used chemistry book and sat at that little open-air coffee shop on the corner, pretending I was studying. Too bad I didn't do more of that when I had the chance. But I never did like studying. I liked the pretending.

Sometimes Vera came over on her day off and stayed with Georgie so I could get out. I liked talking to her when the others weren't around and would have stayed in on those days, but she always insisted. I guess she liked being alone with him, maybe playing with the idea of having her own. One morning, over coffee, I asked if she was happy she'd decided to come back.

"I'm glad I came back, yes," she said. "I don't know that happy is the right word."

"What's wrong with happy?"

"Too hard to define."

"Doesn't seem that hard to me. It's my major goal." I took a sip of coffee. "Not that I'm doing so well. I almost get there, and the next thing I know it's slipping away."

"That's what I mean. It's elusive. Who do you know that you can say is truly happy?"

"Queenie," I said.

Vera smiled, like she knew something I didn't know. "I'd describe Queenie as cheerful, more than happy. Think about it. Would you trade places with her?"

"Be Benno's cook?" I laughed. "No thanks. I wouldn't last a day."

"Your mother," Vera said. "From what you tell me, she seems to do just about what she wants. You think she's happy?"

"Depends on how you define it," I said.

Vera raised her eyebrows and looked right at me, as if to indicate I had proved her point. Then she lit a cigarette and pushed her hair out of her eyes. "Happiness for me right now would be a good haircut. That's the biggest thing I miss about Philadelphia."

"Tell you what," I said, "I'll stop the first girl on the drag I see with a good, sharp cut and ask her where she got it."

"You'd do that?"

"Sure. Why not?"

"I don't know. I usually don't ask things of strangers."

"Then you're lucky to have me around," I told her.

That winter was really the pits. One norther after another, with wind whistling down the chimney and the trees scratching against our roof like some huge cat sharpening its claws. I wanted to keep the fire going in the fireplace all the time, but Fritz said it was a waste to burn all that wood when we had perfectly good central heat. God, I hated sitting around watching my skin get rough and my tan fade.

Fritz had bought a piano for us that Christmas. A family gift, he called it, and said maybe I would teach the kids to play. First I had to remember how, myself.

"I bet it'd come back easy if you'd work at it a little." He was always after me to try harder.

"I'm not that good."

"How good do you have to be to enjoy a little music in your own home?"

"I'm not as good as Sheila."

"I wasn't asking you to be a performer. I grew up with music in my home and I want that for our children. What is it with you, Carol Anne? You misinterpret everything I say."

"Well, I grew up with music in my house, too," I told him, "and to be truthful, it feels a little like having a monkey on my back."

He didn't understand. The damn piano. Every time I walked through the room it sat there, calling my name. Part of me had always wanted to be like Sheila, all that fun and all that attention, but I wasn't about to try and compete with her. Sure, I could sing a little, and play a little, but mostly, I knew the moves. I had studied her so long.

On those long, boring afternoons, when Georgie was taking his nap I'd pull out the Carole King sheet music and entertain myself playing and singing my favorites. When the kid woke up, he'd creep down the stairs and sit with his head between the posts, listening. I pretended I didn't know he was there, but that's when I'd really turn it on, give it everything I had. Not exactly what Fritz had in mind, but it was something to do and it kept Georgie happy.

Some time that winter I began to wonder what was wrong with me. Was it normal to feel so miserable?

"Pretend," the high school drama coach had told us. "Fake it, 'til you make it."

I don't know if he was trying to teach us how to be actors, or how to get along in the world, but I thought he was cool so I tried what he said and found out it worked pretty well. Like, one semester I decided to act like a good student. I sat on the front row, paid attention in class and turned in all my assignments, and when report cards came out, Sheila made a big deal over the improvement. She told me she'd been wondering if she'd pushed too hard on the college thing, but now she knew I could do it if I put my mind to it.

So I decided to pretend I was happy about having this baby and a couple of days later, a miracle happened. Fritz came home with tickets for Las Vegas.

"You and me?" I couldn't believe it. "Big fat me? Well, praise the Lord!"

"It was Vera's idea" he told me. "She thought you might like to catch up with your mother."

"Then praise Vera." I was behind him, on tiptoe, my arms tight around his chest, kissing him on the ear. "But I don't think I want to see Sheila. Not like this."

"I don't understand you two," he said.

I moved around to hug him from the front, but my belly interfered. I rubbed it. "I think I'm bigger this time than last. Maybe our little girl will be an athlete. Would you like that?"

"I wouldn't mind another boy."

"Me neither," I told him. I was just glad to be able to think about another baby and not want to cry.

I went to bed that night with a smile on my face and when I woke up it was still there, and I tried to ignore the little voice that says be careful of quick highs, because you're going to crash and burn. Like, one minute I'm miserable and the next minute I'm so, so happy and I tell myself it's because of this thing that's happened, like Fritz and the tickets, or being invited to a special party, or getting a new car, or some really cute guy flirting with me, but it's not the thing that makes me happy. I can tell, because as soon as I have it, I want something else, or more of the same. All I was sure of was that I wanted off the roller coaster, where life was great one day and horrible the next.

I talked Fritz into exchanging our tickets for some to Reno so I wouldn't have to feel bad about not looking up Sheila. "You can gamble there just like in Vegas," I told him, "and I've always wanted to stay at the MGM Grand."

The hotel lived up to its name. Wide staircases with red carpets, and halls lined with bigger-than-life pictures of Clark Gable, Barbara Stanwyck, Cary Grant, Ida Lupino, all the big stars, some I didn't even recognize. I sat down the first night and got lucky at the blackjack table, and Fritz got jealous I think.

"You're pretty good at that game," he said, when I finally cashed in and went to the room.

"It's easy. "I told him. "I learned to count playing 21 with my mother's friends."

I got tired of gambling after a while and spent my time wandering through the shops and hanging out in the big, plush booths of the cocktail lounge, drinking Cokes and listening to the music.

The baby came about three weeks after we got back. Another boy, that we named Max. Everyone was excited, except me. Boys are wonderful, they say, but I'd counted on a girl. Maybe I wanted someone to talk to, instead of someone else to please. Maybe I wanted something to dress up and play dolls with. Who the hell knows!

That summer I put Georgie in nursery school, found a sitter to watch Max and got back in the swing of things. The country club opened, with a pool, tennis courts and the first nine holes of the golf course. Everyone our age in town was out there, or wanted to be. You never saw the old guard, like Benno and Queenie, but a lot of them showed up for the opening dinner. Queenie even made a speech.

It happened this way. The business partners were looking to Fritz and Benno to help build good will, so there wouldn't be the feeling a bunch of auslanders were trying to take over. They wanted what they called a hometown touch for the grand opening.

"Get Queenie to talk." I told Fritz. "She has good stories and she's fun to listen to."

"What have I to say to such people?" she said when Fritz asked her.

"Tell them about the land, Mom."

"That's simple," she said. "if they want to listen, I can tell them. And how long am I to talk?"

"Fifteen minutes."

"That long? They will be going to sleep."

"Try, once, and see," said Benno. "I've had to listen for fifty years."

"This was once my playground. Now it is yours," she told the dining room filled with new members. "I grew up in this spot," she went on, "in a cabin with my mother and her second husband and his four children. That may sound crowded to you, but it was good for us. We were spending most of our time outside, which is where you will get to go when I have finished my talking." The audience laughed and settled in to listen.

"I remember our first day here. I took my little stepbrother for a walk to see what we could see. We were children and curious and had to climb up on the rocks. That's when I heard the rattlesnake's warning. Very clear, it was, like seeds in a dry gourd, and I pushed back the little one but wasn't quick enough myself. The poor snake did what he knew to do. He bit me. Here, above the ankle. It was a good lesson.

"In time, my second papa came looking for us. He put me on the horse and sent me home, so dizzy I could hardly hold on. Mama doctored the bite with prickly pear pulp and kerosene, a poultice from her cookbook. Still my leg grew to the size of a watermelon and I couldn't walk for a month.

"Every morning papa carried me from my bed to the porch and there I sat. 'Watch everything,' he told me, 'and see what you can learn.' At first I watched the swelling of my leg, and tried to learn patience. When I was done being worried and sorry for myself, my eyes came open.

"So much to see here, on the hill, birds of all sizes that live in the trees and run on the ground and hunt from way on high. And I learned to watch the weather. You know how we say, 'If you don't like the weather, take a little nap. It will change.'

"The land was everything to my people because they came from a place where there was not enough and when there is not enough land, there is no hope. So that may be hard for you to understand unless you grew up hearing the stories about the Old Country. And unless you lifted the rock and dug the well and carried the water and chopped the cedar, you wouldn't realize how hard it was. This was no land of plenty like the storybook had promised, but it was my people's dream, and they held to it. It was like the children, sometimes good, sometimes bad, but always there to deal with. And, like the children, the land is stubborn and full of surprises.

"Out there, through that window, see the pond? The one where the boys fish now for the golf balls. When I was a girl, we caught our dinner there, using heavy string from a spool of thread and a crooked pin. Behind the cliff lie the springs. When the rains come, the rocks will shine and leak for days from the water that hides behind. One winter the cliff froze like a wall of ice, so bright in the sun it blinded the eyes. A sight to see!

"I tell you about this place, and you listen, but the thing to do is walk on it, down the hill, past the oak tree that spreads its legs across the path, down through the tall grasses that grow above a girl's head in the summertime and down to the water, where the cattle stand up to their bellies on a hot day. So when you are not playing games, I invite you to sit a while under the oak tree and watch the squirrel that jumps from limb to limb, or maybe you'll be so lucky to see a young deer rubbing the moss from the buds of its new horns. Go stand on the hill when the wind blows across the valley and watch the lightning holding hands across the sky. See for yourself how this land lives in the heart."

I watched the crowd while she talked. Some were outsiders. Others had lived here all their lives. Some, like Vera, had left and then come back. What Queenie had to say, or maybe the way she said it, brought us all together. On the back row, old men with eyeglasses thick as Coke bottles nodded, chuckled, and clapped their rough hands. And up front, the developers in their shiny suits beamed and wiped their faces. They still had a lot to learn, I thought, like what to plant on the golf course that the deer wouldn't eat. Queenie would be telling them that, too, before the day was over.

"That was good, Mom," Fritz told her when she sat back down at our table and the crowd started to wander outside. She looked pleased. "You know, I never heard that rattlesnake story before," he said.

"Me, neither," Benno grunted.

Queenie put her finger to her lips. "I told it as it happened."

"Only it didn't happen to you," Benno said.

She looked down and mumbled something in German.

"What'd she say?" I asked Vera.

"It doesn't translate," she said, "but it's something like 'poetic license.'"

After the grand opening there was a tour of the clubhouse and the grounds. I walked out on the covered patio to smoke a cigarette.

"Mrs. Jahn."

I turned around. He was tall, dark, handsome, and looked familiar.

I smiled. "Mrs. Jahn is my mother-in-law. I'm Carol Anne."

"I know. We met last summer, at the river. I'm helping your cousin now with her dock. She calls me her consultant." He held out his hand and after a second I reached up with my own hand. I wasn't used to shaking hands with people, especially good-looking Mexicans. I tried to remember to grasp firmly, like I had read in a magazine.

"I remember. Miguel, right?"

He nodded. "Around here they call me Mike."

"How's school?"

"I quit," he said, "when I got a chance to take over the pro shop."

"I guess we have something in common."

"Golf?"

"No. Dropping out of school."

He gave me a polite smile. "Do you play?"

"Tennis."

"I could teach you golf."

I guess I looked at him surprised.

"I didn't mean to be forward, Mrs. Jahn. I'm supposed to drum up business."

Something about talking to him made me warm and nervous.

"I bet you're a natural athlete," he said.

"Me? I was on the swim team in junior high, but then I went into . . ." I could hear myself babbling. "But you don't want to hear about that, you're just drumming, right?"

"If you decide you'd like some lessons, give me a call," he smiled again and handed me a card.

"I'll think about it," I called after him as he headed inside. God, he was gorgeous and I was a married woman with two kids and I shouldn't have been thinking what I was.

Around the swimming pool we turned our beach chairs to watch him on the practice range. Some of the girls had signed up for lessons.

"What do you think?" I asked.

"Very rugged and incredibly refined," Darlene said behind her sunglasses.

"Sounds like an ad for a truck."

"It is," she laughed, "but don't you think it fits?"

I spent the summer working on my tennis game and my tan, trying to get back into shape after Max. Three mornings a week I took Georgie with me to the pool for swimming lessons. He reminded me of a baby bear, standing on the diving board, shouting for me to watch, while he rolled in, head first.

"Carol Anne, he's not coming up," some nervous mother would invariably sit up and announce.

"Wait," I'd tell her, proud that my son was so capable, and then we'd watch together until he broke the surface, almost at the side of the pool and dog paddled his way to the edge. From there he worked his way, hand over hand, to the deep end steps and headed for the board again.

"How can you be so relaxed?" one of the girls asked me. "I worry every day that something horrible will happen to one of my children and Franklin says I'm overprotective, but it's my job, I tell him, and he says my job is to take care of him and the house, and the children will take care of themselves."

"Children are the first priority," someone else said. "Let the men take care of themselves."

"That'll be the day," someone else said. And we all laughed. We were mostly auslanders, girls who hadn't grown up in the area, married to men who had.

Maybe Vera didn't want to talk about sex, but the girls at the pool sure didn't mind. Darlene told about Tom streaking through the bedroom after a shower with a towel wrapped around his head and nothing else. "He thought it was sexy," she laughed. "I told him it was funny, very funny, and that's the next best thing."

Martha said she considered it a duty. She'd put her husband off and then when he was getting really cross or she wanted something, she'd invite him to bed and when they were doing it, she'd take his face in both her hands and say, "Now, are you listening? We really need new living room furniture."

Kathy said she didn't like doing it at home because she was always afraid the kids would walk in on them, so when they went on vacation, they made up for lost time. One time they went to the shore for two weeks and her husband liked sitting on the beach, looking at all the girls in their bikinis. He'd come back to the room really turned on and, in her words, "screw her socks off."

Jennifer confessed something she made us swear not to tell. "When we lived in Austin," she said, "one time we went to one of those couples-swapping meetings. It was at this downtown bar and everyone was checking everyone else out. Really weird. We had one drink and ran like crazy."

"Do you suppose the guys talk like this when they get together?" someone asked.

"They make jokes about it, but what they talk about is business." Everyone groaned.

"Sex is our business," Martha announced. Then we really groaned.

"Try cutting him off and see how long it takes before you're out looking for a job."

"That's an overstatement," Kathy said.

"Well, there wouldn't be many of us lying around the pool all day."

"We even have a little twenty-eight day time clock to remind us what we're about."

"What if you weren't married?" someone asked. "Would you sleep around?"

"Why not?" Sherry said. We had all heard the latest rumor that she was sleeping with the builder who was doing her new house.

"You sure are quiet, Carol Anne," someone said to me. "I heard Fritz was dream man in high school. So is it still good?"

"Ummm," I said and rolled my eyes. I wasn't silly enough to think whatever I said at the swimming pool was private. I might as well put it in the newspaper. Besides, what could I say? "It's okay?" I didn't want my private life to be okay. I wanted it to be exciting. Not likely, with your husband. Still, I read the magazines and hoped. "Do the unexpected," they suggested.

I signed up for golf lessons with some of my friends.

"Welcome, Mrs. Jahn," Miguel said politely.

"Carol Anne," I said and smiled my best smile.

When the six week class was over, he said I was his star pupil. I signed up for private lessons. It was a game, trying to see if I could outdo everyone else who was trying to get his attention. I was winning. The other girls teased me about all the time I spent with Miguel. I liked calling him Miguel because it sounded romantic. Teacher's pet, they called me. Fritz looked at the Country Club bills and frowned.

"First tennis, now golf. What next, Carol Anne?"

"I thought I'd train for a marathon."

"Get serious," he said. "You're spending too much time away from the kids. I wish you'd take your job a little more seriously."

"I wish you'd take yours a little less seriously," I told him. "There's more to life than making money."

"You don't seem to mind spending it."

"Is that what's bothering you? That I'm spending your money?"

"That you're spending it on some damned Mexican golf gigolo that will tell you whatever you want to hear. 'You have a beautiful swing, Mrs. Jahn.' That's a great line. I bet he'd like a swing like that in his back yard."

"That's not fair. He's a gentleman."

"What am I supposed to think? Do you know how many people have come up and politely warned me about what's going on in front of my nose?"

"How many?"

"One is too many. I helped get him that job. You're making me look like a fool."

"So it isn't about me. It's about you and your precious reputation. How about all those women you 'take care of' with insurance?"

"Have I ever given you a reason to doubt me?"

"No. But what I wonder is how you can be so damned charming in a crowd, and when it's the two of us you act bored as hell."

"Grow up, Carol Anne," he said and slammed the door behind him.

That summer Vera had Queenie's old stone cabin rebuilt on her lot. She spent most of her time at the river with the workmen, overseeing everything—the setting of the house, the new roof, putting in the dock, everything. When I asked how she knew so much about building, she told me she studied up in advance, that she informed herself before each step just like she would if she was teaching a class. I'd never known anyone who took things so seriously.

Lunchtime at Queenie's, Vera was there, talking with Fritz about her building project. Even Benno got into the act, giving advice now and then. Only Queenie was quiet. She had made it clear she didn't approve of anyone living at the river. She wasn't too happy about me leaving the baby with a sitter most days either, and was always begging me to bring him to her. Once or twice a week I did. One day I came into her kitchen to find her pacing the floor, with Max in her arms. Her face was white and her eyes were wide open, like bugging out.

"Such a scare," she said. "One minute he is fine, the next it is like a pin is sticking him he screams so loud and before I can check he lets out a long cry and never catches his breath, just goes limp like a rag doll in my arms and no blood in the face. I shake him, I breathe into his mouth. Finally he starts again to breathe like regular and the color comes back to his face. I check then, but there is no pin, nothing to see."

I took the baby from her arms. "He looks fine to me, Oma. You okay, Maxie?" I rocked him from side to side over my head and he burped a little sour milk. I turned back to her. "Don't you wish they could talk and tell you what's the matter."

"I think he would not know. This is for the doctor to know."

"I'm sorry he frightened you."

"Don't be sorry to me," she said. "Keep a watch. I have never seen such a thing."

I didn't think much of it until it happened again. This time we were at Vera's, down at the river bank, where she had dredged a little shallow place and filled it with smooth pebbles to make a wading pool for the kids. She and Georgie were already in, splashing each other. I took off Max's diaper, draped him over my arm, waded in and sat down. He let out a scream when we sat down in the cold water.

I grinned at Vera. "It'll take some getting used to."

Max's scream never finished. It just died away until his head fell sideways and his eyes closed. I took him back in two hands and shook him. "Max," I shouted.

I held him upside down and ran my finger in his mouth to see if there was something caught in his throat.

"Help me," I yelled and started back toward the house.

Vera was at my side then, taking the baby from me, putting Georgie's hand in mine. She stopped and held her head against his chest.

"It's okay," she said in a calm voice. "I can hear his heartbeat. It's regular." Then she cradled him in her arms. "His color is coming back. Look, now, he's breathing normally again. I think he's sleeping."

"This is too weird," I said, still shaking.

"Wake up, little Max," she was cooing to him. "Wake up, *liebchen.*" Finally he opened his eyes and looked around. Georgie came up and made a silly face at him and suddenly he was smiling at us, like nothing had happened.

"Sounds like a temper tantrum to me," Fritz said when I told him what had happened.

"He's only five months old," I told him. "He doesn't even know what a temper is."

"Kids are smarter than you think," he told me. "Sounds like he's found a way to get your attention."

I glared at him and walked into the other room.

Vera called the next day.

"How's the baby?"

"Fine," I said. "As long as nothing upsets him. Fritz says he's looking for attention."

"What do you think?"

"I'm scared," I told her.

"Have you called the doctor?"

"Maybe he'll think I'm overreacting, like Fritz does."

"So what?"

"I don't know what to do."

"Call him," she told me. "I'll come with you if you want."

The doctor listened to my story with a blank face.

"The child looks fine to me," he said, "but we'll run some tests if you want. It could be a temper tantrum, you know, a way to get attention. You could keep an eye on it."

Vera was right there with me. "Run the tests," she told him. "I don't know much about this, but what I saw wasn't normal."

She stayed with me while they greased his little head and attached electrodes to check the brain waves. I gave him a bottle and she patted him to sleep and then we crept out of the room and left him alone. Maybe he'd wake up and do it, I thought, and then they could all see what we were talking about. On the other hand, I was praying he'd never do it again.

We sat in the waiting room, flipping through magazines, smoking cigarettes and making small talk.

"Mike stopped by the house the other day. He told me he was giving you golf lessons."

"Was is the word," I said. "This thing with Max really has me scared. I'm saying right now that I'm going to quit running around so much and spend more time with the kids."

"That's probably a good decision." Something about the way she said it made me wonder.

"Did Mike say something else?"

"That people were talking, and he liked you, but he liked his job, too."

"Oh, shit!"

"I shouldn't have said that," Vera said. "At least, not now. But it seemed like it needed to be out in the open."

"I'm living under a goddamned microscope."

"I know that feeling. But if you're going to do as you please, you've got to be willing to take the consequences."

"Like what?"

"Disapproval," she said, and ground out her cigarette. "What else?" I sat with my head in my hands.

"Are you okay?"

"What's okay?" When I looked up the doctor was coming our way. He said the tests were in the normal range and that the next time it happened I should walk out of the room and ignore it. I was relieved, for sure, but something in me was mad as hell. Mad at the doctor, mad at Fritz, mad at Vera for telling me the truth.

QUEENIE

W hat's wrong with Carol Anne?" Benno asks me. "Not looking so good. Lost her spunk."

I have been noticing too, but decide maybe it is okay she has stopped thinking so much on herself and begins to think of the children. She is worried for baby Max, I know, and his falling out, and so was I when it first happened but the doctors tell us there is nothing wrong. He is a beautiful child, pretty enough to be a girl, with yellow curls and blue eyes set wide, like his Mama, and her narrow jaw and pointy chin and a dimple in one cheek. She took him to the city to have his picture made for a furniture company ad. Carol Anne likes that kind of thing. She told me he might end up in the motion pictures, but the flashing lights frightened him and the first time he lost his breath, the people got frightened and sent her home .

"It is a habit he will outgrow," I tell her.

"I hope you're right, Omie," she says, but still she carries him with her everywhere now and I wonder when will the child learn to walk and talk if she does everything for him.

They say grandchildren are easy because you can send them home. Not so for me. Because they are not mine to raise, there are times I must watch and hold my tongue and that is not easy.

Carol Anne changes like the weather, one day sunny, one day dark.

She is not the child Fritz brought home, but he is different too. Still strong and handsome, his hair moving back on his head, still short, like a soldier's. Serious like a soldier, too, with creases on his forehead from concentrating and eyes always looking away, like there is too much on his mind and no time to see what is in front of his face. Benno is proud that Fritz pays attention to the business, makes good money and is still well thought of. Nothing is more important, Benno says, than a man's reputation.

"Nothing?" I say.

"Nothing you would understand," he tells me and though he says it in his joking voice, we both know it is part truth. We have different ideas of what is important, Benno and me, and that is how we leave it. Some spaces between us cannot be filled.

Fritz tries to be like Benno, but he is not so strong a man, I think, because everything has come easy. I say it is a shame the money has drained the joy from him and Benno says I am talking nonsense, but I know what I see. The test of the flame, my grandfather said, tells what something is made of. Well, I do not wish trouble, but I see it coming and he will have to decide what is important to him and not take his father's word for it.

One day there is a telephone call for Benno.

"Ja," I hear him say and then begin to speak in German, in a shouting voice that he uses for the long distance.

"My sister Greta has died," he tells me when he hangs up the phone. "Her car ran off a bridge, the city's fault because it was not marked."

"How did they find you?" I want to know.

"With her papers. There is a will. They look for Vera, too."

"Vera!" Suddenly I realize this is her mother who has died.

"She is named on the insurance," he tells me.

"Sad," I say, thinking of Greta.

"It happens," he shrugs. Benno is not one to borrow sadness.

"We were all she had."

"Her choice," he says.

Vera stops in at lunch the next day to say she has asked for time off

123

from her job to go to Germany to settle her mother's business. It is very soon since she begins there, but she tells me not to worry, that the institute has agreed. She wants that I should travel with her.

"I will pay for the trip," she says.

"Me?" I say. "To Germany?" I am taken by surprise, and look to Benno.

Vera, too, looks at Benno.

"You go," he says. "It will be good for you both."

I stir the soup and add a little salt and all the while I am thinking. "Is it possible to go on the boat?" I ask.

"Are you nervous about flying?" she says.

"Certainly not. But I have always dreamed to travel on a boat."

"I need to get there as soon as possible," she says. "We'll fly over and I'll try to arrange for us to come back by ship, but it's short notice and it may be more than we can afford."

Quickly I must make ready my things and put the house in order. Benno says not to worry, he will go to the market, but mostly he will eat with Carol Anne and Fritz. She is cooking now, every day.

The airplane is an excitement that sets my heart beating fast and my head pounding, but I get used to it. Not too good for sleeping, but a person of my age doesn't sleep so well anyhow. Mostly, I'm busy thinking ahead. Vera has maps and is making the plans. She looks after our bags and gets us through the customs and rents a car. So many people to deal with, all busy going this way and that. I let her take care of everything and try to ask for nothing that makes her job harder.

We arrive in Bonn and find our way to Greta's house. I am surprised it is so small, not the fine place she had told us of, and not too well kept. I suppose such things will be overlooked when there is no man to take care of. We share the bed, Vera and I, and in the morning are awakened by a knock on the door. Greta's neighbor.

"She spoke of you," the woman tells Vera.

"In what way?"

"That you were now a professor and had asked her to come live with you, but she thought she was too old to make such a move."

Vera and I look at each other over the neighbor's head and say nothing.

"You knew my mother a long time?" Vera asks.

"I was here in this room the day you were born," she tells her. "We were neighbors for a while, but I stayed away at first on purpose, what with him, in the Nazi Party and her, an American. But . . . a baby comes and there is no one else to help. What was I to do? Then I found she wasn't the bad person I had thought, only sad. A lonely girl, back then. Sold her, her father did, like a piece of property, to a man he knew nothing of. And she came, young still, hoping to make it work, but he, your father, was a mean-tempered one, anyone could see that, with little time for family."

Vera looked at me. I wished the woman would stop her talking, but on she went.

"She told me, when you were only a few days, that she thought to send you away. No, I told her, that would be a mistake. 'This baby can be your joy,' I told her. But she insisted. Her brother was a good man, she told me, and she would ask him to take you while you were too young to remember. 'Who knows what will happen here?' she said. And believe me, it was a hard time."

"After the war I told her to go, herself, now that she was free, to make a life with you but she had thought better of it. Again she said no. 'She has a place there,' she told me, and showed me pictures she carried in her purse. 'She won't be pulled and pushed around, as has been done to me. This child will have better.'"

The woman stopped for breath. Vera studied her hands. It did not seem right to me, Greta gone and here we learn of her from another.

The neighbor turns to me. "You are Queenie?" she asks.

"Ja." How would this woman know my name?

"Greta shared with me the packages you sent. During the war."

"A long time ago," I say.

"I remember still. I remember the packages," she said in German. "Sewed shut in heavy cloth that could be used again and again."

"Feed sacks," I told Vera, who looked to me for explaining.

125

"I don't remember that," says Vera.

"You were very, very young," I reminded her. "Through the Hermann Sons we sent packages to family in Germany. I sent to your mother, but seldom was knowing what reached her."

"She got them, all right," the neighbor told us. "And traded the goods to me for fuel stamps. Clothing, coffee, tomatoes dried in the sun, orange peel candy, chewing gum. I had no need for fuel stamps, afraid as I was to go on the street."

"Afraid?" Vera asked her.

"Ja. My husband was part Jew. A teacher, he was, forced to register, then taken early, for telling the truth. The children and I had nothing, except the fear they would come for us next. Why they didn't, I don't know. But nothing made sense. Not the punishment from our own, nor the packages from the enemy."

"My mother helped you?"

"She traded with me, which is more than some would do. Once she even threw in a present for the children. Corn seeds in a tin with a tight lid."

"Popping corn," I nodded.

"'Does she think we are animals?' my children asked, for it looked to us like cattle feed, and I wondered myself why she had brought such a thing. But I did as she had told me, put it over the fire in a little oil, and then their eyes got big. They ate it all and begged for more."

"Did you know my father?" Vera asked.

"Only a little. He never came back from the war. My Alfred came back from the work camp when the war was over, but he wasn't much to see. Teeth gone, and the hair, too, and he weighed less than the twelve-year-old daughter. But in time he was able to work again."

"How could you stay here, where this happened?" Vera kept asking questions. "Why would you stay?"

"Life is hard," the woman told her. "We do what must be done. The rest, we try to forget."

When the neighbor has finally gone, we do not talk but start on the house. It is an unhappy task and best done quickly. I begin in the bed-

126

room and Vera in the living room, choosing what is to be carried away, what goes for sale, and what we set in another large pile that the neighbor will go through.

"Vera," I call. "Come, see."

I have come across Greta's memory box. It holds certificates of merit from her workplace, a newspaper marking the end of the war, letters from Benno and me, with pictures of Vera I sent each year, some dried carnations, and on the top, a small booklet. Vera picks it up.

"You know what this is?"

It is in English, but nothing I recognize.

"The journal I gave her, the one with my published article. I wish," she started but didn't finish her wishing.

"What, *liebchen?*"

"Oh, a lot of things, about Greta." She tapped on the book with her finger. "I wish, for instance, I'd known she thought this was worth keeping."

"One can never know what goes on in another's head," I told her.

When our business was completed, it was good to get on the road. Vera rented a car and drove us along the Rhine. In the Black Forest we stopped to buy gifts. For Benno, a cuckoo clock to replace the one broken by little Max who insists on pulling the weights. This time the opa will know to put it higher on the wall. Vera chooses oil paintings in colors to match with Fritz and Carol Anne's new house, and for the boys, lederhosen, short pants of gray leather, sewed by hand.

On we drove, along first one winding river, and then another, through the southern hills, in places rich and green, in others, layered with rock and small streams. It looked much like home.

"This would be a hard land to leave," I say.

"Unless you wanted to be free," Vera says back to me, like I should know.

After all the years, talking of the homeland, now I have the chance to appreciate its beauty. I allowed Vera to take me where she planned, with no question-asking. Strange it was, having only to look and be surprised.

"Comfortable?" she asked me.

"Very comfortable."

"Anxious to get home?"

"Why would you ask?"

"Fritz and Benno said you'd get restless without work to do, riding in the car and sightseeing."

It was good to be two women, alone. "Men," I shared my thought with her, "don't know everything."

Our trip ended in Bremerhaven, where the ship sat waiting and there we were so lucky to change tickets with a couple who wanted to fly across and come back on the ship. Vera was saying to me, all along the way, it probably won't work, we'll probably be going back on the plane. But I was knowing it would all work out. From Bremerhaven, we left to go through the North Sea and across the Atlantic Ocean, the same path of my grandfather and his parents so long ago.

The ship was very large and very clean, with men in white jackets who would do anything to help. The cabins were not so large, but good enough for sleeping. It was strange, at first, with so much time and so little to do, but then I started to take my walks on the deck and came to know some of the other travelers. Sometimes I sat in the sunshine, as I saw them do, and read books I had brought from Greta's house.

I was watching the sun go down over the water one afternoon, when Vera found me.

"There you are," she said. "I've been looking for you."

"And I am looking for something I cannot find."

"What's that?"

"The feeling of crossing. It's much too comfortable here."

"Now, Queenie, did you really think . . ."

"I know." I covered her hand with mine. "I feel like a foolish old woman, thinking to relive the story I have carried so long in my heart, the hardness of the crossing, the hope, the excitement, the suffering. This," I looked around me, "is much too nice. Such food. And people playing games, lying in the sun. I find myself forgetting what I came to find."

Vera took a seat beside me and there was no talking for a time.

"Such a trip you have given me," I told her. "I'm sorry you had to lose your mother for it to come about."

"It wasn't such a painful loss," she said to me. "I was always curious about her, and angry, too, I suppose. Couldn't understand why she didn't want to know me. Now I have a reason, though I'm still not sure I understand."

"Ja. Some things aren't to understand. I'm thinking your mother gave what she could. And it came out well," I told her. "You have made us all proud."

"You've been the real mother, Queenie. I wanted to make you proud."

"And made Greta proud enough to brag of you to her neighbor."

"I suppose."

"Benno, too."

"Benno never approved of me, from the time I was a little girl."

"He was raised a farmer. A simple life, and hard. He had no good ideas for a smart girl with a strong will. Now he thinks he has done well."

"Fritz always came first in his mind. You know that."

"It's a man's way," I reminded her. "The boy is raised to take care of things when his father no longer can."

I watched the last of the sun being swallowed into the ocean and wished this old quarrel could disappear so easy. Benno and Vera and Greta, the same blood, I thought, the kind that will shut feelings up in a box. "Benno only meant to protect you," I said. "He raised you as his own."

"He separated me."

"To give you independence."

"We both know that wasn't the reason."

"He had his worries. You and Fritz were very close. There were rules."

"Not for cousins."

"Ja. They will grow out of it, I told him. But to Benno, you were brother and sister, and that makes a different story."

PART II

*We do not succeed in changing things
according to our desire, but gradually our
desire changes. The situation that we hoped
to change because it was intolerable becomes
unimportant. We have not managed to surmount
the obstacle, as we were absolutely determined to
do, but life has taken us round it, led us
past it, and then if we turn round to gaze at the
remote past, we can barely catch sight of it,
so imperceptible has it become.*

Proust, *The Sweet Cheat Gone*

Carol Anne

"I'm glad you didn't turn out like your mother," Fritz told me once. He meant it as a compliment. Funny that it rubbed me the wrong way when I was always complaining about her, but it did. Besides that, I wasn't so sure he knew me, or her, as well as he thought he did. Sometimes I'd find myself traveling down one road and then I'd take a sudden left turn, just like Sheila.

When I got scared about my baby, people told me I should ignore him, but what I ended up ignoring was their advice. After a while even Queenie thought I was spoiling him. I could tell by the way she wrinkled up her nose when he wouldn't leave me to go to her, and the way she tried to get him to feed himself instead of let me feed him. Queenie knew a lot about raising kids, but I was the specialist on wanting attention.

Max outgrew his spells, Fritz got himself elected to the school board, and I was den mother for the Webelos, which is what boys are before they get to be Cub Scouts. This involved cleaning up gobs of glue, collecting bottle caps, making Rice Krispie cookies, and painting 1976 on anything that looked like a Liberty Bell.

There were meetings two or three nights a week, field trips on weekends, and Sunday dinners at Queenie's. My life was like the family shows on television, except I kept waiting for that part at the end, where everyone was happy at the same time.

Sheila called from time to time and sent postcards from fancy-looking places but almost never came to see us. Georgie started calling her "the fairy godmother," and Fritz complained about her extravagant presents. "They wish for something, and she makes it appear," he said. "The woman never materializes."

Right after we got into the new house, Sheila did show up. That was before Max was born, and it was the first time she'd come to Schoenberg since Georgie was a baby. She made it a point that she wanted to meet Benno and Queenie.

"Okay if I smoke in front of them?" she asked me.

"Smoking's okay."

"Anything I shouldn't do?"

"I can't believe you're asking me this."

She smoothed her jeans over her tummy and took a deep breath. "I feel a little out of place. I'd only do this for you, Carol Anne."

"It's not like you're giving blood."

She opened the refrigerator filled a glass with ice, and reached under the cabinet for the scotch.

"We've got beer," I said.

She dumped the ice and opened a can of beer. I grinned at her. "Why don't you give me a hand with the salad."

"I can manage that." She arranged herself carefully on the bar stool like she was getting ready to perform and starting chopping celery. When they came, we went to sit in the yard.

Queenie was wearing rouge and lipstick and a new dress and she was real quiet. She had asked us to come to her house and I was thinking maybe I should have agreed, because she sure looked uncomfortable at mine. Benno had a new joke about a man who found a dead horse in his bathtub and Sheila laughed more than I thought it deserved and then told him about the time she was at a hotel in New Orleans and someone brought a horse up in the elevator. Then Benno told his story about the fox in the henhouse and Sheila followed it with one about a baby chick that found itself trapped in a fresh cow patty. I wished she'd slow down a little, but it was out of my hands. Sheila was always working the crowd.

I took Georgie in the kitchen with me and Queenie followed to see if she could help.

"You're dressed up tonight," I said.

"To honor your mother's visit. It's good to finally sit down together. She's a playful person, your mother," Queenie said it like a compliment but I wondered if she was feeling just a little critical. Sheila had no sense of how to take a back seat in a group, like women are expected to do.

I nodded.

"You think she will give us some music, after dinner?"

"Sure she will."

Through the window I heard them laughing. Even Fritz.

After dinner Sheila kicked off her shoes and sat down at the piano, taking requests. Queenie asked for "Harbor Lights." When Benno wanted to hear "Springtime in the Rockies," she played him a whole medley of World War I songs. Georgie was trying to act very grown up for almost five. He asked for "In Heaven There Is No Beer," and insisted that we all sing.

"You must come more often," Queenie said when they were leaving, and I heard Sheila promise she would. Just another gig, I thought.

I had long since stopped flirting with everyone in sight, except maybe on New Year's Eve when I had too much to drink. I envied Vera, who came and went as she pleased and didn't belong to any of the local clubs. She had her own offbeat friends, like the history teacher, who Fritz suspected was a queer, because he had lived in San Francisco and didn't get married, and Miguel, who still gave golf lessons at the club and was trying to get on the big professional tour. She went on trips with people at the institute, like last spring when they went to Mexico to some ancient ruins to watch the vernal equinox come in, or whatever it does.

"You've got it good," I told her. We sat on the river bank with a thermos of coffee, watching the boys fish. They were eleven and seven and on summer vacation. I was about to turn thirty-two and feeling pitiful.

"I don't think you'd like to trade. No husband. No children. Lots of time alone."

"No lovers?"

She smiled what I thought of as her mysterious smile. I was always curious, but she kept things like that to herself. Living out from town like she did, working in the city, she kept her private life private.

"You still think I have something going with Mike?"

"I would if I were you."

"If you were me, you'd be out looking for a husband like Fritz."

"So why aren't you?"

"The best ones are already taken."

"Vera, I'm bored out of my head," I said suddenly.

She nodded, like she had already guessed.

"I need a change. I feel like I'm . . . ."

"Measuring out your life in teaspoons?"

"You can always say it better than me."

"You need to get away. Take some time for yourself. I have some vacation coming and this is a slow time. I'll watch the kids."

"You think?"

"Why not?"

"You could stay at the house," I told her. "It'd be easier than having to run them to town all the time."

"I'll have to bring Val. Her puppies are due any time now."

"That'd be something for the boys to see. Georgie probably could help deliver them, if they come. He goes with Benno every time the cows are dropping calves."

"Angie's having a hard time over her divorce," I told Fritz one Friday night, "and needs me to cheer her up." He frowned but didn't fight me on it. The next day I dropped the kids with Vera and left her to work out the details.

Somewhere outside of Houston, the old energy began to hum. Fritz hates to go there because of the traffic, but it was my freeway and I have this little formula for driving it. I rev it up to about 70 and get in the middle lane. Then, I find a good country western station and sing along. When I want to drive in the fast lane, I switch to rock-and-roll.

Angie and I picked up where we left off, kids again, lying on her bed, listening to music, talking about everything and nothing. She and her husband had split up, but she wasn't having a hard time. In fact, she'd gotten a brand new condo out of the divorce and was feeling her oats. She told me she was going to keep her teaching job.

"Third-grade teacher by day, wild woman by night," she joked. "So what do you want to do?"

"Something outrageous," I told her.

At a secondhand shop we spent two hours trying on everything in sight.

"What do you think?" She came out of the dressing room in a black sequined dress with a hot pink boa and a purple felt hat down over her eyes.

"The hat has to go," I handed her a black velvet job with a veil.

"However," I said, trying the purple hat in front of the mirror, "this has possibilities."

She found me a white silk suit, tight skirt, slit in back, jacket with wide lapels. "I have a chemise you can wear under the jacket. No bra. Dynamite," she said. You take the jacket off when you get hot."

I wiggled my eyebrows at her, trying to look wicked. "So where do we wear this stuff?"

"That's my secret."

Cassandra's was a two-story house in an old, residential part of town. It looked harmless enough, except for the name over the doorway in neon and all the cars parked along both sides of the tree-lined street. Inside, a man who looked like Benno in a tuxedo showed us past a paneled bar, into another room set with tables, where he sat us near the musicians. I thought briefly of home but was distracted by a girl in a long dress playing a harp and singing "Muskrat Love."

"Where'd you find this place?" I turned to Angie.

"A very mod speakeasy," she said with a grin, "except it's not about illegal booze, honey. It's about lifestyles."

I looked around the room. Mostly tables for two. Couples, dressed to the teeth, leaning toward each other, laughing, talking, some holding hands. Some of the couples were men.

"Over there," I said.

"Be cool," Angie told me and adjusted her veil so she could light a cigarette.

We were still there after midnight, watching them come and go, dressed in everything from capes to leather jump suits. The music changed every hour.

"I could stay all night," I told Angie.

"Good. 'Cause it doesn't close 'til 4:00. Look!"

I looked up to see Sheila coming toward me, dressed in a tight black sheath with a short gold jacket.

"Surprise!" she hugged me.

"I thought you were in Barbados."

They both laughed. "That's what we wanted you to think."

"Granger," she said and motioned to the waiter who looked like Benno. "A bottle of champagne for this table. On me."

She ran her hands over her hair and then down across her hips and tummy, which still looked good. "I'm on," she said, and nodded toward the stage. "Me, a trumpet, and a sax. Catch you at the first break."

Her act was smooth, better than I remembered. The audience liked it, too. I looked around. Not a dinner crowd any more. These were after hours people. Sheila used to say the ones who come in after midnight come to feed on fuzz. When I was little I thought that was funny. Even drew a picture of ladies in long dresses and men in hats, swimming under the ocean, nibbling at mossy stuff. Tonight, I got it. The fuzz was alcohol, soft lights, smoke, people talking in the background, music up front that told me to listen. Fuzz. It made everything blurry except what was happening that very minute.

"This stuff runs in my veins," I shouted at Angie over a loud trumpet riff.

She leaned forward, her ear to my mouth, then beamed when she made out the words and nodded as if to say "I told you so".

I slept as late as I wanted the next day, shades drawn, no phone, no kids, nowhere to go, no one to answer to. Then awake, I rolled over in the strange bed and thought how good it was to think about nothing. Angie stuck her head in about noon.

"You awake?"

"I'm unraveling."

"Good," she said. "Because you really are tight around the edges." She walked across the room and picked up the white chemise I had draped over a chair and shook her finger at me. "You never took off your jacket last night. For that, you wear this today, without a jacket."

"Where to?"

"Your mother called. She wants us at her hotel about five."

Sheila had a suite at the Warwick, the kind of place you don't want to walk into unless you're dressed for show. I checked myself in the mirrored elevator, stood up straight, sucked in my stomach, shook back my head to loosen my hair. Angie, doing the same, met my eyes in the mirror and laughed.

"You think we'll pass muster?"

Sheila met us at the door in slacks and a white silk shirt and hugged first me, then Angie.

"You girls are a sight for sore eyes," she said, fingering my chemise, "Hey, I like this." She walked to the sofa, kicked off her shoes and settled in cross-legged. "I want to take you girls to dinner, but sit down first. Let's talk."

She told us about California and how exciting the music scene was, how she played at a little spot in Santa Monica Thursday through Sunday nights and had the rest of the week free. She talked about trips to Malibu and the Hearst Mansion and the wine country, and about her new friend, a rancher in Nevada she had met in Vegas, who'd taught her to ride a horse and shoot a rifle.

"Never thought I'd like the out-of-doors, but you have to keep your options open," she told us in classic Sheila style.

"How's Fritz?" she asked me.

"Successful." I knew better than to whine.

"And the kids?"

"Growing like weeds."

She took a long look at me. "I think motherhood becomes you."

I looked back at her and shrugged. Angie had gone to the bathroom.

It was her and me and I was about to spill my guts when someone knocked lightly on the door and then let himself in, a light-skinned Negro, so tall he had to duck to clear the door frame.

"Leroi," Sheila looked up, beaming.

His head was shaved and shining like a piece of polished wood.

"Baby," he said. He moved across the room in a couple of smooth, easy steps and leaned down to kiss her on the cheek. I checked out his tight slacks and the slick shirt that made his chest look twice as big as his hips, and the gold necklace. He turned to me and raised one eyebrow in a question.

"Baby, baby," he sang softly. "Who is this lovely woman?"

About that time Angie showed up.

"I leave the room for a minute and you all rub the magic lamp." She held out her hand. "Aladdin, I presume."

He smiled broadly and bowed. "At your service, ma'am."

"Girls," Sheila said. "This is Leroi, my latest discovery. Guess what he does?"

Angie acted coy, put her finger to her lips and struck a thinking pose. "Well, let's see."

"Bongo drums," I said, feeling irritated.

"Close," Sheila said. "Steel drums. We're incorporating them into the act. He's terrific."

"I bet he is," Angie rolled her eyes.

Sheila brushed off the comment with her hand, but she was loving it. She stood up suddenly. "Why don't you all get acquainted while I freshen up." At the bedroom door she stopped. "Oh, Carol Anne," she said, "come with me for a minute. I've got something I'd like to show you."

I went dutifully, leaving Angie with the giant who had lowered himself into a white chair and sat leaning forward, giving her all his attention.

Sheila closed the door to the bedroom and got right in my face. Her eyes were dancing. "What do you think?"

"About what?"

"About Leroi and Angie. You think she likes him?"

"Mother! Are you matchmaking?"

She lit a cigarette and leaned over the dresser to check her eyebrows in the mirror. "She's lonely, she's ready for adventure and she's a doll. Leroi's in the same position. I thought they might have some fun." She turned around and looked at me. "You disapprove?"

"I thought you had a claim on him."

"Good Lord, child. He's barely thirty. Besides, I told you about Rocky."

"The rancher?"

"He's great. When I'm having a ball, I want all my friends to be in the same place." She gave her hair a final fluff. "You having any, Carol Anne?"

"Fun? Not much," I said, trying to keep it light.

"I thought as much."

"How come?"

"I saw it in your eyes." She sat on the edge of the bed and pinned me with a stare. "You know, Baby, most people are afraid of getting old, but it's not about getting old, it's about losing your spark. Having fun isn't some kind of crime."

"Tell me about it," I said, sarcastically.

"Stop having fun, that's when you start looking at the world out of shit-colored glasses."

"You think that's what I'm doing?"

She ignored my question.

"My Uncle Eddie," she said, "was a gambler."

I knew I was in for a story.

"Too bad you didn't know him. The man loved the horses. One day he passed out in the men's room at the track and it scared him so bad he said he'd never go back. Settled for hanging out at the bar and using a bookie. One day for his birthday I took him to the races. You were just a baby then. By the time we made it to our seats he was huffing and puffing, bent over, neck all sunk into his chest, his eyes pinned on the floor, wondering, probably, if he was going to make it. To tell you the truth, I was too.

"Well, make a long story short, he bet a long shot on the last race and at the turn, his horse pulled away and left the pack behind. Eddie was standing up, beating his cane on the floor, yelling, 'Go, baby, go.

Run for Papa,' as excited as a ten-year-old on a roller coaster. If he had dropped dead that minute, it would have been okay by me. The next thing I knew, the man who could hardly walk in under his own steam was taking off for the window to claim his winnings."

She grabbed my hand all of a sudden and pulled me up. "Come on," she said with a wink. "Those two in the other room are gonna think we left them alone on purpose."

Angie was sitting on the sofa with her legs tucked under her, looking enchanted.

"*Ganja,*" he said.

"*Ganja,*" she repeated with a giggle, trying to imitate his lilt. She looked up at us. "Leroi's teaching me Jamaican."

"And he cut to the chase," Sheila observed.

"No," Angie insisted. "I asked."

"Asked what?" I had missed something in the conversation.

"If he had any good stuff."

I shot her a look that said she was out of control.

He pulled a leather case out of his pocket and glanced at Sheila, as if asking permission. "Before we go to dinner, would anyone like a toke?"

Sheila shrugged as if to say it was okay with her. Angie nodded like a kid that had been offered an ice cream cone.

"We're talking marijuana?" I asked.

"*Ganja,*" he said again, softly, looking apologetic, as if he had offended me.

"My daughter lives in the heartland," Sheila said. "Where work and beer are the drugs of choice."

"In that order," I said.

Leroi's face broke into a broad smile. "The work, we say, is always there. The music and the *ganja* make it bearable."

"Lead on," Angie said.

"What the hell," Sheila said. "I'm not on stage tonight."

Leroi knelt beside the coffee table, long, brown fingers sifting the leaves into the waiting paper. With a single movement he made a quick roll and lifted the smooth, white cylinder to his mouth. I watched his pink tongue tickle the gummed edge.

"You do that as easy as my mother-in-law makes bread," I said.

His dark eyes shot me a soft arrow. "Practice, practice," he sang.

He passed the joint twice and then put it away, as if to say 'that's plenty'. This is wild, I thought, and I liked it.

We took a taxi to the north side, some place that had been recommended to Sheila. Angie called it cozy. I liked it because no one seemed to be staring at us, three white women with one very tall, brown man. Leroi sat at the table and looked from Sheila, to me, then back to Sheila. "She looks like her mother," he said. "Does she sing like her mother?"

I shook my head.

"She has perfect pitch," Sheila said.

"That so?" he asked me.

"Yep," Angie answered him. "It's weird. Like those people who always know where north is. She always knows where the notes are."

"So where's C?"

I thought a minute and gave him a C.

He looked at Sheila. "Don't look at me," she said. "I get my pitch from a piano."

"How about an A sharp?"

He was testing me. I hummed an A sharp. "Can we stop now? I feel like a dog doing a parlor trick."

"It's a gift," he said, like he was really impressed.

"She used to come up on stage with me," Sheila told him. "But when she was about ten, all of a sudden decided she didn't like to perform."

"I don't have that good a voice."

"She sings all the time," Angie said.

"Shut up, all of you," I said. "I don't want to talk about this. I want to order."

The main course was served family style, so the four of us had to agree, which took a long time and almost two bottles of wine. We finally decided on butterfly shrimp, with artichoke hearts and roasted peppers on what they called "a mattress of steamed rice." Everyone picked his own dessert. Angie and I got chocolate decadence.

"No ice cream on my side," I insisted. "I'm off milk products."

"Oooh," they all crooned in unison, like they were so impressed.

We laughed a lot at dinner, sometimes at nothing, and at one point I caught myself looking around the table, thinking how special these people were and how lucky I was to be with them. Then I remembered the pot. It must have been good stuff. Sheila paid the check, which she

143

said was outrageous. Then she left a twenty dollar tip and had the waiter call a taxi.

"Take us to the water wall," she told the driver. To the rest of us she ordered, "Take off your shoes." The taxi pulled up along a deserted street inside a business park and we stepped out barefoot, and followed her through rows of evenly spaced trees and across the damp grass toward a fancy entrance of arches and columns.

"It's almost midnight," Angie whispered. "You think we're going to get in trouble?"

Sheila turned around. "Drunk, are you?"

"Pretty near but not plum," Angie giggled, straightening herself up. "But can't they get us for trespassing?"

"Who's 'they'?" I challenged her.

"Relax," Sheila brushed it off. "Public art is meant to be experienced. Leroi, you'll be our bodyguard?"

"If you say so," he beamed, white teeth shining in the dark.

"Then you girls get your asses over here."

We followed to an open space in the green, then stood beside her, looking up. She made us guess how tall it was. We guessed five stories. The water bubbled down over a high, curving wall, like an overflowing bathtub. She led us single file around to the front, where archways called us in and we were suddenly surrounded by water that crashed onto stone steps and then rolled into a little trough to be sucked to the top again. Angie read the inscription aloud like she was giving a speech: 'A jewel planted in the heart of the city to remind whoever passes this way that natural beauty and spiritual rejuvenation are ever within reach.'

Angie decided at that minute to run through an arch and plant herself smack in the center of the huge circle. She closed her eyes, stretched out her hands and lifted her face to the stars. "Hallelujah," she shouted. "I bet this spray is great for your skin."

"Big sound," I had to shout over it. "Just like rapids."

"What do you think, Leroi?" Sheila asked, insisting on a reaction from everyone.

"Reminds me of home," he said. "Like waves on the beach. Except, lady, we don't have the smell of Clorox."

Sheila reached over, pinched his nose with her fingers and held it shut. She grabbed my hand, and I grabbed Angie's, and Angie grabbed Leroi's and we danced around in a circle then out toward the taxi where the meter was still running.

I called the hotel the next afternoon to say goodbye and Sheila had checked out. Left a message that her plans had changed and she'd be in touch.

"I thought she wanted to set me up with Leroi," Angie complained.

"That's Mother for you."

"Wouldn't have her any other way. Couldn't," she corrected herself, sitting on the bed with huge rollers in her hair. "Besides, he's not my type."

"Oh, really?"

"I figure musicians have a girl in every port. Me, I want to be numero uno."

"I want to have some more fun," I told her.

She rolled her eyes. "Be careful what you wish for."

"Oh, Angie, you don't even know what that means."

"I've been married, haven't I?"

Driving home, I entertained myself with the game Georgie liked to play with me in the car. We turned everything into alphabetical lists. This time I tried to think of things I'd never done, that I wanted to do. A, act in a play. B, backpack in the mountains. C, curl my hair. I mean serious curls, like Barbra Steisand in that prizefighter movie. D, dive, as in scuba. E, eat watermelon with my fingers and spit out the seeds. Sometimes you have to stretch to make it interesting. F, fly over a city on the Fourth of July to watch the fireworks. M was make love in an elevator. Five days ago I'd have said that stuff was too silly, too expensive, too messy, or too dangerous. Suddenly, I was ready to consider it all. Oh, bless the city, and Angie, and Sheila, I thought. What the hell, bless Leroi, too.

The house was dark when I drove in. It was a little after eleven and no one was expecting me until the next morning. I had planned how it would be, my homecoming, even if it was a Tuesday night. I slipped into the bedroom, and took my time undressing in the dark. I listened to Fritz's even breathing and caught a whiff of the soap from the shower he always took at night. My mind was set on giving him a really sweet dream. I'd slip into bed, fit my body against his, bury my head in his neck and suck up all that wonderful man smell, and before he was completely awake, we'd be connected, without a word being said. I dropped the straps of my slip and was sliding it over my hips when he suddenly sat up.

"Vera?" he whispered.

I pulled up the slip and hit the light switch. "Guess again."

"Carol Anne? When did you get home?" He held his hand to his eyes and squinted against the brightness.

"Too soon for you, I gather."

"What are you talking about?"

"What do you think I'm talking about? You thought it was Vera coming into our bedroom?"

"Hell no. I woke up and someone was in the room and she's the only other person who's been in the house."

"Except the boys."

"I could tell it wasn't one of the boys. For God's sake, Carol Anne, why didn't you tell me you were coming home early?"

"Because I'm some kind of a fool." I stormed downstairs, poured bourbon over ice, choked down as much as I could swallow at one time and sat at the kitchen table, fuming.

"Asshole!" I said to the kitchen sink.

He came to the doorway in his bathrobe.

"Asshole," I said to his face and emptied the glass to impress him.

"Hold it down," he said. "The kids are asleep."

"And Vera? Is she asleep too?"

He held his finger to his lips to shush me and frowned. "Can we please talk this out without waking everyone in the house?"

I waved my arms at him in desperation. "What's to talk out? I think one thing. You're going to try and convince me it was another. My word against yours, you'll always come out the winner. So forget it. Just forget it. Pretend it never happened. Pretend. That's all I ever do in this place anyway. Pretend I'm something I'm not. Pretend I'm having fun. Pretend I'm the happy little homemaker, not a real live person." I was pouring it on, and something inside said I should stop, but there was satisfaction, too, from the helpless look on his face. "You want me to pretend you didn't just call the woman undressing in your bedroom Vera?"

"I can't talk to you like this," he said and left the room.

I took a gulp and followed him into the living room. "You can't talk to me anyway. Truth is, you don't want to talk to me. But you like to talk to Vera. We all know how much you respect her opinion. Well, maybe she'll want to come be your full-time help because I'm tired of the job."

He turned and took me by the shoulders. "Get hold of yourself."

I shook him off. "Leave me alone."

"Let's go outside and talk about this."

"Aren't you afraid the neighbors will hear? We might make the newspaper. For twenty-five cents everyone in town can read about Fritz Jahn's dirty laundry."

He held the door open and waited until I finally got up and walked outside. My legs felt unsteady. Well, fuck it, I thought.

He took the glass from my hand, set it beside the front steps, and started walking me down the street. At the corner I looked up at the street light, all shining with a halo around it, and started to cry.

He reached for my hand. "It was a misunderstanding, Carol Anne. Don't blow it out of proportion."

"You wanted it to be her."

"For God's sake."

"And she's been staying at our house since last Friday."

"At your invitation. What do you want?"

"Everything."

"Then you picked the wrong man."

"I thought you picked me."

"I guess I did."

"So, I guess you're not always right after all."

"At least I try."

"You think I don't?" I thought how excited I had been to get home just a few hours before, how I thought I was going to change things.

"I think you could try harder."

"I think you're an asshole."

"That's where you started. Can we finish this tomorrow? I've got to get some sleep."

"Well, of course. Shall I call your office for an appointment?"

He turned and headed toward the house, and after a minute I followed, barefoot, in my slip, woozy, and hoping he had left the latch off so I wouldn't have to knock on the door to get back in.

The thought of sleeping on the sofa and having to face the kids and Vera first thing in the morning was even worse than lying down in his damn bed. Besides, I thought, it's my bed too. I crawled in and pulled myself into a knot, determined not to touch him even by accident. The liquor helped me sleep for a while, I guess, but I woke to the clock striking two, and three, and four. It was awful, having him sleep there, like nothing in the world was wrong. I wanted to flip on the lights and make him listen to everything I was thinking. I wanted to reach over and choke him until he came up begging for air.

It was mid-morning and the house was quiet when I made it downstairs, feeling like dog-dirt. The kitchen was spotless, and there was a note on the table from Vera.

Max has an ear infection and has been running a fever the last three days. Told me he always comes in last on the swim team anyway, so it's okay if he misses practice. His medicine is in the refrigerator. He had it at eight and gets it again at noon. Hope your trip went well.

I was still looking at her note, feeling mortified, wondering if I owed her an apology and what I was going to do next, when Max peeked around the corner in his underwear and socks, looking forlorn.

"Mommy," he ran to hug me. "I was as quiet as a mouse so you could sleep."

"Yes you were. Thanks." I set him down and put my cheek to his forehead, feeling for a fever. "How 'bout you, buddy? Feeling okay?"

He nodded, still pressing himself to me like he wanted to stick on. "Don't go away so long," he shook one finger, looking very serious. "I need you here."

"I know, baby. I know."

Vera

I never found out exactly what happened that time Carol Anne took off for Houston. I know this, that nothing was ever the same again. My intention hadn't been to make trouble, regardless of how it ended up. I had intended to give her the break she said she needed. After all, she had confided in me.

She called it her demon. You can count on Carol Anne to make it dramatic. I thought she was talking about her period at first. Some women are always talking about their period.

"No." she said, "This comes in bigger cycles, once or twice a year. I wake up one day, miserable. The whole world, black. It lasts for a while, and then I wake up one morning and it's lifting. Sometimes it goes as quick as it comes. Sometimes it comes on slow and gets a little worse every day until I'm finally in the absolute pits."

When I insisted she see a doctor, she did. He told her it was normal for women to get depressed and offered to give her a prescription for it.

"That would freak Fritz out," she told me. "Me taking happy pills. He says I should be able to think my way through it. To tell the truth," she added, "it freaks me out too. So I'm just going to cut out milk products."

"To what end?"

"Maybe I have an allergy or something. I read about it in a magazine."

It seemed unlikely to me, but so did most of Carol Anne's solutions.

The week she went to Houston, the boys and I enjoyed each other. I took them to the library and made them check out my dearest childhood books. They made me watch their favorite television shows and gave me the backgrounds on all the characters. One day I took them into San Antonio to the institute to watch the "Faces of Texas" film, and we talked about it on the way home. Georgie was impressed that Texas had belonged to Mexico.

"They're supposed to teach that in fourth grade."

"I guess they did," he told me, "but all I remember is that there was a big fight at the Alamo and we got massacred, and that's why Texans don't like Mexicans."

"If I worked downtown," Max announced, ignoring our history conversation, "I'd ride the space needle at Hemisfair Plaza every day."

I promised we'd try to do that before their mother got back but Max ended up getting sick, which concerned me. Apparently this was a common occurrence with Max, but it was new for me. For two nights I got a taste of parenting, up at midnight and again at four to take his temperature, put in warm ear drops, and give the medicine the doctor had called in for us. The first night, Fritz was up with us both times; the second night, I thought I heard voices downstairs about midnight and was relieved that Max would have his mother back.

I stopped by the office a few days after Carol Anne returned to let Fritz know he was finally an uncle. "Val had her pups. Four of them. I'm reserving one for the boys."

"We can't handle anything else right now," he snapped.

"Carol Anne okay?" I asked him.

"I guess. Why?"

151

"She hasn't called."

"She hasn't been feeling well."

"Sick?"

"I guess."

"You guess?"

"I don't know, Vera. Ask her yourself."

He was in a bad temper and not inclined to let me in.

"I don't think I'll do that, but you can tell me if you like."

He turned, ran his hands through his hair, then watched something out the window before he finally looked at me.

"She thinks something's going on between us."

"That's ridiculous!"

"That's what I said."

By the end of the month, just after school started, she had gone to California to visit her mother and Queenie had taken over, driving up the hill every afternoon before the boys were due home. She cooked dinner, did the wash and supervised their lessons. I wanted to help but was determined not to set foot in that house again until I was invited.

I did make it a point to drop by the office to see how things were going. Benno was there alone, one afternoon, fussing over the bills. He looked up with a frown when I walked in.

"How are you, Onkel?"

"Not so good."

"Need any help?"

"Queenie always does this," he told me. "Can't figure out what's going on."

"Let me have a look."

"What do you know about books?"

"A little."

"Not this kind of books, you don't."

"Well, let me see." I walked over and peered over his shoulder at Queenie's tidy columns.

He grunted and pushed away from the desk. "Something wrong there. See if you can fix it."

I lowered myself into the still warm chair and tried to rise to the challenge.

"What's going on with Carol Anne?" he said, out of the blue.

"I don't know. I guess she needed a change."

"The girl's never satisfied."

I looked up, surprised. "I thought you liked her."

"Too much troublemaking. First the rumors about her and the Mexican boy. Now she runs off to California."

"Are you talking about Mike?"

"The Mexican, what's his name, at the golf course."

"That got blown out of proportion, Onkel. And it was quite a while back."

"So, what do you know, Missie?"

I hesitated, always measuring my words with Benno. "I know she loves Fritz and the boys."

"Hmmph."

"It's not easy living here, especially for an auslander."

"Best goddamn place in the world!"

"It takes some adjusting."

"She's had plenty of time."

"Onkel, do you want to know what I think, or do you want to tell me what you think?"

He started to roll a cigarette and I went back to studying the books.

"Looks to me like the club didn't make their payment last month."

"Queenie called and they told her it was in the mail."

"So has it come yet?"

He looked down at his desk, cluttered with papers and envelopes and shrugged his shoulders. "Could be. I count on her for that."

"Something else, Onkel."

"What's that?"

"They skipped a payment in July and another one last February. Paid at the end of the month instead of the first, and never caught up."

"Must be some mistake."

"I could call the bank and see if they're paying their other bills."

Benno took a long time grinding out his cigarette, then shook his head. "No," he said.

"Why not?"

"Because these are the people I do business with. I trust them."

"How long are you willing to trust them?"

"Until they prove me wrong."

I closed the ledger and stood up. "Then I guess there's no reason for me to be here."

I left the office and drove home under leaden skies. Winter had come and the hills were almost barren. As I approached the house, circles of leaves danced across the road. I turned the headlights on high to warn the deer I was coming. Grazing safely in my yard, they had become careless.

"Still wants to do business on a handshake and a promise." I thought aloud of Benno. "Should have stuck with what he knew." And in the back of my mind was the question of how Fritz could have let this happen. We hadn't talked in weeks. I waited until after the boys should have been in bed and called.

"Fritz? Vera."

"Yeah?"

"Sorry to bother you."

"No bother."

"I stopped in the office today and tried to help Benno with the books."

"Yeah?"

"Well, I know it's none of my business, but are you aware the development company is behind on their note payments?"

"Who says?"

"I say. I saw the books."

"Must be some mistake."

"That's what Benno said. Why don't you go look for yourself," I told him and hung up the phone.

When my phone rang thirty minutes later, I knew it was him.

"You're right," he said, without saying hello. "I don't like it, not at all. I should have put two and two together. So busy trying to keep things going at home, I forgot to pay attention to business."

"What are you going to do?"

"Nothing I can do tonight. Go home and pace the floor, I suppose."

"If you want to drive out here, we can talk."

"Let me stop by the house first and leave Georgie a note, in case they wake up and wonder if they've been totally deserted."

I turned on the porch light and listened for his truck. Val heard it before I did and left her pups long enough to run to the window and stand guard until I came to release her with a pat. I watched him walk toward the cabin, head down against the wind. When he reached the door, I opened it a crack to let him in.

"You warned me not to set that door facing north," I said, but he didn't appear to hear. He took off his jacket, dropped into a chair and leaned forward to warm his hands by the fire.

"Coffee?

He shook his head.

"Bourbon?"

He nodded. "On the rocks."

I fixed the drink and carried it to him, then waited.

"Those bastards owe us more than $20,000," he said finally. "And it's coming right out of Benno's pocket. Benno's and mine."

"How come?"

"We have notes to pay, too. We've obligated ourselves buying land all over town."

"How could this happen?"

"Because Benno felt safe with the note to back him up."

"The note?"

"The balance of the ranch sale. $450,000. The $7,500 a month you found delinquent."

I nodded, trying to think like a businessman.

"If they've fallen behind," he said, "they're probably in trouble. And if they're in trouble, we're in trouble." He finished his drink and I refilled it.

"What's the worst case?"

"They default on their note. We foreclose. The property goes up for sale and the proceeds go to the first lien holder."

"Who is?"

"The consortium who loaned them five and a half million dollars to build that place."

"And we get neither the land nor the money?"

"That's how it could go."

"How could this happen?"

He looked defensive. "How many times are you going to ask me that? It was a calculated risk. We checked the developers out. They were solid. Three other resorts. A good track record. No reason to believe they'd get in financial trouble."

"So it looked good. What went wrong?"

"I don't know. The lots aren't moving, for one thing. They counted on that for income. Have them priced too damned high, if you ask me. Interest rates keep climbing. Damned inflation. Hell, I don't know."

"There's a way out."

"You tell me."

"You never see places like that sit and rot. Someone will pick it up and make it work."

"And we'll still be in our second position, with egg all over our faces. Meanwhile, our own investments need capital, every month."

I threw up my hands. "It's over my head. Maybe it's best to take your loss and start again from a simpler position."

He gave me a disgusted look. "Think about it, Vera" he said. You know how many people in town have bought into this thing because they trusted us? You know how Pop feels about his reputation? Not to mention losing the money he had counted to retire on." Fritz's face was a mass of lines and shadows in the firelight. We would both be forty next year, I thought, apropos of nothing.

He talked on.

He poured another drink. At midnight, he was still traveling over the same old territory. What he could have done. What he should have done. What he might do. He didn't talk about Carol Anne, but she was there, another thorn below the surface. He paced back and forth.

"You think it was your fault?"

"Might not have happened if I'd paid more attention. I trusted those guys because they knew a lot more than I did."

"You think they set out to cheat you?"

"No, but they're businessmen, not friends. If their backs are against the wall, they'll do whatever they can to come out on top. Tomorrow I put them on notice for back payments. I'll talk to the lawyer, see what I can work out with the first lien holders, a way out. Concentrate on land sales. If we sell two lots a month, we'll be okay."

I thought how he used to be after the team lost a football game, drinking beer, working off the frustration, planning with the guys how to kick ass the next time. "Fritz. Fritz!" I practically shouted to get his attention. "I think you've got things exaggerated."

"No. I've got things fucked. Benno and I need to work our asses off, be three places at one time. Come and help?"

"Me?"

"I need someone in the office I can trust."

"I have a job. A demanding one, in case you're interested."

"You could come in half a day."

"You're grabbing at straws, Fritz. "

He stood up and pulled me to my feet, his hands pinning my arms on either side. He bent down and kissed my forehead. "Vee, I need you," he said.

I smiled and tried not to look patronizing. "You'll think better of it tomorrow, Cousin."

He took me in his arms then. My face pressed against his shoulder. I could turn my head and make my mouth available. I could close my eyes and listen to the crack of the fire, the whine of the wind, and step into some alien place where, for a while, nothing would exist but us. He smelled of cedar and bourbon. His hands were wrapped around my waist, his head buried in my hair. I could feel the warmth of his breath.

"Deja vu," I said, and walked over to refill my glass. "There's too much going on here."

"You think too much," he said.

"That's why you like me."

He ran his hands through his hair and shook his head. "Shit," he said.

The next morning I called and invited Mike to dinner. When he asked if he could bring his girlfriend, I agreed, although I'd hoped we could talk in private. I wanted to find out what he knew about the club's business.

"Vera Jahn, I'd like you to meet Susan," he introduced us proudly. The girl smiled up at me shyly. "I've seen you around town," she said. "I'm Susan Kiesling."

"Otto's daughter?"

"Yes, ma'am."

"You work at the cafe?"

"I used to. I'm in school now. Home on weekends and holidays."

"Susan and I met at the club," Mike said. "We, uh, usually see each other in Austin, but I told her it'd be okay to come here."

"Of course it's okay. Why would it not be?"

They sat side by side on the sofa, the girl looking uncomfortable. Mike circled her shoulder with his arm, looking protective.

"Am I missing something here?" I asked.

Mike turned to Susan. "I told you."

"Told her what?"

"That you wouldn't disapprove."

I turned to the girl. "Mike and I have an ongoing discussion about this. He's too sensitive, don't you think?"

"Not if you know my daddy."

I nodded. I knew Otto.

"Is this serious?" I asked them both in turn.

"We plan to get married," Susan said and looked over at Mike for confirmation. He nodded.

"And your father doesn't approve?"

"That's putting it politely."

"You're not the first couple who's had to face that brand of adversity," I told them. "Give it some time."

Susan looked at the floor.

"Well," I said, "we can't solve your problem tonight. Susan, why don't you help me put dinner on while Mike tends the fire." It was something Queenie would do, finding work to divert people's minds from their problems. I wanted to laugh when I heard myself but decided my guests would find the joke hard to appreciate.

"I think the development company's in trouble up north," Mike told us, over coffee. "The auto industry is dead. People aren't buying the big

American cars any more, much less land. Not taking vacations. Giving up golf."

"Where do you hear this?"

"From the snowbirds who come down from Michigan. Lucky ones who are drawing retirement and can afford to travel. Our people have two big resorts up there, with reciprocal memberships, so it's a good deal for them to come down here for the winter."

"If it's so bad up there, maybe they'll move here for good."

He shook his head. "Snowbirds don't stay. They stick around for the winter, live out of their RVs, and head back in the spring. They hang around the clubhouse and the bar and they love to talk. Stagflation. That's their big, new word. They blame it on President Carter and foreign policy and high oil prices. I don't understand half of it, but they say it's just a matter of time until it hits here. My guess is that the company's stretched thin, trying to cover their losses."

The couple was getting ready to leave when I asked Mike the main question on my mind, "Do you think this club can run at a profit?"

He zipped his jacket, closed his hands into a golf grip and took an imaginary swing at a ball. "I'm a golfer, ma'am, not a businessman."

Part of me was in sympathy with Fritz and Benno. Another part reasoned that they had allowed things to get out of hand and now must live with the consequences. I could remember a time when we had nothing but the land. Surely they could too. If worse came to worse and everything was lost, they would still have a home. And a business. Not depleted. Except for pride, I thought, which was no small thing.

What about my own pride? I was angry with Fritz for grabbing at me like some handy branch he happened to see when he found himself sliding off the cliff. Nevertheless, I found myself doing for him what I would do for few others. Making excuses. And another thing, harder to admit. I had wanted him. But that was a momentary thing. I liked my life just as it was. To value thinking over feeling was the way to avoid those intrusive things that happen to people when they fail to pay attention. What's required is to value thinking over feeling.

Carol Anne

I remember a deer we found out at the ranch one day, with its leg caught in a barbed wire fence. She had herself all wound up, one foot barely touching the ground. Her eyes were wide open and rolling around out of control, drool running from her mouth. When Fritz cut the wire and stepped back, she hit the ground running. Her tail flashed as she went, like she was giving us a sign, and I could feel the life rushing back into her. "Poor thing," he said. "She'd have died there if we hadn't found her."

I was at the car dealer's leaving the station wagon to be serviced when the owner asked if I knew anyone heading west. I didn't pay much attention at first. He always flirts with me.

"I've got an Apple Red '79 convertible on the lot a dealer in L.A. will pay me a bundle for if I can get it to him."

"You're kidding!"

"Nope. Happens that way sometimes. But the people who are free to drive a car across country aren't usually the ones you'd trust with your car, if you know what I mean."

"What about me? Would you trust me, Mr. Baese?"

"Can you drive a standard?"

"I can drive anything with wheels."

"When were you planning to go?"

"Uh, the next few days. My mother's out there, you know."

"Well, give me a call when you're ready. She's a demo, only got a few thousand miles on her. But we'll check her out and be sure she's road-ready for you. All you have to do is drop her off when you get there and deliver the released title."

It was like I was destined to go.

I did some thinking on the way to California. I thought about that deer and how maybe the main thing wrong with me was that I was acting in Fritz's story—waiting for him to save me—instead of my own. I put the top down, turned on the radio and sang along. I lathered myself with suntan oil, put on a tube top and worked on my tan. It was September. I'd be home in a month or six weeks. Meanwhile, Queenie would see to the boys. They'd be busy with school, anyway, and Fritz could cool his heels and guess.

I lit a cigarette, adjusted the rear view mirror and, staring into it real close, tried to look tough. There was a little speech the coach had given my boyfriend in high school and I knew it by heart, because even back then it had struck me as a perfect man-thing, like something they'd say, and something they'd need to hear. "Mister," I said to the mirror, thinking about Fritz, "it's time you put your head in gear and backed it out of your ass."

When I used to hear Queenie and Benno talk about freedom, it was stuff out of ancient history. Driving across the country alone, I figured out what freedom was for me. It was deciding when to eat and sleep, when to drive and when to stop. Was I scared? Not a bit. Depressed? Definitely not.

Sheila was playing in a dinner spot on Santa Monica Boulevard and had leased an apartment at Venice Beach. Leroi backed her up on drums and vocals. I halfway expected to find him staying with her, but she said he was hanging out with friends.

It was the first time we'd spent any real time together in ten years and we both wanted to make it good. The first few weeks, when they weren't practicing or playing, we took in the sights, Catalina, Disneyland, Universal Studios, Rodeo Drive. We combed second-hand shops for jeans and sweaters and a couple of slinky things I could wear at night when I went to hear them play. Their music was different. Bongo jazz, I called it. Not really her style.

"It's a stretch," she told me. "You've got to have a gimmick. Leroi's mine," she reached over and gave a pull on the long gold earring he wore in one ear. "I've been trying to get him to take off his shirt and show off that wonderful body, but he's shy. It would sell. Absolutely."

"I'm a musician, not an exhibition," he told her, in that wonderful sing-song voice.

In mid-October Sheila and I took off early one morning and drove north along the coast. It reminded me of summer trips to Galveston when I was a kid, except this time the scenery was delicious and the weather was dry and cool and Sheila wanted me to drive. After watching a while, she laid her head back against the seat. Her hair was in a loose pony tail, her eyes covered by huge sunglasses. I looked over and thought how her jaw and neck looked drawn and saggy, then cut my eyes back to the road because if she had seen me, she'd have read my mind.

"This place makes me feel old," she said.

"California?"

"Yep! L. A., at least. Funny, I've wanted all my life to get here and now I'm thinking I ought to get out."

"I thought you were loving it."

"Good. That's what I wanted you to think."

"So what's the problem?"

"Ask me no questions, I'll tell you no lies." One of her stock answers.

"Am I overstaying my welcome?"

She sat up and raised her sunglasses. "Baby, you know I always do what I want, and you're welcome to come along. I'm into figuring what I want right now."

"Does it have to do with Leroi?"

"He's talented and I'd like to help him. Brought him out here with promises, but it's dragging me down."

"How so?"

"Can't you see it?"

"See what?"

"They like him more than they do me."

"Mother!"

"Truth hurts. Old blondes are a dime a dozen, but a beautiful, bald, brown-skinned man, with a voice like honey and good hands, now that's marketable."

"So what are you going to do?"

"I don't know, Carol Anne. What are you going to do?" She gave me her city hall smile.

I pulled the car off the main highway and headed toward the beach. "I think I'm going to see what the Pacific Ocean feels like."

The thing that made Sheila fun to be with was that she never let anything get her down for long. "There's always another game in town," she'd say. "All we need to do is find it."

"I wish I'd inherited that attitude," I told her.

"It's not something you inherit, Silly. It's a mental discipline."

"Did you read that somewhere?"

"No. Why?"

"Doesn't sound like something you'd say."

She threw her head back and laughed. "See? Never, never get predictable. That's when people start taking you for granted and the next thing you know, they'll be walking on you. Whenever they think they have you figured out, throw them a curve. It's your best tool."

"Best?" I raised my eyebrows in doubt.

She tapped her temple with a phony red nail. "Don't kid yourself.

Brains count."

I thought of Vera.

It wasn't long after our trip that the restaurant management decided to book Sheila and Leroi in the bar. The hours were longer and later, and the money was less. I wrote Sheila a check for part of the rent and groceries and when she deposited it, it came back, stamped "account closed."

"There's some mistake," I told her and called the bank.

"Yes ma'm, Mrs. Jahn," the girl told me, "Mr. Jahn closed that account last week. There was some problem, lost checks I think he said. He opened another joint account and said you'd be in to sign the cards as soon as you got back from California."

"Son of a bitch," I slammed down the phone.

"Seems pretty civilized," Sheila said when I told her what had happened. "Lots of men would do a lot worse."

"Well, Fritz would never want anyone in town to think he wasn't supporting his family."

"Don't knock it," Sheila said. "Why don't you have an account of your own?"

"Fritz says I don't need one if I don't have an income."

"Well, Sheila says you need to open one." She reached for her purse.

"Here's two hundred to get you started. And the next thing you need is a job."

Sheila got me on as a cocktail waitress at the bar where they played. I made $150 on a good night and never less than $75. It was easy money, dressing up, carrying people their drinks and their change. So when someone pawed me or got rude, I figured I was getting paid for it. And I was having fun. Sheila, Leroi and I, started a little routine going, them from the stage, me from the floor. I'd call out requests, they'd feed me banter. It felt cool and uptown and the crowd liked it.

Every Sunday evening I telephoned the kids. Since the money quarrel, Fritz and I hadn't talked, but I wanted him to know he hadn't hurt me as bad as he thought.

"I have a job," I told Georgie, "at the same place where Sheila works.

Just temporary, of course, to pay for my sightseeing. We went to the desert last weekend. Did you get my postcard?"

"Yeah," he said. "So, Mom, are you going to be home by Thanksgiving? We have two days off from school."

"I'll try, honey, but it may be a little after that. Definitely by Christmas. Can you put Max on?"

"He's pouting in his room."

"He doesn't want to talk to me?"

"You know how he is. He won't talk and then he'll scream when I hang up because he didn't get to talk to you."

"Tell him I'm sending him a present. One for you too."

"Thanks, Mom."

"I love you, kiddo."

"Love you too."

I sent the most expensive presents I could manage, to let Fritz know his nasty trick had backfired. When I called the boys two weeks later, he got on the phone.

"When are you coming home, Carol Anne?"

"Soon. I'm saving my money now."

"You could have saved a bundle on those presents for the boys."

"I want them to know I'm thinking about them."

"If you care about them, you'll get your ass back here and act like their mother."

I wanted to slam the phone in his ear. Who made him the king of the world and me some slave dog woman that was supposed to do everything he said? And how had I let that happen? I said nothing until I could answer in a soft voice.

"What makes you think someone would want to come home to be talked to like that?"

When he answered, I could practically hear him clenching his teeth. "Carol Anne, every day I think of things I want to say. But when you call, I see red. All I want to do is grab you and shake some sense into you." He stopped. "I guess you're right," he said after a while. "We do need to talk."

"You could come out for a couple of days. I don't work from Sunday morning 'til Tuesday night."

"There's no way I can drop everything and come out there. My plate's full trying to keep the business afloat."

"It was only an idea." There was a long, dark silence, both of us waiting for the other to say something, I guess. "Okay, I'll let you get back to your full plate now," I told him.

"You have no idea what's going on here."

"Fritz, I don't even care," I said and hung up the phone.

One night, during their final set, Leroi stood up and pointed to where I stood waiting for the bartender to fill my order.

"You," he called out, like he'd never seen me before. "You play maracas?"

"A little," I called back and made a rolling motion with my hands and hips.

"How about coming up and helping us out on this next number."

I shook my head, and looked over at the manager, who nodded like he wanted to encourage me.

Leroi came forward, his hand held out. "You folks can do without her for one song, right?"

The customers answered with a smattering of half-hearted cheers and claps and he led me up the couple of steps to the raised bandstand and sat me on a stool between him and Sheila.

"Is this a set-up?" I said under my breath.

He ignored me, reached for the maracas, put one in each of my hands and then, his brown hands over mine, began moving my arms up and down in a smooth little pattern. "That's the way," he said. Then he turned to the audience. "Making music is like making love. Everyone can do it. Now I bet you this little lady is good. Very good." They laughed and somebody called out, "Wouldn't you like to know?"

To me he said, "Darlin', you start the beat, like so, and when we're ready, we'll come in."

I looked over at Sheila, who was nodding encouragement too, but I thought she looked as surprised as I was. Then I looked out at the audience and my heart started racing. They were looking back. Nothing to it, I told myself. You've done it a hundred times, on the kitchen stool. Pretend you're Sheila. So I closed my eyes and started swaying and then

I got the beat. I was so into it, I didn't even know when the others joined in, but before long we were a trio. Of course, I was just the maracas. But good maracas, I thought.

When the number was over, Leroi drummed into another before I could get off stage, so I sat on the stool, clapped my hands in time and swayed back and forth, humming along.

"You're a natural, baby," he said when it was over and we were breaking down.

"It was fun. Think I've missed my calling?"

"Maybe so. You never know 'til you try. What do you think, Sheila?"

"I think I'm out of here. You coming, Carol Anne?"

I looked over at Leroi. "How about something to eat?" he asked.

"Sounds good. I'll get a cab home," I told Sheila.

"Suit yourself," she said.

"You upset with me?" Leroi asked her.

"Yeah, but I'll get over it." Then she looked at me. "You be careful," she said.

I saluted.

Leroi and I talked it out over an omelette at an all-night diner.

"She doesn't like surprises," I told him, "unless they're her idea."

"How 'bout you?"

I thought about it, giggled, then covered my face with my hands. "I can't believe I got up there and did that."

"Did what?"

"Impersonated a musician."

"Woman, you are a musician."

"It was exciting. The most exciting thing I've ever done."

"Well, now," he said, "you've led a sheltered life. How come you've never done that before? Afraid you'd outshine your mother?"

He was so slick.

"What are you going to say to Sheila?" I was thinking about the way she had left.

"She'll have something to say to me," he smiled. "It hasn't been working out like we planned, our music. We both know it. It was a matter of time."

"Did you plan that with me tonight?"

"I wanted to see what you could do. Maybe we can put a little act together."

"Spare the flattery, Leroi."

"I'm serious." He reached over and covered my hand with his. "Let's get out of here." He found a cab, opened the door for me and leaned down to kiss me on the forehead. "Sleep on it. I'll be over tomorrow for practice."

"Bring your shin guards," I warned.

Sheila was still up when I got in. Sitting in the dark, smoking.

"You okay?"

"I guess." She looked up at me. "I didn't have any problem with you sitting in, but I don't like surprises like that. He should have told me. It's my act, godammit."

"You're right."

"Sure I'm right. I've spent the last hour convincing myself it's a matter of principle and not a bruised ego."

"And?"

"Time to cut my losses," she said.

When Leroi showed up the next day, Sheila and I were sunbathing. I pulled on a cover-up and opened the door. He looked down at me and nodded approval. I pulled my shirt closed and took him out to the deck where she lay stretched out, facing the ocean. He planted a kiss on her nose. She sat up and lowered her sunglasses.

"Asshole," she said.

"Your servant, ma'am."

"I'm ready to look for something else, Leroi."

He lit a joint and offered it to me. I shook my head.

"We both know this gig has turned out to be yours," Sheila went on, "with or without me."

He looked over and smiled. "Can I keep your pretty daughter too?"

"That's up to her." Irritated, she turned to me. "You're being foolish if you think you can waltz into this business and make something happen without a lot of work."

"Did you see how comfortable she was on stage? I say she can learn the music."

"And fart in perfect pitch?"

Leroi laughed. "Now that would be an act."

Sheila got up, went into the bedroom, and closed the door behind her.

"I need to talk to her," I told him. "Call me later." He blew me a kiss and let himself out the door.

"He's a charmer," she said, shaking her head, as I walked into her room, "no doubt about it."

Sheila didn't tell me what I should do, but it was clear she thought it was time for me to head back home. When I told her I wasn't ready, that I wanted to stick around a little longer because I was finally having fun, that I wanted to try singing with Leroi, to see if I could, she warned me about the music business and about Leroi and about California in general. She said she was going to visit her boyfriend in Nevada, pick up some work in Reno, and from there she thought she'd try to get on the cruise line that goes up to Alaska. That crowd was more her speed, she said. Then she said if I was going to stick around, I should get Leroi to cover the next two months' lease on the condo so I'd at least have a rent-free place to stay.

Everything happened fast. Leroi took over the act and changed the music to fit his style. We practiced together in the daytime. I learned to follow his songs enough to back him up with simple accompaniment. We were spending so much time together and he was paying for the apartment, it only seemed reasonable that he should move in.

"I won't hit on you," he held his hands up, like Mr. Innocence. "This is strictly business, until you want it otherwise."

"How about you?" I asked him.

"I always want it otherwise, lady," he gave me a big smile.

For a while we continued the waitress on the stage act because it gave me a pass to be an amateur. Then, the big holiday weekend after

Thanksgiving Leroi said I was ready to sit in. We were billed as Brown Sugar and Cream, and drew a full house. A guy in the audience came up afterwards and gave Leroi his card. Said he wanted to talk to him about making a commercial. In the third set, I finally began to relax a little and see what I could do with my voice and my body and the energy between the two of us. He was so easy to play off of, so big and electric and sexy. I thought I could feel the women in the audience wishing they were me, and the men wishing they were Leroi. We exchanged knowing looks, pretended there was something special going on between us.

We celebrated by making love. We didn't plan it, but of course everything was leading that way. Once I let him know I was agreeable, I thought it would be fast and frantic. After all, we had waited a long time. But no, he was slow and deliberate and I was wondering how to respond, like when you're thinking in terms of a rock beat, and all of a sudden the music goes Brazilian.

"Relax," he told me. "Close your eyes. Center your body right here," he kissed his fingers and touched me between the legs, "in this sweet cave, which I shall enter with this," he kissed my hand and placed it on his penis, "but not 'til you want it so bad you can't think of anything else." And then with his tongue and his lips and his hands he worshipped my body like he had never seen another woman, and then I heard myself beg. "Now. Please."

Seems like it went on forever and still ended too soon, which was new for me because, much as I liked the idea of sex, I was usually ready for it to be over.

"That was. . . ." I stopped, looking for a word.

"Incredible, isn't it?"

I rolled over and looked at him. "I've never done it like that."

"Never been made love to?" he took his finger, which still smelled of me, and outlined my lips.

"Never slow like that. Never just to please me. Never so stretched out."

"Island pace," he smiled.

Could this guy be for real? I swept the doubts away, too relaxed to care.

Sometimes I'd wake in the afternoons with him beside me and wonder what I'd do if Fritz came to the door, or Vera, or both of them. In my vision, the kids were standing right behind them. Leroi and I didn't talk about much but the music. The pot he was always smoking made me sleepy, so I passed on it, except sometimes at bedtime. When I asked if he thought it made the sex better, he gave one of his big laughs.

"I learned that fact in elementary school."

"Well, you're either a fast learner, or a hell of a liar."

"One or the other," he smiled. "Could be both."

Our appointment with the commercial people got set for Christmas week. I already had tickets to fly home that week and tried to get him to postpone it, but Leroi was so jazzed about the idea I agreed, even though I figured it was a waste of time. We both were disappointed when we saw the office. Dirty hallway, no receptionist, two rooms of cheap furniture. From the front door we could see a fat guy standing beside a desk in the back room. He was talking on the telephone, but waved us in. Leroi took my arm and kind of steered me in his direction.

"My receptionist must've gone to the bathroom," he told us. "But I've been expecting you. Brown Sugar and Cream. I like that name. You two have a great gimmick. Gave me the whole idea for this shot. Skin products, you know, like blacks use. We zoom in on your act, singing, throwing those little flirty looks around, then someone comes up and asks what you're drinking. And you, baby, order coffee. And then they ask you, 'How do you like your coffee?' and you look over at him and say, 'Like I like my men, light, brown and sweet.' Then you lean over like you're telling her a secret and you, baby, you turn your head to one side and look like you're blushing, and then we fade out and onto the product, 'Melanome,' this deep voice says. 'She goes for the look. You'll go for the look. Nothing to lose but your fear of the dark.' What do you think?" He was looking at me.

I said, "I thought this was supposed to be an audition."

"Hey, it's a sure thing. Minute I saw you I knew you were the ones for this job."

"Me, selling a black beauty cream? It doesn't make sense."

"It makes sizzle. You know, the desire for 'the other.'"

"I don't like this big deal about skin color."

"Why so uptight all of a sudden?" he said. "You two are a walking commentary on skin color."

I turned to Leroi. "It doesn't bother you?"

"Sheila capitalized on it," he shrugged like it was no big deal.

"Yeah," the guy said. "I've got places I can sell this one. It's a hot market. For $150 we shoot the commercial. When we sell it, you get fifty per cent of the net."

"You want us to pay to make this commercial?"

"That's the way it's done."

"I don't believe that." I turned to leave.

"It's only $150, Baby, not much for a good idea, and if it sells, we're in."

If Leroi told me that once, he said it ten times. Problem was, the recording studio wasn't available until Christmas Eve, which meant I had to scramble to change plane reservations again.

"There's a seat on a plane that leaves at noon, but I have to be on it." I told him. "I promised the kids."

"Don't worry," Leroi said. "It'll all work out."

"Easy for you to say, Mr. Never Worries About Anything."

"It's a talent," he told me, "like finding things in strange places. Hey," he reached under the bed and came up with a shiny red package with a white bow, "I believe this one's for you."

I unwrapped it to find a zebra striped leotard and a black silk shirt. He leaned back on the bed and lit up. "Try it on?"

"Not now." I was packing.

He took a few hits and laid the joint in the ashtray. "You need to chill out, my lady. I'll be on the deck when you're ready."

I tried to think what I'd need for the trip. Jeans, sweaters, something for Christmas Day, a slip, stockings, earrings. Hell, I had all that at home in the closet. I got a smaller bag, threw in some underwear, my makeup bag and a nylon warmup suit for the plane ride. Then I powdered my naked body and wiggled into the leotard, stepped into high black heels, pulled on the shirt that just covered my butt, rolled the sleeves to look casual, and went out to show Leroi.

He looked up and grinned. "That will sell."

"I need more boobs," I said, looking down. "I used to have more."

"Honey," he stood up and came to me, reached inside the shirt and cupped my breasts in his hands. "You know what I thought when I first saw these?"

I shook my head.

"I thought, now I understand why the Arabs like having those very young girls in their harems." While he talked, he slowly spread his long fingers, making my nipples hard. "You're a woman, Carol Anne, but your body is still like a budding flower."

"You are full of shit," I pulled away, laughing

The recording studio was as sleazy as the office, run by a kid that called himself the engineer. His face was a mass of pimples and his clothes looked like they'd been slept in, which they probably had been, because he was there when we got there at 8:30, and that's real early for anyone in the music business. We warmed up for a half hour, and were ready when the fat producer showed up to act like a director. No script, no helpers, and only one camera. Everything had to be shot two or three times from different angles.

"Don't worry," he told us, "Joey, here, is a genius at editing."

"I've got to be out of here by 11:15 to catch a plane," I told him.

"Honey, it's Christmas Eve, we've all got places to be. Now, freshen up your lipstick and let's do that part again about the coffee." He had me put makeup on my arm and hand and shot it to look like a brown woman was handing me a cup of coffee. When it was finally over, there wasn't time to change. I grabbed my bag and pulled Leroi out on the street where his van was parked and changed clothes while he raced for the airport.

"That stage was so phony," I complained, struggling out of the leotard. "Christmas lights strung around aluminum foil."

"It'll come out looking fine. The camera does magic."

"Weird," I said. "Like it's Christmas Eve, and the car is hot and I can't get any air back here and I'm sweating, and this damn makeup won't come off my arm."

"You're nervous."

"Keep your eyes on the road. I'll be really pissed if I miss that plane."

"We have a date for New Years," he reminded me.

I climbed into the front seat, pulled down the mirror and straightened my hair. I couldn't think that far ahead.

QUEENIE

If the snails crawl up the side of the house, they say, the rain is coming. But even if one watches for snails, who can stop the rain? So much worry I saw on the faces of Fritz and Benno, so many questions in the eyes of Georgie and Max, and all coming at Christmastime. I was for making a celebration.

Every day I go to Fritz's house and make the dinner and wash the clothes. So many clothes those boys have, like they must wear something different every day of the week and more. And every day they are glad to see me but still they ask when their mother will come. Especially the little one. What am I to say?

Georgie is a boy close to my heart, maybe because he came first, but easy he is, and liking his studies, and then there is the other one. I take them to the river to swim and Max gets in for a minute then climbs out to stand on the bank and shivers until I must tell him to wrap in a towel. One day I take him to pick berries and he gets into the stinging nettle and begins to cry. I bring him home and into the kitchen to wash his hands and legs, then put on the baking soda and follow it with the vinegar so he can watch the bubbles.

"You must learn to know the bad plants from the good ones," I told him. Then I told of Mr. Lindheimer who more than a hundred years ago drove his wagon out to collect all the plants of Texas, and pressed them in paper, and gave them names, and put together the ones that were alike, in families, and it all went in a book that is still used today. "It's important," I told him, "to learn everything you can, and to be remembered, especially in a book."

"Were there dinosaurs when you were a girl, Oma?" he asks, and I can see that the time, so clear to me, is in another world for him.

"No dinosaurs, *liebchen*."

"Indians?"

"No Indians in my time, but my opa knew some." He starts to listen and I tell a story of early days in Fredericksburg when Indians came onto the settlers' land and helped themselves to whatever they found. "This was not acceptable," I said, "so our best men were sent to the Indian camp to work out an agreement, while the people in town waited to see what would happen. Up on the hill at the edge of town large fires appeared and burned through the night. My grandfather, a boy then, remembered this. He woke from his sleep and went to his mother who sat by the window.

'They are going to cook us,' he told his mother.

'Who?' says she.

'The Indians, with their fires.'

'No Indians out there,' she told him, 'only the Easter Bunny who has gathered the eggs and is now boiling them in her pots and dying them with wildflowers, preparing a celebration for the boys and girls.'"

"And he believed that?" Max questions my story.

"Of course," I tell him, "A good boy believes whatever his mother tells him."

"But you're not my mother."

"Also what his oma tells him."

"So what happened then?"

"The next morning the fires were no longer burning and in the yard my grandfather found beautiful colored eggs, lying in baskets of fresh green grass."

"Do you believe that?" he asks me, his eyes big with the question.

"Certainly," I say. "That is how it was told to me."

The boy wants to believe that his fears are only the make-believe man in the closet. Doesn't everyone? That is why I'm for making an old-fashioned Christmas, so we all have something good to think about. When I say this to the others, they pay no attention. No time or money to spend this year they say, so wrapped up they are with business. It is only the boys and me. We harvest the pecans, crack them with the hammer and clean them at night when the studies are done. The pieces we save for baking, the large meats we salt and put in a jar, a present for their father. Nights when Benno and Fritz go to the hunting camp, we bake the *pfefferrneuse*. Packed away in tins with tight lids, it is stacked on the pantry shelf. Rum cakes I wrap in cheese cloth and every week we check to see if more rum is needed. On Christmas Day the boys will go delivering to neighbors. I teach the old songs and how to make presents for their teachers. Fresh cloves we stick into an orange for something sweet-smelling to hang in the closet and when they prick their fingers and suck where it hurts, they come away with the smell of clove in their noses and I know they will not forget.

"What about the tree," they want to know and I say that must wait. The week before Christmas, when the boys go to hunt with their father I send Benno to the woods for a juniper, the largest you can find I tell him, and he grumbles, but I know he'll return with a good tree. It is very full, so tall and heavy he must tie it to the ceiling of the living room, where we set it up and then close the doors.

Now here is the hard part. The children know that Christmas lies behind that door, but they are not allowed to look. If they look, the *Weinachtsmann* may not bring gifts and though they say they do not believe, they will think before they look. Just in case, I don't put everything out. But each day I decorate the tree a little more, with cookies, candy, wooden ornaments from the old country, lacy snowflakes crocheted and stiff with starch, polished nuts, dried flowers. Every space I fill with something wonderful to see. All the time I wonder about Carol Anne, and why she is still not here, but I don't ask and no one says.

On the day before Christmas I take out thirty tin candle holders that were my mother's, fill them with fresh candles and set them firmly on the branches, like placing an egg in a nest. It would not do for one to slip and the tree to catch on fire.

At my asking, Benno has carved wooden guns for the boys, guns with clothespins for springs and pieces of rubber tire for shooting, and I have made knit caps for them in their school colors. They must see the good of things made by hand, and not just bought in stores. Fritz has tackle boxes filled with everything one needs for catching fish and Vera has chosen a wristwatch for Georgie and for Max a black cat clock that hangs on the wall and swings its tail with each tick. The presents are wrapped and placed under the tree .

In the afternoon the family gathers and I can see how Fritz listens for the phone to ring. We all listen. Carol Anne, finally on her way, will be calling from the airport. Then the daylight goes and it is time to eat. I ask if I should wait dinner. Fritz looks at his watch and says no.

We have fresh venison and herring salad and black-eyed peas for luck, fresh bread, homemade pickles, and apples baked with brown sugar. The boys pick at their food, but Benno, Vera and Fritz drink some homemade wine and begin to find the spirit. Benno whistles the Santa song and Georgie rolls his eyes and asks if he can have some wine. We pour him a little, now that he is almost a man and for Max I pour red juice and we call it wine. We talk of Christmas when Fritz and Vera were children and I tell of when a visitor came to our house and brought a wondrous log of chocolate candy and the children laugh and say that wasn't so much and I tell them to look under their plates where I have hidden a gold candy coin. They unwrap it and pop it into their mouths and then comes the hot cake with Mother Christmas baked inside and everyone cuts a piece and tries not to get the doll, for that means they must help with the dishes.

"Is it time?" the boys ask, and Benno gets up and slips through the living room door, opening it a crack, but not so anyone can see.

"When the bell rings," I tell them.

"This is stupid," Max says, and I know he is getting anxious.

"It is good to be patient," I tell him.

"We're going to be patients, in the hospital," Georgie says, "if something doesn't happen soon."

When Benno rings the bell, I turn out the dining room lights and the house is in darkness.

"Come now. It is time," I tell them and take the boys across the hall to the front room. Fritz throws the double doors open wide and there is the tree, blazing with candles and filled with surprises.

"Oh," says little Max.

"Wow," says Georgie.

"Lovely" says Vera, and we all take hands and walk into the great room, where the tree calls and Benno stands beside the fireplace, smoking his father's pipe which he saves for special occasions.

Vera

I've never been particularly fond of Christmas, not since I was a child, and that seems very long ago. But Queenie's planning kept the boys involved and gave them something to look forward to when the rest of us had more important things on our minds and that was the good I could see in it. Then Benno threw open those doors and I was carried back in time, like Proust biting on his cookie. My chest began to ache like it needed to expand or burst. This was not joy, whatever that must feel like. It was something between awareness and pain, but hardly something you can think through. I looked down so no one could see the tears that filled my eyes. Georgie held one hand and Fritz the other and we stood before the lovely tree like a picture on a Christmas card, the kind I would never send. When I finally trusted myself to look up, Fritz was looking down at me and grinning as if to say "You're not so tough after all." Or maybe he was simply saying "This is sweet." For it was, and his eyes were wet as well.

That was the moment Carol Anne showed up. She slipped in the front door, listening while we sang "O, Tannenbaum," and no one knew she was there until the song was over and she clapped. Georgie ran to hug her and little Max hung to her leg like a fly to sticky paper. She was again the center of attention, looking beautiful and excited. She carried presents for the boys and as they unwrapped them Queenie brought a plate heaped with food.

"So thin," she said.

Carol Anne laughed. "In California they say you can't be too thin or too rich."

"Hmmph," Benno said and lit his pipe.

Fritz frowned and sat with him arms folded. I saw how he had answered her greeting kiss by turning his cheek.

"You said you'd call," he said.

"I rented a car."

"Liberated," he announced to the group, as if he were looking for a way to belittle her.

"Oh, Fritz, drop it. I saved you a trip and it didn't cost that much."

"Soon we all walk down to the square where the choir is singing," Queenie announced, pulling on her coat. She turned to Fritz and gave him a sharp look, like a warning. "And we shall say a prayer for peace."

"Do you pray, Oma?" Max asked.

"In my way," she told him.

For years I had championed Carol Anne. I had excused her foolishness because she was young and had taken up for her because I thought I knew what it meant to be an outsider. I had watched her take advantage of Queenie's good and generous heart. I had seen her ignore Georgie and indulge Max and all the while I took up for her. She had wanted to be my friend and in my way I had tried to be hers. She came to my house a few days after Christmas.

"I need to talk," she said.

"All right," I said. The last I wanted to hear was her troubles.

"This is very private, Vera."

"Either you want to tell me or you don't."

"I do. It's just kind of sticky, and I don't want you to think bad of me."

"Carol Anne," I said, "start at the beginning."

She hesitated, lit a cigarette, and stared at the table, running her polished fingernail along a grain in the wood. Finally she took a deep breath and began.

"I went out to California because Fritz and I had a big fight."

"You thought there was something between us."

Her eyes opened in surprise and she covered her face with her hands.

"That was so stupid. I wish he hadn't told you that."

"It makes things awkward."

"I'm sorry, Vera, truly." She leaned forward and put her hand on my arm. "Sometimes I get things in my head and I can't see anything else. I was miserable and thought I saw something that wasn't there, but it doesn't matter so much any more because. . . ."

"Because you've found someone else?"

"How'd you know that?"

"I'm guessing. I've seen people split up before."

"It's more than someone. I've got a career started and I don't want to let it go."

"What does Fritz say?"

"Says he'll file for divorce if I go back." She held her hands out in a motion of helplessness. "I have to go back. I'm singing in a nightclub New Year's Eve. Could you talk to him? Convince him to give me more time. I need six months to find out if I can do this. A separation. Vera, please. I know I shouldn't get you involved, but. . . ."

I reached for her cigarette pack and helped myself to one.

"He'll listen to you," she said.

"This is very selfish, Carol Anne." I didn't even try to hide my irritation.

"Sure it is. You know what? I'm tired of trying to do the 'right' thing."

"Does Fritz know about the other man?"

"Leroi?" She put the accent on the second syllable.

"What kind of name is that?"

She rolled her eyes, smiling. "Unlikely, huh? Well, that's me. How about Brown Sugar and Cream? That's our stage name." She took a strand of hair and studied it for split ends. "I don't know if I can be a singer. I don't even know if I want to. But I want to try."

"You have to tell him about this Leroi," I tried to pronounce it her way. "I won't be a party to that."

"Then the whole thing explodes in my face."

"Probably, but you must be honest with him. You can't have your cake and eat it too, Carol Anne."

She frowned. "That's exactly what he'll say. You two are so much alike, except you like me more than he does."

I wasn't sure at that moment how much I liked her and all my talk about being honest echoed in my ears with a hollow ring.

"What about the children if you stay in California?"

"Georgie is rooted here. He'd never be happy out there, but Max would want to come with me, and I could handle that. My mother did it."

"You've thought about it?"

"Enough."

I took a deep breath. "I don't know. I could shake you for pulling me into this. It's between you and Fritz."

"But if he asks your opinion?"

"In my opinion, a family should try to stay together at all costs."

"Then that's all you need to say. It might buy me a little time." She smiled at me, looking relieved, and a little worn. "I wish we could change places, you and me. You like the ties and I want the freedom."

She had no idea what I wanted.

Years ago, before I left Philadelphia, I became disenchanted with the men who passed through my life and shared my bed and made a conscious decision to abstain. The Shakers, I had read, regarded celibacy as a movement toward equality between males and females. This rang true for me. When I was involved with a man, my independence was compromised. I had to make myself available. Much as I might enjoy the physical side, I resented the expectations. Doing without sex was a very practical solution and I had taken satisfaction in the self-discipline. Until recently. Recently, I had reopened the dialogue with myself.

Now here is Carol Anne, simple as a child, but complicated nevertheless, and so involved in her own situation she can't fathom the truth of mine. I am drawn to Fritz. I have always been drawn to Fritz, but I have buried those feelings from a sense of right. I found myself questioning everything. Marriage, sex, love, loyalty. The words floated around in my head, assuming various and awkward shapes. Suddenly nothing was as well-defined or as solid as I had believed it to be.

Tully Fox was a newcomer to town, brought in to head up the reorganization of the town's oldest bank. I first met him at the grand opening of their new building, the kind of social nonsense I make it a point to avoid, except Fritz had asked me to go.

"We're thinking of trying to move and renegotiate our loans," he told me. "I'd like your opinion of this guy. He was All-State back in 1951. Went straight to Korea out of high school. Took a bad hit there, but he came back, went to SMU on the GI bill and ended up playing ball for them."

"Those are impressive credentials for a banker," I said, with more than a touch of sarcasm.

"It tells me he's tough."

"But is he smart?"

"That's what I want your opinion on."

I stood at the corner of the room, sipping champagne from a plastic glass, and watching Mr. Fox from a distance. His reddish-brown hair appeared to be permed. Medium height, sturdily built, wearing an expensive-looking navy sport coat with a white turtleneck, he stood out among the dark suits.

"Does he realize this is Schoenberg and not Dallas?" I whispered to Fritz,who nudged me to shush and edged me toward the group waiting to pay their respects.

"Fritz," he called past the immediate circle around him and started toward us.

"Tully," Fritz grinned and shook the man's extended hand.

"You must be Vera." He pinned his eyes on me, very attentive, but unsmiling.

"How could you know that?"

"Fritz said he'd be bringing you. Look, I have to mingle for awhile, but I hope you'll stick around so we can talk later. Is Benno here?"

I nodded. "Over there."

"Good. In about an hour then?" He turned abruptly and moved toward another group.

I raised my eyebrows and looked at Fritz. "He doesn't mind taking control," I said.

An hour later, as most people were leaving, a black waiter found us and brought us to the atrium where Mr. Fox and maybe fifteen others had gathered.

"Jackson," he spoke to the waiter as if they were a co-conspirators, "let's open up the bar and get these people what they'd like to drink. And for God's sake, get rid of this plastic crap and find us some real glasses."

"Yes sir, Mr. Fox," the waiter smiled indulgently and started around the circle taking drink orders.

There were two doctors, two lawyers, a dentist, the owner of the largest jewelry store, the mayor, who also owned the Ford dealership, and his mother, a widow who owned a great deal of property in town, including that which the bank sat on. I had known these people all my life but I had never had the opportunity to see them being courted.

Tully Fox staged himself in the center of the pavers and addressed the group. Not what I'd call a handsome man, but he certainly radiated confidence. And more. There was an unyielding way about him that made me think of those lions that had called for their breakfast across the freeway, and the angry young blacks on the street corner in Philadelphia, of a steamroller, something you didn't want to stand in the way of. He was, of course, more civilized.

"I feel like someone who has come home," he said. "This town has great possibilities. Beautiful land, plenty of it, and a rich culture of hard work and honesty. If we pull together we can make it grow and prosper."

He looked around. "I know what some of you are thinking. If the town's so good as it is, why try to change it? I'll tell you. Because things are changing whether we like it or not. We've stepped into the '80s, people. You have a resort down the road that's going to bring in visitors from all over the state. All over the country. Hell, all over the world. We have the chance to make Schoenberg an elite community, where only the best people want to live, because it's safe and clean and beautiful here.

He took a sip of his drink and relaxed his stance. "I'm looking for board members, people who can bring accounts and, of course, loans into the bank. Interest rates have been sky high for a while, but prime went down a half point last week and I'm wagering it'll go down again this month. People who've held off taking out loans will be coming out of the woodwork. We'll be pouring money into this community, and this bank will have a say about what's built, and where. I guess the only question is, do you want a part in the prosperity?

"I'll warn you in advance, I'm not an easy man to work with, but I don't forget my friends. I've opened up the second level so you can wander upstairs and see the new offices and the board room. Meanwhile, Jackson will fill your glass if you're empty."

I turned around and looked at Fritz. "We need to talk about this," I said.

"Later," he said. Tully was coming our way.

"Fritz, Benno," he said, shaking their hands, "I hope you took my proposition seriously."

"May I assume you weren't inviting me to be on your board?" I smiled, teasing him.

"It's not out of the question," he said, "but I had something else in mind. Could you come by my office some time tomorrow?"

"I'll be in a meeting tomorrow until five," I said.

"Five forty-five, then?"

I was trapped.

It was the third week in January. Carol Anne had returned to California and Fritz seemed resigned. He told me she was singing with her mother and had a contract until the first of June. I was furious with her for lying to him, but it did make things easier for everyone. Still, it was a broad lie and she was likely to get caught.

It was dark at 5:45 as I navigated the traffic circle, around the bandstand where Christmas lights were still strung, and pulled my car into a newly painted parking space a few steps from the large glass doors of the bank. The building was well-lit, and its shiny image reflected off the wet pavement. A uniformed guard accompanied me through the deserted lobby and saw me into the elevator to the second floor. This was a serious departure from the simple office buildings of our town, the ones I had grown up with. The upper level was carpeted in moss green and decorated with impressive nineteenth-century art. Mr. Fox's pretty, young secretary was still at work and looked up as if she were expecting me.

"He'll be right with you," she said and disappeared behind a wooden paneled door.

She returned quickly and went back to her work. Ten, maybe fifteen minutes I waited, almost to the point of impatience. How much did he have to do at this time of day, I wondered, and was considering leaving when a buzzer rang on her desk and she told me I could go in.

"Vera," he closed a single file that sat on his desk and stood up to greet me. "Thanks for coming. Sorry you had to wait."

I nodded. "No problem,"

He motioned for me to sit down in a comfortable leather chair and I sat, facing him across a wide expanse of well-polished desk.

"I understand you're a student of German literature."

"Language and literature," I said.

"Right," he corrected himself. "And you're with the Institute of Texan Cultures. Their German specialist, I assume?"

"Germans, Swedes, Wends"

"Wends?"

"Wends were Slavs of East Germany who came in with the late settlers. Actually, we're all late settlers when you consider the Indian and Mexican cultures, whose history is incredibly rich."

"Maybe so, but nothing got accomplished until we got here."

"Oh? What's your background, Mr. Fox?"

"Same as yours. Family name was Fuchs, but I changed it when I got to college. You can imagine what kind of harrassment I went through as a jock with a name like that."

"It's a troublesome name," I had to smile, "for English speakers."

"Damned right. My father was furious when I told him I was changing it, but my mother understood. Tully's her maiden name, you see, from Atlanta. I'm surprised she married him, considering she'd have that baggage to carry around."

"I went to school here with a girl named Helen Zushlag," I told him, "who talked about how glad she'd be to get married and rid of her name. She married Carl Zunker, but there's three Helen Zunkers in town, so everyone refers to her as Helen—"

"Zushlag Zunker," he said, anticipating my ending. "Sounds like a sump pump."

Why was I sitting there making polite conversation with this man? My mind was on Val's new puppies and I was anxious to get home. They had a tendency to get into mischief if I ran late and on top of that I had a new toy for them in the car. I was about to ask the purpose of our meeting when suddenly Mr. Fox leaned forward. "You know Arno Leisner?"

"Of course. He's been president of this bank for years."

"How old do you think Arno is?"

"Sixty-five?" I guessed.

"Seventy-eight," he said. "Never guess it to look at him, but it worries the hell out of me. When we took over the bank, part of the deal was to keep Arno on for a year, kind of liaison between the old and the new. He's going to handle public relations for us."

"That's a good idea," I said, "but what does this have to do with me?"

"Hold on a minute and go with me on this. Now my thought is three months, six at the most, is all we'll need him but frankly, I'm worried. He's going to be out in the front lobby. Suppose he falls over with a stroke? A shame, sure, but messy, too. I don't want to risk it."

"He likes the work," I was offended by this man's take-charge attitude.

"Sure he does. All he knows is work. But he's tired. He's as much as admitted it to me. And he knows he doesn't have many good years left. I'll send him out with full retirement, a big party, a new car, a last trip to Europe."

"What does this have to do with me, Mr. Fox?"

"I want you to replace him."

"Me?"

He laced his large, neatly manicured fingers and placed them before him on the desk. "When I came to town, I asked around. Who's the smartest woman in town, I wanted to know, and you were one of the names that kept coming up. Then I saw you at the opening and I knew. You're not just intelligent, you have class. You come from a good family. You're respected. I'd like you to come to work for me. We need women like you in banking."

"I have a job, Mr. Fox, which I like very much, and I'm good at. I have no experience in your business and, frankly, very little interest."

He stood up. "Think about it," he said. "I can beat what you're making."

"How do you know what I'm making?"

He walked around the edge of the desk and put his hand on my shoulder. "Don't say no tonight. Talk it over with Fritz and Benno and get back with me. You'd be a natural with these people and with the people we're going to bring into town. A natural."

After helping with my coat, he walked me down the hall, into the elevator and out through the glass doors. "That your car over there?" he pointed.

"Yes."

"Japanese make, isn't it? Like it?"

"I like it fine. Why do you ask?"

"I know someone who's looking to get rid of a little creampuff Buick. I could put you in it for less than $5,000."

"Why should I change cars? This runs perfectly well."

"For fun. Want to have a look ? See what you're turning down?"

He took my hesitation for a yes. "I'll have it here tomorrow afternoon. Maybe you'll have an answer by then. Come see the car, and then I'll buy you a drink and let you in on the wonders of easy auto financing."

He hunched his shoulders against the mist and hurried back to the safety of the building. Then he turned and waved as if certain I would still be watching, which I was.

Mr. Fox was unnerving. I dreamed that night of counting money, behind bars, counting, counting, while my hair trailed through the bars and hung down into the garden. It was blonde, of course, like Rapunzel's. It irritated me to have obvious dreams. They seemed so ordinary

Tully Fox alternately attracted and offended me.

"Did Fritz tell you I'm interested in building a house on the golf course?" he asked over drinks. He was dressed in slacks and a sport shirt and looked less imposing than he had the other night.

"That's good news! He's looking for sales."

He laughed, shook his head and took a slow sip of scotch and water.

"I'll buy three lots if you come work for me."

"Is that flattery or bribery?"

"Whatever it takes. I don't like to beat around the bush. All you need to do is tell me, Vera, what you want that you don't have."

"I don't know you that well."

"Well, put me on your 'to do' list and when you see Fritz, tell him I've put together some investors who want to talk about a buyout."

"A buyout?"

"The bank will put up the money on the basis of the investors' financial statements. Benno and Fritz put up their financial statements too, become part owners, and then exercise their option to assume the loan. We pay off the note, move it over here, and put our heads and our money together to get the resort back on its feet and push land sales."

"With a lot of new partners."

"It'll work. Where's his wife, by the way?"

"Fritz's wife?"

"I hear she's something to see."

"You hear a lot. I'd rather you tell me about these potential buyers."

"They're solid. They believe, as I do, this project is a little gold mine and they don't want to see it grabbed by those jokers at the S&L across the street who aren't bright enough to protect their rear. We've got them where we want them." His hand was clenched into a soft fist, palm up, and I thought his eyes looked like those of a boy I had watched once, boiling frogs in his mother's wash tub.

I refused to look disturbed. "You have a way with words, Mr. Fox."

"Tully," he said. He reached in his pocket, took a thick fold of cash from a money clip and laid two bills on top of the check.

"You sure you don't want that Buick?" he asked as he delivered me to my own car. "Belonged to the sheriff's daughter. Apparently, she's taken up with the Mexican hotshot at the golf course and her dad sent her back to school without a car so she can cool her heels." He seemed intrigued, and I thought how much I disliked the habit of small-town gossip.

"The sheriff's a bigot," I said.

"I've found him easy to work with," Tully said.

"You consider that a valuable quality for a sheriff?"

"Hey," he said. "That's my first question for anyone. Are you willing to do what's necessary to get along?"

I shut the car door, caught my coat in it and was forced to open it again to extricate myself. He sat in the driver's seat looking smug. Impossible. I wondered how anyone who talked the way he did could have made his way to a respected position. There was no way I would work for him.

Benno smiled at me when I walked into the office the next afternoon.

"You're in a good mood," I said.

"Did you hear about your nephew?" he asked. Georgie had won the sixth grade American Legion award for good citizenship.

I nodded. I had my own news.

"Tully Fox said he's going to make you a deal you can't refuse."

Benno picked up a toothpick off the desk and began to chew on it.

"He's a persistent one. Reminds me of that javelina I shot. Damned thing kept coming at me. Dogs hanging off both sides." He chuckled. "You two should get along well, Missy."

I ignored his comment. "Don't you wonder why he's so interested in your project?"

"It's the best land around. Get this going and the bank stands to make a lot of money."

Why did I even bother talking with Benno? I wanted to ask if he was sure Tully was a man of scruples, if there might be a conflict of interest, why he was courting us, so willing to go out on a limb when he hardly knew us. "He's an auslander," I said. "He wants to change things. Take the best of our town and turn it into some kind of elitist playground for the rich."

He looked hard across the desk at me. "I don't know what a 'litist playground is. What I do know is that boy was shot in Korea, then left for dead. When the soldiers came round with the body bags, someone saw him twitch. That close he was to being sent home in a sack. He's got that scar across his throat where they opened him up and stuck a tube in."

"Where'd you hear that?"

"At the cafe."

"You believe it?"

"I do. And I think about it when I look at him. He comes from money, they say. Father owned a bunch of mills, but the boy had to learn everything the hard way, like going off and getting shot instead of going on to school like he should. What he has, he's earned. Got some pretty good ideas, seems to me. What's wrong with keeping the town clean?"

Who could quarrel with a football player and a risen war hero? Tully Fox had apparently managed to impress the men in town who sat down at the cafe and took it as their responsibility to decide how things should be.

Mike stood on the practice tee, hitting golf balls and I watched from my car. He had lost some of his boyishness and naiveté since I'd first met him, but none of his easy grace. I didn't know if he was serious about Otto's daughter but felt the need to warn him.

He looked up, recognized my car and waved. "You make that look very easy," I called, walking toward him.

"You should let me teach you."

"All I know about golf," I told him, "is that Mark Twain said it was a good way to spoil a nice walk."

"If that was all it was," he said, "it wouldn't have lasted so long. I bet you didn't know they were playing in Scotland before Columbus came to America and it was so popular the King declared it aginst the law."

"What could be illegal about golf?"

"The army was spending more time chasing the little ball around than practicing archery."

From the elevated spot where we stood, I looked down onto a wide highway of grass that narrowed as it climbed to a lush, velvet summit circled by hourglasses of sand. A stream of clear water wandered laterally across my line of view, pooled in a corner beside a cottonwood, then trickled off over a stone dam. I pointed toward the white flag. "If I'm not turned around, my house is on the other side of that bluff."

"So you were in the neighborhood and thought you'd drop by?" Mike grinned, never in a hurry.

"I was hoping we could talk."

He looked around. "Want to take a ride first?"

We climbed into a golf cart.

"Zip your jacket," he instructed. We followed a narrow cement path until it ended, then took off across the close cropped grass, past the stream, the pond, a thick bed of rushes, along stacked stone walls, up a steep gravel incline that led us out across the limestone cliffs, then down into a dry creek bed, through the woods, into a tunnel and back to the clubhouse. I was holding to the cart with both hands when he came to a stop.

"I guess that's what you'd call a whirlwind tour."

"Didn't want you to get cold. So, what do you think?"

"It captures the Hill County at its very best, Mike. Did you lay this out?"

"I wish," he smiled at me. "Designing is a professional's job. I've been watching over the installation and maintenance, though. It wouldn't be a bad business to get into if I can't make it onto the tour. Still hoping," he grinned.

I followed him into the clubhouse and sat at a table while he talked a moment with the boy behind the counter who was pacing like he had a plane to catch.

"I remember when I was like him," he told me, pulling the tabs on two beers he had brought to the table. "I used to be ready to leave when the clock got on the hour. Now I come on my days off."

"How is Susan?"

He looked uncomfortable. "Haven't been able to see her much. I've been getting ready for a tournament."

"You're still serious about this game."

"Got to be," he said. "You know what they say. Can't beat anyone else 'til you conquer yourself."

"And how are you doing?"

He laughed and took a long drink. "Probably better than I deserve."

From the clubhouse window I watched a herd of deer wandering across the green. It was getting dark.

"Are you here to stay, Mike?" I was fishing for information and could hear it in my voice, but he seemed not to notice.

He shrugged. "Who knows? Like to get my name a little better known before I try to move on. That's assuming the club doesn't fold."

"Have you met Mr. Fox?"

He lowered his eyes. "You haven't heard? I thought everyone knew."

"I don't get much town talk."

"A fight," he said. "In the bar. Happened a couple of weeks ago. Mr. Fox, he came in off of eighteen, had a few drinks, then his group went home, but he stayed. Sat at the bar, drinking Jack Black and water and talking with Cassie, the bartender. The more he drank, the more his mouth needed to be washed out. The man talks foul, you know?"

"I can imagine."

"Kept calling her Pussy, excuse me, ma'am, like that was her name instead of Cassie. And that wasn't the worst of it. She couldn't get him to leave. When she wouldn't tell him where she lived, he said he was going to follow her home. That's when I went over and suggested maybe he'd had a little too much to drink, couldn't I take him home. 'Hell no,' he says, pushed me away, fell off the barstool and hit his head on the foot rail. I leaned down to help him up and he pulled me down on top of him and started wrestling. I backed off and he threw the stool at me."

"Did anyone witness this?"

Mike continued to talk as he got up and turned on the clubhouse lights.

"Only Cassie and she quit the next day because she was scared of him. She called the sheriff, but by the time the car got there, Fox had calmed down. Said it was a misunderstanding. Let them take him home."

"Did he say anything to you?"

"Shook my hand and said he'd see me around. He's got it in for me. I can see it in his eyes."

"That's exactly how it happened?"

"I wouldn't lie to you."

"I know, Mike. But I find it incongruous. Why would a successful businessman jeopardize his position with a barroom brawl."

"There are people like that. Lots of them, used to getting by with things. Kind of a macho, Texas thing."

"He and the sheriff are getting awfully friendly. I thought you should know."

"I know, and neither of them likes me. I'm trying to stay out of their way. Maybe this'll pass."

"You think so?"

"Got to play them as they lie."

"I suppose that's golf talk."

"Yes ma'am. You want to know what it means?"

"No."

I stood before the mirror, still dressed in my clothes from work, trying to see the reflection before me as a stranger on the street might. It was an old habit. At ten, I had overheard one teacher say to another, "Vera's a smart girl. Too bad she's so plain." At that age I didn't feel plain but very complicated and important inside and when I looked in the mirror, I liked what I saw. At about fourteen, I accepted the label as accurate. I was never going to be small or blonde or cute. So I concentrated on the other part, being smart. I decided that makeup and primping were a waste of time and basically dishonest.

My first year of graduate school I met a man at a conference in New York in a hotel on 5th Avenue. He was considerably older than me, handsome and well-dressed and comfortable to be with. We had drinks the first night after the keynote address, with a few moments of serious conversation about some obscure issues and a look at the schedule for the next day. He was giving a major presentation the next morning. I was impressed. "Would you like to have lunch with me afterwards?" he asked and I jumped at the chance. I ended up in his hotel room, almost as if it had been planned.

It was 3:00 in the afternoon, with the sun filtering through half-shut blinds. We had passed an unhurried, almost silent, hour in bed together. It had been more exciting for me than for him, I decided, but there was no doubt he had enjoyed himself. I had the feeling he had done this many times before. Now he held me before the mirror. "What a lovely body."

I looked away.

"No. Look at you," he turned my head back toward the mirror, "like a fine race horse."

"Especially the nose," I tried to make a joke.

"You're serious, aren't you?"

He sat on the bed and brought me to sit across his knees. Embarrassed, I buried my head in his shoulder, trying to avoid his eyes. "Let's talk about perception," he said. "I perceive you as lovely. You perceive yourself as not. Who do you suppose is right?"

"I'd rather talk about something else."

"We could play a game," he said.

I looked up.

"Take this," he handed me a hundred dollar bill, "go down the street to Bergdorf Goodman. On the mezzanine is the beauty shop. You may have a little wait, but they'll work you in. Tell them you want to look natural, but not ordinary."

"I couldn't do that."

"All right," he said and took back the bill, smiling.

"All right," I said and grabbed it back. "You won't laugh?"

"Vera, you're obviously very intelligent, but these people can show you something I suspect you've been too proud to learn."

It cost me fifty dollars for a good haircut and a lesson in makeup. With the rest, I bought a simple, black dress at what seemed an outrageous price. My benefactor, whose name I have forgotten, was pleased with the results, and so was I, and if one wanted to consider it taking money for sex, they could, but I've never thought of it that way. It was my official move into the modern world.

The following summer I won a grant that covered travel and the summer's study in Germany. While there, I lived with Hans. For years, since Schoenberg's first Octoberfest, we had written each other, nurturing a hopeful tension. I went overseas as his "American cousin," to live in his apartment and study at his school. It turned out to be more complicated than that, of course. He seemed to desire me more than he'd expected. And I desired him less. He was a very nice boy but not the man I had pictured him to be. He was also more ordinary than I had remembered. When the summer was over, we parted friends.

I turned from the mirror and sat on the edge of the bed to brush my hair. I thought about some of the girls I had envied in high school who had grown fat and sallow. I thought of Mike and wondered if he had broken up with his girlfriend because of her father or if he had grown tired of her. I thought about Fritz and Tully, both wanting my help, and maybe more. I thought about my work at the institute and about my friend and teacher, Donald, and the need he had inspired in me to present the past in a way that had relevance for the present. I finished changing clothes and picked up the phone to call Georgie.

"Aunt Vera," he said, "did you hear the news?"

"That you won an award?"

"No, that Dad and Opa are making a deal with the bank to buy the resort."

"That's not for you to worry about."

"I'm not worrying, I'm celebrating. Dad says if the papers get signed in the next month, he'll take us skiing at Easter. You should come with us. Will you? Please?"

"We'll see," I said, dismissing his invitation but pleased nevertheless. "What's your brother doing?"

"Peeling apples now, but a few minutes ago he was mooning the neighbors from the upstairs window."

"Mooning?"

"You know, sticking his bare butt out the window."

"My God."

"Yeah! Oma caught him when she took up the laundry and she started telling him stuff in German, to stop acting like a *grobber hund* and to come downstairs right away and help her in the kitchen. And now she's got him peeling apples for a pie and I heard her say he's got to take the pie over to the neighbors he was mooning."

"That seems fair enough."

"He's hating it. He promised never to do it again, but she's not about to change her mind. Said a *lausbub* asks for hard lessons. What's a *lausbub?*"

"A young one who thinks he's smart. You've never heard her say that before?"

"Not to me, she hasn't, and I hope she never does."

Fritz called later that night, enthusiastic over the deal Tully was putting together. "He's talking new management in key places. Says there's a lot we can do to be more profitable, attract visitors, buyers, improve our image."

"For example?"

"Nothing specific."

"He's not thinking about getting rid of Mike, is he?"

"What makes you think that?"

"Did you hear something about a fight at the club?"

"Mike was hitting on the girl bartender and got belligerent when Fox tried to stop him."

"Where'd you hear that?"

"At the cafe."

"From whom?"

"The sheriff himself. I know you like this kid, Vera, but he's a hotshot and no one trusts him farther than they can throw him. He didn't even grow up here."

"I trust him, Fritz, more than I trust Tully, or even you at this particular moment."

"Wait a minute."

"You wait a minute. I could tell you some things about Mike."

"I don't want to know."

"Of course not," I was through with the conversation. "Why don't we talk about this later."

I hung up the phone, grabbed a jacket and walked outside to clear my head, down the narrow gravel path that curved its way from my door to the dock. I didn't need the lights. I knew the way by heart. Two steps, then ten paces and two, and ten and two and ten on to the river. Mike's plan. It occurred to me that I equated his design eye with some inner perfection, while Fritz focused unspecified hatred on the boy because women, especially Carol Anne, found him appealing. I sat on the dock, legs over the edge, and listened to the water lap irregularly against the wooden posts beneath while the frogs were busy talking about something and occasionally a fish broke the water's surface with a splash. I consciously drew in the still night air and stretched to capture the sweet, sweet smell of spring.

"What do you want that you don't have," Tully had asked. I dismissed him at the time, but the question haunted me. The truth was, there was nothing I was willing to sacrifice my solitude for. Women have been propagandized into believing they must fulfill their biological imperative, but the times didn't demand that any longer, and I didn't fit the mold. And yes, there was a sense of barrenness that lived with me, but it wasn't about being childless. It was about another kind of sterility. Sometimes I found myself hoping something would happen. It seemed ridiculous to desire the unpredictable at the same time I diligently tried to keep it at bay.

I awoke the next morning to the piercing call of the peacocks. The air was still, the sky overcast. By nine o'clock the wind had begun to gust, circling strong from the north, then later settling into a constant whine against the weatherstripping. I closed the windows and the chimney vent, brewed a cup of tea and tried to concentrate on the papers that lay strewn across my table.

After a few minutes I laid down my pen and walked to the door. The spring norther whipped my hair into my eyes, demanding a jacket. I grabbed one, invited Val to join me, and made my way, head down, toward the car, not sure yet where I was going. The crisp air put a spring in the dog's step. Wisps of steam rose from the river and drifted southward, presenting an otherworldly look to the otherwise familiar landscape. I was still unsettled by concerns for Mike and last night's impatience with Fritz.

At the top of the hill Benno's cows had planted themselves patiently along the fence line, heads into the wind. His truck was parked on the side of the road. I stopped, stepped through the barbed wire, and started across the pasture in search of him. Halfway across the brown, leaf-strewn field I saw him coming from the brush, experienced arms firmly pinning a newborn calf that was struggling to get free.

He looked up, neither particularly surprised nor pleased to see me.

"Thought she was about to drop," he shouted over the wind, "and if I know that mama cow she'll stand there 'til this thing blows over." He put the calf to the teat, brushed his gloved hands, then rolled back his sleeve and checked a place on his arm where the scuffle with the calf had broken the skin.

"Come back to the cabin and I'll get you some iodine for that."

"Got any coffee?" he asked.

I nodded. He climbed into the truck and started down the hill toward my place. Inside, he sat at the kitchen table and watched as I cleared the papers, hunted up the first aid box and put on the coffee pot.

He looked around. "Haven't been in here for a long time," he said.

"What do you think?"

"Shouldn't have set the front door facing north."

Benno's scratch was deeper than it had appeared. I washed it with soap and water and wrapped it with a narrow strip of gauze.

"Remind me of your mother," he said.

I looked up, surprised. "Greta?"

"Ja. She kept the kitchen when I was a boy. Used to pour clorox on my knees when I scraped them."

I winced. "Where was your mother?"

"Gone. When I was four."

"She died early?"

"Nope. Just gone. Too much work, I suppose. So Greta and another sister took over. Kept us fed and clothed. Took us to church."

"Church?"

"Always church," he said.

"I never knew that."

"No need to know. I left it behind."

"Why?"

"Too many rules."

I laughed. "That's serious talk coming from a man of rules."

"Good you didn't know my father."

"Oh?"

"A good man, but hard. That's all there is to say."

"So you left the church?"

"Ja. When I left home. Sixteen, or so. When I met Queenie, she made it okay. Her people believed everyone had to come up with their own rules. I have her to thank."

"You never saw your mother?"

He looked past me. "Once, in Houston. When I started driving the freight, I looked for her when I passed through a town. Found her name one day on a street sign. Hannah Jahn, photographer. I went in and had my picture taken, to be sure it was her."

"Did she recognize you?"

"No, but I remembered, from pictures at home. She looked well."

"And you left without saying anything?"

"What was there to say? That dog carrying pups again?" he motioned to Val.

I nodded.

"Ought to have her fixed."

Benno rolled down his sleeve and refilled the coffee cup.

"What do you think of Tully Fox?" I asked him.

"You asked me that the other day."

"I wasn't satisfied with your answer. You know he's asked me to work for him."

"Smart fellow," he said.

"For wanting me to work for him?"

"That too." His compliments were always grudging.

"I thought you'd say, 'a good man.'"

"He's a good man for us, if he gets us out of the woods, and it looks like he will."

"What if Fox is an opportunist who runs over anyone he takes a mind to?" I asked Benno, and added my concerns about Mike.

"What do you like so much about this Mexican boy?"

"He's a hard worker, Onkel. Worked for me for years, never overcharged me or took advantage in any way." I told how he spoke of his father with admiration, how he wanted to better himself, everything I could think of that might catch Benno's attention.

"If he's so innocent, why don't he take up for himself?"

"Because he wants to keep his job. Because he was taught to respect authority. Maybe because he's dating the sheriff's daughter and doesn't want to rock the boat. What about that?"

"Not so good. I wouldn't want him dating my daughter. Better stay out of this, Vera. Men's business."

"Mike said something like that too."

"So leave it be, girl." He stood to go, hands on the table, pushing himself stiffly from the chair.

Men's business!

I sat in the waiting area of Tully's office, mentally rehearsing the reasons I'd present for not accepting his offer. Negotiations to move the loan were continuing and I felt pressed not to offend the man who held our family welfare in his hands.

"You look very righteous today, Vera," he said as he ushered me into his office.

"That's a strange observation."

"Well, look at you," he made a sweeping gesture in my direction, "black and white, no jewelry, flat shoes. I'd say if you came intending to accept my offer, you'd be dressed a little perkier."

I had to laugh. "That's one point for you."

"So, it's no deal?"

"Yes, you see—"

"No, no, no," he interrupted me. "I don't need your reasons, though I'm sure they're valid. I'm disappointed, though." He looked at me, eyes soft for the first time I could remember and with none of the rancor I had expected.

He leaned back in the heavy leather chair. "Actually, in a way I'm glad you declined because I have a rule against employees getting chummy and," he leaned forward, "I'd like to go out with you. Would you have dinner with me tonight?"

Conversation with Tully was like a chess game. I hesitated, groping for the right move.

"It would be a good way to find out if I'm the barbarian your friend Mike says I am."

I was at a loss for words.

"I know you two are friends. Have been ever since he did the land work at your house, correct me if I'm wrong, and I'd be willing to bet he told you his version of what went down between us the other night. Well, let me tell you this. There are two sides to every story. You get two men alone in a room with a sweet young thing for a couple of hours and they're going to end up pawing the ground. It happens. I'm over it. The chip on the shoulder is his."

"Are you planning to have him replaced?"

"If I say no, will you go to dinner with me?"

"I hope you're joking."

"I hope you're considering."

"Okay," I said, surprised at my own response. He had, after all, been gracious in accepting my refusal. It would surely give me a better idea of who the man was.

He downed two quick drinks before we ordered, then leaned across the table and threw the question at me like a dart at a dartboard.

"You want to have an affair with me?"

"No."

"I know. You think I'm unruly and potentially dangerous. That turns some women on. Too bad. Men like it. Want me on their side. Everyone's a whole lot more comfortable with me on the inside of the tent pissin' out than on the outside pissin' in."

I shook my head. What now, I wondered. After what I thought would come at the end of the evening had come at the beginning.

203

"I'm not looking to get married, Vera. Done that twice and have the scars to prove it. Seems to me you've got your reasons for avoiding it too. Thought we might make a good team."

"You make me extremely uncomfortable, Tully."

"I know. You think I get by with too much, but I give a lot, too. You've never seen me run a bank. Good, clean loans, documentation out the gazoo, and when someone's going down, I cut them off quick." He accentuated his point with the table knife. "Can't be soft-hearted when you're lending someone else's money. I'm responsible, Vera, and I'm good. I can be nice to the little old ladies and I can be mean as hell if the situation calls for it."

"I'm sure of that."

"I can also negotiate."

"Oh?"

"I like the fact you aren't afraid to say no. Not many people do that to me and you've done it twice in one day. I have one more proposition." He emptied his drink glass and waved it at the waiter. "I stopped by the historical society the other day. Dump of a place that reminds me of the goodwill barn, but they have some damn interesting photographs of this town, going back before the Civil War. Ever seen 'em?"

I nodded. My friend Bill and I had spent a month of Saturdays there. It was, as Tully had observed, a treasure in disarray. As the oldtimers died, family members, reluctant to throw away a departed one's keepsakes, brought box upon box of papers to the society. There were letters, newspapers, photographs, books, diaries, wills. Just sorting them by type and century was an overwhelming task for the inexperienced, mostly elderly volunteers who manned the place. Sometimes Bill brought students in to help, but most lacked the interest to stay with it.

"I hate to see that stuff turning to dust," he spoke with convincing sincerity. "They should be sorted, preserved, framed, put on display." he continued.

"The problem is, the people who care about such things can't afford to finance a project like that."

"The bank's going to spring for it. Give us a chance to prove our goodwill. We'll fill those glass cases that line the walls. Fill them, downstairs and up, with a good display and we'll pull people in off the street, make up our investment fast. Question is, will you be there to make it happen?"

"I really can't take. . .".

"I have a healthy budget that includes your time."

"And you'd want it finished yesterday."

"No time frame. Don't you have days off from the Institute? Start with one display case and let it grow. I want something ongoing and I want it notable."

"Maybe there's someone else in town who could. . . ."

"You do it, or no one, Vera. I won't have a half-assed job."

"I'll think about it."

"Say yes. No strings attached."

"Okay," I decided suddenly. As he reached his glass over and clicked mine, I stifled a laugh.

"Let me in on the joke."

"No joke." I was wondering what Fritz would say.

"For an intelligent woman, you do the damndest things," Fritz said. He predicted the project would never get off the ground, he reminded me that I had turned down an offer to work with him, and he pointed out that Tully had gotten exactly what he set out to accomplish, for me to work for him. Then he asked if I would go skiing with him and the boys over spring vacation. There was something frantic and vulnerable in his reaction and I found it interesting to think that Fritz might be jealous of my dealings with Tully.

Each of the boys had invited a friend to go on the ski trip and I went along as another pair of hands, an adult companion, a relief driver, and surrogate mother.

"This is the family trip we never got to take when we were kids," Fritz commented as he paid the dinner bill and we waited in the restaurant lobby while the kids hovered over a game machine that featured an innocuous little circle intent on devouring everything in sight.

"Why pay perfectly good money to sleep in a strange bed?" I mocked Benno's response to vacation requests.

"A strange bed is better than a familiar, empty one," Fritz said, fumbling in his pocket for another quarter as Max approached with outstretched hand.

"You miss her," I said when the boy had turned back to his machine.

"I miss having a wife."

"What do you hear?"

"Almost nothing." He looked noncommittal. "It's over, Vera. I'm only waiting to tell her face to face."

"If she doesn't tell you first."

He dug his hands deeper into his pockets and shrugged his shoulders in a gesture of letting go.

"Last game, boys." I herded our covey together. "We have four more hours on the road."

It started to snow as we crossed into the Oklahoma panhandle. The younger children in back, zipped into their bedrolls, eventually dropped off to sleep. I turned the radio dial, looking for a station, while Fritz bent forward and strained for definition of the unfamiliar and almost deserted highway.

"You like Jethro Tull?" I asked him.

"I do," Georgie, beside me, sat up.

"Go to sleep, son," Fritz said. "I don't know one group from the next," he told me, "but that's a nice flute."

"Goes with the night, doesn't it? Music for hurtling through the darkness. How can you see what's ahead?"

"Want me to slow down?"

"I trust you."

I closed my eyes and let my head rest against the back of the seat. How unreal this all seemed. Me, pressed hip to hip against Fritz, the car full of children, some of them strangers. We appear to be rushing into a void, car lights eaten by the snow, windshield wipers back and forth, a flute rilling in the background and Fritz's hand, yes, I didn't need to open my eyes, it was his hand, reaching in the space between us for my own.

Fingers lacing, we held on as if to say a million things too long unsaid. I turned to him, my back to the boy, lifted the hand to my mouth, brushed the length of it with my lips, and put it back on the wheel. He looked straight ahead and neither of us was quite able to breathe. For all the world, we were sixteen.

He shared a suite with the boys. I had a single room. At night he came to my room for an hour when the boys went to bed. They thought we were watching the news on television. We locked the door and made love in the dark, silent and ravenous, rushing against the clock, blanketed by guilt, never satisfied, never enough. When it was over, we held on, still without words. I turned my head so he wouldn't feel the tears.

In the daylight we were a happy family. We ate breakfast, told jokes, made snowmen, shopped for souvenirs. The older boys took two days of lessons and began to go on the slopes with Fritz. Confident in their bodies, they liked to show off, challenging each other, challenging Fritz, turning to men before our eyes. At dinner they whispered about the girls at the next table. They wanted to shave. I looked at Fritz and smiled. He grinned.

Max and his friend tired of the bunny slope and their lessons. They were content to throw snowballs, to float potato chips in hot chocolate, and to play in the game arcade. But it was the last day of skiing and they decided they wanted to ride the lift to the top of the mountain and back down. Fritz and I agreed to take them and sent the other boys on their way. When the boys had to put on skis, Max complained and did it halfway, so that when it was time to exit the lift his foot wasn't in the ski as it should be. He was so small there, sliding across the ice, like a hockey puck, and when he tumbled over the edge there was nothing any of us could do. Fritz reached him first, a hundred yards down the slope, and I followed the ski patrol, carefully, picking my way. The boy's foot laid at a strange angle like a doll's leg twisted perversely. The leg was badly broken, but otherwise he seemed all right. Fritz, grave with concern, took off his jacket and made a pillow for the boy's head.

"Don't look so scared, Dad. You're scaring me," Max said, and we all relaxed a little.

The boy was amazingly stoic. "That was cool, until I hit the ground. Did Jimmy see?" he wanted to know.

"We all saw," I assured him.

In the helicopter he told me he wanted his mother. "Don't get me wrong, I'm glad you're here, Aunt Vera, but I need her," and the tears that came weren't only from the pain of a broken leg.

Hours later, it seemed, the leg was set and the boy resting comfortably.

"You know why I'm glad it happened?" he told his father, who finally arrived at the hospital after settling the others at the hotel. "Now that I know what a broken leg feels like, I won't be so afraid of it." He was drowsy from the medication and drifted off as he spoke.

Standing at the bedside, I leaned back against Fritz. "We were lucky."

"I'm glad you were here, Vee," he whispered in my ear. "Thank you."

I turned to face him and he wrapped me in his arms and kissed me sweetly. At that moment we were of a single mind, and whatever we had done was right.

Carol Anne

Everyone in L. A. has a story about someone getting discovered and making it big overnight. Those stories pass around like little salted goldfish and people waiting for their big break fill up on them to forget how hungry they are. At the club, between performances, we got fed that stuff every day. Good looking people, dressed like they were somebody, liked us. They called us to their tables and bought us drinks and told us about their connections.

"This is it," I told Leroi, night after night. "I can feel it."

"Sure, baby," he told me and lit another joint. "Keep thinking that way. You're my good luck charm."

"I wish you didn't do that all the time," I told him, waving away the smoke. "We've got to be clear-headed."

"This is what makes me clear," he told me. "Keeps everything in its place, don't you see?"

"All I can see is that I'm running out of time and we've got to explore every possibility. Right now we should be at that supermarket opening the guy invited us to last night."

"That's no fun," he said.

"It's not about fun any more. I've put my marriage on the line for this career."

He roared with laughter.

"What's so funny," I demanded.

"That's your deal. Not mine."

"Cocksucker," I muttered under my breath.

He stretched his long body out on the bed, arms above his head. "Now there's an idea."

I grabbed my billfold and left the house in a huff.

At the market two blocks from the condo a flyer caught my eye. EXPLORE CREATIVE WOMANHOOD, it said, and I wandered into the session a few doors down.

"Close your eyes," an attractive blonde directed, "and breathe deeply. From your diaphragm."

Someone giggled. I opened my eyes. "Here," she said, at my side, her manicured nails pressing below my breastbone. I closed my eyes and concentrated. "Breathe in peace, harmony, success, power. Breathe out stress, failure, fear, anxiety."

I tried. "Again," she said, wandering goddess-like among the five of us assembled.

When do we get to the creativity, I wondered.

"Empty your mind," she directed. "If a thought comes in, let it pass through. Concentrate on your breathing. Only your breathing."

Thoughts kept bubbling up. Leroi, Sheila, the kids, Fritz, performing, being happy, being successful and thoughts about how foolish I must look, sitting on the floor of a room in a strip center, hoping to be visited by the muse. But I did what she said. I let everything pass through, like scenery on a train.

"As I touch your head, imagine I am pouring a can of red paint over you." Oh, great, I thought. "Let it run down, coloring every inch of your body. You are red and shiny, perfect and wonderful."

I felt it. Sort of.

"This time, as I pass, I have a can of green paint. Green is the color of the earth. It is also the color of money. Green is the peace of nature and the recognition of your desires. Without opening your eyes, indicate the part of your body you would like to receive this gift of color and you will be touched in that place. Perhaps it is your hands, your genitals, your eyes. The choice is yours."

I touched my throat and, as she passed, she painted my throat in green. I felt it.

"Leroi," I ran into the house.

"You over being mad?"

"I want to rehearse."

He picked up the guitar. I was anxious to practice what I'd learned, to hear myself sing.

"What do you think?" I asked, after we had been through a couple of songs.

"Umm. Nice," he reached over to stroke my hair.

"No, really."

"You're great, baby. Good sound."

"Anything different?"

"Hot," he said, licking his finger and touching me like he was testing an iron. "On fire."

"You like that?"

"Don't see me complaining, do you?" He put down the guitar and reached for me.

"Wait. Let's do one more."

He strapped the guitar back on, reluctantly. "Keep this up and we gotta change our name."

"To what?"

"Tequila and the Worm."

"Be serious, Leroi."

"Lord, woman, I think you're serious enough for the both of us."

At the next Creative Womanhood session we focused on visualization. "Imagine what you want," the leader told us, "and it will manifest itself in reality."

I was getting better at concentrating.

"But first, you must discover what you really want. We begin with a place of perfect peace. Close your eyes. Breathe deeply."

I did as she directed.

"Imagine yourself walking down a road. It is a sandy road, bordered by green grass. You are barefoot. Feel the sand between your toes. Feel the gentle breeze on your face. You have no concerns, only happiness at being on this road. You walk along until you see a house. It calls you. Walk into the house. What do you see?"

I tried to keep my head right with hers. I imagined opening the door to the house and walking into a kitchen. There was steam rising from a pot on the stove. I walked over and lifted the lid. Chicken soup. Somebody like Queenie was standing at the counter and her hands were dusty with flour. Just like a dream, except I knew I was making it up. The Queenie lady tore dough into little pieces, rolled them in balls, and dropped them into the broth, and she smiled at me. "The children are at the river," she told me. "They'll be hungry when they come in."

I opened my eyes.

"Whatever you saw. Whatever you felt. Trust that place. There is your heart," the woman said.

I walked out of the meeting.

It was about that time I found out Leroi was married. One of his friends went to Jamaica and brought back a letter and a photograph.

"What's this?" I asked.

"News from home."

"Who are the kids?"

"My children."

A knot, like a hot fist, started happening just below my rib cage. I reached down to rub it away. "You didn't tell me you were married."

"I don't recall that you asked."

I stared at him in disbelief.

"Mrs. Jahn has rules about being married?" he smiled at me.

"That's not the point."

"What is the point?"

"Your commitment."

"Commitment," he said the word in parts, feeding it back to me in bite-sized pieces. "A lady's word if ever I heard one. Shall I ask the same?"

"I'm thinking about mine all the time."

"If you have to think about it, it's not much of a commitment."

"I guess," I said, struggling for a place to hold on in this conversation.

"I owe my people something, but not my soul. This man's committed to whatever holds his attention."

"Disgusting."

"You liked it."

"That's the most disgusting part."

Later, in the middle of the night. "Leroi," I said, "what am I going to do?"

"Whatever you want, Baby. Whatever you want."

What I did was the most daring thing I could think of. I had a crescent moon and a single star tattooed just above my navel to remind myself I was a child of the universe. Every time I rubbed it, I felt centered.

What I wanted, or thought I wanted, was to stand on a stage and make people notice. I asked for a sign, like a white cat to cross my path, and I got it. A booking. The grand opening of a roadhouse in Malibu, a huge open-air club overlooking the ocean. We fought about the music and Leroi finally let me have my way, which only involved one song where he backed me up instead of the other way around. My sound was getting better and he knew it. I bought the perfect dress, gauzy and flowing and the color of wet sand.

The bandstand was in an alcove of the dining area, arranged so the music could flow into the bar, the game area, and onto the balcony. I liked the feel of this place. The dinner crowd paid attention and, in spite of constant movement through the room, things were going well. Everyone could hear us and we were giving them what they had come for, entertainment. After the first set my nerves settled down. I studied the audience, and touched my star for luck, like Carol Burnett pulls on her ear.

The final set began with a single spotlight. I arranged myself in front of the mike, head down. Leroi stood behind me in the shadows and began the piece with a soft flute. People at the tables stopped talking. I closed my eyes and pictured the melody line rising up like a snake from a basket. Before I started to sing, I mentally painted my throat green.

It was a Jamaican folk tune, soft, about young lovers. As I started to sing Leroi picked up the beat on the bongos. I gave it everything I had. Everything I'd picked up from watching musicians all my life. I stretched the final note as long as I dared, then lowered my head and held still, eyes closed, and suddenly there was a burst of shouts and clapping off to my left. I opened my eyes and smiled in that direction, like I knew I'd done well but I wanted to be told anyway. People near the side door had gotten up from their tables and were crowding into the game room. Others were clapping politely, and looking past me to check out what was going on.

I turned to Leroi, confused.

"Dart tournament," he shifted his head in the direction of the other room. "I think someone won the big pot. Tough break, baby. You sounded great."

He let me spend a day in bed, alone, and on the second morning he brought me toast and a Bloody Mary.

"Twenty-four hours is all the grieving time that was worth."

"I'll never get over it," I told him and fished in the bedside table for a joint.

He took it from my hand. "This is a fickle business. You can't take it so personally."

"I feel like the world's biggest fool."

He laughed.

"Don't laugh at me."

"What can I do with you?"

"Anything that'll make me stop hurting."

We were still in bed when the phone rang. It was Vera, telling me that Max had broken his leg.

"I'm going back," I told him when I set down the phone.

"Good timing," he said, and it was that easy.

It was raining when the plane set down in San Antonio. I held the magazine I'd been reading over my head and ran toward the terminal. Fritz was waiting, looking solemn and gray at the temples.

"You brought a lot of stuff," he observed as he pulled my bags from the conveyor.

"All of it."

"You're home for good?"

I nodded. He turned away in silence.

I tried to talk to him in the car. "I know I've put you through a lot and I'm sorry. Really sorry, Fritz. I don't know what I was thinking, but I promise you this, I'm a different person than I was six months ago. I'm not proud of what I did, but I had to try. Can you see that?"

He looked across at me, his face blank. "I don't even know you."

"I'm just getting to know myself."

He looked over again, this time disgusted. "Spare me the California bullshit."

I touched my star and started again. "What do you want?"

"A divorce."

I had expected him to be mad, but not like this. "What could I do to change your mind?"

He stared straight ahead. "Nothing I can think of."

We rode along in silence for the better part of an hour. I stared at the limestone hills, the carpet of green, the wildflowers in bloom, the huge sky.

"It's beautiful," I said.

"What's beautiful?"

"This place."

"You've been gone so long you forgot how it looked?"

"Everything looks different. I need one more chance, Fritz."

"What kind of a fool do you take me for?"

"No fool. The guy who carved my name in that table down by the river. The father of my children. We have a history together. Are you willing to throw it away?"

"Your new philosophical personality isn't very convincing, Carol Anne. You're not jerking me around any more."

"I'm not trying to jerk you around. I'm scared. The idea of being on my own, of raising the boys without you . . .".

"Don't think I'm giving up my sons," he looked across to interrupt me.

"They have a voice in this too."

"Some," he said. "But we've learned to get along without you this past year."

"That was temporary."

"You forgot to tell us."

I held up my hands. "Guilty! Damn it! I'm guilty. What else can I say? I'm sorry and I want to change and I want to make it up to all of you. I need your help. I want you to forgive me. I'll do whatever you say. Give me a fucking chance."

"Don't talk trash."

"Sorry." I covered my face with my hands and stopped fighting to hold back the tears.

He reached over and patted me in a helpless way. Fritz always gave in to tears. I didn't like being pitiful and hearing myself beg but I wasn't lying. I had lost something and I wanted it back.

At least the boys were happy to see me. Max insisted on telling me the story of every signature he had collected on his cast, starting with doctors and nurses in the hospital, through waitresses in Amarillo on the way home, his grandparents, the cleaning lady, the teenage girl next door, the paper boy, and his teacher who had stopped by the house to check on him.

"When I get back to school," he told me, "I'm going to have everyone in the whole school sign."

"This leg is getting you a lot of attention."

"Yeah. I like it," he admitted, and I felt a twinge of recognition.

"Dad tells me you were very brave."

"Nothing's as bad as you think it's going to be," he told me.

"Well, you sure got smart while I was gone. Cuter, too. What are we going to do with these curls?" I ran my fingers through his hair.

"I saved them for you. He wanted me to cut my hair," he said, looking over at Fritz, "but I said I wasn't going to do it until you got home."

"And it worked, didn't it?"

"Did you know? Is that really why you came home?"

"I came home because I missed you, all of you guys, and I wanted to be with you."

"About time," Georgie said from across the room.

I looked over. "Hey, I brought you something."

"Yeah?"

"It's in my tote bag. Bring it here."

He brought me the bag and watched as I pulled out a Dodgers cap.

"Cool," he said, and put it on.

"That's backwards, son," Fritz said.

"That's how they're wearing them in L.A.," I told him.

"Looks ridiculous," Fritz insisted.

"It is kind of stupid." Georgie turned the cap around and smiled sheepishly. "I saw somebody wearing it this way on the t.v."

"You'll catch more girls this way," Fritz told him.

"You interested in catching girls, Georgie?"

"Well, you know," he protested.

"He got his share of attention on the slopes," Fritz said, and pulled the cap down over Georgie's blushing face.

Strange, my son getting interested in girls. I wondered how that made Fritz feel.

"What the hell is that?" Fritz asked when I was undressing for bed and he came in to brush his teeth.

"It's called Venus in the Crescent."

He got busy with the toothpaste. "You'll have to have it taken off."

"Have to?

"You think I'm going to sleep with you with that thing on your midriff?"

"Were you thinking about sleeping with me?"

"No."

"Never again?"

He spit in the sink and walked into the bedroom.

I wasn't giving up the tattoo. It was the most independent decision I'd ever made. Everything else in my life, I'd just kind of fallen into. Nope, I thought, he's going to have to take me like this, and then there was this voice that said, what if he doesn't? Maybe if I kept it out of his line of view, he'd kind of forget.

Seven months. That's how long I'd been gone. Well, nine and a half if you count everything. Not very long in the great scheme of things, to borrow Sheila's phrase, but long enough to rearrange my thinking. Everyone else's thinking, too.

People say weird things when they don't know what to say because they can't say what's on their mind. When I went to the grocery store, which was about the only place I showed my face for awhile, I'd always have to face the music.

"How's your mother?" was a regular question. That was a kind of pass, to let me pretend, if I wanted to, that she'd been sick and that's why I'd been gone so long.

Other people weren't so polite, or phony, depending on the way you look at it. They'd say, "You're back!"

Well, what did that mean? Obviously I was back. Did they want an explanation of why I was gone so long? I'd nod and smile, yes, I'm back. And we'd stand next to each other in the check-out line, them wondering what stories I had to tell, me wondering what stories they'd heard.

But the worst, the very worst, was Queenie. When she didn't call or come by, I stopped in to see her one day.

"I wanted to thank you for all the time you spent with the boys."

"No need," she said without even a little bit of a smile. She was cooking swiss steak and onions and washing up the dishes as she went, and wouldn't stop to look at me.

"Yes, there is a need. I was gone much too long, and I'm sorry if it caused you trouble."

"Everyone worried, especially the children."

"I know."

After a long silence I asked how her garden was.

"It's coming."

"You going to need some help when the green beans are ripe?" Every year she called me to help harvest green beans, because when they came, she liked to pick and wash and can them right away and we'd spend a whole day at it and then she'd send me home with the car packed full of beans and other stuff from the garden, and strudel from the freezer, and whatever else she could find to load me up with that she thought the family would like.

"Not so many this year," she told me. "I can manage without."

"Without me?"

"Ja."

I took a deep breath. "Queenie, I know you're mad at me, and I don't blame you, but can't we work through this?" For thirteen years she had been so good to me, without once acting like she disapproved. And now I was getting this huge cold shoulder. She might as well have slapped me and called me a bad name. I'm sure there were names in German for people like me.

Finally, she looked up from the sink and I could see tears in her eyes. "No, I am not mad, as you say. I am sad. You have hurt my Fritz and left your young ones to wonder. I don't know what to think of a girl who treats her family in a way that even the mother cat or mother bird would not do. I have nothing to say, except that this will not go away so easy. The healing, it will take time."

"I know," I said, and I was glad to have it out in the open. I wanted to go over and hug her. Well, I guess what I really wanted was to have her hug me, but she was looking down again.

"Are you all going to marriage counseling?" Angie wanted to know.

"We went once."

"And?"

"The counselor and Fritz decided I needed help. He said I'd always been moody, and I couldn't deny it."

"That's a rip-off."

"That's what I thought, but I agreed to see a psychiatrist if Fritz would schedule another round with the marriage counselor. There's no way I'm going to get him to come around on my own."

"Hmm," she said, like she questioned my reasoning. "So, you've been to the shrink?"

"Yesterday. What an experience that was. He was tall and sharp-looking. Very expensive suit. Told me I had unresolved parental issues."

"I could have come up with that one. What did he charge you for that piece of insight?"

"Seventy-five for the hour and he wants me to come back every week for a while."

"What did Fritz think?"

"He said nothing was worth more than a dollar a minute."

She laughed. "I can think of a couple of things."

"I'm sure you could."

"You talk to the shrink about being depressed?"

"No. Because, you know what? I wasn't depressed in L.A. What do you think that means?"

"I think that's something you should have asked him. Are you depressed now?"

"Yeah. But now I have a reason."

Angie hadn't called just to talk about me. She wanted to tell me she was getting married again.

"Wear your best jeans," she said. "We're doing it very mod, in Hermann Park, with checkered tablecloths and a picnic lunch and mariachis. We're writing our vows, right along with a prenuptual agreement. And I've absolutely forbidden anyone to cry."

"I only cry at first weddings," I told her. "Reminds me of how I felt sending my kids off to school the first day. Brides are so blind and there's no sense trying to warn them."

"I gather you don't think I should enter this with any high hopes?"

I was such a jerk. My best friend, finally excited about her life, and all I could think about was my problems.

Three weeks later Fritz and I went to a second meeting with the marriage counselor, who only charged forty dollars a session, which worked out to sixty-seven cents a minute, Fritz pointed out, which was still high-priced for talking.

I thought the counselor had sided with Fritz in our first session and I told him so.

"Maybe we did double-team you, Mrs. Jahn. I apologize. It wasn't intentional. Men have a tendency to do that to women, without realizing it. So you don't think your moodiness is a crucial factor in your problems right now."

I liked him better. "No, I don't" I said.

"Mr. Jahn?"

"Probably not," Fritz agreed, reluctantly.

"Okay. Let's start again. What do you like most about your husband, Mrs. Jahn."

He caught me off guard. "Well, he's strong, I mean, like steady, and reliable. And I like the way he looks. And he's a good father. Everybody counts on him." I looked over at Fritz and smiled.

"Your turn, Mr. Jahn. What do you like best about Carol Anne?"

Fritz frowned.

"Not much these days," I said.

"Well, she's a beautiful woman. Do you like that?"

"I guess."

"Do you tell her?"

"She knows it."

"It wouldn't hurt to tell her. How is your sex life?"

We were both silent.

"Any specific problem you'd like to address?"

Fritz looked at his shoes.

"We need to get at the source of your conflict," the counselor tried again. "You tell me you've been separated for some time and the thing that comes to mind is that one of you may be involved with someone else."

Silence. Fritz shifted in his chair. Did he know, I wondered. Or suspect?

"These things happen, and they don't always mean the end of a mar-

221

riage," the counselor went on, while Fritz folded his arms and turned one shoulder forward and listened in that attitude that means he doesn't like what the person's saying, "but in order to make things work, you need to be able to talk to each other. I assume you do want to stay together?"

I nodded.

"Mr. Jahn?"

"I don't want to break up the family."

"Your family's important to you?"

"Of course."

"What else?"

"My work."

"What about Carol Anne? Is she important to you."

"I can't count on her."

The counselor looked over at me. "Because she's mercurial."

"What the hell does that mean?"

"Similar to moody, but more like unpredictable. At least, that's what came out on her psychological tests. It may be what attracted you in the first place, especially since she described you as solid, and lots of solid people choose their opposites as mates. But it's a hard trait to live with."

I liked this guy. I liked the idea of being mercurial, rather than moody. But I could tell by Fritz's jaw that he had heard just about enough.

"Mr. Jahn, I'm in the business of trying to save marriages. I'd say it's up to you to decide if you want to save yours. I'll tell you from experience that divorce is more painful, and more expensive, than most people think when they set out to get one. I'd like to see you two go home and try to talk to each other. Say what's on your minds. Be honest. Be fair. Listen to each other and don't interrupt."

In the car on the way home Fritz was silent.

"I liked him," I said.

"Sure you did. I'm surprised you didn't lift your blouse and show him your tattoo."

"Can't you let that be? I want to talk, like he said."

"Carol Anne, I don't want to talk."

"Do you want to try and make this work?"

"I don't intend to pay any more goddamned people to butt into my business."

We were almost home when I broke the silence again. "So you still think I'm pretty?"

He didn't answer.

I leaned over so he'd have to see me and held up my hand like I was taking an oath. "I promise to be more reliable."

"Do you have some need to turn everything into a joke?"

"I'm not joking, Fritz."

Fritz didn't mention divorce after our second session. Maybe he decided to give me the chance I'd asked for, but I had the feeling it was because the counselor had gotten him thinking about how much it would cost. Money and business were the main things on his mind, as far as I could see. He sure wasn't having much to do with me.

"You know what he's worth?" Angie asked me. She had stopped teaching and started selling houses after she got married.

"No idea."

"Never seen his financial statement?"

"Not that I remember."

"What'd you pay in taxes last year?"

"I don't know, Angie." I was getting irritated.

"You sign on them, you know. Get with the program, woman. Don't you realize half of everything Fritz has is yours?"

"I don't think it's that much."

"Oh, right. Just a few little land deals, like a resort with a golf course in the Hill Country. Not to mention a subdivision and then some larger tracts of farm land suitable for what do they call it? Ranchettes? Give me a break, Carol Anne."

"Some of that is his separate property. I remember them talking about it when Queenie divided the land, because, you know, it was her separate property too. Whatever we have is his, as far as I'm concerned. He's the one who worked for it."

"No way, kiddo. Who had those babies?"

I understood her point, but I didn't want to get into it. "Anyway he's been complaining for months about business troubles. The other day he said he might have to cash IRAs and pay a penalty in order to meet some note that's due in December."

"He's trying to make you sorry for him."

"I don't think so. The people that bought the land where they built the resort, they stopped paying on it."

"Well, that's not good. But there's lots of twists and turns in this market. I heard someone say the other day that land was Texas' third wave of wealth. In the 1800s it was cattle. In the early 1900s it was oil. Now it's land. They're wheeling and dealing all over the state and you're in hot territory."

"My God, Angie, you're talking like a wheeler-dealer yourself."

"Honey, going into real estate was the best idea I ever had. I can make $12,000 on the commission from one good-sized house and that's what I used to get paid for six months of wiping noses and kissing the skinned knees of those darling third graders. I loved them, but the cost-to-benefit ratio was too high."

Fritz called from work one Friday with an invitation to go to dinner with Tully Fox.

"This is a surprise," I told him.

"He specifically asked to meet you," was all Fritz told me.

I dressed carefully, intending to make a good impression.

"Carol Anne," Mr. Fox said, looking me over, "I've waited a long time to meet you. Did your husband tell you this is a celebration?"

I looked at Fritz, who was looking at Mr. Fox.

"We closed the buyout on the resort today," the banker told me, "which makes you a part owner. Is Vera joining us?" he asked Fritz.

Fritz shook his head. "Vera had some place else she needed to be, and Benno was tired. It'll just be the three of us."

"You think two men can keep you entertained?" Mr. Fox looked at me pointedly.

"I'll be happy to let you try," I smiled and removed my hand from his. I was wondering if the others didn't come because I was going to be here. Sheila had a favorite comment for thoughts like that: "Don't overestimate your own importance," she used to tell me.

The banker ordered a round of drinks and he and Fritz discussed the resort, while I half listened. They were talking about needing cheap labor for cleaning people and grounds maintenance and then I heard Mr. Fox ask Fritz if he knew how many black families there were in Schoenberg.

Not many, I thought.

"Not many," Fritz said.

"I did the demographics before I came. Ten black heads of household. Course they double up a lot. Probably fifty, sixty, total."

"You're lucky to have inherited Jackson," Fritz said, and it sounded funny to me, like the man was a piece of property.

"That's my man. Stayed on with the bank when I came. Does a shitload of odd jobs around the place and always has a smile."

"You know Jackson's father?"

"The one that bartends at private parties? Gray-haired?"

"That's the one. He's a good man even if he gets a little snarly at times. Then, there's Tom Johnson."

I knew what Fritz thought of Tom Johnson. My God, it sounded like we going to discuss every black man in town.

"I hear he's worthless."

"He is, but his brother's okay. Works on my car from time to time. If he doesn't get it right, I just take it back."

I expected the banker to smile and tell us that "some of them are like children."

"It's good for a town to have a few blacks," Fox was saying. "Just don't want too many. That's when the trouble starts. We sure as hell don't want the kind of trouble here they're having in other parts of the country. We've got enough problems with the Mexicans."

"Mexicans we can handle," Fritz said. "We've always found a way to work out our differences."

"As long as they stay in their place," I said.

Fritz looked over, like he had forgotten I was there. I had lost my strong desire to make a good impression.

"Kind of like women." I faked a sweet smile.

"She's quick." Mr. Fox laughed and patted my hand.

"I think," I began slowly, trying to get out what I wanted to say in an acceptable form.

Fritz interrupted me. "Benno's said for years if we put a good Mexican on the city council we'd have a better bargaining position with that element."

"Wait. I want to hear what Carol Anne thinks," the banker said.

I started again. "I think Schoenberg's a little behind the times."

"Which means?" Fritz had that tone in his voice that meant whatever I was about to say, he was going to disagree with.

"Which means we talk about what a great place it is to live, but there's all these little invisible rules to keep people in their place. Nothing's up for discussion here and that's just not how the world works these days."

"Not in Houston or Los Angeles," Fritz said pointedly, "but I don't plan to live there."

"Unspoken rules are the beauty of a small town." Mr. Fox took a drink without moving his eyes from me. "But, as a matter of fact, change is exactly what we're talking about, honey," he said. "Running a Mexican for city council. Not a bad idea, Fritz. What do you think about that, Carol Anne?"

"Sure." I looked over at Fritz. "Maybe Mr. Mendez." Mendez was a scab, a jeweler who sold junk to the Mexicans at outrageous prices.

"The jeweler? Might work," Fox said. "He's got a good line of credit. Everyone knows the name."

"Not Mendez," Fritz said, looking back at me. "Carol Anne was being sarcastic."

Tully looked from Fritz to me. "Why don't you tell us what you're really thinking," he invited me, almost like a dare.

If I had said what I was really thinking, I'd have told them how full of shit I thought they were. That without the right names and some money in their pockets, they wouldn't be so likely to think they were God's chosen. I wanted to tell them that I hoped my boys wouldn't grow up thinking like that, and that planning the next city council election wasn't exactly my idea of fun.

I shook my head. "Fritz tells me you've helped turn the business around, Mr. Fox. We really ought to celebrate. I think I'd like to order a martini. I love those glasses they come in."

Tully laughed and Fritz managed a grin. "I like this girl, Fritz," I'm not a girl, I wanted to say, but I decided to bite my tongue.

"We could build a house down on the river," I said to Fritz one day. He frowned and didn't answer.

Later he said, "What's wrong with this house?"

"Bad memories," I said.

He said nothing.

Things were better between us, especially since the business had picked up, even though sometimes I wanted to scream at that square-jawed silence. But I was trying hard to keep things on an even keel. We were polite with each other. No fights, but not much conversation either, and no touching. I wondered if it was going to be like that forever. Something had to happen.

"The boys love the river," I said. "And Max wants a dog. We could take one of Val's puppies and not have to worry about the neighbors."

"Not an outstanding reason to build a house," Fritz said. "You'd be running back and forth to town all the time."

"I don't mind."

"We can't intrude on Vera. She likes her privacy."

"It's your land, too. For heaven's sake, she's a half-mile away. We can put in a separate entrance and she doesn't ever have to see us, unless she gets over being such a hermit and decides to come around sometime."

He looked pained. "We'd have to sell this house first."

"That's cool."

"I wish you wouldn't say that."

"What?"

"Cool. It makes you sound like a kid."

"Sometimes I am a kid."

"You said you had grown up."

"I said I had changed."

I didn't bring the house idea up again, but Fritz came back with it a few weeks later.

"Wunderlich's son is going into custom homes. He'll build for his cost and ten per cent," he told me.

"What kind of house?"

"Why don't you get with him and come up with something."

"No limits?"

"Of couse there's limits."

"But you'll leave the planning to me?"

"Just stay within reason, Carol Anne."

"And we can start right away?"

He nodded.

"That's great!" I walked over to where he sat reading the paper and reached down to kiss him on the cheek. "You won't be sorry."

"I hope not." He took my arms from around his neck, stood up, and walked outside.

I wondered what had made him change his mind. Maybe he had a buyer for the other house. Maybe it was about something like capital gains, or maybe he wanted to get away from town too. Maybe he wanted to please me. Not likely, I thought. But maybe.

I was right the first time. I found out a few days later that he had a good offer on our house and, as Angie had pointed out, it was just smart business to take our profit when the market was hot.

"Angie said we shouldn't cut corners on the new house," I told him when I showed him the drawings the builder had come up with.

"Angie should mind her own business."

"She just said it was a good time to get a lot for our money."

"We don't need her advice. I'd just as soon you didn't talk to her about this."

"She's my best friend. I always talk to her about what's going on in my life. She keeps me going."

"What does that mean?"

"Nothing." I didn't want to get into an argument.

"Seems to me you've got just about everything you could want," he said with a flat face. "You've had your fling and now you're getting a new house. What more do you need to keep you going?"

"Oh, come on, Fritz." I hadn't expected that reaction.

"Well, it's not exactly the greatest time to be building a house," he said, "considering."

"Considering what?"

"Considering that you walked out on me and the kids for almost a year. Considering that you made me look like a fool in front of the whole town and now it looks like I'm rewarding you for it."

"If it's so embarrassing, why'd you agree to this whole thing? Because you saw a chance for a profit, I guess. Silly me. I thought maybe it was a new start for us."

"We can't start new, Carol Anne. There's too much water under the bridge."

I started folding up the plans that were spread out on the dining room table, thinking about how excited I had been twenty minutes before when I laid them out for him to see. I crumpled them up and threw them on the floor.

"Forget it," I said. "Forget the whole damn thing. I don't want a part of this."

"Wait just a minute," Fritz put his hands on my shoulders to stop me from storming out of the room. "You're not going to throw a tantrum and leave me to clean up the mess. You wanted this and we're into it and for once you're going to stick with it until it's done." He stooped down and picked up the plans.

"No I'm not. I've done everything I know to do. I've begged your forgiveness, I've held my tongue, and I've tried to make things right. Living with you is like living with a zombie, Fritz. I don't know what you're thinking. I don't know how to reach you. I want our marriage to work more than anything I can think of right now, certainly more than I want a new house, or a career, or even a good time in bed occasionally." I covered my mouth, wishing I hadn't said that.

"You had your share of that in California, I bet."

"Even if I did, I came back here."

Fritz walked over and shut the door to the dining room. The boys were upstairs. When he turned back to face me, his eyes were like gray rocks.

"And I'm supposed to be grateful? Take you back and say it's okay. You played hell with my life, Carol Anne, and I can't forget it. Every time I look at you, I see fingerprints all over you. It makes me sick."

"So why are you even trying?"

"Why the hell do you think I'm trying? Because of the boys. Because I don't believe in breaking up families."

"So you'd turn me into a zombie, too? Going through the motions, just for the boys? I love them, too, in case you hadn't noticed, and they love me. But I'm not willing to have an empty marriage with someone I make sick just to spare them a little discomfort."

"Lower your voice," he said.

"No. Hell, no," I practically shouted. "Let them hear. Parents have fights. Parents are imperfect. If they haven't figured that out by now, it's time they did. I plan to talk to them about life, about their lives and about mine. Get it out in the open. It's all this silence that's no good. All the things that don't get said between parents and kids, between us, for that matter. If we split, they deserve to know why." I walked over to the door and opened it. "Georgie, Max, come down here." I shouted up the stairs.

Fritz's face was as white as the wall behind him.

The boys came bounding down the stairs and stopped in their tracks when they got a look at our faces.

"You all okay?" Georgie said.

"Your dad and I are going out for a while. We want you to stay here and finish your homework. Okay?"

"Sure," Georgie said.

"Okay, Max?"

"Where are you going?" he wanted to know.

"For a drive."

"Can I come?"

"No. We need to talk."

"Will you bring some ice cream?"

"Sure. Georgie's in charge while we're gone. Don't give him any trouble."

"Right," he saluted, stuck his thumbs in his ears, wiggled his fingers at Georgie and ran up the stairs two at a time.

Georgie shrugged at us and chased his brother up the stairs.

Fritz turned to me. "I've had about enough."

"Come on," I said. "We need to finish this conversation. Either here or somewhere else. I thought you'd be more comfortable out of the house."

"I need a drink."

"Then get one. I'll get the car."

We drove in silence, through the subdivision, and down the hill to the park. I didn't know what I was going to say, but I had taken one giant step and wasn't going to stop until I'd seen it through. I found a deserted place by the water's edge and parked, turned to face Fritz and reached for his hand. He pulled it away. I put my hand on his knee.

"Okay. This is how it is. I left because I was restless and bored and because I thought you didn't care."

"I was working my tail off to keep you happy."

"Please. Let me finish. This isn't about you. It's about me. I went to California looking for excitement and I found some with the music and . . . okay, there was a man there and I did sleep with him. Only one. And he made love to me like I was the queen of the earth and I liked that. I liked it a lot. I'm sorry if that makes you sick, but it happened. I didn't love him and I couldn't count on him and I would never have stayed with him. I finally realized where I wanted to be most of all was right here."

"So you came back and expected to wiggle your ass at me and everything would be okay."

"No. I came back, ready to do whatever it would take to convince you that nothing like that would happen again. You've given me security, Fritz, and a place I belong. It's something I never had growing up and it's real important to me. But I won't sell my life for it."

"No, it's not as important as having fun."

"It's not about fun any more. It's about just feeling alive."

"So what am I supposed to say?"

"Whatever comes to mind."

"We need to go get some ice cream."

We drove home in silence. I went up to bed and Fritz had another drink while the boys had ice cream. Maybe he had a couple more drinks because when he finally came up, he was stumbling around the bedroom in the dark.

"It must be nice never to make a mistake," I said sarcastically.

"I've made my share," he growled.

"Yes. Maybe you were sleeping around the whole time I was gone. Maybe you still are. That's why it's so easy for you to avoid me." I don't know why I said it.

"Shut up, Carol Anne."

"I can't. I won't. We have a problem. I'm not going to let it go until something changes."

"You think having sex will make it change."

"It's a start. The way I feel right now, it's either that or a divorce. You want a divorce?"

"I don't think so. I told you that before."

"Well, don't you want to try?"

"Try what?"

I rolled over against him. "Try to feel alive?"

"I can't."

I buried my head in his neck. "Pretend," I whispered.

His hands were suddenly all over me, his mouth on my shoulders, my hair, my neck, hard on my mouth. He smelled of soap and bourbon. His face was against mine, like fine sandpaper, warm and familiar. I don't know what he was thinking, but I don't think he was pretending.

The new house was laid out to look like the old Spanish haciendas, single level stucco, built around a center courtyard with skylights and saltillo tile on the floor. I chose foot-square cedar posts for the outside front columns and the ceiling beams. The back side faced the river with double-paned glass doors that opened onto a wide, flagstone patio, and between the patio and the river we set an old iron gate I'd found at an estate sale. They said it had been part of a Spanish mission.

The builder was young and anxious to do a good job, but he'd worked for his daddy too long. "Ask your husband if he wants underground wiring," he'd say to me, or, "You think Mr. Jahn would be interested in a metal roof?"

"Look," I had to tell him, "I'm the boss on this house. If I don't understand something, you'll have to explain it to me."

When the house was at the finish stage, the boys and I checked every evening to see how it was coming and sometimes stayed to work until dark, putting in shrubs and ground cover, so there wouldn't be so much lawn to cut. That was Max's idea. We laid stone steps leading to the river and low rock walls bordering the steps. Georgie helped and Max mostly watched, and on weekends Fritz came too. We spent whole days there, taking breaks to swim or fish. I liked to sit behind the trees and try to hear what the people floating by had to say about the house. "Wow," "Interesting," and "Different," were the most popular comments.

"Wonder whose house that is," I heard someone say one afternoon, and I smiled to myself.

It was early afternoon on a Monday, but Max had stayed home from school that day and he answered the phone.

"It's for you," he said, with a funny look on his face.

"This is Carol Anne," I said.

"I'd know that voice anywhere, baby."

Max was sitting on the couch a few feet away. "I think you have the wrong number," I said.

"Not a good time, huh? I'll call back in an hour," he said and hung up.

"What was that?" Max asked.

"Wrong number."

"He asked for Carol Anne. Sounded like the man on the juice commercial."

"He wanted Carol Anne Carranza, or something."

"Yeah, like the phone book is alphabetical first names."

"Just one of those weird mistakes." I walked into the kitchen, trying to think of a way to get Max out of the house. What the hell did Leroi want with me. He promised he'd never try to contact me, and I'd believed him.

Thirty minutes later Max still hadn't budged from the sofa.

"I'll give you five dollars to wash my car."

"You know I'm sick today, Mom."

"Seven-fifty?"

"Can I drive it in and out of the garage by myself?"

He had to stretch to see over the wheel and touch the brakes, but I knew he could manage it. "I guess."

"And down the road?"

"Absolutely not."

"Just to the mailbox?"

"No."

"Pleeease."

"Oh, I suppose." Fritz would have disapproved, but I was desperate.

"All right," he said and jumped up.

I sat by the phone to wait and Leroi called back, right on schedule.

"You told me you'd never call," I snapped at him.

"I try to be a man of my word, but sometimes the beat goes on and one has to follow."

"What does that mean?"

"Our commercial, baby. After all this time, someone wants to pick it up. I need you to sign a little release, that's all, and we may be on national t. v."

"Oh my God," I sat down. "Leroi, I can't do that. I simply can't."

"I was afraid you'd say that, so I'm here to offer you what's behind door number two."

"Which is?"

"If you don't want it on the market, maybe you'd like to buy the demo copy from me."

"For what?"

"Five thousand."

"That's not what I meant. Why should I buy it from you?"

"Maybe you owe me something. I don't want to make trouble, but we did have a kind of partnership, now didn't we? I just want to get home. Now, look at you, you're already home. I need money. You have money. I know you know how to be fair."

"Fair?"

"Mom? Where's the Windex?" Max stuck his head in the door.

I motioned under the kitchen cabinet.

"Who you talking to?" he asked.

I waved him out the door and, thankfully, he went. "Leroi, understand this. I'm not signing a release and I don't have any money of my own to buy your copy."

"What about your man? If you're not interested, maybe I should offer this copy to him."

"You don't know him. He's not the kind of man who'd go for something like that. If you bring it up, he won't even talk to you."

"What kind of man wouldn't be curious? Why don't you take a few days to think about this, baby. See what you can do for me."

I hung up the phone with a sick feeling. No one but me knew how much I had changed. When I thought about the past, these days, it was like reading someone else's diary. Sometimes I wondered where the other parts of me had gone, the part that liked to play tennis all day and flirt with cops, the me that smoked pot and danced in the rain, the girl that sang at The Beachcombers' Club in a sand-colored see-through dress and had the tattoo to prove it. I had thought I was out of the woods when I was just in a little clearing.

Sheila

*M*y daddy used to quote a famous line. He pulled it out on special occasions, whenever the shoe seemed to fit. "Oh what a tangled web we weave when first we practice to deceive," he'd say, and everyone listening knew he'd sure as hell learned that one the hard way. It came to mind when Carol Anne told me about her call from Leroi, but to have said it then would have been like shaming her. What I said was, "Take a deep breath, honey, and let's think this thing through."

I was surprised she called me, but, like she admitted, she didn't have any place else to turn. That was about the best thing I could have heard. I haven't been the most accessible mother around, by a long shot, but at this point I liked the idea of her wanting my help. What I didn't like was how frantic she sounded.

"I think I'll head your way. Just hold on 'til I get there."

"You don't have somewhere else you need to be?"

"Not this month. Rocky's gone to Spain to buy bulls and I'm watching the ranch."

"I'm supposed to believe that?"

"Yup."

"It's that good, huh?"

"I think I finally got lucky," I told her. "See you day after tomorrow."

She met me at the airport and we talked, well I talked mostly, on the drive home.

"I've been thinking about this," I told her, "and it seems to me you have lots of options."

"All bad."

"Not necessarily. First of all, I don't believe Leroi's trying to black-mail you, even though he may be trying to scare you a little. You can pay him the money, or you can refuse and hope he goes away."

"I don't have money to pay him and I don't want to take a chance on hoping he'll go away."

"Oh, come on. Surely you've got something you can tap for a couple of thousand. I think he'd settle for less than five."

"I sign on the boys' college savings, but I'm not about to touch that."

"You still don't have your own account?"

"I don't even sign on ours. Fritz never said anything about me going back on, after L. A., and I guess I was afraid to ask. He gives me grocery money, and I have a gasoline credit card, and. . ."

I waved my hand at her. "Never mind. I don't need to know how you all work out your finances."

"So what else do you suggest?"

"Sign the release and see if the damn commercial sells. Most of those things don't pan out. A possible black sitcom they're promoting for next season, with a commercial sponsor attached? How many black beauty products do you see advertised on the telly? Not many."

"I'd hate to take the chance."

"Lots of people would jump at the chance. If you were back singing, you'd be walking around now with your fingers and toes crossed for luck. This ain't the end of the world."

"It would embarrass the whole family."

"They'll have to get over it."

"You don't understand."

"No, honey, you don't understand. Until you let them see you for what you are, a person who's willing to take some chances and make some mistakes, you're going to be remaking yourself every day, according to their image. And, why don't we say Fritz, instead of 'them.' This is about Fritz, isn't it?"

"I'm afraid of losing him."

"You want to spend the rest of your life being afraid?"

"Of course not."

"Then you stand up and tell him. Clear the air."

"I've told him as much as I'm willing to."

"And how's it going?"

"We have a truce."

"Best thing about a truce," I told her, "is that it can lead to peace."

"That's what I'm hoping."

"My God, the sky is big here. Look at that thunderhead. I bet it's a mile high."

"Since when did you start noticing the scenery?"

"Since I took the time to look."

After we drove in silence for a while, I asked Carol Anne, "Hey, what are we having for dinner?"

She looked over, wondering, I guess, why I'd be interested. "I haven't thought about it."

"Good. Because I brought a suitcase full of our choice steaks. They should be just about thawed by now. How are my grandsons?"

"I think you'll be surprised."

I was. Georgie was a handsome fifteen-year-old, reluctant to look me in the eye but interested enough to sit in the room and take in the conversation. Max was eleven, skinny and blond, with a quick lip.

"So where are your cowboy boots?" I asked him when we were alone for a minute. Both Fritz and Georgie wore boots.

"I'm a surfer type."

"And just where do you surf?"

"It's a style, you know. There's the kickers and the surfers."

"Kickers?"

"Shit-kickers. They're the ones who wear boots," he informed me.

"I get it. So, you're into tennis shoes. And what else?"

"Cars. Music. You're a musician, aren't you?"

"Sure 'nuf. You like jazz?"

"I like rock and roll. You know any stars?"

"Fogelberg?" I was stretching. We had shared the same stage once.

"No kidding?"

I nodded.

Georgie didn't say anything directly to me until we were at dinner. Fritz complimented me on the veal steaks.

"We had a bumper crop of calves this year," I said. "Rocky only has a few bulls, but they stay busy, if you know what I mean."

"Problem is knowing when to move them to a new field," Fritz said.

"We don't let ours run. Too much to lose if they get hurt. So Rocky brings the cows to them. He ties a fat red magic marker around the bull's neck and when the deed is done, the cow's got a mark on her back, then out she goes, and in comes another."

"That would work in the field, too, Dad," Georgie looked up.

"Got the idea from the ag school," I told him.

"It's a good one, Grandmother" he said, very manly, like it's pretty grown up to talk about animal sex, when you've got a reason to.

"Call me Sheila. It's just another name."

He blushed. "Thanks, Sheila."

"Oma Sheila," Fritz corrected.

"Can I call you Sheila, too?" Max asked.

I looked over at Fritz.

"Oma Sheila," he insisted. To me he said, "A little respect never hurts."

I guess I couldn't quarrel with that.

Carol Anne's new house was pure class. The other one had been showy. I've seen lots of showy houses. This one was big, but didn't shout at you. It had a personality like a grand piano. Santa Fe on the river, I named it, and told the boys the three of us should sit down and write a song about it before I left.

After dinner the kids went their own ways and the three of us moved out to the back patio with our coffee. We stretched out on lounge chairs, and watched the water slip on by.

"What a place," I said.

"Carol Anne gets most of the credit," Fritz told me. "She knew what she wanted and stayed with the builder until she got it."

Well, I liked the tone of his voice. I looked over at her and remembered why I'd come. And I was beginning to see what she had that she didn't want to give up. It wasn't just about Fritz, I was thinking. It was about a place, and, I guess, a way of life, she was afraid of losing.

"What brings you our way, Sheila?" Fritz was asking me.

"Oh, I've got a little business proposition for Carol Anne. Thought we needed to talk about it in person."

She looked over at me with a worried look.

"What kind of business proposition?" Fritz wanted to know.

I turned to Carol Anne. "Remember that commercial we made when you were in L.A.?"

She closed her eyes for a minute, then opened them and looked at me like a calf being forced into the slaughtering pen. Fritz straightened up in his chair.

"What commercial?"

"Oh, something I talked her into. For a skin-lightening cream. We used her and a Jamaican fellow that played bongos for me and I put up the ante."

He turned to her, "You never told me about this." She shrugged her shoulders, like she hadn't thought it was important.

I reached for a cigarette. "Forgive me if this sounds rude, Fritz, but I doubt you tell Carol Anne about everything you do."

He didn't answer, didn't even look my way. He didn't approve of me, I knew, but I didn't much give a damn.

"I was doing a lot of promotionals back then," I rattled on, "Most of them never come to anything, but the people that shot this found me the other day and say they've got a buyer and want a new contract. As it stands, we get fifty percent of whatever they can sell it for."

"Which is?"

"Hell, middle five figures, I'd guess."

"Carol Anne, on television, advertising a beauty cream?" Fritz sounded interested.

"Yeah. They want to hook it in with a black sitcom."

"A black sitcom?" Fritz repeated. He still didn't have the picture. Maybe I was being too subtle.

"Carol Anne's the draw. It's aimed at black people, assuming they want her creamy white skin, just the flip side of the quick-tan lotions they sell to white people who want to look dark. Thing is, I took a jar of the stuff to my dermatologist and he said it wasn't any different than any other skin lightener on the market. Mostly Vaseline, and the result's minimal." I turned to Carol Anne. "I don't think we want a part of this."

She shook her head.

"Well, why in the hell did you do it?" Fritz asked.

"It was a chance to make some money," she said.

That's my girl, I thought.

"What makes you think you can get out of it?" he finally looked my way.

I gave him my version of the truth. A smart lawyer, I said, had advised me to put an escape clause into my contracts, whenever I could. (This was true.) And this one had an option for a buyout. (Not true, as far as I knew.) The people we were dealing with were middle-men, I told him, and not too stable a bunch at that. (Almost certainly true.) I thought they'd settle for a bird in hand, rather than three in the bush. They had something marketable in Carol Anne's commercial. "She's a natural to sell skin products," I laid it on.

"Have you seen the commercial?" Fritz wanted to know.

"It's good. Trust me, or they wouldn't be interested. But, they're peddling it to one bunch, who's trying to hook on to another bunch, you know how it goes, and frankly, I think they'll give it up if we make them a reasonable offer."

Fritz stood up. "I'm going to get a drink. You?"

Carol Anne shook her head and I asked for a scotch and water. When he was out of sight, she rolled her eyes at me and said, "Mother!"

"Hush," I told her. This is going to work."

"This is the business proposition you came to talk to Carol Anne about?" Fritz asked as he handed me the drink.

"Not really. I came all hyped to get on with the deal and see if we could make some bucks, but I took a look at my grandsons at dinner and I thought to myself, maybe this isn't such a good idea. These boys should have a mother, not a singer who's taken on an acting part, selling a half-assed product that says one skin color is better than another."

241

I took a drag from my cigarette. "Isn't that what her coming back was all about?"

Fritz stood at the edge of the patio, looking at the river, but listening. Thinking, too, I hoped.

"I think they'll take $5,000," I went on, "and I'm prepared to put in $3,500, because it was my idea, to get into it in the first place and now to get out. But I could use some help with the rest."

"Fifteen hundred to buy out of something she shouldn't have gotten into in the first place?"

"Ever forfeited earnest money on a real estate deal?" I asked him.

"A few times, when it didn't seem right."

"Was that your money you forfeited, or Carol Anne's?"

"It was our money, but—"

"This isn't much different," I told him before he could finish his sentence.

We went to bed about midnight. I'd been up for eighteen hours, but I'd turned in a good performance. At least I thought I had.

Carol Anne showed up about 9:30 in the morning with a bedtray. A Bloody Mary, cheese toast, and a check. It was a nice touch.

"I did good," I told her.

"You're amazing, Mother. I've only got a few questions."

"Too early to think," I told her. "Come back later."

"No," she sat on the corner of the bed. "I need to get this straight now. What are you going to do with this money?"

"I'm going to put it with my own, hunt up that Jamaican bongo boy and set him straight. He may not even have a tape, but if he does, he's going to give it to me in exchange for his passage home and if he ever shows up again, I set Rocky on his tail."

"Rocky's not mafia." There was a hint of a question in her voice.

"No, but Leroi won't know that. He wasn't ever bad to you, was he?"

"Not until now."

"Good. I got to thinking about that midway through my spiel and I'm not about to extend him any charity if he was."

She leaned over and gave me a hug. "Thanks, Sheila. I'm going to pay you back."

"I'm only going to offer him three grand. That way, as far as I'm concerned, we're even."

"Not exactly."

I pretended to frown and waved her out the door. "Don't mess with Oma Sheila."

QUEENIE

When Benno got sick, I wanted it to be me. Always so strong he was. Then one day he falls from the bed is not able to get up or talk sense or think things out and it is up to me, so I call the doctor. Sounds like stroke he said and sent the ambulance to carry him to the hospital and Fritz and I followed in the car.

"Mrs. Jahn," the doctor says to me and I am looking at his face trying to remember from where I know him. "Mrs. Jahn," he says again, like I didn't hear so well, "Benno has had a stroke."

"So what are we to do?" I ask and look into his eyes for an answer. Now I see it is the Henke boy who used to live down the street, a boy whose diapers I changed not so many years ago.

"Wait and see," he tells me. "We must assess the damage."

My head is angry. Inside, everything is weeping. I want to slap the young man who tells me empty words, but I can see he is hurting too. Maybe he thinks of his own parents.

"Tell me what I must do," I say, but I am still angry.

"Go home and rest," he says. "I will call when I know something."

The next morning Fritz came early and again we went to the hospital.

"Good news," the doctor said. His face was broad with a smile and he lifted Benno's arm and leaned down and shouted in his ear.

"Move your fingers, Mr. Jahn."

Nothing happened. I watched closer. Benno laid still like the wooden puppets, the side of his mouth pulled down like it was broken. "This is good?" I asked.

"Wait," he motioned for me to come and stand beside him and gave again the order for Benno to move his fingers. I saw them move then, like so, a little wave, like the tops of the corn stalks when the air is still and I thought, this will never do.

A good sign, the doctor told us. The storm in Benno's brain was over and with time some of the lights would come back on, but he couldn't say how good or bad it would be. Myself, I wasn't too hopeful and I didn't like this white hospital bed with strangers poking needles and tubes in his arm and women he didn't even know changing his gown.

"It would be better that he died," I said and Fritz put his hand on my shoulder and the nurse looked up with a frown.

"What's to frown about the truth?" I asked her and took myself near the bed and picked up the rough old hand that I knew better than anyone. It felt cold to my fingers.

I pulled my chair up close on the side where his head was turned so he could know I was there. People came and went. I said no one but family and doctors could come in the room. I wanted no one else to see him like that. I could wash the body, I said. I could change the sheets. "We will do what we can," I told them, "but we won't do it with everyone looking."

All that evening I sat beside the bed. When I looked up from my mending, it seemed his eyes were seeing.

"What happened to me?" he said.

"A stroke," I told him.

He shut his eyes and said nothing.

"Benno," I told him loud, like supper is ready and he is reading the paper, "you will get better and I will help you." He nodded his head but his eyes stayed closed.

I moved to the hospital room. Every day I rubbed the arms and legs and pulled the fingers and toes to make them work. Every day they worked a little better. I fed him with a spoon and wiped his mouth where the soup fell out. I read to him from the newspaper, in German. He didn't talk so much to me, but he listened, and when the doctors came and asked him questions, he began to make answers. A week later he was able to lean on me and walk to the bathroom alone. When he started to complain about the food, I gathered up my clothes and put them in the suitcase.

"Where are you going," he asked.

"Home," I said.

"Not without me."

"Ha!" I said and he looked like little Georgie looked on the first day of school, but I continued to pack up.

"Send in the nurse," he said.

I nodded.

"The pretty one with the soft hands."

I looked up and saw a smile. It sat crooked on his face, but it was a welcome sight.

There was work to do at home and I needed time to gather my thinking. Fritz and the boys came to the house and built a ramp for the wheel chair they bought. Max sat in the chair and Georgie wheeled him around the house while they discovered what it could do.

"Look, it fits right up to the sink," Georgie said while Max leaned up to turn on the water and pretended brushing his teeth.

"You know Opa has false teeth," Georgie said and Max grabbed a glass and pretended to take out his teeth and put them in the glass.

"Let's see if we can get into the refrigerator," Max said and off they rolled toward the kitchen. For the back of the chair they made a sign. *"Der grosse opa,"* it said. I laughed and shook my head.

"You boys get out here and stop bothering Oma," Fritz called from the front porch.

But I needed their foolishness. I started to plan my cooking for the day we bring Benno home. Not so much meat, the doctor has said, so we will have chicken. And dumplings, I decided. And red cabbage and for dessert . . .

"Mom," Fritz called and I went to see. "See if you can handle this." And Georgie sat in the chair while I wheeled it down the ramp and back up.

"Good," I told him.

He put his arm around my shoulder. "Are you okay?"

"Of course."

"Call me if there's anything you need."

"Of course," I said again, like I couldn't think of anything else to say.

"Georgie will come tomorrow and cut the grass while I look over the books and pay the bills."

When they had gone I poured a glass of milk and sat at the kitchen table. Through the window I saw my garden had gone to weeds. The zinnia's heads were drooping from want of water, but the butterflies were coming still. Almost September and time to plant fall vegetables. I could see in my head where the lettuce and squash would go in rows. I thought of last year's yellow seeds saved in an envelope, and the spot out by the garage where the faucet drips, a good spot for a pumpkin. Two hours of daylight remained. If I start now, I thought, I will have a bed turned and ready to plant in the morning.

And so I was busy at work when Emil came and rang the front doorbell, and I didn't hear. He walked, then, to the side of the house, so when I lifted up from the spade I jumped to see him.

"Emil Zipp? That is you?" I had to ask, so different he looked, with a bald head and gray beard, not a nice one, but a few days of roughness, and still those round eyes with questions that couldn't make.

Right by the back steps, he stood, with his straw hat in both hands, and looking red-faced like his father, Peter, had looked so long ago, except not quite so big in the belly. No woman cooking for him, I suppose.

"Ja. You want I should help with the garden?"

"No, *danke.*" I put the spade down and pushed the hair back from my eyes. "It's a surprise, Emil. So long it's been. Thirty years, maybe more."

247

"I heard at the feed store that Benno had a stroke."

"He gets better every day now."

"Thought a stroke meant dead."

"Not this time." Poor Emil, so much about the world he didn't know. "I'll take care of you, if Benno can't."

"There's no need," I told him and he looked down the rows and nodded. "But it's good to see you. When Benno gets home, you'll want to stop again."

He put his hat back on. "I don't come to town much. Busy with the animals," he said, and he turned to go.

He was past the front rose bushes when I thought to call him back.

"Wait up a minute." He stopped and turned. "I have stollen in the freezer. Strudel, too. I'll get you some."

"Ja. You do that." He smiled, like he was the one surprised this time, and I could see some of the teeth were gone, but that wasn't so important. It was good he was finally over being mad.

Nothing is so bad as some people make it. So many friends. They came to the house with kind words and food and wondering what they could do, for me, or Benno.

"Such a shame," they said.

"It could have been worse," I told them.

A few stopped by with long faces to ask about Benno, but ended up talking about themselves.

"When my husband had his stroke, he never spoke and he lived for seven more years," the lady from the church told me. "Poor man, locked up behind those eyes. I could see him calling for help, but he couldn't say a word. Not a word."

"Thank goodness Benno can speak," I told her.

"Can he feed himself?"

"Ja. Now he can."

"And, you know, go to the bathroom alone? A real mess, you know."

"I'm sure."

"Well, you call me if I can help you, Mrs. Jahn. I know what you're going through. It's like having a child to take care of. And sometimes they get so confused."

When she had gone, I took a long drink of cool water to get the bad taste from my mouth. Benno gave money to the church some time back to help and fix the old building that had stood so long. Good for business, he told me. The woman who came showed me the card from 1972, like she wanted to remind me we had once given. Eleven years ago, and still on the visiting list. At the time, the young minister, himself, came to our door to say *'danke.'* He said we should attend the next Sunday to pray for God's help in winning the war.

"Why not pray for peace?" I asked him.

"We must think of our own," he told me.

"I have seen the war on television," I told Benno when the man was gone. It is as bad for the ones on the other side. I will not hope for winning, like a football game."

"Someone has to win," Benno told me. To the minister he said, "We go to the river on Sunday mornings," and so we did, until the flood.

Against the church lady's sour talk, I decided we will have a party at the river for Benno's coming home. All the family and some friends as well, with plenty of food, and beer to drink. A little will be good for him, I think. Carol Anne always asks that we come to her new house. Maybe, now is the time. Every few days she comes by in the mornings before I go to the hospital and wants to clean and do the wash and bring groceries, like to be a part of the family again. At her new place we can set up tables and chairs by the pecan trees so Benno can see how the crop is making. The young ones can swim and float and the old one, he can watch, and fish and maybe play some dominos. Perhaps we all do some healing.

"Are you sure he'll be ready for this?" Fritz asked me.

"I asked him today at the hospital and he said it would be good."

"I don't know if he's up to it."

"Up to what? Your father needs the *gemütlichkeit.* Now here's something important I need to know."

"What's that?"

"About the gasoline for the car. There used to be boys to put it in. Now they say serve yourself but I'm not knowing how."

He laughed. "That's easy, Mom, but you shouldn't have to do it."

"Well, why not? I'm the driver now."

"I'll send Georgie by to fill your car every week."

"Good. And he will take me and show me how the pump works, in case."

A month after the stroke, we took Benno from the hospital. He was ready to leave, dressed and sitting in the chair when I got there. Fritz came to help.

"Give me my cane so I can walk out," he said.

"No, Pop, let's do the wheelchair, to see how it works."

"Don't want to be pushed around in that thing all the time."

"It's the only way you're getting out of here today."

He sat in the chair, with his back straight and held the cane across his lap, so anyone could see he would get up when he wanted. I handed him his straw hat and he put it on. He carried a white handkerchief and wiped at his mouth on the left side.

"Drooling like a baby," he said.

"No one will notice if you don't tell them," I said.

"You look good, Pop," Fritz told him.

"Twenty pounds lighter than when I came in."

"Mom's cooking will take care of that."

"The doctor says that's what got me in trouble in the first place."

As soon as we left the hospital I got afraid. So weak and thin he was, his body bent like a broken kite. He sat in the front seat with Fritz driving and I sat in the back.

"Where are we going?" he asked.

"To the river for a picnic. I've been telling you," I said.

"Oh," he said.

"You feel up to it, Pop?"

"Up to what?"

"The river. A picnic."

"Sure. Is there a bathroom there?"

"Do you need to go to the bathroom?"

"No."

Confused, the church lady had said. Like a child, she had said.

I leaned up to his seat. "Hungry yet?"

"Ja."

"We have a lot of food and beer."

He reached up and took off his hat and I could see the shaking in his hand.

"I could use a beer," he said.

Everyone had their own feelings about Benno and I saw how they tried to help. Max took to coming by every day after school on his motor scooter. He stopped in the kitchen first for something sweet to eat and then found his way into the front room where Benno watched his stories on the television. A silly story that came on in the middle of the afternoon the boy got Benno to watching, about a bad man in an old house, making trouble for the town people.

"Why would you want to look at such a thing," I asked, but they watched it together every day, and laughed when I walked through the room and frowned.

"It's cool, Oma," he told me.

"*Schwartze*," I told him. "So dark I cannot even see the faces."

"*Schwartze* Shadows," the boy jumped on my word. That's what we'll call it from now on. Right, Opa?"

He wanted to spend his time with Benno and I was glad for that. Even still, I wondered where were his own friends. After the show they played dominos, every day until dinner time. From the kitchen I heard the sound of their playing. No words, mind you, only the sound. It reminded me of long ago.

I was five when my mother and I went to live with my grandparents after my first Papa died. My mother and grandfather ran the schoolhouse and my grandmother and I tended the house and garden.

My grandmother was a sour woman. Like the juice of lemons, she made everything turn to curd. My mother said she was pretty once but when I came to live with her I could see only a face like a sad iron. A smart woman, she had been, with money and education and her head filled with the wanderlust and ideas of a great, golden land she had read in books. With her brother, she came at age nineteen, bringing a piano and fine furniture and china plates, and then came the war and the quarrels over slavery and talk of separating the country and to the north she asked to go, but her brother thought to stay where he was, but true to the Union, and make right what was wrong. No man should be a slave and no country should be divided was what he believed, what he had learned from the problems in the old country, and for those ideas the brother joined with others and for this their property was taken and the brother was killed on the road one night and thrown into a pit. And he was not the only one. To think that would happen here, like a bad dream!

She was twenty-five and had lost everything, even her hope. After the war she married my opa, who had come sooner to Texas, though he was not so old as she. He was twenty-two and thought better, that a new land takes new rules, and when the fighting was on and the Germans in the Hill Country were called traitors because they were against such things, my opa joined with those who believed a newcomer should not meddle. It was an old problem, they said, and maybe we don't understand it so good, but we are not traitors. And for that they escaped with their lives and their land. Two stillbirths my oma had after, then a child who died of the smallpox when she was two, and then came my mother, and disappointed she was to have a daughter. My mother said that giving the babies had torn her woman parts so bad that everything there was hanging down and causing her such pain. It makes her bad nature easier to forgive.

My oma didn't allow my going to school with the others. She would teach me what was needed, she said, but I could do nothing to please her. If I planted seeds in the garden, they were too deep or not deep enough. If I sorted the beans I left in too many stones. When I tried to make lace, she saw only knots. She made a frown when I laughed. She fussed when the wind blew and was unhappy when it was still, was angry with the mud when it rained, and with the heat when the sun was shining. A complaining woman is like a barking dog, the men say. More nuisance than help. I decided that no matter how bad things come, I will find something to be happy about.

On Saturdays my grandfather sometimes took me to the meeting house where the men gathered to play dominos and drink beer. When I got tired of watching I crawled beneath the table and went to sleep to the sharp noise of their laughing and the rap of dominoes on wood. Rap, they click the domino. I play on your play, it says. Pay attention.

And I thought of this while I paid attention from the kitchen to the click of their dominos. The boy I knew so little and the man I knew so well. Both kept their distance. So I cooked for them and let them have their time. Benno, he got to looking for Max to come.

"Where's the boy?" he says after lunch.

"He comes when the school is out," I told him.

One day Max said to me, "Opa wants to go for a drive in the car."

"Later," I said.

"I'll take him," he said.

"You don't drive yet."

"I can drive, Oma. I've been driving for years."

"Years?" I laughed at him. "How come I've never seen?"

"Dad lets me drive all the time at the ranch. Let me take Opa out to the ranch. It'll be okay. All I need's a big pillow."

"No," I said.

"Come on, Omie," he said, "he'll really like it."

Such a fool I was, letting them go off like that. I watched them pull from the driveway and right away I was sorry. I called Fritz, but he wasn't at the office. I called Vera.

"I'm glad you're there because such a mistake I've made," I said, and told her what had happened.

"I'll watch for them," she told me.

Later she brought them in the pickup truck and Max went home on his scooter.

"It's okay," she told me, because she sees I am upset. "But you mustn't let Max have the keys again. And Benno shouldn't be driving, either."

"Benno, driving?"

"Max let him. I found them in the pasture, chasing cows. I don't know what we're going to do with that boy."

"It's better to say nothing to Fritz," I told her. "I will handle this."

The next thing I knew, the boy was stealing from me. I found money missing from my purse and at first thought nothing of it. So much to remember these days, sometimes I forget where the money goes. But it happened enough that I knew it wasn't my forgetting, but a problem. And the only answer was Max.

"Did you take money from my purse?" I asked him.

"No," he said, and would not look at me.

"Max," I said, "I am your oma and I will see that you have whatever you need. Now you must tell me, did you take money from my purse?"

"Yes," he said, and still does not look.

"Look at me," I said, and he looked at me then.

"*Liebchen*," I said and brought him in my arms and his body was stiff, but he didn't push away. I held him then at arm's length, "Listen!" I said. "Whatever you want, I will help you get it, but you must not take what is not yours to take. It's not right."

He laughed a silly laugh.

"I need five dollars," he said.

"For what?"

"For cigarettes."

"Cigarettes don't cost five dollars."

"Two packs for me and two packs for Opa," he said.

"Opa isn't supposed to smoke. The doctor says he shouldn't."

"But you know he does. You buy them for him."

"Only a package a week."

"We'll keep them here and only smoke when we're watching *Schwartze* Shadows. How's that?"

"Does your father know you are smoking?"

"Sure."

"What does he say?"

"That it's not good for me. But I do it anyway, and he knows it."

"So, if you buy these cigarettes, you will smoke only here?"

"Sure."

"Do you promise?"

"I promise. Is it a deal?"

"A deal," I said, and the word was strange on my tongue, "but you must never take from me again without asking."

I handed him the money and he started out the door.

"*Liebchen,*" I said, and he stopped. "This is the only time I make such a deal."

"That's cool," he said and smiled like an angel, out the door.

The next time Fritz stopped by I talked with him.

"I've been thinking about Max's birthday. What would he want?"

"Who knows?"

"A car?"

"Sure, he wants a car, Mom, like they all do, but he doesn't get his license for two years, and I'm not sure he'll be ready then"

"What if I put money away for a car, to buy when you say he's ready, of course."

"Did he put you up to this?"

"You think I have no ideas of my own?"

"I know he's spending a lot of time there. Is he giving you trouble?"

"Not trouble. No, not trouble."

"But?"

"But, he's not like Georgie. Not like you were as a boy. He's a hard one to understand."

"I know," he said.

"What do you think?" I asked him.

"I don't know what to think, Mom," he told me and I saw he was worried.

"It will be okay," I told him. "Children go through such things. Every one is different."

"That's what Carol Anne says."

The next time Max asked for money I took him to the bank and we opened a savings account.

"This is for your car," I told him, and he liked that, I could tell. He began to collect pictures of cars and bring them to show me what he liked, and he asked every day for money and every day I put aside a dollar until he said that wasn't enough.

"The one I want will cost at least $3,500," he told me. "Only five dollars a day, and by the time I have my license we can go pick it out. What color do you like, Omie," he asked. "I'll let you pick the color."

He thought I didn't know what was going on.

"For five dollars a day," I said, "I'll expect much help around here."

And so I put him to work, afternoons and weekends, weeding my garden, cutting the lawn, washing the windows, turning the beds, whatever I found that needed doing. He was a smart boy and worked steady, once I got him started. Each Friday I gave him the money and the bank envelope and he brought back to me the envelope that showed it had been deposited. In six months there was almost $1,000.

"Red," I told him. "I think the car should be red."

"Cool," he said.

One day I came from the grocery and Max and Benno were watching the television. I saw they had Benno's old cigarette papers out.

"What is this?" I asked.

"We rolled our own," Max said and gave me a silly smile. I looked at the two of them and thought something was wrong. Benno was talking to the television and laughing. Max looked like a child who had been caught licking the icing. I turned on the lights and raised the window.

"Did you get any cookies?" Max asked me.

"Dinner will be soon," I told him.

"Need cookies," he said. "Right, Opa? Cookies! Cookies!"

Benno chuckled and nodded.

I walked to the coffee table and picked up a little can of green leaves. "And what is this?"

"Weed," he said to me.

"Answer me so I understand," I said.

"It's a weed," he said again. "It's harmless. A friend of mine found it growing in his back yard. It makes you relaxed, so I brought some to Opa."

"Go home," I said to Max. "I am tired and it is time for you to go."

He looked up, surprised. "We smoked it outside, back behind the garage. No one saw."

"You think that makes it okay, smoking this 'weed'? You think I am an old woman who knows nothing that goes on in this world?"

"It's perfectly safe, Oma. It grows in the earth," and he held out his hand for me to give him the little can.

"So does the Jimson weed grow in the earth." I unhooked the screen to throw his weeds in the flower bed, and then in his hand I put the empty can. "And that makes the cattle crazy and they end up dead. Go home now and don't come back until you've found some brains and some respect."

I didn't want to lose the boy, but there is only so much one can do. Besides, I think, he'll be back. There is the bank account, and the car, and Benno. I picked up the nasty rolling papers and threw them in the trash.

When Georgie was in grade five, he was so different, even then wanting that I read to him, in German yet, and wanting to know how it was when I was a girl. It made me happy to tell him, because it's important for a child to know where he comes from. Happy for another reason, too. Because I like the remembering. Max makes me think always of just now, and with him I worry for the tomorrows.

Vera

H e called one night, from the club. It was almost eleven.
"Your Mexican friend needs to see you," he said.
"Tully? Where are you?"
"At the club. You better get down here quick."
"I'm not coming there at this time of night."
"If you aren't here in fifteen minutes, we're coming over."
"I'm turning out the lights and locking the door."
"Then I guess we'll have to figure out a way to wake you up." He hung up the phone.

I dressed hurriedly, irritated, trying to still my concerns about what I might find.

Tully and Mike sat in the otherwise deserted bar. They both had drinks in hand and as I walked in, Tully called for another round.

"What are you drinking, madam?" he shouted across the room.

"Nothing."

"Gotta have something."

"Coffee," I said to the girl and took a seat at the table, beside Mike.

"My buddy and I have been talking about you, so I decided you needed to join the party."

Mike shrugged his shoulders and grinned helplessly at me.

"This is a party?"

"Now that you're here, it is. We've decided you're the woman we'd most like to have—"

"Stop right there." I stood up.

Tully grabbed my hand. "Oh, sit down and get off your high horse. Character, that's what we said. You're a woman with character."

I sat, hoping to avoid a scene.

"Vera," Tully said. "Means truth, doesn't it?"

I nodded, trying to decide the best way to deal with his drunkenness.

"Well, let me tell you some truth, Miss Jahn. I drink too much. But tomorrow, I'll be sober and I'll remember everything that went on here tonight and I want you to witness our friendship. Cheers, Mike."

Tully lifted his glass, and Mike did the same.

"To what do we attribute this breakthrough?"

"You mean, what's the deal? You tell her, boy."

"I won the qualifying round today," Mike told me, suddenly beaming. "To play in the Texas Open. Mr. Fox backed me."

"Tully," he corrected.

"Yes, sir," Mike said.

"Shot a sixty-two," Tully stumbled over the words.

"That's good, I gather."

"Good? Damn near perfect."

I stood up again. "I'm happy for you, Mike, but I think I came to this party a little late."

"Nope." Tully pulled me down again. "Want you to hear the part about you. We've decided we respect you more than any woman we've ever known."

"Except my mother," said Mike, who had obviously been drinking too.

"Can we talk tomorrow?" I looked over at the clock. "I need to get back. I think Val's going to deliver tonight and I want to be there."

"Why do you let that dog keep having pups? Isn't this the third time? Ought to have her fixed. Don't you think, Mike?"

"This is the last."

"Seems like that's what you said last time."

"They're a lot of fun, aren't they?" Mike said.

I nodded, completely aware, and slightly embarrassed by the fact that my affection for Val's pups looked like a spinster's substitute for children.

"Take me home, Vera," Tully begged. "Can't risk a DWI."

"Mike?" I gave him a look, asking for help.

"I shouldn't be driving either," he said. "That's the good thing about living on the grounds."

I drove Tully to his townhouse, but first he insisted I drive past the site where he was breaking ground for a new house.

"You live right on the other side of that cliff, don't you?" he said. "I could slide down and keep you company on cold nights."

"It would be a steep slide."

"There's a road there. I checked it out."

"A cattle path," I told him. "It wouldn't be kind on your Lincoln."

"Oh, well," he sighed like a baby bull. "I'll find a way."

"Tully, you're impossible."

"I know. Wound up almost as tight as you are, but in the other direction."

"I don't manipulate people."

"Nope. Don't cut them any slack, either."

"I'm glad you've changed your attitude toward Mike."

"Hell, the Mex is good. I'm thinking about backing him for City Council. Good thing he broke up with Otto's daughter, or we might've had a little problem there. But these golf hustlers have women hanging on them wherever they go. Little girl like that couldn't hold him anyway."

After I practically pushed him from the car that night I found myself wondering, once again, why I was willing to put up with Tully Fox. I had said I would never work for him, yet he was basically responsible for my most satisfying work. The displays I was meticulously piecing together at the bank were working their way into a written and pictorial history of German Texans the Institute had agreed to publish. It would span from the early 1800s, through the Civil War, and World

Wars I and II, to the present, and would address, without amplification, the inventiveness and energy of these settlers, the technology they developed, the dams and roads and permanent buildings they constructed, their contributions as merchants and bankers, beermeisters, and photographers, their devotion to government, and most of all, to education.

Tully had opened doors for me, even when I asked that he not. He was infuriatingly honest, often mean, sometimes surprisingly kind, and continually linked with some woman, which no longer offended nor threatened me. "Power," he liked to quote Kissinger, "is the only aphrodisiac."

Queenie asked once if there was a chance for romance.

"No." I laughed at her choice of words.

"An intelligent man," she said. "And nice-looking, in his way."

"He's crude," I said.

She questioned my word.

"Rough. Unpolished," I told her.

"I've seen," she said. "What else?"

"He chases women."

She shook her head like I was complaining about the sun being hot. "Men do that."

"He manipulates people," I said in frustration, holding my hands before me and wiggling my fingers like a puppeteer.

"We all have a worm in our apple," she told me.

The truth was, he had an interesting mind, complicated and unpredictable. That was why I put up with him. But to be anything but a sometimes friendly adversary and a business associate would be a mistake. Tully was one of those men who liked the chase. If I allowed myself to be caught, even for one night, the mystery would be gone and our present relationship would degenerate into something much less satisfactory. What we had was somewhere between a grudging respect and a contentious flirtation; it was going nowhere.

For a few months after Carol Anne returned from California, Fritz and I continued to see each other. He came to the cabin in the late afternoons and we talked and touched each other and walked along the river. Sometimes we tried to make love, but it was too complicated, a wall standing between us, and always the guilt. We even talked about trying to make a life together.

"Have you thought about this?" he asked one day not long after she had come back. "If I divorced Carol Anne, could you marry me and face Benno and Queenie and the kids, and the town?"

"It would be awkward. Could you?"

He looked incredibly pained. "I try to imagine it, and I can't get through the first step."

"Which is?"

"Telling Benno."

"The guilt went in with the nursery rhymes, before we were old enough to understand."

"I guess."

"Fritz," I took his face in my hands and made him look at me. "If it makes it easier, marriage isn't what I want."

"Maybe it's what I want. You've been like a mother to the boys."

"No. Listen to me. I love you. I've never told another man that, and I don't expect that to change. But there's no place for us to go with this."

"No place that won't hurt us more than we're already hurting," he said, and we both knew he was right.

It was a relief, in a way, to have it settled. I devoted myself to work and kept my distance with Fritz and Carol Anne. I was upset by the idea of them building on the river, as much as Queenie was, for different reasons. I had a long time to get used to the idea. The house took more than a year, stretching over two summers, and during that time I was visited regularly by Georgie and his friends.

"This is my Aunt Vera," he'd tell them. "She's writing a book." And I could see them showing off for me, hoping, I suppose, I would write about them. It was our private joke, Georgie's and mine, and we never mentioned that the book was about history, the subject they all groaned about.

"I don't get it," he said to me one day.

"What's that?"

"My dad. I used to think he was always right."

"Something in particular cause you to change your thinking?"

"Yeah. My friend Mondo. Dad said something like I shouldn't be spending so much time with a Mexican."

"What brought that on?"

"Oh, we kid around. Mondo calls me a Kraut and I call him a Beaner, and Dad heard us for some reason got all bent out of shape. 'You're known by the company you keep,' he told me."

I shifted my position on the dock and allowed my attention to be captured briefly by the minnows swarming in the shallow wading pool, remembering how Fritz used to mimick Benno's voice.

"You have to be true to yourself," I told him.

"But I have to be true to my parents, too. Mom thinks it's funny because it's food names we're calling each other, but Mom's not my problem."

"I know."

"So what do I do?"

"I can't give you advice."

"Now you sound like Oma Sheila."

"What did you ask her?"

"If she thought I ought to be a rancher."

"And what did she say?"

"She said, 'Suit yourself, Kiddo.'"

Georgie sometimes brought his girlfriend with him. She was a good-sized girl, almost as tall as he, and captain of the volleyball team, he told me. I watched them play in the water, him, climbing to the tallest limb and diving out, trying to impress. She, doing the same, sometimes better than he. They laid on the dock in the sun to dry and sometimes I saw them curled against each other like two spoons. They never hid from me, and I appreciated their openness, but wondered at their liberties, happy not to be a parent.

One day he came alone.

"Where's Kelly," I asked.

"It's her period and she has cramps," he told me. I was surprised, thinking when I was in school a boy and girl would never talk so freely. Things had changed. I hoped for the better.

Max came to see me too. Well, perhaps not to see me, but when I looked out the window, sometimes he was there, fishing from the dock, or when I drove in from school he might be sitting on the steps. Sometimes I paid him to help me with the yard work. He was saving money for a car.

"Think you'll like the new house?"

"It's okay," he told me. "Almost finished. You ought to come over and see it."

"I will."

"I don't think so."

"What makes you say that?"

"Because you don't like my mother."

"That's not true."

"Okay," he shrugged. "But you like my father. A lot."

I stopped and brushed the dirt from my hands. "What are you trying to say?"

He would't look at me. "It's like one of those stories on television. I saw the way you kissed him that time I was in the hospital. I'm not stupid."

"I know you're not, Max, but you are mistaken. Your father and I grew up together. I love him in a way no television story could ever explain."

"If you say so," he said in a flat voice. "So I guess that's why you never come see us any more."

We had fractured. Max and I. Fritz and I. Carol Anne and I. Betrayed each other in so many ways one could never count them all, or begin to place blame. But Benno's stroke brought us together under a new regimen. Forced into a different pattern we brushed against each other at the hospital, at Queenie's house, at Carol Anne and Fritz's new place on the river, that day they brought him home. I got a tour of their house that day and was impressed at the good taste it reflected. And I observed a different Fritz, one openly proud of Georgie, gentler with Max, more respectful of Carol Anne.

Benno and Queenie decline slowly. Every few months another of their old friends and neighbors dies, and one or the other of us accompanies them to the funeral home, or to the house, to pay respects. They complain that Schoenberg isn't like it used to be. It bothers Benno that the merchants don't sweep the streets or talk to him in German any more. Queenie says the bakery strudel is tough because they don't roll the dough thin enough and she misses the German newspaper. On the other hand, our boys are quickly becoming men, though it comes easily to Georgie and is a struggle for Max. I am struck by the constantly changing nature of people and things and have decided it is unproductive to impose yesterday's judgments on today's reality.

Carol Anne

*A*fter Benno had his stroke the doctor said he shouldn't drive. You could take one look at him with half of his parts not working so well and know he shouldn't be out on the road, even though most of his friends were still driving, some so shrunk and bent over they could hardly see over the steering wheel.

"Grey hairs driving in our lane," Max called it, and I had to laugh, even though I shouldn't.

"Have a little respect," I'd tell him.

"*Jawohl*," he'd answer, and shake his blond curls down over one eye with a Hitler salute. Where he got all this, I'll never know.

The problem with Benno was, no one wanted to tell him he'd never drive again, so we kept hem-hawing around it, like you do with a kid that wants something you know isn't good for him. One day Benno read in the paper there was a good interest rate on new savings accounts and he decided he needed to go to the bank. Queenie told him Fritz would take care of it, but he insisted he could still do his own business and demanded the keys. When Queenie said she couldn't find the keys, he finally gave in and let her call me. I guess that option was the least degrading. I also guess that meant he had forgiven me, or forgotten that before the stroke he didn't like being in the same room with me.

The clerk at the New Accounts desk was right out of high school, with long silky hair so smooth I figure her mother had ironed it. Her fingernails were painted hot pink and she wore a little diamond engagement ring. The nameplate on her desk announced her as Miss Zipp, which made me think of a joke. But Benno liked it. A good name, he told her. It was good, too, that she knew to speak slow and loud enough for him to understand.

"You're allowed one free withdrawal per month, Mr. Jahn," she explained like she had memorized her speech, "but after that, there will be a slight charge for each additional withdrawal."

Benno brushed his big freckled hand in front of his face like he was shooing gnats. He wasn't opening any savings account with the intention of making withdrawals. "Ach, that's not important," he said.

Tully's girls had been trained to listen to the customer. She leaned forward, so anxious to please. "What is important to you, Mr. Jahn," she asked with a sweet smile.

Benno sat and thought for a minute. At 78, he still liked a pretty face and an audience. He leaned forward, too, and locked her eyes with his. "Freedom and the land," he told her. She smiled indulgently, and when he was busy signing the account card, she leaned over to whisper to me.

"He's so cute."

Listen, I wanted to thump her on the forehead. That's not cute. It's something to remember. You can tell it to your children, the ones you're going to have with that guy whose ring you're wearing, the one you iron your hair for, the one you're rubbing against in the back seat of the car. Tell them that one day you asked an old rancher with shaky hands and hair growing out of his ears what was important to him and he answered right off, and didn't have to think for even a minute, because for him it's always been the same. Freedom and the land.

One afternoon I picked up Queenie to take her to the farmer's market. She had a new photograph on the wall, one Vera had brought her from the heritage collection. I recognized her grandfather, the one with the bushy beard, and beside him was Queenie's mother, the school-teacher, with her hair piled on her head and a high-necked white blouse. And Queenie was there, just a little girl, peeking out with bright eyes, like watermelon seeds, like Max's eyes, from behind her mother's long, skirt.

Looking at the picture made her think of her mother and she asked if I'd take her to the cemetery.

"The one in town?"

"No. The one out on the ranch, where Benno used to take me. It's been a long time since."

"You'll have to help me find it."

She nodded.

The old dirt ranch road was crisscrossed with new ones, cart paths, cul de sacs and driveways. Three kids were whizzing dirt bikes up a huge mound of fresh earth, where construction was going on. Bulldozed trees, crushed and still green, were piled up like bonfire makings on somebody's building site.

"There. No, over there." The changes had her confused.

We circled around until she said to stop the car and wanted to walk. She took off across the fairway and I was looking to see if any golfers were coming in our direction. She went in a straight line toward the pond, then turned right, like a witching stick was pulling her.

"Here," she said. "Close to here." She was standing on the thirteenth tee, a little circle of high ground bordered by live oaks. The land dropped off to a ditch below and a skinny kid, wading barefoot in the muddy water, looked up to see if we'd be hitting at him. I waved, friendly, and when he saw we weren't carrying clubs, went back to his business of retrieving balls. Queenie stood in the short grass, her old brown oxfords wet with the morning dew. She looked in all directions then pointed behind her.

"Down there is the cemetery."

I remembered talk about a cemetery, but hadn't paid much attention. Something about sacred ground on the golf course. The original buyers offered to pay for moving the bodies, but Queenie wouldn't hear of it, so they built around it and closed it in. I went with Fritz once to see how it was going, but had stayed in the car to watch Miguel giving lessons to some high school boys.

"You want to go down?" I asked.

She nodded. "I think I see the path."

It was a narrow path that cut through a thicket then opened onto a grove backed by limestone cliffs. The area wasn't any bigger than my bedroom, with a cedar elm as tall as a three-story building smack in the center and another smaller one that had doubled itself almost to the ground in order to survive in the giant's shadow. Queenie reached out her hand and we steadied each other and stepped over a low wall of stacked grey stones. There were rectangles of graves and small cement markers flush with the ground. The air was chilly and very quiet, like walking into a church on a weekday. Birds flushed when we came near, then settled again on trees nearby and began to call.

"Talking about us," Queenie said. She was convinced that birds communicated, and never failed to point it out when it happened. By now, I believed it too. In this spot you could believe almost anything. Sunlight filtered through the leaves and lit up a carpet of green moss that clung to the bent-over tree, like fur on its back. I rubbed my hand across it. Tough and spongy, like Astroturf.

"How many people buried here?"

"Six," if I remember right," Queenie said. She walked around, not reading the headstones, just remembering. "Peter's first wife, one of their children, before he married my mother, then Peter, my opa, my oma, and my mother." Suddenly she was busy stepping off the space in the far corner of the little plot. "Room for two more," she said. "Benno and me, I would wish."

"I like this better than that place on the highway with the plastic flowers, but there's a law now against private burial spots."

"Ashes you can put anywhere," she said, like she had given it some thought. "Benno wouldn't want that, but I think I should like it."

"To be cremated?"

"Whatever it is called. Me in a blue glass jar, in this place," she reached down and stuck a stick in the ground, "under the tree."

I lifted a stone from the top of the fence and set it beside the stick. "There you are."

She laughed and motioned with her hand. "Over some, so to get the morning sun."

I rearranged the stone. "Like so?"

"Ja."

269

I picked up another stone and set it at an angle beside the first. "I think I'd like to be right here, myself," I said.

She took my hand in both of hers. *"Liebchen,"* she said, but she looked away and didn't finish her sentence. I guess, like she had told me, she didn't want to spend too much time thinking about endings. "We must be getting back. Benno will be wondering."

"We'll tell him we were harvesting pecans," I said. "He'd snort at us if we told him the truth."

Queenie and I had spent longer than I'd counted on at the cemetery, and I was late picking up the boys after football practice. Georgie was there, but Max had started walking to Fritz's office.

"I told him to wait, that you'd be along, but he said he wasn't going to count on it."

"Sometimes I get the feeling he's still punishing me. How come you don't feel that way?"

"I don't know. I just don't." Georgie never wanted to talk about the year I had spent away.

"It wasn't so bad for you, I guess."

"Aunt Vera was there and Oma and Opa, and, well I missed you but I knew you'd be back."

I reached over and patted the football pads where his shoulder should be.

"Georgie, you know what they say about people like you? They say you're old beyond your years."

He shrugged and I knew I was making him uncomfortable. "Sorry I made things hard for you," I said because I wanted him to know. "You know it wasn't about you."

"You told me that."

"You'll understand some day."

"I understand now."

"How's your love life?" Max says one day when we're driving home. I looked over at him and I'm sure my eyes were bugging out.

"How's your love life," he repeats, and points at the bumper sticker he's reading from.

"None of your business," I told him and stuck out my tongue.

"How's Dad's?"

I looked over and could tell by the look on his face it was a serious question.

"About the same," I'd say. "How's yours?"

"Not so good. The hormones haven't really kicked in yet, I guess. I like watching."

My hands started to get sweaty on the steering wheel. We stopped at a red light and I lit a cigarette.

"I saw Georgie and his girl making out after football practice."

"Making out?"

"Yeah. You know, kissing, rubbing around."

"In broad daylight?"

"Everybody does it. In the halls at school. The teachers have to break them up sometimes. It's really funny."

Jesus, I thought. I'm not ready for this. "So, is there something you want to know?" I asked him.

"Does everybody have to act that way?"

"It's pretty normal, I guess."

"You think I'm normal?"

"Max, there's no such thing as normal, but your time for girls will come."

"How come I never see you and Dad kissing?"

"That's really none of your business."

"You're my parents, aren't you?"

"Some things are private."

"Well, do you kiss in private?"

"Sometimes."

"I saw him kiss Aunt Vera."

"They've always been close."

"Close," he repeated, with a knowing sneer.

I pulled the car into the driveway. Max jumped out, picked up a frisbee and tossed it to the dog while I sat and stared at the house. My brain was like sawdust. Thoughts struggled to the surface like little bubbles, then drifted away. It had always been there, the jealousy of Vera, the idea that she and Fritz had been closer in many ways than he and I could ever be. But those thoughts had been packed away with my mini-skirts and that zebra jumpsuit.

Still, there was something hidden between the two of them. I had noticed how they hardly looked at each other any more.

When I was in fourth grade I made up a story about my father. He was in the war, I told everyone. A marine. A hero, purple heart and all. I cut a picture of a handsome man in uniform from Life Magazine, glued it to a piece of cardboard, put it in an old picture frame and took it to school for show and tell. The teacher called my mother and it really pissed her off.

When I got home she was waiting for me.

"Your father was no hero," she said. "He was a jerk."

I nodded and started to cry.

"Let me see the picture," she demanded.

I pulled it from my school bag and handed it to her.

"Good choice," she said, and she ran her hands across the page, smoothing out the bubbles where paste had dried. "You pretend he's your Daddy all you want, keep his picture by your bed, talk to it, kiss it goodnight, write him letters if you want to, but it'll be between you and me and we'll know it's pretend."

"What's so bad about taking it to school?"

She sighed. "Oh, hell, I don't know. Because if you lie to people, they get upset with you."

"They didn't get upset, they liked it. Everybody wanted to see."

"How do you think they're going to act when you tell them that isn't your father?"

"I'm not going to tell them."

"The teacher already knows. She wants you to come back tomorrow and set it straight."

"I can't. I just can't." I was destroyed, imagining having to go in front of my class and say I was a liar. "What am I supposed to say? 'This isn't my father. I don't have any pictures of my father, because he was a jerk?'"

"Don't get smart with me."

"I'm sorry."

"What if I come?"

"And do what?"

"Help you out."

"What are you going to say?"

"I'm not sure," she said, "but I'm good with an audience."

The next day at 10:00 o'clock the classroom door opened and Sheila tiptoed in. She was dressed in a leather mini-skirt and a vest and was carrying her guitar.

When it came time for Show and Tell, the teacher introduced her and everyone turned around and looked at me.

"Hi," she said to the class and pulled up a tall stool to sit on. She pulled out the picture I had brought the day before and I scrunched down in my chair.

"Yesterday, Carol Anne showed you this picture and told you it was her father. Well, it's not really her father."

I hated her. A girl at the front of the room turned around and gave me a snooty look. Some of the boys laughed.

"It's someone she'd like to be her father, because we all like heroes, don't we?"

The class nodded in agreement.

"Since Carol Anne doesn't know her father, I told her she could pick anyone she wanted to be a father she'd be proud of, and this is who she chose. I think she did a real good job, don't you?"

"My father is a marine," one boy shouted out.

"And mine's a helicopter pilot," someone else said.

Sheila ran her hand across the guitar and the talking stopped. "I brought my instrument today because I have a song for you. A song about war and the men that have to fight. I want you to listen real carefully and see what you think it's trying to say. It's called "Where Have All the Flowers Gone." And when she sang the class listened real close and some of the girls even cried.

That night at dinner I asked her. "Before yesterday you never told me I could pick anyone I wanted to be a father. So, when you said that to the class, wasn't that kind of a lie?"

"Would you rather I hadn't?" she said.

"No."

"Then let it be," she smiled. "I did good, didn't I?"

Maybe Max had fabricated the kiss to get attention, like I had fabricated the story of a father I never knew. Maybe his interest in 'watching' had interpreted an affectionate hug as something more. Maybe he was trying to make trouble. It was so complicated it made my head spin, for about three days. I claimed to have the flu, hid out in the bedroom and thought of going straight to Vera. I knew she wouldn't lie to me, but I didn't know what I would do, if it was true.

I went back to the source.

He was sitting on the steps, bouncing the basketball.

"Can we talk?" I asked.

"What language?"

"English will do."

"Cool."

"Max, remember the other day in the car . . ."

"I know what's coming." He stood up and started taking aim at the hoop.

"Sit down, please."

He plopped down and started low dribbling in rhythm.

"So what is it you think's coming?"

"You want to know when I saw Dad kiss Aunt Vera."

"Yeah, I'd like to know that."

"Do you think that's any of your business?"

"You've made it my business."

"Well I didn't see it. I made it up."

"Just like that?"

"Yup."

"Why?"

"To see if it'd get you stirred up. Guess I went too far. Made you worry for three days. If it was true, what would happen?"

"I have no idea."

He waved the basketball at me. "Want to play HORSE?"

"You always beat me."

"Maybe it's your day."

He was graceful, like a colt is, skinny, gangly, arms, legs, elbows and knees, and somehow able to jump, spin in mid-air and put the ball through the hoop. It was fun to play with Max because he threw himself into every game, not really caring how anything came out in the end. I felt deliriously relieved. He had made it up. Made it up.

Sheila

*B*ack when I was still with The Knights and Carol Anne called to say she'd found her true love and, by the way, was pregnant, I started on a song. Wanted to call it "You Say New, I Say Blue." That's as far as I got, just a title. I fiddled with a melody on the piano a couple of days, but what I was really trying to do was get the thing in perspective. Hell, it wasn't the first time some daughter got married before she knew better and it wasn't the first time some woman had to answer to grandmother just when she was hitting her stride.

Eighteen years later, I had changed my tune. My boys, I called them, and thinking about them, well, it was like popping a butterscotch kiss, those little soft, hard candies that give a lot of flavor and make you feel good without sticking in your teeth. Seed of my seed. Eggs of my egg, I guess. Whatever the metaphor, I sure got a kick out of watching them grow, and not being responsible for the weeding and watering.

Georgie called one night around Memorial Day to say he was going to tour the Grand Canyon for a graduation trip and wanted to stop in and see me. It was a first.

"You driving?"

"I'm flying to Flagstaff and renting a car there. Didn't want to put all the miles on my truck since it has to last me through college."

"Eighteen-year-olds aren't supposed to worry about things like that."

"I wasn't worrying. It just made sense."

"Well, call me when you're headed my way, Kiddo, and I'll put the welcome mat out."

"Thanks. Now all I have to do is decide whether to take the mule trip down into the canyon, or the helicopter ride over it."

"If it was me?"

"Yeah."

"I'd do both."

He called a few weeks later to say his mule trip had been cut short. An older man in the group had gotten sick about two-thirds of the way down and Georgie had helped carry him out on a stretcher.

"That's pretty impressive stuff," I told him, "and here I was worrying that you'd have trouble finding the ranch." I gave him directions to Warm Springs, and he showed up at our door three hours later.

Georgie and Rocky hit it off right away, like I knew they would. Rocky's what I call a guy's guy, not good at small talk, but able to do just about anything in the outdoor line and has been real successful at turning a buck. He fixed Georgie a big platter of steak and eggs and they were still talking ranch stuff when I turned in at midnight. The next morning, they had the horses saddled before I could get my first cup of coffee.

"You all go on without me," I waved them off. "It's uncivilized to get up so early." So while they toured the countryside, I slept in, puttered around the greenhouse, and wondered what was the best way to show a good time to an eighteen-year-old. Rocky would be gone most of the afternoon and evening at a Breeder's meeting.

"Anything you'd like to see while you're here?" I asked him at lunch.

"I was thinking about Hoover Dam," he told me.

"We could do that."

"I guess you've seen it."

"A couple of times."

"I could go by myself."

"Over my dead body. But what do you say we go to Vegas instead?" He seemed hesitant.

"You really want to do Hoover Dam?"

"Aunt Vera said I ought to, if I'm this close."

"You got a sport coat and a white shirt in that suitcase?"

"Sure. For the airplane."

"Indulge an old lady, Kiddo. Let's dress up and do the town. We can take my Caddy . You drive. We'll spend the night and come back tomorrow. And I'll buy you some postcards of the Dam. "

"I can drive the Biarritz?"

"You got it," I fished in my purse and threw him the keys. Then I went back to my bedroom and dressed to the teeth. Long black skirt, sequined top, velvet jacket, gold jewelry.

"Wow," Georgie said when I walked out. He was in the sun room, reading a magazine.

"You're lookin' sharp, yourself, Kiddo. Why don't you carry our bags to the car while I lock up."

On the drive down, I told him the game plan. "We'll catch an early show, have dinner and hit the tables after that. The casino doesn't start hopping until eleven or so, and I hate it when it's dead."

He looked nervous. He also looked good, dressed up, behind the wheel of my Cadillac. I didn't want this to be any ordinary old trip. I was pretty excited too.

"You know, Georgie," I told him, "we don't worry much about speed limits out here in the desert. If you kick it up to eighty-five, we'll have more time to see the lights."

We left the car with the valet and walked in through the lobby like we owned the place.

"People are looking at us," Georgie whispered, while the girl at the desk was taking my credit card.

I turned my back to the counter so she couldn't hear our conversation.

"They think we're *somebody*. People come to Vegas dressed in jeans and polyester pants suits and anyone who's dressed up, especially in the afternoon, they figure that's a star. I've done it lots of times. Works like a charm. Gets you good tables, too."

He grinned. "So maybe you can pass for a star, but what does that make me?"

"Pretend you're my bodyguard.

He straightened his back and puffed out his chest.

"And you ought to call me Sheila."

"And you can call me George."

I took the keys the girl had slid across the counter to me and handed him one. "Your key, George."

We looked at the shows that were in town and he thought he'd like the Neil Diamond concert. I thought he was being polite.

"Diamond's a good show, but The Review is hot," I told him. "Lots of skin. Little shiny costumes and long-legged girls that'll take your breath away."

He looked down, trying not to blush, I think, which made me think I was getting a little carried away. "Ever been to a rock concert?"

He shook his head.

I handed him a ten-dollar bill. "Run in the drugstore and pick us up a couple of lighters."

"I never smoke," he told me. "That's my brother's game."

I laughed. "This isn't about smoking."

The concert was terrific. At the end, when they turned out the lights, we all stood up, lit our Bic candles, and the auditorium became one giant birthday cake. It was a good moment, hundreds of us, swaying together, pulled in by the music and mellowed by the spirit. My grandson and I turned and looked each other in the eye about then and he grinned that precious grin and I thought to myself, it don't get much better than this.

After the concert I got us both a roll of quarters and we played the slots until they were gone.

"It seems kind of a waste," Georgie said, "like throwing a ten-dollar bill out the window. And some of these people look like they can't afford it. I'm not sure I can. Maybe I'll just watch."

"Suit yourself," I told him. "I always look on it like Christmas. I come once a year, I indulge myself, and never look back."

It was almost eleven when I slipped into a seat at a friendly-looking blackjack table and got hot. Georgie stood behind me and watched and in a couple of hours the chips had piled up pretty good. I traded four stacks for four singles and handed them to him.

"Would you go cash those in for me."

"How much is that?"

"Four hundred."

"That's what I thought."

"If you'll go down to the underground level, you'll find a bunch of neat shops. Why don't you go see if there's anything down there that calls your name."

He looked down at the chips and then back at me, like he wanted to protest. "This isn't up for discussion, George. Easy come, easy go," I smiled and waved him off.

He showed up some time later with a good-sized sack and a plastic garment bag over his arm. "I think I'm going to the room," he said. "I've been up a long time."

I looked at my watch. "God, it's almost three. Let's meet about noon and we'll have lunch, or breakfast, whatever you want to call it, and head home."

Driving back the next day, he kept glancing over and checking the bag that hung in the back seat, like he wanted to be sure it was still there.

"What'd you get you're so proud of?"

"Look and see."

I unzipped the black bag decorated with a classy gold crest. It was a fine, camel-colored leather jacket. "Hey, good choice."

"I got some stuff for Mom and Dad and Max, too," he told me, "but I spent most of it on myself."

"You feel bad about that?"

"Nope."

"Good. You feel bad about not seeing Hoover Dam?"

He laughed. "Only about what I'm going to tell Aunt Vera."

"You don't want to disappoint her."

"No. She's always interested in what I do. All my life she's been like a—"
He stopped in mid-sentence.

"Like a mother to you? Hey, that's okay."

"A second mother," he rushed in to fill the gap.

I unbuckled my seat belt, kicked off my shoes, and turned sideways in the seat so I could watch him while we talked. "I've only met your Aunt Vera a couple of times, but she strikes me as someone who doesn't have much fun."

"She's serious, yeah, but she's not boring. I think you'd like her if you got to know her."

"Now why do I have the feeling she'd disapprove of me?"

"Because she might, but I know what she'd like about you."

"What's that?"

"That you're independent. That you say and do what you want to and don't live by other people's rules."

"Maybe I've been reading her wrong," I said, "but she could still loosen up a little."

"Maybe she doesn't want to." He looked over at me, like he thought I should have been able to figure that out.

I reached over and patted him on the shoulder. I was so proud of him. "You're a smart boy, George. And I can't wait to see you in that leather jacket."

Carol Anne

*T*had learned to watch the weather, along with everyone else. Still, we didn't see it coming, not even Queenie, who had finally stopped worrying about floods. It rained every day that spring until the ground under our feet was like a damp sponge. The air got so heavy even the birds stopped singing. Didn't build their regular nests. For weeks Max had been checking the rain gauge outside his room and posting the measurements on the refrigerator with a magnet. But no one paid attention to Max when he was in one of his spells. At fifteen, he spent a lot of time in his room with the shutters closed, listening to rock music on the radio and writing in a journal I was forbidden to touch.

It was a Friday evening. Georgie was home from A&M for the weekend to get his clothes washed and see his girlfriend. He was getting dressed to go out when we heard the thumping.

Fritz lifted his head from the newspaper and listened toward the front door. "What's that noise?"

I turned off the television, where they were predicting more thunderstorms, and tried to hear.

"Georgie," he called. "I think that's the back gate banging. Go lock it, will you?"

Georgie came down the hall carrying his boots. While he pulled them on, he and Fritz discussed the possibilities.

"It's the boat hitting against the roof of the boathouse," Max shouted from his room. Georgie looked at Fritz and rolled his eyes.

"Could be," Fritz said.

"He says he can see in the dark," I said.

"Certainly gets enough practice," Georgie grinned. He pulled on a slicker and headed out the front door. After a minute Fritz went out to see if he needed help.

When the water began to trickle in under the glass door I headed to the bathroom for towels. I stopped to knock on Max's door, then opened it.

"I need some help."

"Won't do any good," he said in a flat voice.

"C'mon, Max. I don't have time to argue."

By the time I got back, the carpet was squishy. Dropping towels along the sill I knelt and bunched them up, trying to dam the stream. The rain had picked up again. I cupped my hands around my eyes and tried to see out into the night but caught mostly reflections from the inside lights. From the patio our yard sloped gently down to the river for more than thirty yards. I was looking for a large standing puddle, but what I seemed to be seeing was a solid lake of water lapping against the glass door, five or six inches high. My eyes were confused, I thought, and where in the hell were Fritz and George? The pounding of my heart began before my head got clear.

"Max," I shouted. "Get in here."

He came, followed by his pup, Hilda, who was the only welcome guest in his room. Still wearing his swim trunks from earlier in the day, he had a strange expression on his face. "A twelve-foot wall of water, coming down the river, the radio just said. What do you think that looks like?" he said.

"I don't have time to think," I snapped. "Grab the chairs and help me set them on the table."

He obeyed.

"Get as much as you can off the floor so it won't be ruined," I told him and ran to see if it was coming in the master bedroom. Mud, I thought, on the white carpet. Crud!

"Mom," The tone of Georgie's voice brought me running back. It was everywhere now, pouring in from beneath the side door too, bubbling up from the atrium drain. Max stood with water covering his ankles, his long, bare legs sticking up like saplings.

"Coming fast," Georgie said, out of breath. "We got the boat tied to a tree and Dad got the truck started and pulled it to the top of the drive. Got to get out. Now."

"Let me find my purse. Max, go get a shirt."

"No time," Georgie barked. "Come on."

The front of the house was two feet higher than the back. Even so, we struggled through water almost to our waists, up toward the top of the driveway to where Fritz sat gunning the engine of the pickup and honking the horn. We grabbed hands, Georgie first, then me, then Max, and worked our way against the swirling current. A plastic hose brushed against me and I screamed and pushed it away. Georgie kept hold of my left hand, but I lost Max and turned back, straining to see him in the dark. He was swimming away from us, toward the house, back to where he saw something we'd missed. Hilda, whimpering and paddling for dear life, was madly trying to follow. We had forgotten our pet. What else had we forgotten? Georgie pulled me to the truck and started back for Max. "Go on, Dad," he screamed and motioned wildly in the direction of high ground. "I've got to get Max."

Fritz jerked the driver's door open and started after Georgie. "Drive up to the bend in the road," he shouted at me. "Turn around so the headlights face the house and keep the motor running." He slammed the door and hit the truck hard as he moved away. I've seen men hit a horse like that to start it running.

I scrambled into the driver's seat and did what he said. Drove to where the water wouldn't reach, at least to where it wasn't likely to reach, and I waited. I was maybe thirty yards from them and could see the house and shadows and reflections in the water rushing around it, trees and trash floating by, stuff I couldn't make out. The rain pounded on the truck cab. I checked the gas gauge. It was about half full. I checked the clock. Eight fifteen. I bent over the steering wheel, straining to see, hitting my palms against the dashboard. "Come on. Come on. Come on." It was all I knew to say and it came out like a chant. Too bad I didn't know how to pray. I felt like I was drowning in a wave of panic. My chest was tight, my breath coming in fast, shallow gulps, a pulse pounding in my temples. Eight twenty two. I leaned back, closed my eyes, covered my ears, and took a deep breath. I thought of Queenie, how she had always been so careful about the river, how we had teased her and made light of her worries, how smart we all thought we were. I just didn't realize, Queenie, I found myself trying to explain to her. I didn't know how quick it could come, how mean it could be. I flicked the lights to high bright. Why hadn't I thought of that before. I heard Sheila's voice. Get hold of yourself, Carol Anne. Eight twenty-four. It looked like the water was halfway up the columns now and then the house lights suddenly went out and I opened the car door and stepped out into a couple of inches of water. "Fritz. Georgie. Max," I screamed into the dark.

It was another five or six minutes, before they appeared in the headlight's beam, struggling toward me, like thin, soaked, scarecrows. Fritz had his head down and his arm around Georgie, who had no expression on his face and a wild look in his eyes I'd never seen before. I ran to them and Fritz looked up at me and shook his head.

"No," I said quietly, my hands to my mouth. Then louder, "No. No. No."

"Help Georgie," Fritz said.

We got in the truck and the three of us sat shivering in silence. Georgie, still out of breath, sat staring straight ahead.

"I saw him," he said finally. "I headed back in the direction the current was going and was up to my waist when I saw him swimming toward me. He wasn't any more than ten feet away. I yelled at him and tried to plant my feet and reach out and then this tree came out of nowhere. Big, goddamned tree. Washed right between us, kind of half sideways. Knocked me down and I went under for a minute and thrashed around trying to get free of the branches and then Dad was there, pulling me back. We kept on looking and yelling 'til the lights went out, and then we couldn't see for shit and had to come back." When he stopped talking, he leaned forward with his hands cupped around his eyes and put his forehead to the windshield. "I think the water's still coming up," he announced in a flat, shaky voice. Fritz put the truck in gear.

"What are we going to do?" I asked.

"We'll try to make it to Queenie's."

I was glad he could think about that because my brain had gone on freeze. I tried to think about Max, but when I did, a brick wall slid into place. I'd get a vision of him in that churning water and click, the wall appeared and, even though I wanted something more, I couldn't take the picture any further than that.

At the edge of town we stopped at a sheriff's car that sat in the road with its lights flashing.

"Where you folks headed?"

"My mother's house, in town," Fritz told him."

He shined his flashlight in the truck. "That you Mr. Jahn?"

"Edmund?" Fritz opened the truck door, stepped out into the rain and stood talking with the deputy.

I slid over and got out. "We lost our son back there in the water," I yelled at the officer. "Someone's got to get him."

"Yes ma'am, Mr. Jahn told me. I'm awfully sorry to hear it and we'll do everything we can, just as soon as it's light. Sometimes folks are lucky. You try not to give up hope, Ma'am," he told me and walked back toward the patrol car.

"They're talking like he's already dead," I said to Georgie.

He stared straight ahead like he couldn't look at me, and in a shaky, whisper he said, "He probably is, Mom."

The brick wall began to crumble. Tears came streaming from my eyes, my heart was racing and I couldn't stop trembling. Beside me, I felt Georgie's shoulders shaking. I needed to hold it together for him, for Fritz. My body seemed to be out of control but my mind was getting clearer.

"I'm sorry I said that," Georgie said.

I reached for his hand. "Something terrible has happened, Georgie. Or is still happening, like in slow motion. Like a car wreck. I see it coming, but it hasn't quite hit yet. It's coming and there's nothing we can do." I wiped my nose on my shirt. "My God, I don't even have my purse with me. Not even a toothbrush. Our things are gone. Maybe our house. Maybe Max. Probably Max."

"Maybe he got hold of that tree and can ride it out, like the guy said," Georgie offered.

"You think?" I wanted to believe it.

"I don't know, Mom," he rested his forehead on his hands and took a deep breath. "I guess he could."

Fritz got in the truck. "The river bridge is out," he told us. "The park's under water, but we can get to Queenie's on the high road. They think the worst is over."

"The worst isn't over," I mumbled.

When we reached the house, all the lights were on and Vera's truck was there.

"My dear ones," Queenie hugged us one by one as we came in the door, while Benno stood by. "But where is Maxie?"

"Max didn't get out, Mom," Fritz told her.

Queenie put her hand on her bosom and sank into a chair. *"Gott in himmel,"* she said. She was struggling for breath. "Georgie," she motioned toward the kitchen, "my pills. Little white ones."

Vera followed Georgie to the kitchen and came back with a glass of water for Queenie. She brought us an armful of towels and then hot coffee and a bottle of brandy. We sat around the kitchen table.

"How high is the water now?" Benno wanted to know.

"It was halfway over the columns when we left," I told him.

"Columns?"

"The ones in front, Pop."

"Halfway over the columns," he repeated.

I heard Fritz ask Vera what time she got out.

"Before dark. I went to the dock to check the water level and it was rising fast. Should have called before I left, but I imagined you'd be watching, too. As soon as I got here, I tried to call, but. . ."

"It happened so fast," I said. "Max heard on the radio . . . ." I stopped. We all looked at each other.

"I will think good thoughts until I know otherwise," Queenie said softly and raised herself slowly out of the chair. "Let us think now, who will be sleeping where."

"I can't sleep, Queenie," I said.

"Me neither," Georgie echoed.

"I don't think any of us can," Vera said.

"But we must try," Queenie insisted. "We'll be needing strength for tomorrow."

About midnight we finally settled down. Vera and I shared her old bedroom. Fritz and Georgie were in Fritz's room.

"How are you doing?" Vera asked me.

How was I doing? I had to think. "Numb," I said, taking off my shoes and starting to undress. "For some reason I keep thinking about that time I had a lump in my breast and had to wait four days to find out if I had cancer. Remember the big deal I made? It was nothing compared to this, but it's the same kind of feeling. Waiting for my life to self-destruct." I sat on the bed and stared at the wall. "Vera, I don't know how I'm going to get through this."

She nodded, like she understood. "One minute at a time" she told me. "We're all in this boat together, if that's any help."

"All in the boat except Max."

"Shhh," she came over and put her arms around me and I leaned against her.

Queenie insisted on leaving the porch light on, in case, she said. And all that night, every time I opened my eyes, I could see that light shining into the wet darkness, like we were calling him home, and I pictured what it would be like to see him come walking in, all wet and grinning about his adventure, and that made my chest ache and I'd start to cry, and then I'd shake it off and calm myself down. Then I'd look out and it would all start again. Vera tossed in the bed beside me. I could feel her wiping her face quietly so as not to disturb me. It was really too soon for us to grieve and it hurt too much to hope.

They found him eight miles downstream the next afternoon. Fritz and Georgie went to do the identification, even though the rescue people that found him said we should send someone else to do that, because the body was so messed up. I wish they hadn't told me that. I wish Fritz and Georgie hadn't gone, because now they'll always live with that memory and I'll live with my imaginings, and I don't know which is worse. After they came back to tell us what we all knew anyway, Fritz and Georgie sat in the back yard and drank a case of beer. We could hear them out there talking, shouting, cursing, then real quiet sometimes. Georgie got sick and Fritz laughed at him and woke everyone in the house trying to get him into bed, when he could hardly walk himself, and Queenie didn't say anything to shame either of them.

I wanted it over quick, the funeral. And I wanted it quiet and private, but it wasn't that easy, because the graveyard was flooded and the ground was too soft for awhile and everything was going slow because the town was torn up in places and so many people were calling on the phone or knocking at the door and bringing things like whole hams and cakes and fresh-baked bread and they brought clothes and shoes and even underwear and Suzanne from the beauty shop brought over some makeup and shampoo and conditioner and a hair dryer because she knew Vera and I were staying there and she figured Queenie wouldn't have a lot of stuff like that. The photography studio called to say they had negatives of our last family portrait and would print us another if ours had been ruined. Tully Fox brought cash and some temporary checks and wanted us to know he had started a memorial fund for Max and then more people came with barbecue and huge pots of baked beans and potato salad, and they stayed to talk and eat and tell stories about this flood and other floods and the deaths of other children they had known, or sometimes their own. It helped and hurt at the same time.

We weren't the only ones hurt by the flood, but I guess we were about the worst. People had lost their homes, and pets and livestock and some had already started their cleaning up, but they all seemed to feel lucky when they looked at us. For two days the house was full of people suffering some strange kind of guilt, or just plan compassion, or a mixture of both, and they wanted to talk about it and they wanted to help us, and I guess they did help because sometimes we laughed with those people and sometimes we cried and when night came, we crawled into bed tired and glad to be alone and we slept a little, a few hours at a time. Whenever I woke up, it all came back and I had to fit the pieces of my life in place just like a jigsaw puzzle, but every time, it was a little more familiar.

At the funeral Sheila sang a song she had written for Max, a song about a spirit wild in a well-loved child, now forever free. I guess he was a wild spirit and maybe I had something to do with that and maybe it would have all come out the same, no matter what. I had hold of his hand one minute, and he had slipped away the next. And his smile, and his sweetness, would never leave me, no matter how foolish or troublesome or careless he had been. And no matter how much we all thought about how we could have made things different for Max, from before he was born until the moment he decided to go back for that puppy, we had to go on with whatever he had left us. Which was a lot.

Vera

The day after the funeral we started cleaning up. The whole town was cleaning up. Those who hadn't suffered from the high water showed up to help those of us who had. It didn't matter that no one was up to it. We had no choice. We started at Fritz and Carol Anne's house and then moved to my cabin, working in teams, first to move the furniture out, then to deal with the mud and to search for smaller things and see what could be salvaged. At night, I awakened regularly, remembering favorite books, fountain pens, bills, hastily scribbled telephone numbers I had wanted to keep, photographs from long ago, impossible to replace. And always with us, thoughts of Max. Everywhere, reminders.

I watched Fritz salvage a black tennis shoe, wedged under the front gate, half-buried, and walked over to take it away from him. His face was wet with tears.

"The earth is sinking under my feet," he said. "Always thought I knew what was important. Now? Nothing. Nothing but questions. How could it happen? Why did it happen? It makes no sense."

"There aren't any answers." I put my hand on his shoulder. "At least not for right now."

"That's about what I've decided. I'm not sure there'll ever be any. Maybe for someone else. Not for me."

Sometime after noon on the first day, Tully arrived at the river with two men in the back of his truck.

"Thought you could use some help," he said, and motioned toward the vehicle where the men hunkered, hands between their knees, heads down.

I brushed my hair from my eyes, knowing my face was probably smeared with dirt. "You thought right."

He whistled and waved, and the two climbed from the truck and headed our way.

"Wetbacks," he said, before I could complain.

I looked at him in irritation.

"Twenty-five dollars a day. It's good money." I was in no mood to argue.

All afternoon the workers were at our disposal, relieving Fritz from some of the heavy lifting, and more willing than most to wash carefully whatever was handed them. Tully directed their activities and, when there was no more light to work by, he paid them.

"Thanks for the thought," I told him, as the men loaded the shovels and water jugs, then themselves, up into the truck bed.

"Have them back tomorrow," he said.

"No need," I told him.

"We'll be back," he said.

"Then wear your old clothes," I told him. "Tomorrow, I'll expect you to get your hands dirty."

He showed up around ten the next morning, dressed in jeans and boots. The rest of us were exhausted and had begun to get on each other's nerves. Four displaced persons, camping at Queenie's house, six of us trying to share two bathrooms.

"We'll take Alfredo and go to your place," Tully said. "You need to be working there."

We left the other man with Fritz and headed for my cabin, where the water had pushed more than a foot of mud through the frame of the absent front door and shifted the house on its foundation.

"Came through pretty well," Tully said.

"I never should have set the front door due north."

"Same thing would've happened, wherever the door was," he said. With the heel of his boot he kicked away the crusted top of the mud and tested the dirt beneath. He looked up. "You know what's wrong with you, Vera? You're always trying to make some sense of things. Take my word for it. It's a thoroughly unpredictable god damn world and—"

I was in no mood for lessons, or platitudes; I didn't want pity or advice. If anyone could understand that, it should be Tully and apparently he did, for he suddenly stopped talking, rolled up his sleeves and reached for a shovel "Come on," he said, in a softer voice. "Let's clean up this shit."

Fritz and Carol Anne came over one afternoon and found me sitting on the dock.

"Weird, isn't it?" Carol Anne said. "Like time is standing still, and all you have to do every day is clean up, but it's never going to get finished. Like those guys that paint the Brooklyn Bridge."

I looked up and smiled at her fitting analogy.

She smiled back. She was holding up well, better than I would have predicted. And Fritz? It looked to me as if he had shut something down inside. Well, hadn't we all? It would take time.

Queenie and Benno came later that evening and Queenie brought dinner, which we ate out in the yard. As Carol Anne and I helped put the food on the table, I saw Queenie glance up regularly to check on Benno, who had become so careless and forgetful, we were all reluctant to leave him alone. The weather had turned dry and mild and Benno wandered down by the river with Val following at a respectful distance. The dog had learned early not to get in the way of Benno's cane, which he used as a walking aid and a weapon against any perceived obstacle. As I watched, he stopped to prod the earth with the cane, investigating some half-buried object. He stood there a moment, as if deep in thought, then moved on to inspect the pecan trees, knocking with the cane again at what was probably a hole in the bark, squinting up to check their new, green growth.

"Val will keep an eye on him," I told Queenie.

"Someone needs to," she said, letting the tiredness, for once, creep into her voice.

"Where's the boy?" Benno asked when he came back for his dinner.

We all looked away, waiting for the other to answer.

"The boy's gone, Papa," Queenie said.

Five minutes later he asked again. "Where's the boy?"

Carol Anne looked across at me with tears in her eyes and shrugged. "Gone fishing, Pop," she told him and he nodded in approval.

It was getting dark when Tully appeared.

"Sorry I'm so late," he said.

Carol Anne looked at me and raised her eyebrows, as if to ask what he was doing there. I shook my head at her as Fritz stood up to shake hands with Tully across the table, glad, I thought, for a new face.

"Any word on government relief loans?" he asked.

"I'll take in the plates," Queenie made herself busy.

"Mr. Jahn," Tully stuck out his hand and walked over to where Benno sat.

"What brings you out?" Benno said, looking up and adjusting his glasses with the tip of his index finger.

"Needed a break," Tully spoke louder to accommodate Benno's hearing.

"Can't make the loans fast enough these days. Your people are sure anxious to start things going again."

Benno nodded. "Good for business."

"Don't know what it will do to sales at the resort. Just have to wait and see how the auslanders react."

"Auslanders come and go," Benno said, and waved his hand as if to dismiss them. "Some will stay. Some always do."

"So you think we'll survive this, sir?"

"Oh, sure," Benno told him. "I've seen worse."

"Papa," Queenie called. "Time to go."

Benno lifted himself from the bench heavily and fingered his moustache. "When that boy gets back," he told Carol Anne, "tell him to come see me."

In the spring of 1987 we found our lives irrevocably changed. The world population reached five billion that year, President Reagan challenged Gorbachev to tear down the Berlin wall, and in Schoenberg, we began to rebuild. The flood had more than disrupted our lives, it had exploded them, dislodged our established systems, sent the pieces flying, and there they floated for a while, as if trying to decide whether to come to rest in the old patterns, or new ones.

I moved back into the cabin within a couple of weeks and Fritz and Carol Anne took an apartment in town. They had decided to sell their house and build a new one on some high land bordering the canyon. Carol Anne, he told me, was unwilling to live on the river again and had decided she wanted another baby.

"Is that what you want?" I asked.

"That's too much starting over for me," he took a deep breath and ran his hand through his hair. "Tully offered her a job at the bank and she's thinking about taking it."

That's trouble, I thought.

"I know what you're thinking," Fritz told me. "I'd like to say I didn't give a damn, and maybe I don't. We both know she's going to do what she wants. And she should. We're trying to get over this thing, but unfortunately, we're not very good at helping each other."

He put his arm around my shoulder as we walked to the river's edge. The water was once again calm and green and new grass was making its way up through the silt. "You and this," he said. "Solid places in my life, Vee."

"I know that."

"If I did what I wanted . . . ." The unfinished sentence hung between us, not uncomfortably.

"Things take time," I said.

"You sound like Queenie," he shook his head and smiled.

"And what's so wrong with that?"